JOURNEY TO A DIFFERENT DIMENSION

by

Demian Schatt & Stan Schatt

JOURNEY TO A DIFFERENT DIMENSION

Published by Subliminal Editions

Copyright @2013 by Demian Schatt and Stan Schatt.

Cover art by Indie Designz

First Printing: July 2013

First Edition: July 2013

Table of Contents

INTRODUCTION

It's possible to play Minecraft for hours every day and never get bored because there's so very much to learn. How do you craft what you need to survive the first night? How do you fight monsters that can spawn faster than you can kill them? How do you brew the right potion to counteract a witch's potion? What can you do to counteract a village overrun with zombies?

To make Minecraft even more interesting, you can build virtually anything you can possibly imagine whether that includes castles, tree houses or skyscrapers. You can use redstone technology to create elaborate machines and even link devices to TNT to create awesome weapons.

This book is really two books in one. It's an exciting story in which you can follow the adventures of Paul, Ryan, and Tiffany as they find themselves pulled into Minecraft's world and struggle to survive. It's also a user's guide because you can learn survival skills and crafting skills by following these adventurers' examples.

Minecraft is the property of Mojang Game Studio and the authors claim no ownership to it. The references in this book are for learning purposes only.

CHAPTER 1

Becoming a Part of Minecraft

"Just eat it!"

Ryan Sims heard his mother's order and shuddered as he stared at his plate and wished he could make it disappear. It was some kind of Hamburger Helper mess, and it smelled awful. Ryan thought about his favorite game, Minecraft.

The food in that game was a lot more appealing than anything his mother cooked. He wished he could use redstone wire he had found in Minecraft and attach a lever linked to TNT. He imagined what it would look like to watch the glump on his plate blow up into a million pieces. Ryan thought Minecraft was far more fun than his real life because, when his older brother wasn't picking on him, his mother always seemed to be in a bad mood.

Ryan looked at his older brother, who had a smirk on his face. Frank was three years older and in 9th grade. He had started out at his new school with grades just as bad as the ones he had brought home in San Francisco. He took his frustration out on his younger brother, punching him repeatedly when their mother wasn't home. Ryan had learned to defend himself, but he just wasn't strong enough to fight Frank on equal terms even though he was big for his age.

Ryan saw his mother's eyes focus on him. "Did you go to your fencing lesson after school?"

"Yeah. Why do I have to take fencing? It's boring. People don't even use swords anymore if you've noticed."

"It will help you make the fencing team in high school."

"Why would I want to do that? I just told you that fencing isn't fun for me."

"If you make the team, it will help you get into a really good college so you can make something of yourself, unlike your father."

Ryan knew better than to answer; his mother had not had a good word to see about his father since the divorce. His mother meant well, but she was always pushing him to do things he didn't

want to do because they were "good for him."
He'd be happier if she just let him do what he
liked. He could play Minecraft for hours; it never
bored him.

"Have you both finished your homework?"

Once again, Ryan heard his mother's voice
and recognized she was using her boss voice.
Sometimes he felt like he was just another one of
her employees. He had hated moving from his
old school, but his mother said that they needed
the extra money because of the divorce. All she
ever thought about was her job. He was proud
that she was the new Vice President of
Computron, but now she never had time to do
anything fun with him or his brother.

Frank nodded that he had completed all his
homework, and Mrs. Sims gave him a hard look
as if she knew he was lying.

Ryan had hoped to wait until his mother was
in a better mood, but it was now or never. "I'm
all finished. Is it ok if I go over to Paul's house?
We wanted to play Minecraft."

"It's a waste of time. I'd almost feel better if
you wasted your time watching television like
other kids. I don't understand what you see in
that game."

"It's stupid," Frank added.

"That's because you don't know how to play,"
Ryan told his brother. "Mom, it's educational. I
learn lots of stuff playing it. Besides, I don't

have any homework."

Mrs. Sims pursed her lips as if she was trying to make up her mind. "Are you sure Paul's family doesn't mind you coming over this evening. Doesn't he have homework to do?"

"He's super smart and finishes his homework when he first comes home. He called me before you came home and told me his parents don't mind."

"I guess I should feel grateful that you've made one friend anyway. Your brother can't seem to make friends anywhere. You may go, but be home by nine."

"Paul's a loser just like Ryan," Frank said. He balled his hand into fist but didn't take a swing at his brother because he knew how his mother would react.

"Boys, I know the move has been hard on all of us. Things will get easier. I'll feel better when things calm down a bit at the office. Meanwhile, let's all try to get along."

Mrs. Sims began clearing the dinner dishes. Her dinner experiment had not been a success. Ryan picked up his sweater and headed to the door. Paul Richards lived two blocks away. San Diego was much warmer than San Francisco, but the evenings turned chilly, since they lived near the ocean. He hurried to his bike and rode down the street; he was happy he had a place to go and didn't have to spend the evening with his brother. Sometimes he felt envious of Paul. He knew that Paul's mother didn't care what her son did. She really was only his stepmother, anyway, and she lavished most of her attention on her baby.

Ryan parked his bike on the lawn close to the house and knocked. Mrs. Richards opened the door. She had dyed her hair a bright fire engine red and looked much younger than his mother. Her arms cradled her baby. When Ryan eased past her, he noticed that she smelled like baby powder, and decided she probably had just finished changing the baby's diapers.

"Paul's in his room. Don't make any noise. I'm expecting a friend."

Ryan walked down the hall past the master bedroom where his friend's parents slept and past Paul's room until he came to the computer room that Paul shared with his father.

He waved at his friend through the open door. Paul Richards looked up from his computer monitor and smiled.

"Your Mom let you out of prison for good behavior?"

"Very funny. I have to be back by nine, but at least there's time to have some fun. Where's your Dad?"

"He's at a convention in Las Vegas. That's why my stepmother invited a friend over."

"Your Dad knows more about computers than

anyone I know."

"Yeah. We don't talk much about anything but computers. He's got a lot on his mind because he's behind schedule on the program he's writing for the supercomputer, and his boss says it has to be delivered on time and bug-free."

"Can we play Minecraft now?"

Paul nodded. He was a Minecraft systems administrator with his own server. His small desk barely had room for his gigantic monitor and his very fast PC. Ryan thought that playing Minecraft at Paul's house compared to playing the game on his small iPad at home like riding down Space Mountain in Disneyland compared to riding on one of those baby trains in front of the supermarket.

Paul and Ryan did not look like sixth graders who could be friends. Paul wore wireless glasses that made him look a bit like Harry Potter. He had blond wavy hair and was so thin that he looked like a good San Francisco wind would blow him away. His blue eyes were clear and shiny, and he always had something to say. Ryan had noticed that their teacher would always turn to Paul if the class couldn't answer a question in math or science. He never bragged, but he had a quiet confidence that Ryan liked.

Ryan took after his father, who had played football in college. He had wide shoulders and muscular arms, although he was a bit shorter than Paul. Ryan wore his dark hair as short as possible so that he never had to worry about combing it. As far as he could tell, he was average in just about everything except sports. He could throw a football as far as any eighth grader, and he ran fast enough to be on the school's track team. The one thing that brought the two boys together from the very first day Ryan had come to Evergreen Middle School had been their love for Minecraft. Ryan had seen Paul playing the game on an IPad during lunch. He had walked over and started a conversation.

The boys complemented each other. Paul had been quick to volunteer help when Ryan had trouble with his homework while Ryan had stepped in when a seventh grader had begun pushing Paul. Ryan stood about a head taller than the older boy, who quickly backed down. Word had spread the two boys were friends, so whatever bullying of Paul that had taken place in the past had stopped.

The sound of a doorbell interrupted the boys. "It's Marilyn," Paul said and rolled his eyes.

"Who is she?"

"Just one of my stepmother's friends. They spend all their time talking about babies; it's sickening."

Soon the boys heard footsteps approaching. Mrs. Richards stuck her head in. She had one of those phony smiles mothers use when they want you do something that they know you don't want to do.

"Paul. Mrs. Peters came to visit. She brought her daughter Tiffany along. Say hello to her."

Mrs. Peters stepped aside revealing a tall girl with long blond hair and a very pretty face that was twisted into a pout.

"I told you I didn't want to come. Why couldn't you take me home from Girl Scouts before coming here?"

"Tiffany, don't embarrass me in front of my friend. Say hello to the boys."

Tiffany gave them a reluctant "hello," and they responded with greetings of their own. They stared at the girl. Ryan recognized her as clearly the most popular girl in their class. She had a large group of girl friends that followed her everywhere. They ignored him and Paul and only smiled at the other kids who were popular.

Mrs. Peters told her daughter to behave herself and then went to join her friend. Tiffany wore a stylish purse over one shoulder. Their school required all students to wear a uniform. The light blue blouse and dark pants looked good on Tiffany. She ignored the boys for a moment while she studied the room, observing the posters of Minecraft, a creeper lamp on the desk where Paul sat and a creeper jacket and hood that hung from a hook on the door. The only non-Minecraft item in the room was a large poster of the San Diego Supercomputer that his father had hung on one wall.

"You guys are part of the nerdy Minecraft group that spends all their time at lunch playing that stupid game."

Tiffany spoke as if she was merely stating a fact that invited no argument. Paul and Ryan exchanged glances. Both had been stunned to see the girl, since they doubted she ever bothered to learn their names.

Paul shook his head. "It's not a stupid game. Spending all your time trying to be Miss Popularity is stupid. Have you ever even played Minecraft?"

Tiffany shook her head and took out her phone. "No, and I don't want to start now. I'm stuck here, but I don't have to like it. I'm going to sit in this chair and text my friends. You guys can do whatever you want."

Tiffany sat down and stared at her phone as if to say, "I don't care what you do. Just leave me alone." The boys sat down in front of Paul's large monitor.

"It should really be cool to play tonight," Paul said. "Dad has just put in a direct connection to the supercomputer at his work. It's got the power of a 10,000 PCs. I'm going to put us in hard-core mode, so we'll have to really be careful. That means there will be monsters everywhere!"

"Monsters?" Tiffany couldn't help being curious.

"All kinds. Come over here and look over my

shoulder," Paul said as he attached his computer to the supercomputer's link. Tiffany rose reluctantly and stood just behind Paul, glancing over his shoulder, as the boy connected his computer to the fastest computer in the entire country.

Suddenly there was a brilliant flash that almost blinded them followed by a booming sound. Then there was only silence. Gradually the three teens came awake. Paul opened his eyes first, and then he blinked because he thought he was dreaming. His room was gone, replaced by a completely different world. He saw that he was lying on green grass staring up at a blue sky. He raised his head and saw he was in a forest, surrounded by very large trees. Paul looked to his side and saw that Ryan and Tiffany were both opening their eyes and reacting with much the same surprise he had shown.

"What happened?" Tiffany shook her head in an effort to clear it.

"Where are we?" Ryan asked.

Paul studied the forest and then he turned even paler than usual. "I don't believe it," he said.

"What?" Ryan and Tiffany stared at Paul.

"The only explanation that makes any sense is that somehow we're now inside a Minecraft game. Look at the trees; they're just like in the game.

"What exactly are you saying?" Tiffany said. Her voice sounded small, and she was shaking visibly.

"I'm saying that we're part of the game we were starting. We're trapped inside, and I'm not sure how we can get out."

"Could we just play and win?" Tiffany asked.

"You don't really win," Paul said, "but we could get to a different dimension like the one we came from. There's one problem, though, I put the game into hardcore mode. Remember? I've never been able to win in that mode because it's so hard."

"What happens if we lose?" Tiffany said.

Paul looked very serious. "When we play the game and it's not hardcore mode, you die, and then you can spawn back at the same place and play all over again. The problem is we're in hardcore mode, and I'm not sure what the rules are when you're in the game. If we die, we just might stay dead."

The three were silent for a few minutes before Ryan spoke quietly but clearly with some fear in his voice. "It's going to start getting dark soon."

Paul nodded and started to move towards a large tree. Tiffany put her hand on Ryan's shoulder to get his attention. "What happens when it gets dark?"

"Monsters come out, and we're absolutely going to die unless we can find a safe place to spend the night. Let's go help Paul."

"You were joking about monsters, right?"

Ryan looked at Tiffany for a long moment before replying. "Think of your worst nightmare and just double it. We're talking everything from creepers that can blow you sky high to zombies and skeletons, and those are just the beginning."

Tiffany looked up at the sky. It would not be long now until the monsters came out.

CHAPTER 2

Monsters Come Out at Night

Paul stood in front of a large tree. Clearly he was trying to decide how to act inside a Minecraft game since he didn't have a mouse or keyboard. He tried snapping his fingers, but nothing happened.

"What are you going to do with that oak tree?" Tiffany directed her question to Paul who turned in surprise.

"How did you know what kind of tree this is?"

"I'm a Girl Scout. I've earned all my camping and nature badges."

"Maybe you'll be more help than I thought," Paul said. "I'm going to bang my fist against the trunk. If we really are in the game, the tree should fall." It took Paul three very hard punches before the tree fell to the ground. He repeated the action several more times and watched as other trees fell. Each tree yielded a block of wood. Paul knew he could craft four wood panels from a wooden block. He turned to the others and said, "We could use fifty wooden blocks, but there might not be time. Get as many as you can."

"I'll get some wood from that birch tree," Tiffany said. She walked over to a towering tree and imitated Paul. Ryan began to chop down some trees as well.

"What are you going to do about an inventory or crafting area?" Ryan asked.

"There's got to be a way, or we wouldn't be able to be here," Paul said. He bent his head down and closed his eyes.

"What's he doing?" Tiffany whispered.

"That's the way Paul thinks when he has a really hard problem to solve," Ryan said. He watched his friend who seemed to be talking to himself, muttering words that didn't make much sense. After a while Paul raised his head and opened his eyes.

"We don't have a keyboard or a mouse, but we do have our fingers." Paul picked up a stick and scratched the letter "E" into the dirt. Suddenly an inventory appeared on the ground along with a crafting area. He dropped some wood into the crafting area and smiled as he saw the wood crafted into wooden planks.

Paul lined up one plank into each of the four squares in the crafting area. His smile grew even larger when he saw a crafting table appear. "We're in business! Maybe we can survive after all." Paul was swaying from foot to foot, so excited that he had to struggle to keep himself from jumping up and down.

Ryan had been knocking down trees while covertly watching his friend. Seeing the crafting table appear, Ryan turned from facing the trees and began walking away from the forest, studying the ground as he walked. He picked up something off the ground and pointed it out to Tiffany. "Find more wool like this. We'll need it for our beds."

Tiffany delivered the wool back to Paul who had begun making beds. Ryan had another sudden thought and began running towards the grassy area that bordered the trees. He disappeared from view while Paul showed Tiffany what to do to craft beds. Paul crafted some sticks from a wooden cube and crafted a wooden pickaxe and a wooden shovel. He used the pickaxe to turn fifteen stone blocks into cobblestone, and then used that to make a cobblestone pickaxe, sword, and a furnace that required eight pieces. He dug into the soft earth, careful not to dig in a straight line. Soon Paul had dug an area large enough to stand in.

Tiffany noticed some stone blocks with flecks of gray and black in them. "That's weird," she said, pointing at the specks.

Paul became very excited. He realized these specks represented coal and mined it. He used some wood to make charcoal as well. He then sat down with a strange expression on his face.

"What's wrong?" Tiffany asked.

"I'm feeling weak. I think all the work has worn me out. You'll start to feel it soon as well. We have to find something to eat if we want to survive."

Just then Ryan returned. Tiffany saw that the boy's muscles were strained as he carried two large pieces of meat and two pieces of leather. "I found a cow and killed it," he said.

Tiffany wrinkled her mouth in disgust. "Yuk," she said.

Paul divided the meat up into smaller pieces and put them in the furnace, using charcoal to heat it. Soon the three were happily eating their first meal in the new world.

As Ryan held his piece of meat, he noticed that he was still wearing his watch. Curious, he moved his wrist closer to his face to study it. His look of puzzlement caught Tiffany's attention.

"Why are you staring at your watch?"

"It's changed." Ryan showed it to Tiffany and Paul. Instead of twelve numerals, the watch's face was divided into two equal halves and two very small shaded sections.

Ryan thought for a minute and then realized what the watch now represented. "The two large areas represent a Minecraft day and a Minecraft night. The two small shaded areas are sunrise and sunset. We're almost at sunset."

"We better figure out where we're going to sleep," Paul said. I think we can do better than the hole I started to dig. He pointed at a clearing through the trees. Tiffany looked at noticed a hill that rose from the grassy plain.

"You expect us to sleep out in the open?"

"No, but we'll need the hill to make us a hidey hole."

Ryan picked up a shovel and pickaxe and began walking towards the hill. It was further away than it looked, and the sun was growing noticeably lower in the sky when they reached it. Ryan began digging into the hill. He used his pickaxe to make a short hallway that was two blocks tall and one block wide. He then broadened the hallway, making it four blocks long and began hollowing out the area to create a room. Paul picked up a shovel and made the room even wider.

The teens headed back to the area where they had arrived (spawned) and began dragging their inventory over to their new house. They placed the furnace next to their crafting bench and placed some wood planks in the bottom square to make more charcoal. They then began making torches from sticks and charcoal.

Tiffany had caught on quickly to how to craft objects. She crafted a door, and Ryan helped her place the door at the opening of their home. They made several trips back and forth until all their possessions were now in their home. Paul made a couple of chests and combined them to make one big chest. He then began piling their possessions into it. As soon as they placed the objects inside, it magically went into their Inventory where they would reappear when one of the teens drew an "E" on the ground.

The boys dug some more, making the shelter even more spacious. They began to make torches and placed them throughout their shelter. Ryan had a terrible thought. He pantomimed walking like one of the zombies he had seen in a movie. Paul nodded. They added a block to help block off their front hallway.

When Tiffany raised her eyebrows, ready to ask what they were doing, Ryan replied with one word. "Zombies."

"You've got to be joking!"

"I wish I were. They can break down doors."

"Then why did I bother to make a door?"

"Because it keeps out other monsters," Ryan said.

"That's just wonderful," Tiffany said with obvious sarcasm. "I wish you started to play Monopoly or some other game where there weren't zombies and monsters!"

Tiffany seemed to remember something and began rummaging in her purse. She pulled out a small package that was wrapped as a present and handed it to Paul. "I almost forgot. It seems irrelevant now but my mother brought a present for you since she said she didn't know you had your birthday last week."

"It was a small party," Paul said. He blushed, clearly embarrassed that he had not invited her and that she knew about the party.

"It's ok. I probably wouldn't have come anyway. I'm not mad at you," Tiffany said.

Paul nodded and began opening the present, surprised that the present had survived its trip into a new dimension. His eyes lit up when he realized what Tiffany had given him.

"It's the best present you ever could have given me!" he said.

Paul held up a book and read the title aloud: *Secrets to Surviving in Minecraft: Recipes for Success.*

"I heard that's the best book on Minecraft," Ryan said.

"I. B. Winner wrote it. He's the guy who has his own website for Minecraft hints and cheats," Paul said.

"Can I see it?" Tiffany asked.

Paul handed the book to the girl who began thumbing through it. Her face broke into a smile. "I know how to do a lot of these things in real life, and now I can do them here. This is unbelievable!"

She passed the book over to Ryan who also looked through it. He whistled when he saw recipes for all kinds of food they could cook as well as special weapons they could craft.

The three lay in their beds. In the middle of the night Tiffany woke up because she heard a horrible sound coming from the door. Her curiosity overcame her fear, and she decided to take a closer look. She didn't notice that Ryan had also woken up and had decided to follow her, figuring she might need help. He grabbed the cobblestone sword and moved silently behind the girl.

Ryan saw the shadow of a figure outside the door. He realized with a start what it was and dove at Tiffany's legs. She screamed, startled by the boy running into her and knocking her to the ground. Just then something flew over their heads, barely missing them.

"What's that?" She asked.

"It was a skeleton. They can shoot their arrows through the glass part of doors. Let's squeeze through the opening in the hall. We'll be safe there."

Tiffany realized just how much there was to learn in this world and just how dangerous a world it was. She followed Ryan back to where their beds were and picked up the book she had given Paul. She decided she'd better study it carefully. She read far into the night while the two boys slept peacefully. Tiffany was blessed with a photographic memory. She never forgot anything she read. As she read the book, she committed key parts to memory. She promised herself that she would be the one to save them the next time they ran into trouble.

Sunlight started to seep into the house as dawn broke. Ryan insisted on taking the sword and leading the group; after all, he was the only one who actually knew how to use it. The three teens moved the block away from where it was blocking the hall and they opened the door. No monsters were in sight.

Tiffany looked at the rolling plain in front of her that bordered the dense forest. She saw that there was a stream nearby as well. "It's going to take us a long time to get back home, isn't it?"

Paul nodded. "Even if we manage to avoid getting killed, we have a lot of mining and crafting we'll have to do in order to have what we need in our inventory to make it all the way to the portal."

"Will anyone come looking for us?" Ryan asked.

Paul shrugged. "Maybe my dad will come back

from his trip and realize what happened. He's good enough with computers to figure out a way to bring us back."

"You're forgetting something," Tiffany said. "I read the book cover to cover. Each twenty-four hour day here is only twenty minutes long in Earth time. We could be here a week, and it would only be a little over two hours back home."

"What about Notch?" Ryan said.

"I don't know. We can hope he can see this game as well as all the others on Earth, but I find it hard to believe," Paul said

"Notch?" Tiffany asked.

"He's the inventor. Word is that he has created ways for him to view multi-player games whenever he wants. He's sort of like God of the Minecraft world he created," Paul said.

"Maybe we should play the game like we would at home. If we divide up what we have to do, we might be able to move faster than any one of us could by himself," Ryan said.

Paul looked around them. "Let's start with where we are. We have a few tools. I wish I knew more about farming. I never bother to do any farming when I play because I think it's boring compared to mining."

"I have my agriculture badge from Girl Scouts, and I have a vegetable garden in our backyard. I'll take the lead on creating our farm if you guys will help with some of the digging and seed gathering." Tiffany spoke with obvious excitement as she produced a pen and pad of paper from her handbag and began to make a list.

Ryan scanned the ground near their door and then pointed. "Look! Zombies were here last night, and they left some of their rotten flesh. We can use it. If we touch it, then it will go into our inventory."

"You touch it. I feel like throwing up just looking at it," Tiffany said as she wrinkled her face in disgust. "Do you actually expect me to eat THAT?"

"If we're starving, we might have to eat it even if it makes us sick. We'll keep it because we might also need it to feed any wolves we find."

"Wolves?"

Ryan smiled, ignoring Tiffany's question, touched the rotten flesh and wasn't surprised when it disappeared. He then noted something else. "That skeleton that shot at us left some bones; we can use the bone dust to speed up our farming." He touched the bones and they disappeared.

Paul went back into their home and returned with two gardening hoes and a bucket he had crafted. The three teens walked towards the flat land that bordered a stream. Ryan began breaking tall grass blocks and gathering the wheat seeds as they walked.

"We'll have to add carrots and potatoes later after we do some exploring," Paul said.

"Here's a plan I drew for our farm," Tiffany said. She had drawn a plan that included neatly tilled rows and canals that brought water from the stream.

Ryan and Paul began tilling the ground and creating the canal. Tiffany followed by planting the wheat seeds. She also walked over to the stream and gathered some of the green reeds that she recognized as sugar cane and planted them in the dirt where they would have access to water. She placed some bone meal over the wheat seeds to speed up the plants' growth.

Ryan crafted a fence that he placed around the farm to protect it from animals and monsters. He then walked through the grassy plain very slowly, careful not to scare the chickens he was hunting; he returned with three chickens, and Tiffany placed them two of them in a separate area so they could mate and fed them some wheat seeds. Ryan killed the third chicken and placed it in inventory, figuring they'd cook it later. He walked back into the field this time searching for wild pigs he has spotted earlier; he returned with some pork chops that he also placed into inventory.

Paul walked back to the forest and looked around until he saw some apples that had fallen from the trees. He placed those in inventory as well. Hopefully they would never become so desperate that they would have to eat the rotten flesh they had gathered earlier in the day.

Days go by quickly in Minecraft, and hunger comes very quickly to players. The three teens retreated to their house and ate dinner. They felt secure and warm in their little house, especially because they had torches to give them plenty of light. They slept securely and woke, ready to start another day. They walked to the farm and stared in horror. Someone had broken down the fence and stolen their crop.

"I thought you said monsters can't get in if we build a fence," Tiffany said.

"They can't," Paul said looking at Ryan. "You know what this means, don't you?"

"You're saying that we're not alone in this game?"

"That has to be the answer. Someone else is in this world, and they're the ones who stole our food. They could do a lot worse things to us. They could dynamite our house with us inside or set it on fire while we're sleeping."

"We have to find them before they can do any more damage," Ryan said. He ran back to the house and gathered the sword and the pickaxe and shovel. He wondered who had stolen their food and if they were even human. Maybe aliens from other planets also could somehow get zapped into the game. His heart began beating very fast. He couldn't help thinking how lucky he was that his mother had made him take fencing lessons; he probably could handle his sword better than anyone they met. Of course, they might have weapons far superior to a mere sword.

CHAPTER 3

Robbed

Tiffany stared at the ruined farm and her hands folded themselves into fists. She felt furious that all their hard work had been destroyed.

"Why would anyone want to ruin our farm?"

Ryan just tightened his grip on the sword. "Some people are just mean. They can't stand to see anyone happy. Of course, that's assuming they're human."

Tiffany stared at Ryan. The thought had never occurred to her, and it was more than just a little frightening. "Are there non-humans in the version of Minecraft you play?"

"No, but nothing is normal here or we wouldn't be here. What if aliens play a version of Minecraft on their planet? Then, maybe they could wind up here too.

Paul thought about it. "Once I was playing Minecraft, and I was working on building a house. Someone joined my game and dumped dirt blocks on my head until I was buried and died. I never found out who did it. I never thought about aliens being part of this world, but we better do some exploring. We don't want to be trapped out here at night."

Ryan built a large pillar and placed a torch on top before they left. That way they would be able to see the pillar from far away and find their way back to their house. They also took some food and tools with them in case there wasn't time to make it back to their house.

The three teens walked slowly, trying to save their energy. When they climbed a small hill, they saw an enormous house below. It was the strangest dwelling they had ever seen. The building was at least seven stories high with lips jutting out from each level. Paul explained that they were designed to keep spiders from climbing up the structure. The building looked like it should be a ride in Disneyland's Tomorrow Land. The fourth level contained a bridge that connected the building to another similarly looking one. Tracks ran along a bridge lit up by dozens of torches. The house was set back behind at least three hundred feet of green grass.

"Look!" Tiffany pointed to the green belt on the left hand side of the house. Someone had used some of the wood taken from their house to fence in the chickens they had stolen. The wheat and sugarcane that had been ripped out of their fields lay on the group inside the fence.

"Well, now we know who stole our food," Ryan said. His heart beat quickly as he studied the massive building. He noted the door made of stone as well as the windows lit up by torches and realized that they weren't dealing with beginners. These people, or whatever they were, knew enough to be very dangerous.

"The stone door is strong enough to keep everyone out," Paul observed. "They must have lots of stuff in their inventory. I wonder if they rob other people as well."

Ryan's first impulse was to rush the house, but he realized he wouldn't even be able to get past the stone door. He approached the house slowly, just ahead of his two companions. He wondered briefly if the area might be booby-trapped. Ryan crouched down when he saw a cow walking towards the house. Maybe the people inside had stolen the cow as well. It walked very slowly, stopping occasionally to munch on the grass that, apparently, it thought was delicious.

"Don't move any closer. Let's see if there are any traps," Ryan said. Just then the cow made a loud mooing sound as the ground it stood on collapsed. It fell several feet into a deep pit. The sound of the cow in distress was followed shortly by a bang and then a whooshing sound. Ryan waved frantically for his friends to move back. He turned and ran after them. He looked back at the house just in time to see a bundle of TNT land in the pit and explode.

Ryan huddled with his two friends as they studied the terrible damage the trap had inflicted. There was now a large crater where the cow had stood.

"They know how to use redstone technology. They must have dug a pit and then covered it after putting a tripwire across it. When the cow fell into the pit, he triggered the tripwire, and that set off the TNT cannon. I'm not sure we know enough to fight these guys," Paul said.

"We can't just let them take our food," Tiffany said indignantly.

"No, if we don't do something, they'll eventually build a trap that we won't see, and that will be the end of us," Ryan said.

"So, you're saying we'll lose if we fight them and we'll lose if we don't?" Tiffany asked.

"Ryan's just saying we have to think carefully," Paul said.

"We can't sleep in our house tonight. Whoever lives in that house might come back to kill us," Ryan said.

"We won't," Paul said and led the group away from the mysterious robbers' house. When they reached their home, the group gathered up the rest of their possessions and began a long walk away from the house. Paul reminded them that monsters never spawn near where people have their house, and they needed monsters badly for his plan.

When the group had gone almost thirty blocks away, they began digging. With the three of them all working hard, they were able to dig an enormous trap that dropped down twenty-six blocks. Then they began covering the hole with thin twigs and foliage so that it would be invisible at night. Satisfied that the trap was the best they could do, the three then walked until they came to a small hill. They dug into the hill and then down far enough to create a temporary home that they completed with new beds and a new door that they crafted. After a hurried dinner, the group settled down for the night after first lighting some torches.

That night was the worst yet. All three teens kept hearing horrible sounds ranging from moaning to screaming. Each one of them imagined the worst. They thought they heard the door opening, but it didn't. Of course, the monsters weren't their only concern. The temporary home they constructed had a very low profile so that it would have been very difficult for the robbers to discover it.

When morning came, Ryan grabbed his sword

and opened the door slowly. He saw that monsters had been all around the door and that the noises they heard had been real. Once again, the group gathered skeleton bones and rotten flesh. Ryan led the group cautiously over the hill and down into the plain towards where their trap had been set, taking a ladder with them that they had crafted for the occasion. When they came close to their trap, they saw that they had a treasure trove. Skeletons had falling in as well as creepers. Ryan started to cheer when he saw the gunpowder the creepers had left, but stopped when he realized that there still might be some monsters nearby. Ryan climbed down into the pit and added all the elements to their inventory.

Meanwhile Tiffany had been busy walking through the thick grass of the plains. She smiled when she saw her targets. She grabbed several chickens and brought them back to the temporary home. Ryan killed the chickens and added chicken and feathers to their inventory.

The group then trekked to the sand that bordered the nearby stream. Ryan began digging sand and adding it to the inventory. They then continued digging until they had gone quite deep. Paul grabbed a torch and began exploring. He shouted a few minutes later and Tiffany and Ryan rushed to join him. He pointed to some rocks. "That's gravel. We'll have to keep mining it until we're lucky enough to find flint." He began digging. When he tired, Paul took over and then Tiffany joined in. Soon they had all the flint Paul felt they needed.

"One last thing," Paul said. He pointed down into the deep it that had served as a trap. "We'll find some iron ore in there. Use the stone pickaxe."

Ryan soon found the iron ore they needed. They took the iron ore back to camp where they crafted a furnace and used coal as a fuel. They smelted the iron ore into iron ingots. Paul used two iron ingots to create a shiny pair of shears. Tiffany studied the shears. "What do we have to cut?" she asked.

"You're going to love this," Ryan said with a smile. "We need to go back into the cave I found near our new home and find some spider webs. I saw some over in the corner where it's very dark." Tiffany quickly handed the shears back to Ryan as they trekked back to the cave. Ryan then climbed down the ladder and soon found the spider webs he had remembered. He cut them and saw that his efforts resulted in several pieces of string going straight into their inventory. He climbed out of the pit and saw the sun was setting.

"Quick, let's take everything into our temporary home," Paul said. They gathered up everything they could handle, including the crafting table and furnace, and brought them back inside the dwelling, careful to close the door behind them. It was warm and snug with the torches they had lit. They took time for a chicken dinner to replenish their strength.

"It kind of reminds me of camping," Tiffany said. Ryan rolled his eyes. It was one thing to play Minecraft; that was fun. It was very different when you were living in a Minecraft world, surrounded by all kinds of monsters and facing robbers who might be looking for them this very minute.

Paul began crafting a bow and then turned his attention to making some arrows. He also crafted a wooden button and then began the arduous task of crafting TNT. "Be careful," he told everyone. "We don't want to blow ourselves up."

Tiffany contrasted this camping experience with her experience at Girl Scout camps. There she had brought all kinds of things she needed. Here in this Minecraft world they had to make everything they needed.

While they all worked the group went over their plan. It wasn't very good, but it was the best they could do since they had limited supplies in inventory. Paul explained that his first idea was to brew an invisibility potion and then begin punching the robbers so that they might begin fighting among themselves, but too many necessary items were still missing from their inventory. He then had thought about making a sophisticated redstone weapon like the trap they robbers had set, but their inventory didn't even have any redstone dust to create a redstone powered cannon. They would have to make something a lot more primitive.

The group talked far into the night, planning for the morning. They weren't even sure if the robbers were home; maybe they were traveling and looting other people's homes. The thought that there might be other people in this world besides the robbers was chilling but eventually everyone finally fell asleep. They all slept fitfully because their dreams were not pleasant.

The next morning the group began their journey back to the robbers' home. They took the long way since they decided that there was less likelihood that there were traps in the back of the house. They saw that a much smaller fence surrounded the back of the home. Ryan used a ladder to climb the fence and peer over. What he saw made his blood run cold.

Two men were laughing as they gazed at a pile of material. Ryan realized they must have just brought the stolen loot back to their house. The men were truly frightening to see. They both were very large with muscles bursting out of their tee shirts. Both had shaved heads, and their arms were covered with tattoos.

Ryan whispered, "I saw those same tattoos on TV in a show about prisons. They must have been in prison. He realized that the men were much too strong for them to fight. Not only were the men much stronger, but they also had redstone dust, potions, emeralds and even diamonds. The men were drinking from what looked like whiskey bottles. Both men needed shaves, and Ryan could see that their teeth were yellow with black spaces where teeth were missing.

The men began placing the valuables in a large chest before disappearing back in the house. Ryan saw that the men had not spent nearly as much time worrying about protecting the back of their house as they had with the front. The small fence ended in a corner where a block was missing.

Ryan climbed down and shared what he had seen with Tiffany and Paul. Then the three crept around the fence to where the chest lay. Quietly they dragged the chest through the opening in the fence. Just outside that opening they dug a deep hole and placed the TNT in the hole along with a wooden button they had attached to it. Then they covered the hole with twigs and leaves. They dragged the chest further away from the trap but still close enough so that the men would see it when they walked through the opening in the fence.

Paul seemed nervous. "I know it's my plan and it's the best one I could come up with, but what if I miss? I've never been very accurate."

"I'll do it," Tiffany said.

The two boys stared at her. She had a very determined look on her face. "I have an archery Girl Scout badge; I scored 95% on my test."

Tiffany picked up the bow and the arrows. It was one thing to shoot a bow in practice, but another when grown men might be chasing her. She wished she had extra arrows to use for practice, but she didn't.

Ryan took his sword and walked around the trap through the opening in the fence and rapped on the back door. He shouted, "You stole from us, so we're going to steal from you." He turned and ran through the opening in the fence and around the trap.

Ryan's shouting had gotten the attention of the two men. They opened their back door and stared at where their chest had been. They were furious. They disappeared back in their house and soon returned, this time with iron swords and armor that made them look even more frightening as they ran through the opening in the fence. When the men saw the three teens standing several feet away next to their chest, they shouted and ran toward them.

The trap opened and the men fell through. Quickly Tiffany used their ladder to climb to the top of the back fence so that she had a clear view of the TNT in the pit. She took a flaming arrow, prayed as she aimed towards the wooden button, and then fired.

The flaming arrow stuck into the TNT but

nothing happened immediately. Paul had told her to climb down and run as fast as she could because there was a delay. She did so, then she heard a huge explosion and turned to see smoke coming from the pit. She joined Paul and Ryan who hugged her, thrilled that she had been so accurate a shot.

The teens took turns dragging the chest back to their house along with the wheat and sugar cane that had been stolen from them. None of them spoke, all their thoughts focused on the men they had destroyed.

Finally Ryan broke the silence. "They must have stolen from lots of people," he said as he strained to pull the very heavy chest.

"At least they looked human," Paul said. He wouldn't admit it, but he had been afraid that the robbers would turn out to be green monsters from some other planet.

"I hope we never have to do anything like this again," Tiffany said. She was still shaking. It was even worse now that it was over because she felt badly that she had been the one to blow up the men. She tried to tell herself that the men probably would have followed them and killed them without any remorse.

That night Paul noted everything that now had been added to their inventory. "I think we have enough to leave this place now and begin moving in the direction that will take us home," he said. That was the best news Ryan and Tiffany could have heard. They smiled for the first time since the TNT had exploded.

CHAPTER 4

Village of the Zombies

Paul led his friends through the open back door to the house the robbers had built. The two men must have stolen from many people in a wide range of Minecraft worlds. They saw chest after chest filled with wonderful things including one chest filled entirely with emeralds. Paul began adding the items to their inventory. He smiled as he realized that the items would give them a much better chance of making it to the end of the game. Then what? Paul didn't want to think about that because there was no guarantee that they would instantly be sent back to where they had started. He decided to bring up the subject.

"I wonder if it's possible to go from one world to another like we do when we create worlds in Minecraft. I still remember some seeds that could take us to another world, but I don't know if we could make it home from there."

Ryan agreed. "We'd better stay in this world. Since we hadn't chosen a biome yet, maybe this world will have all the different environments in it."

"There's only one way to tell," Ryan said as he pointed towards a mountain in the distance. "I think mountains here must serve as natural dividers. I bet if we climb the one in front of us, they'll be other biomes on the other side."

"Biomes?" Tiffany leafed through the book and then said, "Never mind. I understand. You're just talking about different environments like jungles or oceans or forests."

The boys nodded. They built a very high pillar with a torch at its top and then drew a map so they could return to this now vacant house. Ryan locked the doors and took a key. They began the trek to the mountain, carrying as many valuables as possible with them.

The mountain was not as high as they had thought. They found a path and reached the summit by midday. Looking down, Ryan shouted and pointed to a very unusual scene. A jungle lay directly below them, but they could see plains, a forest, and even a distant desert as well as another mountain in the distance. The teens had already agreed that they would gather what they needed from each biome and then face their final battle that would either result in their deaths or their successful creation of a portal that would take them home. None of them even wanted to think about the possibility that the final portal might send them to whatever place the robbers had come from.

The three teens climbed down the mountain and soon found themselves in a jungle so filled with trees and vines that they barely could see ahead of them. The trees with their massive trunks towered over them.

Paul pointed at one tree that disappeared into the sky. "The jungle trees in the game go up thirty blocks or more. It's all relative, but I can't even see the tops of these trees."

Ryan looked around him and frowned. "Do you see how dark it is where the trees are the thickest and block out the sun? Do you know what that means?"

Paul nodded. "Monsters love the dark. We'll have to be extra careful and be sure and find a safe place to sleep."

Tiffany was studying the plants around them. She had always enjoyed working in her vegetable garden in her backyard. The jungle was lush and filled with exotic looking plants. She noticed a brown pod filled with what looked like seeds or beans growing on the side of a tree. She brought out the shears they had crafted earlier and cut the pod and began examining it.

"Cocoa beans," Paul said. We can plant some near the house we build and grow it quickly if we sprinkle it with some of the bone dust we have."

The group stopped besides a huge tree. Ryan signaled to the others and they began cutting trees around it and crafting wood panels. Then Paul crafted a set of stairs. They climbed up the huge tree and began shaping it into a tree house by first building a wooden platform. Then they build a large wooden shack on the platform using wood panels. Tiffany focused on crafting some more torches.

Suddenly Tiffany froze when something large and low to the ground ran past her. "What's that?" she asked.

"It's a wild pig," Ryan said. "I think this is a main path for them." He grabbed the shovel and began digging a pit right in the middle of the jungle path. He pointed to leaves and twigs and the others helped him cover the trap.

They heard the pigs before they saw them. Several pigs running at top speed started to cross the path and then fell into the pit. They made an awful sounding din.

Ryan began to use wood panels to build a fence. He then led some of the pigs into the pen where they could mate and serve as a pig farm. He killed the others so they could serve as food for dinner as well as trading supplies. Paul set up the furnace and they began to barbeque some of the pigs for dinner. Ryan remembered the ribs his grandmother used to make and felt sad. It seemed so long ago and so far away. He focused on the task and soon they were eating and laughing.

The sun began to set, casting large shadows from the enormous trees and making the entire area suddenly very spooky. The teens climbed up to their tree house and settled in for the evening. Since they had used their crafting table to craft beds, they were comfortable. Paul had pointed out how dangerous it was to build much higher than they had because of the danger of lightning. He described how he had died in one game when lightning had struck the tree. He also explained why it was so important for them to cut down the trees closest to their tree house so they would have time to escape should other trees catch fire.

That night was probably the worst one so far for the group. They heard more noise than they ever had heard before. Several monsters must have congregated at the foot of the stairs, because in the morning they found rotten flesh and bones that had been dropped. The stairs had stopped the monsters in their tracks.

Ryan saw a blur speed past them as they

climbed down to the ground. "That's much too fast for a pig," he said.

"I heard the game now has ocelots," Paul said. They're supposed to keep creepers away."

Tiffany already was thumbing through the Minecraft book she had given Paul. "It says we can make friends with them, but we need to feed them fish."

Paul crafted a fishing rod and the group walked to a nearby stream. "I've never fished. Do any of you know how?" he asked.

"I fished with my dad," Tiffany said, taking the fishing rod. She walked to the bank of the stream and began casting the rod. Time after time she came up empty. Tiffany didn't seem discouraged. "It can take hours in real life to land a fish," she said.

Suddenly she pulled hard and shouted as a fish flew up out of the water. They quickly added it to their inventory and Tiffany cast her rod again. She did so until she had accumulated a large number of fish. She took one from inventory and they headed back to where they had seen the ocelot. About 20 minutes later they saw an ocelot slowly approaching them. Tiffany took several steps toward the animal that then bolted away.

"I read that you have to let it come to you," Paul said.

"Why didn't you tell me that before," Tiffany

said with some exasperation. She held the fish out in front of her and didn't move. Soon another ocelot approached and finally took the fish from her. The ocelot began wagging its tail after devouring the fish. "We have a new friend," Tiffany said with some pride.

"It's great having a new pet, but we need to hunt for a village where we can trade for some of the things we'll need to make it home," Paul reminded the group.

They gathered up their emeralds since Ryan had told them that most villagers only trade for emeralds. Ryan climbed up a tree until he could get a better view of what was around them. He shouted and pointed west, and then he slowly climbed down. It wouldn't help their chances of making it home if he broke his leg.

They proceeded through the jungle slowly, hacking their way through very thick vines. Suddenly the underbrush cleared and they saw a large village around one hundred feet ahead of them. Ryan seemed to have had the most experience trading with villagers while playing Minecraft, so he studied the village carefully.

"I know some people who play Minecraft just kill all the villagers and take over everything, including the village," Paul said.

Ryan and Tiffany both looked at him. "We can't do that. We might be in a game, but the villagers look like real people. Besides, they never have done anything to hurt us like the robbers did." Tiffany had raised her voice because she felt strongly about not hurting innocent villagers.

Ryan nodded and put his finger over his lips to indicate she needed to keep quiet so the villagers wouldn't hear her. Once again he studied the village before describing what he saw.

"They're real villagers. The zombies haven't gotten them!" Ryan whispered. He signaled for them to follow him, and they headed down a road into the village.

"It's beautiful!" Tiffany exclaimed as she saw the neat little village. Tall lampposts were scattered throughout the village. Each lamppost had four torches affixed to them. They passed small huts and houses. The houses had cobblestone floors and flat roofs. Ryan pointed to fenced balconies that the villages accessed by climbing the ladders attached to them.

Paul pointed to a group of much larger L-shaped houses that had doors attached to them. "That's where two farmers spawn, at least in the game," Paul added.

Ryan smelled meat and called everyone's attention to the butcher shop standing on his left. It had small seating areas made of wooden stairs with a table between them. The double stone slab counter looked like the place where the butcher cut his meat. Through the open door the group saw a fenced off backyard that Ryan speculated was probably used to keep the butcher's animals.

Paul always had loved libraries. He immediately recognized the library next to the butcher shop. It was far longer and narrower than the other buildings, and the large windows revealed a row of bookshelves and a librarian. He thought about stopping to visit the library, but realized there was still so much the group had to do before sunset.

The group kept walking and then saw a building that had to belong to a blacksmith. Three cobblestone stairs lead from the road up to a porch that contained a small pool of lava surrounded on one side by iron bars. The teens noted the two furnaces as well as a worktable composed of one double stone slab. Ryan could see a small room with a chest through the open door on the porch. He thought about exploring the chest, but knew they were here for trading and not stealing the villagers' possessions.

Beyond the village spread a number of little farms neatly laid out. Tiffany recognized wheat, potatoes and carrots growing in fields that were separated by a row of water. Before they reached the fields, though, Paul recognized a tall building with stairs used to shape an interior altar that could only mean they had found a church. The building contained a small three-floor tower equipped with ladders and glass panes, with a balcony on the top. They glimpsed a villager in a purple robe that Paul recognized as the priest.

The three teens had compiled a list of items they needed and hoped to obtain by trading with the villagers. The box of emeralds that they had taken from the robbers meant that they had plenty of trading material.

"They're tough traders and they never take your first offer," Ryan said. "Let's start with the toughest items to find and the ones we must have to get home." He walked up to the priest and began negotiating. It took several minutes until they agreed on prices. Ryan purchased the following items:

- Eyes of Ender

- Bottle o' Enchanting

- Redstone

- Glowstone

Paul headed to the blacksmith with his list. Once again, the smithy proved to be a tough negotiator. Finally Paul parted with more emeralds than he had estimated he would need, but he purchased the following items:

- Diamond swords

- Diamond pickaxes

- Diamond helmets

- Diamond chest plates

Tiffany had her own list. She stopped first at the library and negotiated with the Librarian. She walked out several minutes later with an enchantment book. She stopped at the butcher's shop to purchase steaks, and then bargained with a farmer and walked away with flint and steel, arrows, and cookies. The last item was something that wasn't on the list, but they never had a desert since they landed inside the Minecraft game. She convinced herself that they deserved the cookies because they had survived so far.

The teens carried their new purchases back to their tree house, but it was still early in the day. The village was quite far away, a point that was in their favor according to Paul since otherwise zombies would swarm all over them. The three teens returned to the village, carrying their crafting table, wood, and other needed tools.

Paul had expressed fear that zombies would take over the village unless they saved it. He pointed out that they had set their game for hardcore before being swept into the game. There was probably a 100% chance that zombies would take over the villager's bodies and possess them. There only chance to save the villagers was to build protection for them from the zombies and then make it back to the safety of their tree house before dark.

Paul began making torches that he added to the village's existing lighting; he placed the torches inside as well as outside buildings and even on some of the flat roofs. Meanwhile Ryan was busy building a fence to enclose the village with gates to make it easy to go in and out.

As the last villager went inside their homes, Ryan and Tiffany focused on rehanging doors so they faced outwards. They also were careful to remove steps from in front of the doorways or to lower paths to ensure that every door had a drop in front of it to keep zombies from reaching them.

The sun was growing lower and lower in the sky as the teens raced home. They reached the tree house just before sunset and realized they were famished and felt weak. They ate quickly and immediately felt better.

That night was filled with even more groans and other horrible sounds. As dawn broke, Ryan grabbed one of the diamond swords and climbed down the stairs, followed by his friends. Tiffany screamed. A zombie stood directly in front of them. He had just started burning as the sunlight broke through the trees. Ryan ran up to it and finished it off. He looked around quickly but didn't see any other zombies.

Their pet ocelot sat quietly on the ground near the tree house. Tiffany took a fish and fed it. She was thankful that the ocelot had kept the area free of creepers.

"We'll have to go back to the village. We have to let the villagers out," Paul said.

The group hurried to the village, careful to keep in well-lit areas. They opened the doors and let the villagers out. Paul explained the danger the zombies presented to the villagers and explained why it was important to lock their gates and close their doors. He also warned them of checking before locking their doors for the night to make sure no zombies had spawned within them.

They left the village to the cheers and well wishes of all the villagers. Ryan felt a little bad that some gamers took advantage of villagers and slaughtered them to steal all their goods. He felt good that they had helped these poor creatures.

"One thing bothers me," Paul said. His face had gone white.

The two looked at him, not sure what to expect. Paul paused and the said everything in one breath. "The villagers told me there's another village a couple of miles east of here. There hasn't been any contact in several days, and they're afraid the zombies might have gotten to them."

Ryan studied their inventory list. "We don't have some of the materials we would need to brew a potion to change the zombie villagers back to villagers," he said.

"I know," Paul said. "We just can't leave that many zombies so close to our new friends. We have to try to help them."

"What do you want us to do?" Tiffany said.

"I'm not much of a fighter, but I think we have to go fight the zombie villagers to keep them away from this village," Paul said.

"That's crazy," Ryan replied. "They'll just spawn more zombies. It's never-ending."

"We have to buy these villagers enough time to learn to protect themselves," Paul said.

Tiffany was quick to take Paul's position. The thought of being taken over and turned into a zombie was frightening to her, and she couldn't imagine sitting by and letting it happen to others when she could help prevent it.

"At least we have the strongest possible arms," Paul said, pointing to their newly purchased armor as well as the redstone they had purchased.

They soon saw the village. It looked much like the village they had left. They caught a glimpse of someone in a doorway, and it made their blood run cold. The creature was green with empty sockets where his eyes should have been. He walked as if in a daze. The three teens began to whisper as they planned their strategy.

"It doesn't sound like it will work," Tiffany said, sounding very skeptical.

"It's a redstone cannon," Paul said. It will work as long as we're careful and don't blow ourselves up."

They approached the village as quietly as possible. Paul pointed to some large stones and Ryan joined him in lifting the slabs and placing them in a large rectangle. They had crafted a water bucket and filled it with water. Now they hollowed out the rectangular slab and filled it partially with water. At the far end of the rectangle they placed two large stone blocks, adding a button they crafted to the outer side of one of the blocks.

Paul sprinkled redstone powder on one side of the rectangle. On the other side of the rectangle Ryan placed a redstone torch on the blocks at the far end of the rectangle and then added four redstone repeaters to side opposite the side where they had sprinkled redstone powder. Paul added a block to the block that had the redstone torch attached to it. Tiffany set the delay to maximum on each of the repeaters, careful to follow Paul's instructions.

Paul carefully placed four TNT blocks in the trench and then added one TNT block on the end block. Nothing happened for a few seconds, and then there was an enormous explosion and the TNT was blown high in the air. It fell rapidly and landed right in the middle of the village. The explosion shook the ground.

"We're in luck," Paul said. "All the zombies were in the houses to avoid the sunlight; the TNT landed right in the middle and blew up the houses."

The teens watched as a few zombies tried to flee from their houses, but the sunlight caused them to catch on fire. Their horrible moans were almost unbearable to hear. A couple of zombies headed in their direction. Ryan had put on his diamond armor and used his diamond sword to dispatch the zombies quickly.

The teens walked through the now-deserted village now that the zombies were gone. They scooped up chests that had survived the explosion and began to open them and inventory their contents.

Soon they had finished the ghastly task and now they were ready to move on. Gathering the tools and materials they would need, the teens headed away from the jungle, unsure what lay ahead of them.

CHAPTER 5

Giant Mushrooms and Witches

As the teens reached a top of a hill, they saw that the jungle cleared below and beyond a body of water they could see the outline of a small island. They trudged down the hill and headed to the shore. Maybe the island would move them a step closer to getting home. The teens began cutting trees that lined the shore and crafting them into planks. Paul crafted a boat as well as a wooden bowl. They loaded the boat with supplies including plenty of wood, tools, and food, and headed out into the water.

The day was clear with a sky so blue that it was almost blinding. The sun shone with even more intensity when they were on the water since light reflected up from the water. Soon they reached the small island and pulled the boat ashore. They took a few steps on the ground and looked at each other with surprise.

"This doesn't feel like grass," Ryan said. "It's spongy and different somehow."

"It has to be mycelium. I've heard other players talk about it, but I never thought we'd find a mushroom biome," Paul said.

"I thought it was just a story other kids made up to brag. I even tried seeds on some of the websites, but they never worked," Ryan said.

Tiffany took the Minecraft book out of her bag and began thumbing through it. Soon she found the section on the Mushroom biome and read it quickly to herself. It sounded like a really exotic place. One sentence really caught her attention.

"No monsters here," she said.

"That's what they say," Ryan said.

The three teens began walking towards huge structures that clearly were not trees. As they moved closer and looked up, Ryan realized what they were seeing. "Giant mushrooms! The island is filled with them," he said.

"I never thought mushrooms could grow in bright sunlight," Tiffany said as she bent down and studied a brown mushroom.

"It's the mycelium," Paul said. His eyes caught on the biggest mushroom he had ever seen. It was larger than the three of them put together. He felt like he had landed on another planet where everything was alien.

"Are we completely alone here?" Tiffany asked.

She listened and thought she heard a strange sound, one she knew she had never heard before. She pointed in the direction where she heard the sound.

Ryan picked up his sword and motioned for Tiffany to pick up the bow and arrows while Paul grabbed a sword as well. They walked quietly in the direction of the sound. Suddenly they saw something so strange that if it had landed in a spaceship it would have seen perfectly normal.

The animal seemed to be composed partly of a cow and the other part a mushroom. The overall effect was startling. The teens moved closer since the animal seemed to be ignoring them. Tiffany took out her Minecraft book and found the section on the Mushroom biome and smiled. She had remembered the crafting recipe correctly.

Tiffany ran back to the boat and returned with the crafting table and the wooden bowl. She crept up to the creature that she now knew was a mooshroom and plucked a red mushroom from the animal. It did not seem to notice.

She picked up a brown mushroom from the ground and then used the red and brown mushrooms along with the wooden bowl to craft mushroom stew. Proudly she offered the results to her friends who were reluctant at first to taste it. The boys began eating after Tiffany's prodding and soon were eating with relish. The stew was delicious!

Ryan studied a giant mushroom in front of

him. "I read that you can hollow out these mushrooms and make a house. We could sleep in there," he said.

Tiffany stared at him for a few minutes and then finally burst out, "You don't really care about getting home as fast as possible, do you? You enjoy exploring like it's a game. I have a life back at home and I want to get back there as soon as we can. There's nothing else here for us that will help us get home."

Ryan protested. "There might be some things we can use. You never know. I'm not sure what we'll find if we just explore..."

Paul interrupted him. "I think Tiffany's right. We could spend forever just exploring Minecraft, but we do need to get home. Let's pack up and leave while there's still plenty of daylight."

Ryan bit his lip. He started to say something but then decided to keep silent. He trailed the other two teens as they headed back towards the boat. He wondered what their hurry was. It was true that exploring in this Minecraft world was far more fun than anything he could possibly do in the world he had left.

The teens did not talk as they pushed the boat back into the water and climbed in along with their tools and provisions. They headed back toward the mainland but moved farther south in the hope of finding a biome other than the jungle. Soon the vegetation changed. They saw vines, but clearly they no longer were in a jungle. The vegetation was dense, though, and water flowed onto the land and mixed with the dirt and grass to form a very unattractive mix.

"We found a swamp," Paul said. He remembered swamps he had visited while playing Minecraft. His mind flashed over his past games and he quickly realized some of the dangers. There were lots of valuable items they could find in this biome, but it wouldn't be easy. He had died several times while exploring swamps.

Ryan also had recognized the biome as a swamp. He checked over their weapons because he also had battled to stay alive while playing in swamp biomes. He still remembered being killed when slimes spawned near the house he had built. Tiffany had looked up swamp biomes in the Minecraft book and she was studying the chapter. She shuddered when she read about slimes; they sounded hideous.

Once they had dragged their boat ashore, the group began exploring the area. The saw shallow pools of water with floating lily pads everywhere they looked. The trees surrounding them were covered with vines; all the vegetation was of a far darker color than what they had seen in the jungle biome.

Paul pointed to a clump of mushrooms growing on the ground nearby. "Perfect mushroom-growing environment," he said.

Tiffany saw some large green stalks growing

near a pool of water. She broke off a piece and tentatively licked it. She smiled and raised her had in the form of a fist. "YES! I was right. These vines are sugar cane. I thought I recognized it."

Ryan looked up at the sun that already had passed midday. "We'd better find a place to sleep before the slimes come out."

Ryan put on his armor and helmet and carried his sword. He motioned for Tiffany to carry the bow and arrow as well. The boys had agreed that she was the best archer in their group; besides, she was much more comfortable shooting arrows than using the sword.

Tiffany felt proud that the boys had openly admitted she was a better archer. She had added arrows to her inventory that she had purchased from the villagers, so she felt well armed.

The thick vegetation made it difficult to see far ahead of them. After walking what seemed like forever, the group approached a strange looking structure. Two fences decorated the front of the building with spruce wood stairs leading up to a platform covered by a roof.

A strange looking creature stood on the platform. Clad in purple and green robes with brown leggings underneath, the creature had a large nose with a single wart and lavender-colored eyes. A tall hat with a green buckle on it covered much of its head. Ryan gulped when he realized they were looking at a real witch.

"She's a witch," Ryan whispered. If we don't kill her, she'll spawn into dozens of new witches."

"Stand back. She's going to throw some potions at us," Paul shouted. The teens jumped back, well out of range. They saw the witch drink an evil-looking potion. Her nose pointed forward as she began to drink a second potion.

"Now!" Paul shouted to Tiffany. "Shoot her, Tiffany."

Tiffany placed an arrow in her bow, drew it back its full length and fired the arrow. It landed on the witch's chest. Quickly Tiffany repeated the process again and again. Finally the witch fell to the ground. Paul signaled for Tiffany and Ryan to rush forward.

They noticed several items lying on the ground near the witch. "It's a potion of healing," Paul said, gathering a bottle and placing it into their inventory. "We caught her before she could drink it."

He began picking up and naming the other items on the ground. "We hit the jackpot," he said. "I see glowstone dust, gunpowder redstone, spider eyes, and even some sugar. He pointed to the stairs, and the teens climbed up and began to explore the witch's hut.

Inside the building they found a large pot that seemed to contain some kind of mushroom. They also found a crafting table and a cauldron. After exploring for a while, they headed down the stairs.

"We need to build some shelter before nightfall, Paul said as he noticed the sun was hanging low in the sky.

The three teens felt like experienced homebuilders by now. They used wood planks to build a home that would protect them from the monsters they knew would spawn that night. They crafted a door and beds, ate dinner, and retired for the evening.

The noise that night made it very difficult to sleep. Tiffany had never seen a living, breathing slime, but the boys' description of what the creatures looked like in the games they had played made them sound awful.

Ryan put on his armor and helmet and grabbed his sword when morning came. He opened the door slowly and took a few steps away from the house. Suddenly he saw what he had feared. A group of strange looking figures in the shape of large green cubes began hopping towards him. He shouted a warning to the others and moved to meet the slime directly in front of him.

The creatures moved rapidly towards Ryan. He slashed repeatedly and saw one creature fall, but that only seemed to anger the others who started to attack him as well. Paul joined in the fray while Tiffany reached for her arrows. The number of creatures seemed to increase no matter how many the boys killed. Still, they began to make progress, and soon only a few creatures remained. Ryan dispatched the last one and felt his strength fade. He was exhausted.

Ryan turned his back and shouted, "We've won!"

Paul shouted a warning just as a single slime, moving very rapidly, seemed to come out of nowhere and struck Ryan who fell to the ground. Tiffany struck the slime repeatedly with arrows and saw it fall to the ground. She and Paul rushed to the stricken Ryan who lay very still.

"He's still breathing," Paul said, "but he seems very weak."

"We need to save him," Tiffany said.

"I know. Maybe we could craft a milk bucket and feed it to him. Let me go get the crafting table. I hope there's still time," Paul said.

"Stop!" Tiffany shouted. "I have a better idea." She looked in their inventory until she found the wellness potion that the witch had brewed. She took it and fed it to Ryan.

Tiffany and Paul stood over Ryan and watched him closely. After what seemed like an eternity they saw color begin to return to Ryan's cheeks. His breathing became more noticeable. His eyes flickered and then opened.

"How are you doing?" Tiffany asked.

"What happened?"

Tiffany explained that he had been wounded and that the wellness potion had revived him.

Ryan struggled to his feet. "I feel fine now. That stuff really works! I don't feel tired anymore either."

"Do you feel well enough to explore?" Paul asked.

"I'm ready," Ryan said. He shook himself the way a dog shakes itself after coming out of a pool of water. His eyes were clear and alert.

Paul studied his friend. "If we were playing the game, we could see just how healthy we were. All we can do in this world is to guess just how healthy we are and make sure we don't let ourselves become too hungry and weak.

"Let's hope we don't run into any more slime," Tiffany said.

"Swamps have more slimes than dogs have fleas," Paul said. "We'll try to explore as quickly as we can and then head back to the mushroom island to sleep. We'll be safe there. We can even do what Ryan suggested and build ourselves a mushroom house."

After three hours exploring the swamp the group headed back to their boat and began the journey back to the mushroom island. For one of the few times since they had arrived in this world, they felt safe. The strange cow-like mooshrooms were no threat to them. They chose a giant mushroom and began to hollow it out. Soon they had a room big enough to sleep in. They crafted beds and torches. They ate a dinner including some of the steak they had purchased from the villagers what seemed to be so long ago.

That night Ryan thought he heard some sniffling. "Are you all right?" he whispered.

"I'm fine. It's just that it's been a few days here even though it's only a few hours at home. If we count the days, tomorrow should be my birthday. How would you like to spend your birthday here?" Tiffany asked.

Ryan felt awful. He had been selfish, just thinking about himself. He imagined how Tiffany must feel. There had to be something he could do. He thought about it far into the night and then had an idea. He awoke far earlier than Tiffany or Paul and hurried outside. He was thankful that they had brought a crafting table with them as well as their inventory of possessions. He placed what he needed on the crafting table and checked off the items:

- 3 Milk Buckets
- 2 Sugar
- 1 Egg
- 3 Wheat

Ryan took a cake consisting of white icing and red frosting off the crafting table. The recipe had made six slices, enough for the three of them to have desert twice. When Paul came out the door, Ryan quickly filled him in on his plan. Finally Tiffany came out the door. The boys began singing "Happy Birthday" to her as Tiffany felt tears roll down her cheeks. It was such a sweet thing for them to have done for her. Just as they finished singing, a mooshroom bellowed as if it were joining in.

Paul admitted it was one of the best cakes he had ever eaten. His mouth had craved sweets for so long that he was telling the truth. The cake melted in their mouths, and the world seemed a little brighter. The teens began packing up their possessions and headed towards their boat to begin their next adventure, hopefully a step closer to finding their way home.

CHAPTER 6

We Are Not Alone

The teens were anxious to get away from the swamp, since they knew that there would always be too many slime and witches for them to live safely. They also knew that the sooner they explored other biomes, the sooner they would gather what they needed to travel home.

As the teens reached the summit of the mountain that separated the swamp from other parts of this Minecraft world, they saw a beautiful sight. Far below they saw a rolling valley with tall trees that Tiffany identified as spruce. In contrast to the dark colored vegetation in the swamp, the grass below was so green that it almost sparkled in the sun.

As they descended into this new world, Ryan pointed to some snow that clung to the leaves of some of the trees. "It must be the Taiga biome," he said. Paul agreed. They explained to Tiffany that it was one of the newest biomes in the game. Neither had played a game in that biome yet.

"It looks so peaceful. It reminds me of a Christmas card I once saw," Tiffany said.

The group realized that they had plenty of wood available, so they set out to make a house, one that would protect them from the cold. They worked quickly and soon saw a house that filled them with pride. They used some wool from their inventory to craft beds and also filled the house with torches they pulled from their inventory. When Paul saw snow on the ground, he added snowballs to their inventory.

They had plenty of food, including the food they had purchased from the villagers, so they didn't feel any need to hunt. They explored briefly around the house but didn't see any animal tracks.

"We're alone," Paul said with some feeling of relief.

The climb down the mountain had tired them out, so they ate and then went into the house to sleep. Paul and Ryan fell asleep quickly. Tiffany could hear their soft, even breathing. She had a terrible feeling, but couldn't pinpoint it. Something definitely was bothering her. She had inherited a certain talent from her mother, who always seemed to know who was calling before she answered a call. She also seemed able to anticipate unpleasant events before they happened.

Once her mother had warned Tiffany to not wear her new jacket but to put on an old one because "something was going to happen." That afternoon the two of them were walking on a sidewalk nears a ladder. Tiffany observed a painter high above painting a house's trim. Suddenly the man shouted a warning and his paint bucket fell. The bucket missed mother and daughter, but paint splattered all over her jacket.

Now Tiffany had one of those feelings. She tried to think what it could mean, but she couldn't put her feelings into words. She finally fell asleep after tossing and turning for hours. Paul and Ryan awoke early and decided to let Tiffany sleep while they prepared breakfast. They were setting the food on a table when she appeared bleary-eyed.

"We thought it would be a good idea to go exploring today," Paul said. Ryan voiced his approval. They both looked at Tiffany, who seemed different somehow.

"Something bad is going to happen," she said. "I don't know when or how, but I can feel it."

Paul and Ryan looked at each other with some confusion. Since they didn't know about

Tiffany's ability, they thought she was just acting kind of crazy.

"What do you think we should do?" Ryan asked.

"We just need to be careful," she said.

After breakfast, the group walked down a natural path strewn with trees and leaves. At one point Ryan thought he heard something and strolled off the path. Soon they heard a shout from him and rushed to follow him.

Ryan pointed to a cave entrance that jutted out of some rocks. Ryan had stumbled onto it by accident. They decided there wasn't time to explore it now, but they would return the next day.

As the teens walked back to camp, Paul noted just how quiet it was. They could hear their own breathing. The air had turned colder as well; they now could see their breaths. As the path turned and wound its way back to their house, Ryan motioned for them to stop and to be quiet. He pointed in the direction of a clump of trees.

Tiffany looked in that direction. At first she didn't see anything, but suddenly she saw a pair of very intelligent eyes staring at her. She craned her neck to get a better view.

"It's a wolf," Paul whispered.

Tiffany remembered something she had read in the Minecraft book. She whispered, "Give me three bones from our inventory. You know, the ones we found after the skeletons tried to get into our other house."

Paul silently handed the bones to the girl. She walked very slowly until the girl and wolf were not too far apart. She held out the bones. The wolf eyed her, and then slowly approached. Ryan readied his sword just in case the wolf attacked.

The wolf finally accepted the bones and then assumed a sitting position near her. A red collar magically appeared on the animal. When Tiffany turned to head back onto the path, the wolf rose and began to follow her.

"I think you have a new pet," Ryan said.

Tiffany smiled as she looked back at the animal. "I miss my dog. I think I'll call this guy Rufus even though it's a funny name for a wolf."

Tiffany spent the rest of the afternoon teaching the wolf tricks. She realized it would make a good protector as well. That night the teens ate and prepared for sleep. The wolf chose to sleep outside. Once again the boys fell asleep quickly and Tiffany struggled with that same unpleasant feeling of dread. She just knew that something awful was going to happen.

The next morning Tiffany felt shaky. She joined the boys for breakfast. They talked excitedly about exploring further down the valley. She hesitated and then decided to speak.

"I have a terrible feeling. I've learned that when I feel that something awful is going to happen, it always comes true. The worst thing that could possibly happen besides us getting killed would be for us to lose our inventory. If something happened to it, we'd have to start all over and might never make it home."

Paul looked confused. "What are you saying? What do you think we should do?"

Tiffany took a deep breath because she knew the boys wouldn't like her answer. "I think we should take all the chests of goods we've accumulated and drag them over to the cave where no one could find them. I'm afraid of leaving the chests here at the house."

"But there's no one else in this world. Besides, the chests are heavy," Ryan said.

"We have to do it!" Tiffany said. She folded her arms in frustration. How could she make the boys understand?

Paul didn't say anything for a while. He studied Tiffany's face. Finally he spoke. "Better safe than sorry. I don't want to take the chance of having to start over. Let's get started."

"You're crazy! It will take us all morning to drag them to the cave," Ryan said with some exasperation.

Paul shrugged his shoulders and began dragging one of the chests. Tiffany struggled with a chest and began dragging it down the path. Ryan shook his head and then finally relented. He grappled with the largest chest and began following his friends. The wolf followed behind them.

The teens returned to their home once they had hidden their inventory. They began smoothing the leaves on the path so no one could see their footprints and follow them. Finally they were far enough away from the house to just walk normally.

"Are you happy now?" Ryan asked with some resentment still in his voice.

"Yes," Tiffany said. She decided not to have an argument. She knew her request must seem unreasonable to the boys. She was thankful that Paul had taken her side. She looked at the boy with new appreciation. He never said much, but when he did it always made sense. She had a sudden realization and turned to him.

"You're in my algebra class, aren't you?"

"Yes." Paul said. He didn't mention that he had recognized her the minute she had come into his room. She always sat on the other side of the class, surrounded by the more popular kids.

"You got an A on the last test, didn't you?"

It almost sounded like an accusation, but Paul answered anyway. "I did."

"I did too. We were the only ones," Tiffany said with a smile.

Paul looked at her as if he had never seen her before. She actually was smart. He hadn't thought of her as anything but a popular girl.

"You're good at other things besides Minecraft," Tiffany said with a smile.

"I guess," Paul said, not knowing what else to say.

Ryan had watched the exchange quietly. He felt left out. "Let's concentrate on exploring over there," he said as he pointed to a path that snaked through the spruce forest.

The teens spent the afternoon exploring and then trudged home. As they turned in the bend of the path, they saw nothing but broken wood planks where their home had been. The teens looked with growing disbelief at the destruction as they approached cautiously.

"What could have happened?" Tiffany asked.

"You're the expert on predicting bad things," Ryan said. He felt a wave of fear go through him as he realized that only TNT could have caused that much damage. TNT meant they were not alone in this world.

Paul had come to pretty much the same conclusion. He looked down at the dirt and shouted for the others to look where he was pointing.

"There are at least three different footprints. Look at how large they are!"

Ryan walked up to the closest footprint and stuck his shoe in it to compare sizes. The footprint's outline was much wider and longer. Ryan knew he wore a large size for his age; that meant that whoever did this had to be an adult. Three adults had attacked their house if the footprints could be believed.

Paul and Ryan stared at Tiffany almost as if she were a witch. She shrugged. "I'm just glad we weren't inside or that we had left our stuff here," she said.

Paul began lifting some of the wood to get a better idea of what had happened. He stopped when he saw a sign that hadn't been there when they had left the house.

Someone had taken the time to scrawl this on a sign where he figured they would find it:

WE'RE SORRY YOU WEREN'T HOME. WE'LL FIND YOU AND KILL YOU. HAVING FUN PLAYING THIS GAME?

"They sound pretty immature," Paul said.

"Yeah, but they're mature enough to know how to use redstone technology," Ryan said. "They're also much bigger than we are."

Suddenly the teens heard a horrible human like scream. They looked up and saw that their pet wolf had fallen through a hole in the wood and banged its head on the bed's headboard. The wolf lay still, and Tiffany saw that its tail had begun dipping. She had read that a wolf's tail was a sign of its health or lack of health.

"We have to save Rufus," she said.

"I have an idea," Paul said. He ran down the path towards the cave. By the time he returned dragging two large milk buckets, Tiffany was sitting on the ground holding Rufus'large head in her lap.

Help Rufus drink," Paul ordered.

Tiffany lifted the wolf's head towards the milk bucket and smiled as the wolf began lapping up the milk. She noted that its tail began rising until it was finally standing straight up.

"He's better!" Tiffany shouted and gave Paul a smile of appreciation.

"Whoever did this might come back," Ryan said.

The two teens looked at their friend and realized he was right. They decided to spend the night near their cave. They returned to the cave and dug what Ryan called his "hidey hole." They slept fitfully. The next morning they were ready to leave this world. They hoped their enemies wouldn't be able to follow them.

CHAPTER 7

The Deadly Temple

The teens trudged down the mountain that had taken them most of the day to climb. Below them they saw as different a landscape as there could possibly be compared to what they had just left. Instead of tall, stately trees with snow glistening on their branches, they saw a desert that stretched across the horizon. Besides sand, the most common sight was the hearty cactus plant that dotted the landscape and added a green texture.

"I've played the desert biome," Ryan said. "We probably can find some valuable treasure here, but there's also a lot of danger. I've been blown up several times by creepers, and once I was shot by skeletons."

"It's a shame we went into hardcore mode," Paul said. "Sometimes it's fun to just explore and not have to worry about being killed, especially when you can't just start the game over again."

"The position of the sun says it's already late afternoon. If it's as dangerous down there as you say it is, we better hurry so we can make ourselves safe by sunset," Tiffany said.

The teens picked up their pace and soon were on the desert floor. The sand kicked up as they walked through it. They stopped in a large open space where there weren't any plants. Paul pulled out the crafting table, and he began the boring task of crafting sandstone from sand.

Paul indicated after an hour of crafting that he thought he had enough sandstone to move to the next stage of home construction. The teens dug a very large square in the sand and then began placing sandstone in the gap. Soon they had a sandstone floor for their house. They then turned to linking up the sandstone blocks to create walls. They finished the home's frame by creating a roof using the sandstone blocks.

Ryan turned his attention to creating a door in one of the outer walls. He kept the door space narrow enough so that the teens could squeeze through but monsters would find it too narrow.

Paul picked up a pickaxe and began digging a stairway a little way from the house. Soon he had the beginnings of a mine for coal or iron. He took out a number of torches from their inventory and used them to light the house's interior as well as the mine he had started. He then used their crafting table to fashion a door that he then attached to the house.

The teens stepped back and admired their work. It was cool inside because the sand sheltered them from the sun. They crafted beds from their inventory of wood and wool and then prepared dinner.

Tiffany was unusually quiet during dinner. Paul looked over at her, his eyebrows raised in question. "You're not getting any more of those feelings that something terrible is going to happen, are you?"

Ryan stopped eating and waited for Tiffany's reply. He now believed that whatever special power she had was real.

"No. I was just thinking about the people who tried to kill us. I don't think they even looked to see if we were inside before they set off the TNT. In fact, I think they were hoping we were inside. What makes some people so cruel?"

Ryan shook his head. "I don't know. Some kids I know go into multi-player games and spend all their time trying to destroy what other kids build. I don't understand it either.

It's like they can't build anything themselves so they don't want anyone else to be able to do it,"

"Do you think every biome in this world has people like that, just waiting so they can hurt us?" Tiffany said.

"Maybe there are others in this game, but that doesn't mean they're all bad people," Paul said. "We have swords and you have your bow and arrows, so we should be all right as long as no one sneaks up on us."

That night the wind howled through the desert and Paul thought he heard other, more unearthly howls and groans. He glanced at his two friends and saw that they had wrapped their pillows over their heads to blot out the sounds.

The next morning Ryan opened the door carefully, holding his sword in front of him. He ducked as an arrow whizzed by him. He saw a skeleton on fire; clearly it had been caught in the sun's bright rays. It fired one more arrow and then toppled to the ground. Ryan looked around carefully but didn't see any other creatures, but he did see lots of rotting flesh near the door.

"We did have visitors last night," Ryan said and pointed out the evidence.

The three teens packed some tools and food and headed west, away from the rising sun. Soon they came to a strange structure rising from the desert floor. Made of sandstone that glowed from the sunlight, the structure resembled an open hut. Ryan took a closer look and then returned with his findings.

"It's a well. There's plenty of shade inside, so it might be a place a monster goes to get out of the sun. Since we still have plenty of water, I think we ought to ignore it for now."

The teens continued walking as the sun rose overhead. The outline of a large structure began to crystallize in the distance. As they drew closer, the sheer size of the structure filled them with awe.

"Who do you think built this?" Ryan said.

"Hopefully people who no longer live here," Paul said.

The symmetrical design intrigued Tiffany. She carefully noted the two large windowless buildings that seemed to be directly connected by a closed passage to the middle of the structure, the only one that had a door. Strange red markings covered the two windowless buildings.

Paul studied the red markings. "They look vaguely familiar," he said.

Tiffany stood near him and studied the markings as well. "You're right. Remember last year when we studied ancient Egypt? This looks like some of the hieroglyphics we learned."

"The ones that were on mummies," Paul said with some awe.

"At least there aren't any ancient Egyptians in this game," Ryan said. He didn't understand why the markings excited his friends. He was far more interested in exploring the building and looking for treasure.

He headed towards the front door. "Let's see what's inside," he said.

The three teens entered the temple. The darkness was overwhelming since the open door cast only a small ray of light. Ryan thought he saw something moving in the shadows. He had his sword in his hand. He peered into the darkness and then shouted.

"Get back. It's a creeper. If he explodes, he'll take all of us with him."

Tiffany and Paul retreated towards the door. Ryan turned and raced in the direction of the creeper. He veered off just as he struck it. He avoided letting the creature touch him. He repeated the same strategy twice more before the creeper collapsed.

"I remembered from playing the game that you can't give them a clear shot at you," Ryan said. He had trouble speaking because he was out of breath, partly from exhaustion and partly from the adrenalin flowing through him. It was the same feeling that fueled his energy when he fought his much older brother using much the same strategy. His brother was much too strong to fight directly, so Ryan always relied on hit and run attacks, hoping to tire out the older boy.

Paul hastily took a torch from their inventory and lit it. The large room seemed empty now except for a large blue block, surrounded on both sides by large orange blocks. Ryan studied them. He had played the game enough times to know it's better to be careful.

"They look like they're made of wool," he said.

Ryan started to reach for one.

"NO!"

Ryan stopped just before his hand touched the blue block. Tiffany had screamed the warning.

"What's wrong?" Ryan asked.

"I remember reading something about the blue block, and it wasn't very pleasant."

Tiffany took the Minecraft book out of her bag and began thumbing through it. Her face turned white.

"You would have gotten all of us killed if you touched that block," she said.

The two boys crowded around her and began reading the page silently while she read it aloud.

"It says that there's a pressure plate attached to the blue block that is tied to nine blocks of TNT," Tiffany said.

Ryan whistled. He shuddered as he realized just how close he had come to ending their lives. He also thought about what would have happened if the creeper had exploded and set off the TNT.

"Does it say what to do?" Paul said.

"The easiest and safest way seems to be to dig from outside the temple and then harvest the TNT. It says there is probably treasure in a hidden passage."

Ryan was excited. He led the group outside and picked up a shovel. He handed shovels to his friends. "Let's get started," he said. "The sand doesn't look very hard so it should be easy digging."

The sun rose higher in the sky, and the teens began to sweat as the hole grew larger and it snaked its way under the temple. Suddenly Ryan broke through with his shovel and he saw the TNT.

Ryan turned to Paul. "You're the careful one. Why don't you see if you can harvest it for us."

Paul harvested the TNT. Then he pointed to the pressure plate stone that had been placed right under the blue wool cube. "It was a perfect trap. Can you imagine what nine blocks of TNT would have done?"

The teens moved carefully into the secret passage. Tiffany shouted and pointed at four large chests that lay before them. They moved cautiously towards the chests. "Let's see what we have," Ryan said.

The teens pried the first chest open. It was difficult because it felt like the chest hadn't been opened for hundreds of years. Ryan moved a torch closer to the chest so they could view its contents.

"Yuk," Tiffany said, her mouth curling in disgust.

Paul peered in and began naming what he saw. "It looks like bones and rotten flesh," he said.

"Maybe a mummy was in it a long time ago," Tiffany said, her imagination soaring as she imagined an Egyptian Pharaoh's mummy being placed carefully in the chest so very long ago.

"I hope we have better luck with the others," Ryan said. He and Paul pried open the second cabinet and Tiffany held the torch up so they could examine its contents.

"Now that's much better," Ryan said, shouting with glee.

The chest contained a pile of emeralds and diamonds. The three teens made sure they placed all the precious gems in their inventory.

The teens repeated the process with the remaining two chests but except for a few gold ingots they appeared to contain nothing but more rotting flesh and bones. Paul noticed something hidden under the rotting flesh and scrapped the flesh aside. He saw two enchanted books. He grabbed them eagerly and added them to their inventory; he knew they'd need the books later.

The teens headed back towards their home.

Paul had been pondering something ever since Ryan had killed the creeper. He turned to Ryan. "Do you know how when we play Minecraft we get experience points when we do certain things?"

"Sure. It's important so you can go up levels in the game."

"Do you think we earn experience points in this world?"

Ryan had never considered the possibility. The more he thought about it, the more sense it made. They had done all kinds of things that normally would have earned them experience points. They had trained ocelots and wolves, killed monsters, done mining and smelting; they must have a lot of experience points so far.

"Is it important?" Tiffany asked.

"It is if we want to go home," Paul said. "Let's hope this world works the same way as the game we play at home."

When the teens arrived back at the home they had constructed of sand, Paul pointed to a cactus plant. "Let's plan a little surprise for our monster friends so you don't have to kill one trying to catch us coming out the door in the morning."

"I remember how dangerous this stuff is from the last time I spawned in a desert biome," Paul said. He showed his friends how to dig carefully under the cactus to harvest it. He then began laying down a zigzag pattern for the cactus plants until he had assembled a fence around their house.

"If you touch it, the plant will kill you," Paul warned. "I doubt we'll see any monsters tomorrow morning," he said.

That night the teens heard the same horrible sounds they had grown accustomed to hearing from monsters, but there was an added crescendo of sound, almost a constant shrieking of pain.

The next morning Ryan opened their door with his sword in hand. He saw that there wasn't any rotten flesh near it. As he moved closer to the cactus plants, he saw the damage the plants had inflicted. He saw more rotten flesh than he had seen ever before along with more bones. Their cactus fence had done its job.

The teens gathered their possessions because it was time to move on. They felt they now were almost ready to face the most serious challenges of this Minecraft world. They headed towards a distant mountain range that should lead them to yet another biome.

CHAPTER 8

Fight to the Death Underground

The teens were heading towards a distant mountain when Paul spotted an opening in the side of a hill that looked man-made. He walked over to investigate, joined by Ryan and Tiffany. They all had agreed that they needed to earn experience points and find scarce items to add to their inventory before they left the outer world and went into the nether.

"It is man-made," Ryan said. He took a torch and moved slowly into the opening, careful to keep one hand on his sword. What he saw was breathtaking.

"Look!" he shouted. He pointed to a mine cart and tracks that led deep into the ground. As he moved further into the abandoned mine, he saw that it was brighter than he had expected. The lighting the miners had left was still working.

"Before we go much further I think we need to be careful not to get lost," Paul said. "If we can find some Lapis Lazuli, we'll be able to dye wool using some of the cobwebs as string to make wool. Until then, we need to make some signs and leave them with arrows pointing the way back."

"This mine could go down miles. I think I can give us some transportation," Ryan said. He took out their crafting table and crafted some powered rail track. He found a passenger mine car and furnace mine cart and put them together. The teens climbed in and they began heading down into the bowels of the earth.

"Have your weapons ready," Paul said. "Abandoned mines are supposed to be filled with cave spiders and their spawners."

"I HATE spiders," Tiffany said.

"Stop right here," Ryan said.

The group piled out of the cart and looked around them. Now they were in a long, narrow corridor with several passageways branching off. They took additional torches from their inventory and began walking slowly down the corridor, peering down each passageway they passed.

Tiffany looked down one passageway and signaled for the others to stop. "I see something about halfway down and in the middle," she said.

"Look out for outcrops or bridges because the spiders can jump on you. If they sting you, it could be the end," Paul said.

Tiffany thought about a spider falling down the back of her blouse and immediately buttoned the top button and pulled the garment closer to her body. She had always hated spiders. She noticed that even Ryan seemed anxious and kept looking up for possible places where the spiders might ambush them.

Paul moved closer to the object and saw it was a chest and wondered what the miners had left in their hurry to leave the cave. He motioned to the others who moved to the other side of him so they could help him lift the lid.

Ryan whistled. He spotted several items all thrown together. He wasn't about to put his hands into that mess and have a spider sting him so he pulled a shovel out of inventory and began shoveling the items out of the chest and onto the mine's dirt floor. He was shocked at the variety he saw including the following:

- Iron and gold ingots
- Pumpkin seeds

- Lapis Lazuli
- Redstone dust
- Wood planks
- Bread
- Diamonds
- String made from cobwebs

"Why would they leave diamonds?" Tiffany asked.

"Something scared the miners enough to make them run for their lives," Paul said. "I have an idea. Let's move this stuff to the mine's opening. We need to do some work outside before we can proceed."

Paul turned to Tiffany when they reached the mine's opening. "You told me you earned a Girl Scout badge for growing vegetables, so you can really help us now." He handed her the bag of pumpkin seeds. He rummaged in their inventory and also handed her some bone dust.

Ryan picked up a shovel and broke up some earth near the cave's opening. Tiffany got on her hands and knees and carefully planted the pumpkin seeds, covered them with bone dust, and then took a water bucket and watered the plants.

There are other things we can do while we wait," Paul said. He took the string and created wool. Then he took the Lapis Lazuli and bone meal and crafted some light blue dye. He then used the dye and wool as crafting ingredients to craft some light blue wool.

"It's pretty, but why bother?" Tiffany said.

"It's our way to keep from getting lost. We'll leave it along the path we take so we can retrace our steps," Paul said. "Instead of 'follow the yellow brick road' like in the Wizard of Oz, we'll follow the 'blue road.'"

The sun was setting, so the group created a makeshift shelter, a hidey hole, and blocked the opening with a large rock. They placed torches inside. All that night, though, the three teens imagined they heard the steps of eight-legged spiders squeezing their way through what they imagined must be holes in their door. No one slept very well.

The next morning everyone felt a lot better. After breakfast, Tiffany was astounded that pumpkin shafts were shooting up. It still would be a while before they had pumpkins, however. They waited another day and then harvested the pumpkins in the form of Jack 'o' Lanterns. Paul used them along with torches to create Jack 'o' Lanterns.

"These will be easy to spot, so we'll use them along with the blue wool so we won't get lost," Paul said. He added, "I've heard stories of people playing Minecraft and going into an abandoned mine and starving to death because they can't find their way back."

"You're actually going in looking for cave spiders?" Tiffany couldn't believe what she was hearing.

"We have to do it," Ryan said. "We need to earn lots of experience points, and this is the fastest way."

"It might be the fastest way to die," Tiffany said. She whispered something to Paul who nodded in agreement. He disappeared and soon reappeared carrying some milk buckets.

"Just in case we need it," Paul said.

The group began to investigate some of the passageways they had passed the first time they visited the cave. They marked their paths with lit Jack 'o' Lanterns as well as blue wool. They continued down a long passageway until it seemed to come to a dead end.

"Should we turn around?" Paul asked.

"Not so fast," Ryan said. He picked up their iron pickaxe and began striking the gravel. Nothing happened at first and then the passageway opened up again. "The gravel must have collapsed years ago," Ryan added.

The group continued down the passageway and then made a sharp left turn. The passageway grew narrower and then they saw something white glistening when the light hit it.

Ryan clenched his jaw in recognition. "Spider webs, hundreds of them," he said. He warned Tiffany to be ready with her bow and arrows as he approached the webs.

"Hand me the shears," Ryan said. He held the shears in one hand and his sword in the other. He began cutting the webs. Soon he saw something small and very fast heading his way. Its black body contained splashes of red.

Ryan swung his sword, and it sliced through the small but deadly spider, killing it instantly. He continued his work, but soon stepped back.

"There must be a spawner in there, buried deep in the webs. It's producing spiders faster than I can kill them."

"What should we do?" Tiffany asked.

It's almost bedtime, but we don't want the spiders to keep growing in numbers while we sleep," Ryan said.

"Follow me!" Paul ordered, clearly with a plan in mind. He led them several feet back from the spider webs. Then he reached into their inventory and pulled out some iron blocks and a pumpkin.

"I'm not hungry," Tiffany said, staring at the pumpkin and the spider webs in the distance.

Paul laughed. He laid the pumpkin down and then added iron blocks in the form of a T. Suddenly the figure sprung to life, much to Tiffany's horror. The monster rose and began moving in the direction of the spider webs.

"It's an iron golem," Paul said in explanation. "It will keep destroying spiders so that they can't overwhelm us in numbers while we sleep," he said.

"It's like creating Frankenstein's Monster," Tiffany said, staring at the massive figure that kept moving slowly but relentlessly toward the spider webs.

Paul motioned for them to follow him and led them to another passageway where he began ripping wood from the passage's supports. He used their crafting table to make beds and then built up walls and placed a wooden ceiling over them. He finished up with a door.

"It's a safe room," Paul said. "I read about them on a Minecraft board. This way we can be safe while we sleep without having to leave the cave."

The teens finally fell asleep. Ryan had reminded them that all the lights made an abandoned cave a very bad place for monsters. Cave spiders were the only threat, but they definitely were a threat.

The next morning the group found that the golem had worn itself out. It lay on the ground, completely still. Paul reached into their inventory and pulled out some flint and steel and set fires among the massive nest of webs. Ryan watched approvingly as web after web burned away along with the spiders attached to them. Soon there were only a few webs left.

Behind them the teens could see a blue object that Ryan identified as the cause of all their problems. It was creating or spawning new cave spiders.

Tiffany took the shears and reached over Paul's shoulder to cut a web.

"WATCH OUT!" Paul shouted but it was too late. Tiffany had not seen a cave spider on the very top of the web. It dropped neatly onto her hand and stung her before she could move her hand to safety.

The poison moved quickly through Tiffany's body. She turned white and then started to fall to the ground. Ryan caught her in his arms and carried her away from the webs before placing her gently on the ground.

Paul ran to where he had left the milk buckets and brought them to where Tiffany was lying. He reached down and gently lifted her head. He brought the bucket to her lips and watched the milk disappear. The white death like pallor that had given her the look of a corpse began to give way as color flooded back into her face.

Tiffany's breathing began to slow down. She had been hyperventilating. Soon her eyes opened and she looked into Paul's face.

"It bit me, didn't it?" she said.

"Yes. You should be all right now," Paul said.

"Are you sure you feel strong enough? We could wait a few hours until you feel like yourself," Ryan said, concern obvious in his voice.

"Thanks, but the milk worked like magic. I feel fine now. Let's get this over with," Tiffany said.

The teens returned to where the few webs remained. Paul used his sword to cut the webs and kill the spiders. When there was a clear path to the spawner, Ryan picked up their iron pickaxe and swung it with all his might. He felt the tool connect solidly with the spawner and then saw it break into dozens of pieces. Paul stepped in and used his sword to kill the few remaining spiders.

"I think we've gotten everything we can from this cave," Paul said. Ryan and Tiffany agreed, and they began the trip back to the mine's opening.

CHAPTER 9

Battling Monsters in the Nether

That night the teens slept soundly in their safe house and then headed out of the cave. The morning was crisp and clean, and the desert landscape looked beautiful with the sun hitting the sand. Ryan surveyed the scene and then his eyes stopped when he saw an anomaly. Something did not look right. He pointed it out to Paul and Tiffany, and the two friends followed him in the direction he had pointed.

Tiffany tried to understand what had attracted Ryan's attention, and then it hit her. "The sand looks like someone moved things around, and there are so many more cactus plants in this one area. What does it mean?" she asked.

"I think it means we have endermen in the area," Paul said. He thought for a minute and then added, "We need to find and kill several of them in order to get some ender pearls so we can make eyes of ender."

"Why? Tiffany said.

Both boys answered at the same time. "We need the eyes of ender to help us get out of the End and go home."

That answer was good enough for Tiffany, but she never had heard about endermen, although their very name sounded intimidating. "Are they hard to kill?" she asked although from the boys' expressions she guessed the answer was probably yes.

"Really hard," Ryan answered.

"Think of a creature larger than us who can teleport away before you attack it. Sometimes it likes to teleport directly behind you so it can kill you before you know it's there," Paul added.

"They can explode and destroy you," Ryan said.

Tiffany thumbed through her Minecraft book and then stopped, stunned by what she read. "It says here they won't bother you unless you bother them first," she said.

Paul looked at the girl and frowned. "Do you want to spend the rest of your life here in the Minecraft world? We will never go home unless we have what we need to make it through the hardest stage of the game."

Tiffany relented. It was against her nature to bother someone who wasn't bothering her, but she reminded herself that these were monsters and not people. "Ok, so how do we kill them without getting killed ourselves?" she said.

"We need a whole bunch of them, so we'll need a strategy that maximizes the number of them we can kill and minimizes the danger to each of us," Paul said. He began to detail a plan that was forming in his mind. As the others listened, Paul saw that his friends were beginning to smile as they realized that the plan had a good chance of succeeding, if they were lucky of course.

"The endermen always disappear at dawn to get away from the sun," Ryan said, looking at the position of the sun in the sky, revealing it was still morning.

"We have the rest of the day to get ready," Paul added.

The teens began by building two pillars. They then used their enchantment books to add Fire Aspect enchantment to both their diamond swords and Tiffany's bow and arrow weapon. They also took an anvil out of inventory and placed it with their other weapons. Their preparation had taken most of the day. They ate dinner and spent the night in the safe house inside the mine.

They awoke while it was still dark and walked cautiously out of the cave and towards where they had built the pillars. Tiffany took her enchanted weapon and climbed to the top of one pillar while Paul took the heavy anvil as well as his sword and climbed up the other pillar. Ryan stood on the level ground, gripping his enchanted diamond sword. He put a pumpkin over his head and explained to Tiffany that to the endermen, he would look like one of their own.

Paul and Tiffany had agreed to scan the desert floor and look for signs of endermen. Shortly Tiffany noticed some movement in the distance. She saw several creatures with very long limbs extending from thin bodies. Their skin appeared to be black, but their most striking and frightening aspect were their eyes that appeared to be glowing purple. Paul had told her to stare at them because that would irritate the endermen and cause them to attack.

Sure enough, within seconds the strange creatures seemed to appear as if by magic. Tiffany remembered that they had the ability to teleport from place to place. The creatures ignored Ryan for the moment since he appeared to be one of them. Instead, they tried to reach the two teens on their pillars. Paul strained as he lifted the heavy anvil and dropped it right on the head of an enderman who fell to the ground, killed instantly.

Tiffany kept shooting flaming arrows into the heads of the endermen, reducing their ability to teleport as they burned. Ryan suddenly attacked the endermen around him and began hacking at their legs. He sliced cleanly through an enderman, but his mouth opened in surprise as he saw the other enderman disappear.

"WATCH OUT. IT'S BEHIND YOU, RYAN!" Tiffany shouted.

Ryan spun around, using a move he had learned in his fencing class. He sliced through the enderman that had teleported behind him. Paul climbed to the ground and stood back-to-back with his friend so no enderman could sneak up on them. They swung their swords as they battled the creatures. Tiffany kept firing her arrows, but she couldn't help but admire how gracefully Ryan handled his sword. Paul hacked at the creatures while Ryan seemed to be dancing as he moved so gracefully.

The endermen emitted horrible sounds, but soon they became muted. Paul surveyed the damage they had inflicted and then calmly began collecting the ender pearls he knew they needed.

When there was nothing left to collect, the teens headed back towards the abandoned mine. Paul pointed to a flat, vacant area near the mine's opening. They saw some shards of broken obsidian blocks.

"Do you know what that means?" he asked.

Ryan studied the damaged blocks. "No, but I'm sure you'll tell us," he said with some sarcasm in his voice. He was growing weary of Paul showing just how smart he was. In this case, it just meant that Paul had played Minecraft a lot longer; it didn't mean he was really smarter. Of course, Ryan knew deep in his heart that Paul really was smarter; he just hated to admit it.

"It means that someone built a nether portal here and it was destroyed by a ghast," he said.

"You mean there are more strangers in this world?" Tiffany said, dread in her voice.

"It also means they've been here long enough to accumulate what they needed to get this far," Ryan added.

"Could it be the ones who destroyed our home in the taiga?" Tiffany asked.

"It would be an amazing coincidence if they found their way to exactly where we are, but it's possible," Paul said.

Paul's remarks caused the other teens to stare mutely at the broken blocks. Who could be waiting for them in the nether? No matter who it was, they had to go on.

Paul took diamond pickaxes out of inventory and distributed them to his friends. He led them into the abandoned mine and pointed to a passageway that went down at an angle. "I think that's the best place for us to dig for obsidian. We'll need twelve blocks to make a portal."

The teens moved down the passage and stopped where miners had been digging previously. They dug silently until Paul pointed to blocks of a slightly different color. "That's what we need," he said.

The group worked hard even though they realized it would have been impossible without their superior tools because the stone was as tough as metal. They piled up the blocks they needed and added them to their inventory. They then headed out of the mine.

"Why are we building right where they built? Tiffany said.

"Whoever built the first portal picked a good spot. It's flat and out in the open. We don't want to build a portal in the mine," Paul said.

Paul and Ryan seemed to know what they were doing so Tiffany watched as they built the portal that resembled a large door. The boys stepped away from their handiwork and Paul pointed to it. We can use our flint and steel now to set it on fire," he said, "but first we need to craft some medicine in case we run into trouble."

Paul took out the crafting table and loaded it with an apple and gold ingots, producing a golden apple. He repeated the process until they had a healthy supply of the bright apples with their magical restorative powers.

Ryan turned his attention to the flint and steel and soon he had the portal on fire; the middle turned a brilliant purple. Tiffany had the strangest feeling that she was riding on an elevator that was going down at a hundred miles per hour because suddenly she felt like she was flying. She closed her eyes. When she opened them, she thought she was in the Hell that our minister talked about every Sunday at church, since what she saw matched the description he used to scare the smaller children.

The teens appeared to be in a huge cave that seemed to stretch forever. While the cave was dark, it was illuminated somehow by a red glow. What sky Tiffany could see was a dull red. Ryan pointed to glowing stalactites that hung from the high ceiling. "That's glowstone," he said as he reached down and collected some glowstone dust that was forming below the glowstones.

"We don't have much time to protect our portal," Paul said as he began taking out the cobblestone they had brought with them in their inventory. The teens used the portal to form part of their ceiling and used the cobblestone blocks to build a shelter large enough to hold them. They placed a crafting table and chest in the corner.

"What about beds?" Tiffany asked.

"They don't work here like they do in the

outer world," Paul said. "They explode."

Tiffany shivered. This world was sounding more and more like Hell. She saw that Ryan was crafting a wooden door. Just as he hung the door, she saw a strange sight. A creature that looked a little like a jellyfish seemed to be floating through the air. Suddenly it flung a fireball at the teens. Ryan saw it and slammed the door; they all felt a thud as the fireball hit the cobblestone wall.

"Its fireballs can't hurt us in here, but we need to kill it," Ryan said. Paul nodded in agreement.

The teens stepped out of the shelter at Ryan's signal. Tiffany fired an arrow at the creature but missed badly because it moved so quickly.

"You have to lead it by shooting where you think it will be when the arrow gets there," Ryan said.

"I know that," Tiffany said tersely, not liking to be told how to shoot her weapon. She tried but missed once again.

"I have an idea," Paul said. He pulled the fishing rod out of inventory. "Be ready to fire as I drag it closer," he said.

Paul cast the fishing rod and began dragging the creature towards them. Tiffany fired as soon as she had a clear shot. She hit it, but it was still alive so she fired two more arrows. The creature went limp.

"So much for ghasts," Ryan said. "If it had hit our portal before we protected it, we'd be stuck here."

Tiffany stared at the ground around their shelter and saw that it included patches of gravel and sand as well as mushrooms that seemed to be growing there. She saw red, steaming pools with steam rising from them and realized they must be composed of red-hot lava. Paul pointed to a narrow passageway that seemed to serve as a bridge over a lava river.

"I think that's the way we need to go," he said.

By now the group was accustomed to Paul taking charge, so they formed a single line behind him. Ryan held his sword in his right hand, ready for action, while Tiffany carried her bow with her arrows in a quiver on her back. They carried what they thought they needed and left the rest in the chest in their shelter.

Paul pointed to a passageway that looked different from the others. "It looks like someone made this," he said. "I think this is the direction the people who built the portal took. We'll try to sneak up on them," he added.

The teens followed the passageway and noted it wasn't as tall as in the main cave. "I think they built this to create the Wither," Ryan said.

"You've got to be crazy. Why would they do that?" Paul said.

"You tell me why else they built this. I didn't say these guys were smart. I'd just as soon not create a three-headed monster that throws skulls that explode," Ryan said.

Tiffany listened to the conversation and wondered what they were doing. Why head towards that kind of monster? They turned a corner and saw that someone had added a door. Paul opened the door slightly and looked in, and then he slammed it and stepped back.

"I saw the Wither in there along with three dead people."

"I have an idea this time," Ryan said with some pride. He explained his idea both teens nodded. They retraced their steps and brought the materials they needed from their shelter. Paul built three iron golem that were just small enough to fit through the door. He headed them in the direction of the Wither.

"Will they kill the monster?" Tiffany asked.

"Probably not. The Wither might even get a little strong, but I think overall it will be weaker. The problem is that we don't have what we need to enchant our golem and make them faster. The Wither is lightning fast."

The teens waited while they heard horrible sounds coming from the room. The sounds continued for a couple of hours and then stopped. Paul peered in again and signaled for his friends to follow him. They entered and saw the monster was still alive. The teens had put on diamond armor to go with their diamond swords.

Three ugly skulls glared at them. The teens spread out so the monster would not be able to kill all of them with one shot. Suddenly all three skulls began shooting out smaller skulls. The tiny projectiles missed the teens who ducked, but they exploded when they hit the wall.

Before the Wither could begin shooting again the teens were on top of it with their diamond swords smashing into the skulls. The creature struggled. As it began to fall to the ground, the monster shot a small skull that missed Paul but exploded against the wall behind him, sending rocks flying. A jagged piece of rock hit Paul in the head, and he fell to the ground.

Tiffany rushed to his aid. The boy's eyes were half-closed.

"Give me one of the golden apples," he whispered.

Tiffany hastened to obey. She handed him the apple and saw that he seemed to regain some color when he began eating the magic apple. Soon he appeared to recover completely.

Ryan was examining the bodies of the people who had been killed. They lay near the bodies of the iron golem. Ryan saw the same tattoos that he had seen on the robbers several days earlier. The men had shaved their heads and one had a

Nazi swastika tattooed on his neck. They were large, scary looking men.

"It looks like they're friends of the ones who stole our things," Ryan said.

"They might be adults, but they made a lot of mistakes," Paul said.

"I hope these are the last of them," Tiffany added.

The teens retraced their path back to the main cavern and then continued their journey. They seemed to walk for hours. Paul had explained that they still needed some materials that only were available in the nether. He hoped they would get lucky; meanwhile, they had to be on the lookout for ghasts as well as all kinds of other creatures who populated this world.

Ryan raised his hand, alerting the others to stop. He pointed at an enormous structure that seemed to cover every inch of the area in front of them. It appeared to be made of bricks and consisted of a series of interlocking bridges with pillars on the outside supporting them and large corridors within the structure.

"That's the most amazing building I've ever seen in Minecraft," Ryan whispered.

"It's a fortress. We should find the Blazes we need in there," Paul said.

"Blazes?" Tiffany whispered.

"Creatures with yellow skin and black eyes that are able to shoot fireballs," Paul whispered.

"Of course. Why don't you ever tell me we're going to see little furry animals that wag their tails and want to be your friends?" Tiffany said with a slight smile.

Ryan led the group to what looked like an entrance. As they entered, they noted brick like fences that served as windowpanes. Ryan led them to a staircase and pointed to the sand and funny looking plants growing on either side. "Those are nether warts growing in soul sand.

"Pick the nether warts that are dark red," Paul said. "We'll need them for some potions."

"Don't step in the soul sand. It'll be like trying to walk in really thick mud. It'll slow you up," Ryan whispered.

The teens passed a room with a large expanse of red liquid that sent billows of smoke into the air. It smelled awful.

"That's a lava well room," Ryan said. He felt good being able to point out some stuff to Tiffany rather than deferring to Paul.

"I think what we need is next door," Paul said. "Be sure you have your weapons reader." He whispered some strategy he had used when playing the game at home. The others nodded. Tiffany thought to herself that if she had to be thrown into a Minecraft world, it helped to go along with a Minecraft fanatic who played it so often that he knew all the ways to survive.

The teens kept low as they ran into the room. They headed for large blocks that we scattered throughout it. Tiffany caught a glimpse of a Blaze just as it shot a fireball at her. It followed with two others bursts. Two other Blazes repeated the process.

"They can only shoot three fireballs in a row and then they have to reload or something," Paul whispered. "That's our chance. We'll each take the one in front of us. When it stops to reload. Attack and strike at its legs first."

The three teens waited, hearing their hearts beat as the fireballs slammed into the stone near them. They heard the metallic sound that Ryan had said was the way they breathed. When the Blaze in front of each of them stopped shooting, they ran towards it and attacked with their diamond swords. They killed the creatures and snapped up the Blaze rods. Suddenly they saw more Blazes appear. They hurried back behind the stone.

Paul pointed to an apparatus in the corner. They saw that it was spawning new Blazes.

"Let's do it again and then let's upset the spawner," Paul said. He handed each of them two torches. "We need to put these all around the spawner so the light will make it inoperative while we have a chance to silence it for good."

The teens attacked once again and dispatched the additional Blaze creatures and then converged at the spawner where they placed their torches. The mechanism stopped launching new creatures; meanwhile, Paul pointed to some stone blocks. They hauled the blocks to the spawner and covered it completely.

"We should have plenty of Blaze rods now," Paul said. "All we have to do now is get out of here alive."

The teens headed out the door and passed another room. Tiffany stuck her head in and then yanked it out. "There are a bunch of very large black creatures in there," she said.

"That's what we need; the little magma cubes won't give us any magma cream," Paul said.

The teens huddled to develop their strategy and then ducked as they entered the room. Tiffany had her bow strung with an arrow as she ran for a distant corner of the room. She saw one of the large black cube-like creatures jump high in the air. She fired her arrow at it and dove for cover. She looked back and heard a strange sound. She saw that the creature had landed where she had been standing. She had missed. These creatures moved with surprising agility. Tiffany fired two more arrows and saw them land in the creature. Ryan swung his sword and finished it off.

Ryan struck a large magma cube and saw it break into two mid-sized creatures; when he struck it again, it divided into even smaller versions of itself. He swung his sword and realized the smaller ones were easier to kill. The teens continued to brandish their weapons until all the magma cubes were dead. Paul happily added magma cream to their inventory. He muttered something about adding "experience points," but that didn't mean anything to Tiffany.

The teens headed down the stairs, and then they began to retrace their steps. As they grew closer to the shelter where they planned to spend some time sleeping, Tiffany saw the strangest sight, even by the nether's standards. She saw four creatures that walked like men and had faces that bore pigs' coloring. She started to reach for her bow.

"No!" Ryan whispered. "The zombie pigmen won't bother us unless we bother them first."

Tiffany shook her head. There were just too many rules and not enough time for anyone to explain them to her. They reached their shelter and lay down on the floor. Tiffany fell asleep thinking she would give everything she owned if only she could have a bed that wouldn't explode with her in it.

When Ryan calculated that it was morning outside, the group readied itself to leave the nether. Paul looked closely at the portal and smiled. "No fire damage from ghasts," he said. "We should be able to just step under it and get transported back to the outer world."

The three teens stepped under the portal, careful to take their belongings with them. Once again they felt dizzying speed and disorientation. When they opened their eyes, they saw blue sky. Each of them was thrilled to be back in what seemed more like the world they had come from, but no one said anything.

"We have some work to do," Ryan said. He took out the crafting table.

He and Paul began by crafting Blaze powder from Blaze rods. They then crafted several eyes of ender as well as an ender chest. Tiffany watched, thumbing through their Minecraft book occasionally to check on the recipes. From everything she was reading, they were on a path that should lead them to the End, if only they could find a stronghold and then build what they needed to create a portal to that last world between this game world and the world they had left so abruptly.

Paul waited until they had packed up everything they would need. He then tossed an eye of ender in the air. When it landed, they picked it up and continued to throw it up in the air. Just when Ryan had concluded that this feature of the game wasn't working and he was beginning to despair, they saw the eye of ender glistening and reflecting light into a cave directly in front of where it had landed.

"They're always underground," Ryan muttered. He was getting tired of the dangers associated with heading below ground.

"I never found a stronghold when I played Minecraft," Paul said, his voice filled with excitement and anticipation.

Ryan lit a torch as he realized that the dark meant that creepers and various other creatures might be lurking in the shadows. He took the lead, holding his sword in the ready position. Since he had done so much fighting, the sword felt natural. He silently thanked his fencing teacher for all the times the man had yelled at him for some sloppy moves. He had improved because he just got tired of being criticized. Now his hard-won skills meant the difference between life and death.

The group proceeded down the dark, cool passage until they turned a corner. Then they stopped in amazement. The stronghold, apparently built with impenetrable blocks towered high above them. Paul silently pointed to a gate that hung open.

The teens crept quietly through the gate; the silence hung over them until it was almost overwhelming. Paul thought of war movies he had seen when it became almost too quiet just before an attack. He looked over at Tiffany to see if the girl was having one of her bad feelings, the kind that always gave warning just before a catastrophe, but her face didn't show any emotion.

They walked through a courtyard and then into the stronghold itself with their steps seeming to echo loudly against the stone floor as they walked down a long hallway dimly lit by torches. Paul pointed to a half-open door and Ryan peered in with his sword ready.

He whistled softly and motioned for the others to look as he pushed the door open. The passageway contained rows of cells with iron doors that hung open.

"No prisoners are here anymore," Paul said almost to himself.

The teens continued down the main hall and soon it widened into a large room with balconies looking down upon it. Ryan pointed to a large staircase, and the group began climbing. The floor consisted of one very large library with a glittering chandelier hanging down from the ceiling and torches hanging from the walls.

Tiffany saw something that excited her and headed in that direction. She stooped down and then motioned for the boys to join her. She was staring at a huge chest but did not open it until her friends arrived.

Ryan held his sword in readiness while Paul opened the chest. He gave a shout of glee when he saw some of its contents. He reached in and began adding its content to their inventory including the following:

- Redstone
- Ender pearls
- Golden apples
- Bread
- Diamonds

"We hit the jackpot!" Ryan said as he helped Paul add the inventory items. "We especially need the extra ender pearls and golden apples."

The group descended the stairs and headed down another hallway. They passed a room with an open door, and Paul stopped to peer in. His sigh caught the others' attention and they looked over his shoulder. The room had chains coming from the walls. One even had a skeleton still attached to the chain.

"Dungeon," Paul muttered. He thought of what it must have been like to be chained to that wall until your flesh melted away and only your bones were left. The body must have been there for a very long time.

"Do you think he came here from our world?" Tiffany said. "If he did, I wonder who chained him."

Ryan shook his head. "Everything is getting so complicated. I don't know if there are people who always have lived in this world or if they all came from someplace else."

"We need to find the End portal and watch out for the silverfish," Paul said.

"What's so scary about silverfish? They're just little bugs," Tiffany said.

"Not here," Ryan said. "They come in swarms and could kill us. The only way to avoid them is to leave the monster eggs alone."

Paul pointed to the large stone blocks all around them. "Some of them are really monster eggs that will spawn the silverfish. The only way to know is if he breaks more easily than stone. Hopefully we don't have to break any blocks."

The teens continued down the hall and then turned a corner. Directly in front of them were several blocks that had been shaped into something that Tiffany recognized as a portal.

"It's the End portal," Ryan said with some awe. "I've heard about it but never seen one."

Paul was carefully examining the portal. "We're in luck. It's undisturbed. If some blocks were missing, it wouldn't work. Quick. Let's put an eye of ender in each of these blocks."

As Tiffany inserted an eye of ender into the one remaining block without one, something magical happened. They no longer were in the same world.

CHAPTER 10

Fighting the Ender Dragon

Tiffany opened her eyes and saw a purple sky that seemed to go on forever and a landscape devoid of anything but large stones. She saw that her friends were also recovering and viewing their surroundings.

Paul hurriedly looked in their inventory and pulled out several items; he found snowballs they had collected from digging blocks of snow during their time in the Taiga biome and pumpkins they had gathered.

"If you see any endermen, don't look at them without wearing one of these pumpkins," Paul warned.

Ryan placed a pumpkin on his head. "I can't see that well," he complained.

"If you don't want to wear it, just be really careful about not looking at endermen, because we're going to have our hands full just fighting the dragon," Paul said. "We'll need the snowballs to destroy the dragon's crystals," he added.

Tiffany saw movement in the distance and saw that endermen were beginning to converge towards them. She put her hand on her head to reassure herself that she was wearing the pumpkin. At Paul's request, she began taking extra arrows out of inventory because he told her that the dragon would be very difficult to kill.

Paul and Ryan concentrated on dragging obsidian blocks out of their inventory along with a diamond pickaxe. They built a bridge towards a large stone platform that towered over them. Paul kept looking around, searching for the dragon since they were vulnerable while building. He sighed in relief as their bridge reached the platform. The boys then dug into the obsidian and created sunken footholds for the three of them where they could stand without getting knocked over into the void that seemed to stretch forever below them.

Ryan pointed up at several crystals that were shining brightly above them. He picked up one of the snowballs and then threw it with all his strength. He had been on his Little League's All

Star team, so he knew he had a good arm. The snowball struck the crystal, and it shattered. He repeated the process until all crystals were destroyed. He knew that would keep the dragon from being able to regenerate its enormous strength.

Just as the last crystal broke into dozens of small pieces a shadow seemed to blot out the sky. Ryan recognized the enormous wings of the dragon as it headed right towards them.

"Hit it with your arrows," he shouted to Tiffany.

Flustered by the dragon's sudden appearance, Tiffany shot and missed. The creature moved with surprising speed. The three teens ducked as the dragon went directly over them; had they remained standing, it would have knocked them into the void.

The dragon turned and came at them again. This time Tiffany's arrow struck the creature, but it didn't seem to do any harm. Ryan slashed at it, and then he fell to the ground as if hit by an automobile. Paul dragged his friend to safety and managed to hand him a golden apple that revived him.

"We can't keep fighting it like this," Paul gasped. "It's still much too strong for us, but I have an idea."

Paul pulled several beds out of their inventory and began laying them out in a large rectangular pattern. He was breathing heavily.

"We have to bait it to attack us where the beds are," Paul said.

The three teens carefully climbed into the space between the beds; they realized that if the dragon caught them there when it landed, they would all die in the explosion that would follow.

"It's like a battleship," Ryan noted. "It's so big that once it starts moving on a direct line towards something, it can't change direction that fast. It's our only chance."

The dragon soared high above them and then began its dive.

"NOW!" Paul screamed and the teens jumped from between the beds and dove for safety just as there was an enormous explosion. Pieces of rock pummeled the teens. Paul's face was lined with dirt and some blood. He saw the dragon slowly rise into the sky. It was moving much slower and seemed to be wounded. He looked over and saw that Ryan and Tiffany were checking themselves for injuries.

Ryan looked at Tiffany and started laughing.

"What's so funny?" she asked indignantly.

"Do you see how Paul and I look with all the dirt and blood on us? You look just like us. I've never seen you looking anything but perfect before."

Tiffany didn't know how to react. She stiffened

and then just decided not to be angry. She was happy all three of them were still alive. She looked up and saw that the dragon was beginning its dive once again. She picked up her bow and fired three arrows in rapid succession and saw that two landed, one on the dragon's head.

Ryan picked up his diamond sword and stood bravely facing the beast. He swung as hard as he could and could feel his sword cut deeply into the creature's head just as it hit him. Everything went black.

The dragon started to rise, but it seemed to realize it no longer had the strength to fly. It began to fall, barely missing the platform where the teens lay. It kept falling into it disappeared from view. Paul looked up and saw a portal had appeared on the platform. It had to be their ticket out of the End.

Paul turned and saw Tiffany bent over Ryan. He lay there motionless. He rushed over and laid his head against his friend's chest. He listened for several minutes.

"I think he's still alive; I can barely feel him breathing. Do we have any more golden apples?"

Tiffany looked in the inventory and her face turned white. "We used the last one earlier."

Paul just looked at her with a helpless look on his face. Tiffany suddenly had an inspiration.

She pulled a milk bucket out of inventory and poured into over Ryan. Nothing seemed to happen. Desperate, she repeated the process with two more buckets.

Ryan suddenly began coughing. He opened his eyes and lifted his head.

"Are you trying to drown me?" he said.

"I was trying to save you," Tiffany said.

"Is it finally gone for good?" Ryan asked, looking around.

"We can leave this place now," Paul said.

The teens stood beneath the portal and felt the same rush of air. When they opened their eyes, they did not see what they had hoped. They saw tall trees all around them and realized they were back to the place they had spawned when they left Paul's room.

No one said anything. How could they possibly spend the rest of their lives fighting monsters and never seeing their homes again? How could they stand it?

"Maybe this is just the next step towards getting us home," Ryan said, but he didn't really believe it.

Tiffany noticed the sky had suddenly darkened noticeably as if it were behind a cloud. The sky was turning black, but it had just been morning when they arrived. What was happening? She felt a strange tingling sensation.

Ryan felt himself spinning and then saw what looked like a tunnel rushing towards him. He was flung into the tunnel and heard a whooshing sound that blotted out everything. *Maybe I'm dying*, he thought.

When Paul opened his eyes he saw that he was back in his room. He saw Tiffany and Ryan also had arrived, dazed but apparently unhurt. He looked at their faces and then grew concerned.

"Quick, we need to wash our faces before anyone sees us," Paul said.

The teens rushed to the bathroom near Paul's room and splashed water over their faces and then dried themselves before returning. They could hear Paul and Tiffany's mothers talking in the other room. Ryan looked at his watch and gasped. He had to go home! It was almost ten o'clock. He pointed to his watch and said goodbye to his friends.

Tiffany studied Paul who sat at his desk staring at his computer screen as the credits for Minecraft ran across it.

"Did we dream all this?" she asked.

Paul reached into his pocket and felt something small and very hard. He pulled it out and stared. Then he handed it to Tiffany.

She took the small object and moved her hand closer to her eyes to get a better look.

"What is it? She said.

"They look like very small gold ingots. I remember when I was putting the treasures we found in the Fortress into our inventory I dropped a few gold ingots. I felt rushed, so I just stuck them into my pocket. Tiffany, we really were there."

Just then Tiffany's mother knocked on the door and make it clear that it already was far too late and they needed to head home. She turned to her daughter. "I hope you had fun playing," she said.

Tiffany looked at Paul and rolled her eyes.

"Let's have lunch tomorrow at school," she said. "We have lots to talk about."

ABOUT THE AUTHORS

Demian Schatt is a student at Laurel School in San Mateo, California. He plays Minecraft with his friends whenever he can. Demian is training to be a Minecraft Systems Administrator and soon will be managing his own server.

Stan Schatt is the author of *The Smartest Kid in the World* and lives in Carlsbad, California.

CPSIA information can be obtained at www.ICGtesting.com
Printed in the USA
BVOW02s1901161213

339295BV00001B/101/P

SPEAK FOR THE DEAD

A VIKING NOVEL OF MYSTERY AND SUSPENSE

SPEAK
FOR THE
DEAD

MARGARET YORKE

VIKING

VIKING
Published by the Penguin Group
Viking Penguin Inc., 40 West 23rd Street,
New York, New York 10010, U.S.A.
Penguin Books Ltd, 27 Wrights Lane,
London W8 5TZ, England
Penguin Books Australia Ltd, Ringwood,
Victoria, Australia
Penguin Books Canada Ltd, 2801 John Street,
Markham, Ontario, Canada L3R 1B4
Penguin Books (N.Z.) Ltd, 182–190 Wairau Road,
Auckland 10, New Zealand

Penguin Books Ltd, Registered Offices:
Harmondsworth, Middlesex, England

First American Edition
Published in 1988 by Viking Penguin Inc.

1 3 5 7 9 10 8 6 4 2

LIBRARY OF CONGRESS CATALOGING IN PUBLICATION DATA
Yorke, Margaret.
Speak for the dead.
(A Viking novel of mystery and suspense)
I. Title.
PR6075.07S7   1988   823'.914   87–40626
ISBN 0–670–82403–8

Printed in the United States of America by
Arcata Graphics, Fairfield, Pennsylvania
Set in Palatino

1

It was the old woman in the large Victorian house half-way down Elmwood Road who called the police.

Carrie had pressed the bell and waited while the door was unbolted, then opened on the chain. Two bright blue eyes beneath a crop of white curls peered through the gap at Carrie, who smiled winningly.

'I've come for the envelope,' she said. 'For the kids. You know. Got it ready?' and she waved a small buff envelope in front of her own face.

Mrs Fitzmaurice unhooked the door and opened it wider, taking in the spectacle of the thin young girl in jeans and loose white jacket, her blonde hair sprayed into stiff spikes round her head.

At that moment the telephone rang somewhere within the house.

'No, I haven't. You'll have to call back,' said Mrs Fitzmaurice, and shut the door.

She dealt with the telephone call, which was from someone wanting to sell her double glazing, and then searched for the charity envelope pushed through her door some days earlier. She didn't approve of that method of raising money; Mrs Fitzmaurice preferred the tin held by the licensed collector as used by most charities.

Licensed!

That girl with her punk hair wasn't like the usual door-to-door collector, and she'd brandished one of the envelopes, not a permit. She'd been offhand, even brusque, too, though that could have been merely contemporary conduct since manners in general had deteriorated in recent years. If she wasn't a regular helper, she could make a tidy pile gathering envelopes from trusting householders.

Mrs Fitzmaurice dialled the local police station.

Carrie had collected several envelopes before she saw the white police car travelling slowly towards her. She did not wait to discover if she was the quarry but turned into the nearest gateway. Most of the houses in Elmwood Road had front gardens planted with shrubs and trees to shield them from the gaze of passers-by and offering plenty of cover. Carrie ran down the short drive past the side of the house, avoiding a dustbin, into the long back garden. In the darkness she stumbled over a flowerbed, catching her jeans on a rose bush and cursing as a thorn stabbed her shin. A prowling cat sprang out of her way, squawking. There were lights on in the house behind her, but the curtains were drawn and no one heard the small skirmish, or, if they did, paid any heed.

Being hunted was exciting. It had happened to Carrie before when, as a small child, she had gone out collecting for Guy Fawkes with her friend Arlene and Arlene's small brother. At one house, while the occupant went off to get her purse, Carrie had sped in over the threshold, looked around and picked up some oranges from a bowl on a table in the nearest room.

The returning householder had seen her and given chase as the three children ran off, Carrie giggling but Arlene rather shocked, their guy almost falling from the pushchair lately used by Arlene's brother in which it was strapped. Its fierce features – a luridly painted cardboard mask with a hooked nose and attached grey wool hair beneath a woolly cap – seemed to smirk at their prank. They had enjoyed eating the oranges.

Carrie chuckled as she remembered this now. Still, the police were something else; she wanted no hassle with them.

She took off her white jacket and plunged her fingers into her hair, destroying her elaborate coiffure. Then she waited a while, lips parted, even white teeth gleaming in the darkness, heart beating fast as she listened for sounds of pursuit. All she heard was the distant noise of cars passing along the road. At last it seemed safe to leave the garden. The cat stalked her, its back arched as it minced along in her wake. Carried turned and hissed at it, and it hissed back, spitting.

She left the white jacket in the bushes by the gate, then, hands in pockets, her head back, slight body inconspicuous now in a dark sweater, she walked confidently into Elmwood Road as if she were a legitimate resident.

Cars were parked here and there along the road and one passed her as she emerged, but there was no sign of the patrol car. Carrie ran lightly in the direction from which it had come, took the next turning towards town and was soon on a bus heading towards Durford, where she lived with her mother and stepfather and their three children.

She had transferred her spoils from the white jacket into her jeans pocket: several fifty-pence coins, some tenpence pieces, a pound, and some coppers. People were mean, but she'd got enough money to go up to London again.

She'd learned about the envelope collection at school. One of the teachers had mentioned that she would be delivering them in Meddingham, where, as all the girls knew, she shared a flat with her boyfriend who worked for the Water Board. Carrie had innocently inquired if the teacher's collection area was large and had learned that it covered Elmwood Road and several other streets in the neighbourhood.

She did not push her luck too far. If the teacher went back and found the envelopes had already been collected, there could be trouble, so this was her sole such enterprise. As the police had more pressing matters to deal with than a possibly bogus collector, they made no special effort to trace her and she got away with it. She even rescued her white jacket the following evening, taking a carrier bag with her to put it in. It had rained during the day, and the jacket was soaked, but it came up as good as new after a wash.

Carrie Foster liked going to London. She would travel up on a Saturday morning, telling her mother and stepfather that she was spending the day with Arlene and that maybe they'd go to the ice-rink or to the cinema, activities no one could object to. Her mother, who had her younger children to deal with and also, at weekends, quite often the two children of her husband's first marriage, had given up expecting help with them all from Carrie. It was asking a lot to expect even natural brothers and sisters to get on together all the time, much less those acquired by marriage. If Carrie couldn't fit in, and increasingly she seemed unable to do so, she was better absent. She quite often stayed overnight with Arlene, who was a nice girl of whom Carrie's mother approved.

Carrie's mother did not know that her daughter sometimes stayed not with Arlene but in London.

Her early trips to the West End were innocent. She window-shopped and ate in sandwich bars and tried on clothes. Later, she found discos and clubs.

The first time she was propositioned she went into peals of laughter and refused, but one evening she met an Italian who told her that he worked at the embassy. He was quite attractive if you liked older men; she hadn't tried one before but there had to be a first time, so why not?

Carrie was fortunate with that initial experience. The Italian was, in fact, a waiter who worked in a small *trattoria* owned by his wife's family. He had had a major row with his wife and had walked out of both home and job. All this was a world away from Carrie's fumbling encounters with schoolboys, and she met Antonio several times before he told her that he was returning to Italy. In fact, he had had a tremendous and emotional reconciliation with his wife. Carrie felt really sorry when their affair ended. Antonio had given her ten pounds each time they met, taking her to a small hotel near Paddington. In the morning, he had always departed before she woke up; she assumed he was due on duty, but the truth was that he had gone guiltily off to mass. After their last night together, she found a twenty-pound note on the dressing-table, and that did a lot to console her.

There were other fish in the sea.

Carrie met Gordon Matthews three years later.

By this time she was working in Marks and Spencer's in Durford. Her experiences of a wider life had made her impatient to leave school, and as soon as she began earning – she found work in a factory packaging toiletries – she moved first to a hostel and then, with three girls she met in the factory, to what they grandly called a flat – two rooms, one with cooking facilities, and a bathroom shared with tenants on the floor below. At first she maintained close contact with her mother, and often went home for lunch on Sundays because she was certain of a good meal and a welcome, but gradually the intervals between her visits grew longer. For a while she went to evening classes to learn typing and shorthand, but she did not persevere: as when she was at school, she let other things distract her. She liked buying clothes and make-up, and tapes for her cassette player. Cash in and out of the hand was her style, not any long-term plan, unlike Arlene, whom she still saw once or twice a week.

Arlene had gone straight into Marks and Spencer's when she left school. The store gave opportunities for advancement if you had the ability, and there were all sorts of benefits for the staff such as subsidized meals and hair-do's. It was she who suggested that Carrie should apply for a vacancy, pointing out that in addition to all the welfare schemes for employees, you got first peek at the new lines.

Carrie was taken on and she had not regretted the change. All sorts of opportunities came her way.

When she first noticed Gordon, he was buying a suit.

Carrie, unloading a new stock of sweaters in the nearby men's knitwear section, saw him fingering a grey jacket, then looking round as if to check if he were being observed before taking it off its hanger and trying it on. Was he going to steal it? Surreptitiously, she watched as he held the matching trousers against himself to see if the length was right. She was almost disappointed when he took the garments to the pay desk. She had often managed to filch things herself; you had to be careful but everyone knew it went on. It wasn't like stealing, after all; no one went short.

That evening she was meeting Lennie, her current boyfriend, at a café near the cathedral. They'd have a snack before deciding how to spend the evening. He'd want to go ten-pin bowling, probably. She didn't mind. You met a good crowd there but it lacked the glamour of London.

When she entered the café, the man who had bought the

grey suit was sitting at a table alone drinking coffee and studying the *Durford Evening News*. He was wearing the suit. She'd thought him quite old in the store, for his hair was grey like his suit, and he had a small, soft moustache, but now she saw that after all he was only mature. Ever since Antonio, she had liked older men, and on the expeditions she still made to London in search of extra funds she always went for them. They were much more considerate than the young ones, she'd found, and they had more money; sometimes they took her to dinner first. Over the years she'd met other girls who were on the game in the same casual way and she'd learned a bit from them. As long as you didn't poach on their patch, they were quite friendly. She'd once nearly been arrested, but she had talked herself out of it that time and subsequently had been more careful, relying on pick-ups in bars and avoiding kerb crawlers however smart their cars. She sometimes thought of setting up with her own flat and acquiring a regular clientele, but she was nervous of pimps, and a little reluctant to make such a complete break with home.

Gordon noticed the pretty girl with the springy blonde curls take a table across from his but he was startled when she spoke.

'Pleased with your suit, are you?' she asked. 'It looks ever so nice.'

Gordon stared at her, not understanding, and Carrie laughed.

'I work in Marks,' she said. 'I noticed you trying the jacket.'

'Oh, did you?' Gordon's self-absorption was pierced. 'I'm glad you think it's all right,' he said. 'I'm starting a new job tomorrow and I need it for that.'

'Made redundant, were you?' Carrie thought that was such a nice way of describing getting the sack.

'Yes.'

'That's bad,' she sympathized. 'What's the new job?'

'Marketing stationery.'

How dull, thought Carrie.

'Useful,' she said.

'Yes. It's a firm of office suppliers, really,' said Gordon, and added, mundanely enough, 'Do you come here often?'

'Now and then,' Carrie replied. 'I'm supposed to be meeting someone, but he's late.'

'Would you like to go to the cinema with me instead?' asked Gordon.

Carrie glanced at her watch, then looked round. There was no sign of Lennie.

'All right,' she said, and added, 'There's a payphone here, by the gents'.'

'Have you got to make a call?' He sounded surprised.

'No, but haven't you? To your wife?'

He laughed then, but he didn't sound amused.

'No,' he replied. 'My wife's left me.'

'Oh dear,' said Carrie, and wondered if it was true; she'd heard that line before.

'I don't know what's on at the cinema,' he said as they left together. He had paid for her coffee as well as his own. 'Let's have a drink first, while we decide.' He had only been whiling away the time in the café until the pubs opened.

They went to the Pig and Whistle, where he lit a cigarette after offering her one. It was a pity about that; she preferred a non-smoker, but still, it didn't do to be too choosy. They had several drinks while they decided which film to see; there was one about India at the refurbished Plaza and Arlene had said it was good, so Carrie chose that. She expected the evening to end in the same way as when she went to London, but it didn't; Gordon took her to the Crown afterwards, where they served bar meals, and they both had sirloin steaks, with a bottle of red wine. Then he took her back to the flat in a taxi, apologizing because he had no car. His wife had taken it when she left, he said, and the children too.

They arranged to meet again two days later.

Carrie felt quite elated when they parted. He hadn't tried anything on in the cinema, and had barely pecked at her cheek as he said goodnight. Fancy a man taking you out for the evening and spending good money without expecting anything in return! She wondered if he was gay, but he'd looked at her with normal appreciation as they sat near a roaring fire in the lounge bar at the Crown, and as he helped her on with her coat his hands had lingered on her shoulders. He knew what was what, she was sure, and decided she rather liked his shy but experienced management of the evening.

Carrie knew that she could look after herself. She wondered if he could.

2

Hannah Matthews sat in a leather armchair in what had once been the dining-room at 51 Eggleton Road and which she now called her study. She was reading about life in Russia at the turn of the century, when valiant young Englishwomen made the journey to become governesses in noble households where it was fashionable to employ them. Had she lived in that era, she might have been such a one; as it was, she had become a teacher in a small private school where elocution had been her main subject. What adventures some of those women had had, fleeing from the Revolution to China, for instance. Today, in Russia, the family was still important. Television had introduced Hannah to harmonious scenes in admittedly small flats, where it seemed that parents and children pulled together to cope, often humorously, with the problems of day-to-day living, and made no complaints about what would be called, in the West, material deprivation. There was wonderful scenery in that vast land. She had watched shots of hunters in sub-zero temperatures going after game, setting traps, returning to their solid log cabins with faces and beards wreathed in frost, healthily tired after expending their energies in the natural pursuit of food and of skins for trading. The whole of Siberia was not, as the Western press implied, given over to salt mines and punishment cells. Life would be richer elsewhere if more people had clung to first principles. The use of machines for mundane tasks only resulted in excess leisure time in which discontent flourished. A busy person was a happy one, and Hannah thought the West could learn a lot from Russia, where strikes were unknown and there was no unemployment. Here, it was grab, grab, all the time, and the devil take the hindmost.

She was going to Russia soon. At last she would see for herself the beautiful city of Leningrad, built by Peter the Great upon marshland noted only for mosquitoes in summer and extreme cold in winter, a triumph of human endeavour. True, there was still some degree of religious persecution but greater tolerance was evolving and new priests were being recruited. Why, even notorious dissidents were now being allowed to leave the country.

Hannah believed in strict discipline. Rules were needed for the smooth running of any society, and within the family. When forming judgements, the customs of others had to be considered and respected. Russia, with its past history of predatory neighbours, had every reason to fear encroachment. Look at how Sweden had challenged Peter the Great! And later there had been Napoleon, dispatched at last by scorched earth and General Winter. That same relentless warrior had defeated Hitler in her own lifetime. So large and diverse a country required firm rule, just as the human family needed to look to its head.

She heard the front door opening and, with a sigh, laid down her book to listen to the shambling footsteps of Donald, her husband, entering the house and shuffling across the hall to the kitchen with the shopping. Since his retirement he had gone rapidly downhill, but then he had always been weak-willed. Where he would have got to without her to drive him onwards, she did not know, but she had seen that he rose in the light engineering firm he had joined after the war. She had made him go to night school and pass exam after exam, gradually climbing the ladder of commercial success until he became works manager.

She had driven the children, too. What was right was set before them and wrongdoing was punished severely. It was a pity that Monica and her husband had emigrated to Australia so soon after their wedding, but they seemed to be successful there. Gordon had gone against her advice in marrying that pale, puny Anne and naturally it hadn't worked out, but now, with a change of job and a new environment, he would build his life again. He was better off without that feeble wife and the two whining children.

As for Hannah, she'd never liked children much, not those she taught and not her own; but she had one at home now, an elderly toddler who could barely remember what she had sent him to buy at the local shops.

Irritably, because she wanted to finish her book and move on to a study of Catherine the Great, she rose and pursued him into the kitchen to detect his sins of omission.

James walked down the road from school to the village shop, where he lived with his grandparents. His friend Stephen was with him. Stephen intended to buy some crisps in the shop and he hoped Mrs Randall would invite him to tea, as she sometimes did. She was an ace cook, in Stephen's opinion, and always produced home-made scones and jam and squishy sponge cakes, even thought the shop was full of the sort of things you needn't prepare and which you'd think she'd just take from stock. Stephen's own mother wouldn't be home yet. She worked in an office in Rushbridge, typing invoices and sending out letters she constructed on her word processor. Stephen was interested in this and was keen to go to her office to try it. He usually let himself into the house in Church Way, a small private estate in the village of Little Foxton. His mother was never long in coming home as she worked through her lunch hour in order to leave early because of him, but he liked spending the interval at the shop where all sorts of intriguing things went on, like Mr Randall coming back from the cash and carry with stores and delivery men arriving with goods, which meant the shelves had to be filled. He and James often did that, especially in the holidays when Stephen spent a lot of his time with the Randalls while his mother was working. Mr Randall would sigh over the sell-by dates on the deliveries. Wholesalers often dumped nearly expired wares on small individual shops, keeping fresher goods for bulk orders at supermarkets, but naturally customers didn't want yoghurt which must be eaten within a few days when they could get fresher tubs on their regular journeys to Rushbridge, and Mr Randall lost sales through this practice.

Mr Randall was nowhere about today, and Mrs Randall, serving alone, was busy, but she was pleased to see the boys.

That was a nice thing about her, Stephen thought; she always took time to make you feel welcome. He was too young to realize what an asset this was to a shopkeeper.

'Tea's on the table. Help yourselves,' she said. 'Charlotte's practising her recorder – tell her she can stop now, James,' she added, and turned back to the woman whose order she was putting up.

Charlotte, three years younger than James, came out of school a quarter of an hour earlier, delivered by a mother with a similarly-aged child whom she collected daily by car. A good mutual support system in the village operated among the mothers, and they all admired the Randalls who had undertaken the care of their orphaned grandchildren and taken on the shop to provide a new income at a time when most people were retiring. The younger women helped Mary Randall by having the children to play in the holidays, and in return Mary would often baby-sit or take in an extra child or two overnight.

When the shop was closed and the books done, the family would have supper together. It was cosy in the flat above the shop, with the curtains drawn against the night and everything scary shut firmly outside. James remembered the bad time, when that wicked man had made Mummy die, and Daddy too. He could remember Mummy, but Charlotte couldn't and had to look at old photographs to discover what she had looked like. James liked thinking of Mummy but not of Daddy, who'd so often been angry and shouted at all of them.

The Randalls just made a living from the shop. They had turned the loss sustained by the previous owners into a steady gain and sometimes Oliver Randall imagined he might build up a good business to hand over to the children. In a different mood, he would picture James becoming a doctor or lawyer, and Charlotte perhaps a dental surgeon. Girls needed good careers; they might be left with children to support. But the main aim was to keep things going long enough to get the children settled in life and on their way to independence.

When the tragedy happened, Oliver and Mary were looking forward to his retirement. He was a chartered surveyor working in Birmingham. They had planned to move to the coast and take up bird-watching, painting and other leisurely pursuits. Instead they had been catapulted into taking full charge of their grandchildren. That was five years ago.

Stephen had at first been embarrassed, hearing that James's parents were dead. That was worse than the divorce which had parted his mother and father. You never saw them again after death.

'They were killed in a car smash,' James had told him. 'A wicked man made them crash.' Once, he'd woken from a bad dream and come downstairs looking for comfort. He'd heard his grandparents talking.

'Of course he was drunk,' his grandmother had said.

He'd asked if they were talking about the man who had caused the crash and they'd said yes. Then Granny had made him a hot drink and tucked him back into bed.

James was glad they had not gone to live with Uncle Rufus, who was very strict. He was much stricter than Granny who insisted on washed hands and brushed hair before meals but didn't fuss unduly if you interrupted someone else's conversation when you had something urgent to say, or spoke with your mouth full. She and Grandad both said that discussion was very important and it was a pity if good ideas were lost because there was no time to air them. But there was plenty to do at Uncle Rufus' and Aunt Hilary's house. They had a swimming pool and there was a pony, but their children were boring, always full of complaints and ailments. They had an elaborate train set on trestles in an attic, but this could only be used under supervision because it belonged to Uncle Rufus himself and was of historic importance. James and Charlotte went to stay in the summer holidays, but they were always glad to return to the shop in the main street of Little Foxton.

'Where's Grandad?' asked James this afternoon.

'Gone delivering,' said Charlotte. Their grandfather put up orders for people who lived out of the village or were old and couldn't carry heavy shopping, and took them round in the back of his Peugeot estate car.

'He's late.'

Mary Randall, too, had begun to wonder where Oliver was. Her abiding fear was that some dreadful fate would befall him and that she would be left alone to cope with the children. If that happened, Rufus would try to take over their guardianship; he might even prevail on the law to intervene. Such things occurred, even in families. Indeed, terrible things could happen within families.

She was three years younger than Oliver and fit for her age, but she had begun to tire more quickly than before, and she worried. Sometimes she lay awake at night fretting about the future and reliving the past with its griefs and pain. Oliver did, too. His steady snores would stop and she would know he was lying there across the narrow gap between their twin beds sharing her own fears, but neither dared express them aloud, for to do so might cause the whole structure of their world to crumble.

He had not returned by closing time. She turned the sign on the door and locked up, and began preparing the simple supper they had every evening. Stephen was still there, having refused her suggestion that he should telephone his mother to let her know where he was.

'She'll guess,' he explained. 'She'll ring up fast enough if she's bothered.'

He and James went up to James's small room under the eaves to begin their homework. They didn't have much to do: just the spelling of some words to learn and a passage to read. They would both move up from the village primary school together in September, and then they'd have plenty, but that was months away. Charlotte was too young for homework; she settled down to some painting. She was good at drawing; perhaps she had inherited her mother's talent.

Mary Randall peeled potatoes and scraped carrots, and all the time she waited for the knock on the door that would herald the police bringing bad news.

It had happened before.

Oliver had arranged to meet the man in Rushbridge.

'Cheaper if you come to the office,' the man had said. 'I'm afraid I'll have to charge expenses if I travel.'

'I can't spare the time,' said Oliver. The man lived in Lentwich, twenty miles to the east. Oliver did not want to be seen entering the premises of a private inquiry agent closer to home, where he might be recognized. He had found Michael West's name in the yellow pages and was drawn to the fact that he seemed to operate as an individual, not part of some large concern.

Oliver left the car in a pay-and-display park and walked along the main street and down a side road to the Primrose Café. He ordered tea. He had been sitting there only a couple of minutes when the man took a chair opposite him.

Oliver looked up sharply, like a hound pointing, the man thought.

'Mr Randall?' he said. 'I'm Michael West.'

He caught the waitress's eye and asked for tea for himself. He had been standing some distance from the café watching various people enter and had known that the thickset elderly man with white hair, wearing a tweed cap, must be his client.

Mr West was younger than Oliver had expected a private detective to be. He was slight and red-headed, and he wore a dark padded anorak and very clean jeans. He could have been anything from a schoolmaster to a navvy.

'I want you to trace the man who was responsible for killing my daughter,' said Oliver Randall in even tones, low enough not to be overheard at the neighbouring tables.

He had planned this moment for years, and had decided to postpone it no longer lest fate take a hand and deny him his chance for revenge, the vengeance that justice, so-called, with its lily-livered sentences and indifference to the rights of victims, had failed to deliver.

'Tell me about him,' said Michael West, and prepared to listen.

When Oliver finally returned home, Mary was cross and snapped at him because he was so much later than she had expected. He told her that the car had not been running smoothly and he had taken it into the garage.

'You could have rung up,' she said.

'You shouldn't worry,' he answered, and suddenly hugged her. He had lied to her, which was wrong and he felt guilty, but life was precarious and could end abruptly. People who loved one another should not quarrel.

3

Michael West had left the police force after a disciplinary inquiry which concluded that he had questioned the orders of his superiors on too many occasions for the matter to be ignored.

A member of the CID, he had objected to the routine harsh interrogation of persons suspected of crime only on the grounds of circumstantial evidence, and had protested when a grief-stricken man who had come home from work to find the dead body of his wife lying in a pool of blood in their kitchen had been mercilessly grilled while the real culprit escaped and clues were obscured. It was true that most murders occurred within the family, but there were exceptions, and to decide on this occasion that the husband was the killer without first questioning neighbours as to whether the pair got on well, and when there was not a trace of blood on his clothing, was not only inhuman, in Michael's opinion, but also exceedingly stupid. It seemed to be more important to make an arrest than to discover the truth. At first he had hoped to change the system; eventually, it broke him.

Since then he had tried various jobs. He had been a security officer at a factory, a hospital porter, even a driving instructor, but had found satisfaction in none of them. His wife, who had not liked the anti-social hours of his police work, had soon tired of his attempts to find another niche and one evening he had arrived home to find all his belongings stacked in the garage of the house on which he still struggled to keep up mortgage payments, and the doors locked and bolted to keep him out. After ringing and knocking and making enough noise to cause several neighbours to come out of their own houses to see what was happening, with one of them threatening to call the police if he didn't stop creating a disturbance, he left, with the sobs of his children clearly audible from within.

Listening to Oliver Randall relate how his grandchildren had been abruptly orphaned, Michael felt pity and admiration for the old man.

'They made out it was all her fault in court,' said Oliver. 'That she was to blame for her own death.'

'Some people have a death wish when life gets too difficult,' Michael said. 'They put themselves in positions of danger – cross roads dangerously – take chances driving. That sort of thing.'

'She loved her children. She wouldn't knowingly do anything that could put them at risk,' said Oliver. His sunken blue eyes flashed with anger as he spoke. 'Justice is turned on its head when lawyers put forward completely false versions of events, and juries aren't told what really happened.'

Michael nodded. Here was a true kindred spirit.

'And honest citizens are given such a going-over in the witness box that it's no wonder people don't want to get involved,' he said.

'Make a living at it, do you? This gumshoe business? That's what you're known as, isn't it?' Oliver asked.

'Just about,' said Michael. 'A lot of it's routine stuff. Getting evidence for divorce cases, detecting frauds – people who say they've no funds and are reneging on their mortgages and maintenance orders when they're merrily moonlighting. I'll be glad to take on this case, Mr Randall.'

They arranged that Oliver would telephone Michael in a week's time.

'I don't want you ringing me or writing. My wife knows nothing about this,' he warned.

'I understand.'

Before they parted, Oliver handed over a large manila envelope.

'These are copies of some of the newspaper reports there were at the time,' he said. He had taken them out of the black tin box in the wardrobe, photocopied them at a pay machine while supposedly at the cash and carry, and returned the originals while Mary was having a bath. He didn't think she ever looked at them now, but he did: he wanted his anger to endure.

Michael drove back to Lentwich along the main road, the rising wind catching his car on the long exposed stretches where there was no land mass to break its impact as it blew from the sea. He lived in a flat above a betting shop in a seedier part of the town, since rents were too high elsewhere. It was convenient in many ways, for there was a fish-and-chip shop on the corner and a launderette opposite. Back in his flat, he studied the cuttings, in one of which was reproduced a photograph of Anne taken just before her marriage. It showed a young, untried face, with a high forehead, deepset eyes under curved brows, a soft mouth; there had not been time for life to etch in lines of defence or despair, nor even of joy.

Why had defence and despair been the first things to come into his mind? The girl looked wary and vulnerable, but when the photograph was taken she should have been hopeful and happy.

Oliver Randall had revealed that the marriage had not been a success.

'Intimacies. I don't know. He liked his own way,' he'd said, his voice gruff.

Michael waited.

'She held on. There were the children, you see. She was a serious girl who wouldn't throw in her hand lightly.' Oliver frowned. 'Today, I suppose you'd say they were incompatible. They met at university. She never went out with anyone else, as far as I know. I've never understood what she saw in him.'

'You didn't like him,' said Michael.

'No. But then it's common for fathers to think no one good enough for their daughter,' said Oliver.

'Did he have affairs?'

'I don't know.' Once, many years ago, Oliver himself had been briefly unfaithful to Mary with a woman he'd met at the golf club. His guilt was so huge that ever since then he had been seeking to make amends to Mary, who had never known what had happened. He still felt shame at the memory.

Carefully, Michael read the reports, noted dates and

addresses, checked ages. The man would be thirty-eight now, his own age; they had grown up in the hedonistic sixties for which posterity was paying the price with the horrifying increase of violence and the advent of an appalling disease. He sighed over his inability to mend the world. It had been a desire to maintain law and order that had taken him into the police force and out of it again.

He had other work to complete, bills to make out, a report to write for a man who suspected his wife of two-timing him. During the hours when her jealous husband imagined her to be in the arms of a lover, she was visiting a chiropractor, exactly as she had told her husband.

Perhaps the chiropractor was the lover?

Michael dismissed the idea, but would the husband? At least the treatment was working; she walked less stiffly already. Perhaps she would become strong enough to quit her marital prison, thought Michael. She was only forty-four and her children were both at college. She was a good-looking woman who could make her own way if she had enough nerve. You couldn't own somebody else, as her husband appeared to think he owned her.

He finished his report and put it, with his account, in an envelope, then went downstairs and into the street to post it at the box down the road, hoping the bill would be settled promptly. He might never know the outcome. Michael regretted that. The trouble was that he always got involved and that was what had ultimately wrecked his police career.

'You're in the wrong job, matey,' he told himself, walking on to the fish-and-chip shop. There was never time to cook.

Two days later Michael was seeking information on a housing estate in the West Midlands. He had already discovered, by consulting the electoral roll, that his quarry was not living at the address given in the newspaper reports but it had been the obvious place to begin his search. Someone there might know the man's whereabouts. He found the house, 47 Ridgmount Way, and rang the bell, but there was no reply.

The next thing was to ask the neighbours. He tried Number 46, the other half of the semi-detached pair of tiny, box-like houses, and a fair young woman with a two-year-old clutching her legs opened the door and looked at him suspiciously. Michael could see her registering the knowledge that she should have kept the chain up.

He did not want to give the true reason for his visit but used a ploy that had worked before. He held a clipboard, with a wodge of papers attached.

'Excuse me,' he began. 'I'm conducting an inquiry into population mobility. Would you mind telling me how long you've lived here?'

'Three years,' replied the young woman. 'We'd just got married.'

'Ah.' Michael made a note on the page before him. 'And who lived here before you? Where did they go, do you know?'

'Their name's Williams. They moved to Goldsmith Crescent,' said his informant. 'This place got too small for them and they're on their way up, anyway.' She smiled, revealing attractively uneven teeth.

'No one's at home next door, I see,' said Michael, indicating Number 47. 'It's the same as this, is it? Not altered in any way?'

'No. It's just the same, except the other way round,' said the woman. 'Like in a mirror.'

The toddler now began to whine.

'It's all right, pet. The man's just going,' said the young woman, about to close the door.

Michael had to take a chance.

'You didn't know the Matthewses, did you? They lived next door,' he ventured.

'Oh no. That was before we came,' said the young woman. 'And the house has changed hands twice since. It's as if there's a jinx on it. Both the other couples split up. The new people seem all right so far.' She shuddered. 'Terrible about them, wasn't it? You obviously know what happened.'

Michael decided he would like to hear her version of events. He turned on his most winning smile and gave his car keys to the toddler, who immediately stuffed them in his mouth.

Two minutes later he was seated at the kitchen table with

a large mug of coffee in front of him, hearing the local folklore.

The Williamses were, as had been implied, upwardly mobile. Their detached house in Goldsmith Cresent was three times the size of the small box from which they had moved. A line of well-established cupressus trees which would one day cast too much shade bordered the wooden fencing dividing it from its neighbour. There was a garage and car-port. A child's bicycle was propped against the front porch.

Mellow chimes sounded within the house when Michael rang the bell.

He used the same spiel about population movement when Mrs Williams came to the door. She agreed that she and her family had moved here three years before. She was a teacher and had gone back to work when her youngest child started school. Her husband had become disillusioned with the teaching profession and now worked in a food-processing factory ten miles away.

'He earns a lot more,' said Kate Williams. 'He's in the testing department, so I suppose what he does is useful.'

Michael agreed that it probably was. He asked some routine questions, making entries on his paper.

'You knew Anne Matthews, I suppose,' he said, after inquiring about the number of bathrooms the Williamses owned.

'Oh, yes. That was dreadful. She was a dear,' said Kate Williams, and as she spoke her eyes filled with tears. 'Those two poor children. Goodness knows what became of them. They just vanished, afterwards. I suppose Anne's brother took them on.'

'I gather it wasn't a very happy marriage,' Michael suggested.

'I don't know how she stuck it,' said Kate. 'She was either a saint or a fool. Depends which way you look at it.'

Michael decided on a gamble. Mr Williams, if he kept normal office hours, wouldn't be home for a while.

'I'm not really researching into the population,' he confessed. 'Or not in quite the way I've implied. I'm sorry to have misled you, but I'm making some inquiries into her death for an interested party.'

'Who's that? Some insurance company? They don't pay for years, do they?'

'Something like that,' Michael temporized. 'I'm a private detective. Here's my card.' He produced it, and for the second time that day was led into a warm kitchen, this one a good deal tidier than the last, its fitments made of wood. A dishwasher was plumbed in by the sink, and a utility room adjoined.

'I'll tell you what I can,' said Kate. 'The children won't be back for an hour or so. One's got a piano lesson and the other two are with friends. They're twins,' she added, with some pride. 'Boys. Little terrors, really.'

'I've got a boy,' said Michael. 'He's nine.'

Bonded thus, they beamed at one another.

'The newspaper reports made out that she was to blame for the marriage problems,' Michael said. TRAGIC DEATH OF NAGGING WIFE, one headline had stated.

'It wasn't true,' said Kate. 'I was shocked when I saw that. I wish I'd spoken out at the time but I didn't know when the case was going to be heard. I didn't recognize the Anne I knew in the papers. It was all lies to get that devil off the hook.'

'You call him a devil?'

'Wasn't he one? Look at all the grief and misery he caused,' Kate answered. 'He got off relatively scot-free and all by – by –' she searched for the right words. 'By defaming Anne's memory,' she declared.

'Suppose you tell me all you can about her,' Michael invited.

For Anne Matthews had not died in a road accident. Her husband had attacked her savagely, beaten her and finally had strangled her, and though he had been charged with murder, a plea of guilty to manslaughter had been accepted, on the grounds of excessive provocation by the victim.

4

Donald Matthews wandered round the hardware store peering through his bifocals at ranks of tools – screwdrivers and wrenches, secateurs and trowels, garden forks and clippers. Paints and varnishes, too, held his attention; the colours nowadays had such exotic names that there was no way of knowing what they meant without consulting the relevant chart. These modern coverings were easy to apply: thick emulsion that did not drip, gloss paint that dried swiftly and evenly, fillers that adhered despite the most inept application. It had all been different when he worked in this very building as a lad. In those days a tiny part of this large store had been his father's small ironmonger's shop, and Donald had expected to take the business over in due course, but rents had risen and a multiple which already owned the neighbouring property had set up in competition. His father had sold out after the war and Donald had entered the light engineering firm wherein Hannah had made sure he succeeded. His parents had bought the house in Eggleton Road with the proceeds of the sale and had lived comfortably there until they died within weeks of one another. Donald and Hannah had lived in it ever since, although the house was, Donald thought, dark, old-fashioned and gloomy. He would have liked a nice new bungalow within walking distance of the centre of Yelbury instead of being out in the suburbs. But Hannah considered Eggleton Road to be a good address, and it was convenient for the grammar school which the boy had attended. Monica was sent to a convent school where Hannah said she would mix with well-brought up girls and learn nice manners. Monica was not as good at her lessons as the boy who, Hannah said, must aim for a profession. He had gone to university, but once there had appeared to drift, switching courses several times and in the end failing his final examinations.

Remembering this, Donald sighed heavily and, to distract his thoughts, examined a bottle of selective weedkiller. Manufacturers had become very ingenious these days, devising chemicals that picked out only certain targets. Holding the bottle, he looked across at the till to see if Mrs Francis was busy. Donald saw her hand a large package to a customer and smile at him. What a nice woman she was, always so friendly. He moved towards her.

Behind the protective shield of her counter, Mrs Francis's spirits sank as she saw him coming. He was her cross, her albatross. For his part, Donald stiffened his ageing spine, twirled an imaginary moustache and accelerated his customary shamble to step out as smartly as he could, bearing down on the plump, grey-haired woman in her blue overall with the badge pinned to a lapel stating that she was Mrs F.J. Francis. What did the F stand for? Felicity? Donald longed to ask her, and he would one day, when he plucked up enough courage to invite her to the Bird in Hand for a sherry. He'd done that sort of thing as a younger man; why not again?

'Keeping well, then, Mrs Francis?' he began.

'Oh yes,' Mrs Francis replied. 'Mustn't grumble.'

She turned to tidy up her Sellotape and credit-card machine, her scissors and other bits and pieces, praying for another customer to come along and save her from this dreary old man.

'Warm for the time of year,' offered Donald.

'Going to do some gardening, are you?' Mrs Francis inquired brightly.

'Later, when the longer days arrive,' said Donald.

'But they have,' Mrs Francis said. 'They soon draw out after Christmas. It's just the mornings that get darker.'

'I put some bulbs in,' Donald told her.

'That's nice. What were they, then? Daffs, was it?' Mrs Francis could keep up this meaningless dialogue without much effort, her mind ranging meanwhile over what to get Ted for his supper and wondering if he'd remembered to ring up the plumber. Ted was asthmatic and had been forcibly retired two years ago. They depended on her job for the holiday in the sun they took every year, and other extra comforts.

Donald's script contained no Ted. In his scenario, Mrs Francis was a brave and lonely widow.

'Going away, are you, this year?' he asked her. There were bleak weeks to get through when she took her leave.

'Portugal, probably,' she told him, and suppressed a sigh of relief as a genuine customer proferred a wire basket full of purchases.

Donald faded into the background again, eyeing casseroles. There was such a lot to look at in the store; he was never bored while waiting for each chance to talk to his beloved.

Poor old soul, thought Mrs Francis when at last he shuffled out after bidding her what he thought was a debonair farewell. She instantly forgot him.

Donald's next call was at the Bird in Hand, where he fortified himself with a pint of bitter against his return home.

Hannah soon found that he had forgotten the potatoes. She sent him out again directly after lunch, which was a meat pie with a heated up tin of tomatoes.

'I believe you do it on purpose,' she declared.

Sometimes he thought so too: it gave him a reason to escape from her again.

Michael West had just parked his car a little further up Eggleton Road when Donald emerged from Number 51 that afternoon. He saw a bent, elderly figure in a shabby grey raincoat, a muffler round his neck, a tweed hat on his head, shopping bag in hand, heading towards the bus stop on the corner.

Michael waited until he had gone some distance before ringing the bell at the house he had just left.

A woman in a turquoise wool two-piece and a pearl necklace opened the door to him. She had fiercely black hair and heavily painted brows etched in on bald flesh above her small brown eyes.

'I buy nothing at the door,' she told him sternly, preparing to close it before he had even begun his patter.

Michael, his trusty clipboard at the ready, knew instantly that she would not accept his hitherto successful approach: she would want to see his authority, and he had none.

'Excuse me – are you Mrs Warrender?' he asked at random.

'I am not, young man,' said Hannah Matthews.

'I'm very sorry. I must have come to the wrong address. This is Meadow Road, isn't it?' Michael put on his most disarming smile.

'It is not. This is Eggleton Road, as you could find out for yourself if you read the sign at the corner,' Hannah told him curtly.

She shut the door in his face before he could utter another word, and, inside the house, briefly considered telephoning the police to have him investigated. There was something fishy about him, and she might have thought he was a nosy reporter trying to hark back to all that tiresome business if he had not apologized so politely. A reporter would have thrust his foot into the doorway and pushed his elbow round as well. They did not give up without a struggle.

Hannah did not want to resurrect the past, nor did she want dealings with the police. She went back to Catherine the Great.

Michael had again consulted the electoral roll, a good way of discovering who lived in any particular house. Hannah and Donald Matthews were listed as the sole residents of 51 Eggleton Road, which indicated that their son had not moved in with them. Then he had gone to the offices of the *Yelbury Gazette* to look at the files, and he had found a reporter who had been the area correspondent for over ten years, doing some stringing on the side. Over a beer at the Three Pigeons, Barnaby Duke had told Michael what he knew about the Matthewses.

'The mother was a tartar,' he said. 'Is one still, I'm sure. Used to be chairman of the Townswomen's Guild – good at it, too – stood no nonsense from the committee. But even she couldn't ride out that storm and she had to resign. I'm surprised they stayed here afterwards. Of course, they'd both lived here all their lives. It's said she grabbed Donald when he got back from the war and wouldn't leave go of him as she knew she'd never get anyone else. Most people have forgotten it now, I expect. Other scandals have happened since. It's five years ago, after all. Life goes on.'

'For some,' said Michael. 'Not for Anne. Any idea where Gordon is now? Does he ever visit the parents?'

'He's out, is he?'

'Been out six months or more,' said Michael. 'He got remission for good conduct and he'd already served some time on remand, so he was only in for about four years.'

'I expect it seemed long enough to him,' said Barnaby. 'It was a seven-year sentence. That's quite a lot for man-slaughter these days.'

'How did his parents react?'

'Stood by him, of course. The mother was willing to testify about the girl asking for it but she wasn't called. Wouldn't look too good – the mother-in-law, you know.'

'What about the father?'

'Went to pieces. Started drinking. Took early retirement,' Barnaby said. 'He's quite a nice old boy, or used to be. I should think they spent a lot on Gordon's defence.'

'He'd have got legal aid.'

'Mother would have made father stump up for the very best,' said Barnaby. 'Blamed it all on her. On Anne. Couldn't have been true, of course.'

'Why do you say that?'

'She was sweet,' said the reporter. 'I met her once. I knew him too – went to school with him. That's why I remember such a lot about the case. You don't meet many murderers in your lifetime, and he was one. As a boy he was a moody devil. People like that don't change.'

Two people now had described Gordon Matthews as a devil in as many days.

'Why didn't you say so at the time?' demanded Michael.

'Got no chance. It wasn't heard locally, remember. They weren't living here. I didn't know when the case was coming on.' He'd slipped up over that; he could have made a corner in it if he'd taken the trouble to find out; maybe that was why he was still in Yelbury and not in Fleet Street, or even Wapping. 'Gordon pleaded guilty to manslaughter. I'd no evidence to give. I couldn't do a thing.'

'Doesn't throwing marriage dirt around make a good story?' Michael asked. 'You could have chased up her friends – got denials from them over what was said in court about her.'

'That sort of story doesn't get much space in the *Gazette*,' said Barnaby. 'You're right, though. I missed a chance.'

'He wrecked a lot of lives.'

'Yes.' Barnaby tapped the table restlessly. 'She kept them both. They met at university but he never got his degree and never stuck to anything after that. It must have been difficult after the kids came. I can't see Gordon as a housefather looking after them while she went off to work. When it happened the little girl was only a baby.'

'I want to find him,' Michael said.

'Why?'

'For various reasons, which I'm not at liberty to tell you.'

'Is there a story in it?'

'What sort of story?' Michael asked.

'Oh – setting the record straight. That sort of thing,' said Barnaby, with guile.

'There might be.'

'The parents probably do know where he is, but the mother wouldn't talk to me. I might get something out of the old man, though. I could write it up,' said Barnaby. 'On Anne's birthday, or some other such occasion – the anniversary of when it happened, for example.'

'You've just said that's not your paper's style.'

'There are others.' Perhaps he might yet reach a wider circulation, and with his own byline. 'Look, I'll see what I can do, providing you cut me in on anything you discover as a result of what I find out.'

Michael crossed his fingers.

'All right,' he said.

'I'll give you a ring in a few days' time,' said Barnaby. 'OK?'

'OK,' said Michael. 'Thanks.'

5

Carrie liked being married at first. After all, it was what happened to you when you were round about twenty or so. Most of the girls in Marks had gold bands on their fingers and now she had one, too. She'd enjoyed the fuss of the wedding, though it had been rather low key because of Gordon's divorce which meant that a church ceremony was out. Still, she didn't go for that sort of thing much so it was no great hardship to make do with the registry office. She'd had a lovely new outfit – a wide-brimmed straw hat and a gauzy dress in a cyclamen pink – and they'd had a reception at the community hall. Gordon had paid for the drink, which was really thoughtful of him; he'd been quite upset when he saw how her mother lived. She'd felt proud of him, taking him home to meet the family. He'd worn his new suit, with a blue shirt and pale blue tie and matching handkerchief in his breast pocket, looking for all the world like a moustached younger edition of Sir Alastair Burnet, she'd thought.

He was getting on well with his new job. His firm supplied stationery and office equipment over a wide area and employed several salesmen and service engineers as well as the clerical staff at the branch headquarters.

They'd got a ninety per cent mortgage on a brand-new maisonette in Newnham Close on the southern outskirts of Durford. Gordon had a firm's car in which he travelled to work every day. His firm was based right across town to the north, on an industrial estate with several large factories and some smaller units dealing in a wide variety of products. He and Carrie had a joint bank account and both contributed to the mortgage payments. Carrie had never lived in such comfort before. Though the house was tiny, with only one bedroom, a minute bathroom, one living-room and a diminutive kitchen, it was all so spankingly new and bright that it took very little time to clean. Now she shared the bathroom only with Gordon, not a group of girls and their occasional overnight men friends. Any washing that hung to dry on a plastic airer standing in the bath was merely hers and his. It was a joy to run round with the vacuum cleaner on Saturdays and spray Pledge on the furniture they had bought at a discount warehouse. Gordon washed the car and caught up on his paperwork at weekends while she did the domestic chores. Then they'd go to the pub.

She wished he didn't smoke so heavily. The living-room was always stuffy with fumes in the morning, and because they both went out so early, it never got properly aired. Sometimes he drank more than was good for him, too; he'd got into bad ways after his wife left him and it might take some time for him to change these habits, but he would, in the end, she felt sure. She didn't let them bother her much.

The only flaw in the first weeks was when Carrie was requested to leave Marks and Spencer's after there was a query over money missing from a till, and two pairs of lacy briefs, still with their price tags, were found in her handbag without a receipt. However, no charges were brought. She told Arlene, who had married earlier and had left the store to have a baby, that she had felt like a change.

She soon found a job in the fashion department of Brice's, Durford's big independent store where one of the perks was a discount on purchases made in the store.

There was not a lot of socializing among the residents of Newnham Close. Most were young couples or single people, and they all went out to work so that the place was deserted during the day. Carrie was on nodding terms with a few people who travelled on the same bus from Bridge Street into town.

Carrie basked contentedly in her new circumstances for a while until she began to think that a car of her own would be nice. It would make visiting Arlene easier. She lived in a suburb to the west of Durford and the journey meant changing buses in the town centre. A car would be useful in other ways, too, and would give her more freedom. It wasn't an impossible idea, and in preparation she could soon learn to drive.

She'd always liked wearing nice clothes, especially underwear, and Gordon appreciated her taste. He'd surprised her in that way. He looked so quiet and controlled but he could become a veritable tornado when aroused. She enjoyed leading him on, teasing him. He'd wanted to know where she'd learned such tricks but she'd kept her counsel.

'You surely didn't expect me never to have been anywhere?' she'd answered.

'Who was he?' Gordon demanded. 'Who was your other lover?'

He'd looked quite fierce, but she'd soon made him forget what was on his mind, though he often returned to the topic.

'You're jealous!' she diagnosed. 'I don't keep asking about your wife. That doesn't bother me. Why should anything I've done worry you? What counts is now, and it's good.'

She could always calm him down. Sometimes it was quite exciting to have him in such a mood.

'When are you going to start a family?' asked Arlene one day.

'I haven't thought about it,' said Carrie. 'Anyway, we can't afford to at the moment, with the mortgage.'

'He's not getting any younger, your Gordon,' said Arlene. She had been very surprised at Carrie's sudden marriage and was anxious about the age difference, but Gordon was an improvement on some of the men Carrie had gone out with before. Perhaps, as she'd lost her own father, she was better suited to an older man, and as he'd been married before he would probably be extra keen to make things work out this time.

'Well, he's had kids. He must know all about broken nights and that sort of thing.' Carrie herself didn't fancy a sopping wet child climbing into bed with them in the night, which was what happened regularly to Arlene and Tom. Babies were often rather disgusting, all that sick and milk and stuff. She didn't really want one at all, now she came to think about it. Arlene wasn't nearly such good company since she had become a mother; she'd let herself go and wore shabby old clothes, and her conversation was all about Jackie's new tooth or latest verbal achievement. It was quite hard to get her gossiping about times past or interested in what went on at Brice's.

Gordon had had a shock when he discovered that Carrie was no cook. That became evident very early in the marriage when she opened tins and heated up prepared dishes bought from freezer departments. He expected a proper roast on Sundays, and she could not cope with such a challenge. Crispness eluded her potatoes, and her brussels sprouts turned grey and soggy while she waited for the meat to cook. He complained about every culinary failure, as he had during his first marriage, but Carrie, unlike Anne, did not cringe or burst into tears. She answered back.

'I've never done much cooking,' she told him. 'My mum did it at home and we all muddled along at the flat. Rosanne was the best – she did all the fancy stuff, not that we went in for it, much.' Takeaway food had been their main diet.

In those early weeks, Gordon was soon pacified in bed. Carrie crooned to him that she loved him, and she did; he had brought her the first real security she had known and in return she was prepared to be forgiving.

She complained to Arlene about Gordon's untidy ways. Even on their honeymoon – a long weekend in Brighton – he had thrown his clothes about and left them for her to pick up. She'd accepted this, at first, as the consequence of ardour, but later, when the custom continued and he left his discarded garments on the bedroom or bathroom floor, she blamed his upbringing. But not to him: never that. Somehow, she didn't know quite why, she never dared.

'Men,' said Arlene. 'That's all they want – someone to cook and clean for them and go to bed with when they fancy. It's what you have to do for your meal ticket in life. What else is there?'

But Carrie had seen Arlene's husband, Tom, washing up; had heard that he paced the floor with the crying, teething baby.

Gordon got tired, of course, she made the excuse. He had a lot of responsibility at work and was fourteen years older than Arlene's Tom. He'd come round in time.

Marriage had not been in Gordon's plans when he met Carrie in the café several weeks after his release from prison. His probation officer had found him a place in a hostel and an office job, but he had taken up neither. He had decided to start life again in a new area.

Then Carrie came along, and her pretty, piquant face and friendly manner had at once attracted him. Soon after their second meeting he saw her in a pub with another man, a young fellow with a mop of wiry fair curls rather like Carrie's own hair. They were sitting on a bench seat with their heads close together and Gordon felt a sick surge of envious jealousy. It occurred to him that he could attempt to cut out the youngster, and to do it he would have to marry her. Why not, anyway? He needed to return to the domestic order of earlier years.

In youth, his mother had imposed a strict routine and had sent him off to school each day in a spotless shirt with a clean white handkerchief in his pocket. He returned from school on time and was given a nourishing meal before being dispatched to his room to do his homework, for he was expected to succeed. Good manners were taught at home and there was a punishment for every mis-demeanour, however trivial. For spilling his tea, Gordon had to put sixpence in his mother's missionary box. For losing a gym shoe the penalty was ten shillings. Other offences merited appropriately adjusted penalties. He was never beaten, but he was shut in the cellar for contradicting his mother, and again for lying.

This treatment provoked in Gordon a desire to punish others. When he saw a schoolfellow stealing money from another boy's blazer pocket in the changing-room, he blackmailed the culprit and as a result was kept in sweets for two terms, until his victim outgrew him and called his bluff. After that, Gordon found someone else to torment.

At their church wedding, Anne had conventionally promised to obey him. She soon found that she had let herself in for a life of subservience to a bully, but because of the children there was no easy escape. At first she expected things to improve. If Gordon found work, he would be less demanding, she reasoned; but any job he got never lasted, and he became even harsher and more intolerant as she grew crushed and defeated.

Too late, Gordon realized that Carrie would not so easily be brought to heel. She belonged to another generation conditioned to different ideas, and ever since she left school she had lived away from home in what Gordon considered to be unsuitable circumstances. He had collected her from the flat more than once and had frowned at its noisy disorder, unable to perceive the happy co-operation among the girls, who lent each other clothes and looked after one another when unwell, and generally observed a spirit of give and take. Carrie, in particular, was generous, often giving presents to the other girls or buying treats for supper. It was always Carrie who produced an occasional bottle of wine or a supermarket gâteau. Sometimes she had stolen them.

Carrie decided that a microwave oven would transform her life. She could heat ready-made meals in a twinkling and if she first helped them on to plates, Gordon could be deceived into thinking they had originated in her kitchen.

She asked Gordon to give her one for Christmas and he rounded on her angrily.

'Those things cost money and are simply an excuse for laziness,' he told her sternly. 'You'll learn to cook – and economically – like every woman has to.'

Carrie flounced out of the room after this exchange and would not speak to him for the rest of the evening. Gordon left the house later, and did not return until nearly midnight. The next evening she gave him cold ham and coleslaw. When he said he expected a hot meal after working all day, she said she'd been working, too, handed him a tin of soup and told him to heat it up himself.

He walked out of the house after that, and by the time he returned, she was in bed, her back turned to the centre, but she wasn't asleep, though she kept her eyes closed. She could tell from Gordon's floundering movements that he was drunk; this was the first time she acknowledged the signs in him. After crawling into bed in a lumbering way, he reached out for her.

Carrie decided to give in, and Gordon was not too drunk to reflect that he had taught her a lesson she wouldn't forget in a hurry.

It was after this that Carrie changed her hours at Brice's so that she had a day off in the week. She worked some Saturdays instead. Soon she began going to London again. She didn't intend to return to her former ways, or so she told herself, but from devilment, or perhaps her growing boredom with Gordon, she went to a hotel where she had often found custom before.

An opportunity came her way and she took it.

Soon she was going to town every week. She bought Arlene a new sweater and a big cuddly panda for Jackie, and she signed up for a course of driving lessons.

Gordon became increasingly silent on the rare evenings when he was at home. Carrie, puzzled by his moroseness, began to wonder about her predecessor and several times tried to get him to talk about his first wife, but in vain.

'It's a shame you don't see the kids. Couldn't they come and stay?' she ventured, though she did not at all want the work and the mess they would make.

'She won't let them,' said Gordon.

'But surely you've a right – ?'

'It's impossible,' he snapped. 'I don't wish to discuss it.'

Carrie called up an image of two rosy-cheeked children with excellent manners eating bought treacle tart and custard – she could make that – watching television and playing card games in harmony, although experience had taught her that such unison among siblings was wished for more often than attained. She could manage an occasional weekend, if it would make Gordon happy. His surly behaviour might be due to secretly pining for them.

She discussed it with Arlene, who agreed that it was possible. Maybe at Christmas their mother would relent and allow them to come.

Carrie raised the subject again and was sharply told to mind her own business. After that she lost patience with Gordon's moods.

For want of another idea, it was agreed that they should go to Carrie's mother for Christmas Day. It was, after all, supposed to be a family occasion. Carrie took presents for everyone – small electronic toys for the children, a blouse for her mother and a bottle of whisky for her stepfather.

Gordon behaved impeccably while they were celebrating. He poured out the burgundy he had brought for the meal, even helped dry the dishes, wearing one of her mother's aprons to protect his grey suit. Then, to Carrie's amazement, he played Snap with some of the children, but he would not accept being 'snapped' by Tina, aged six, when they both appeared to speak simultaneously. Carrie saw her little sister in tears because, she said, Gordon had cheated.

The incident seemed trivial, and was missed by the other adults as Carrie consoled the child.

'She's only a little kid,' she said to Gordon. 'Couldn't you let her win? It's Christmas, after all.'

'The child has got to learn,' Gordon said coldly.

For a moment he seemed just like a stranger, sitting there scowling.

They made it up that night, however, and Carrie resolved to become a better cook in the New Year; then he'd have no cause for complaint. Things were fine, otherwise.

Weren't they?

6

On his way back from the magistrates' court where he had been covering the morning's hearings, Barnaby Duke saw old Donald Matthews shuffling along the pavement, a shopping bag in either hand. He turned into the hardware store, and Barnaby, following, was in time to witness him exchanging pleasantries with the plump, grey-haired woman on duty behind the till.

'Mr Matthews, isn't it? Good morning!' Barnaby, a small, neat man with spectacles and thinning dark hair, hove to behind Donald, dropping anchor beside him. 'Barnaby Duke, chief reporter on the *Gazette*,' he added, nodding to Mrs Francis. 'Might I have a word in your ear?'

Donald Matthews stared at him with two brown pebble eyes which held an expression of utter dismay.

'What about?' The words were ground out. There could be only one subject connected with him that the press would wish to discuss.

But Barnaby's answer surprised him.

'The old days in Yelbury when your father owned the ironmonger's,' said the reporter blithely. 'I'm hoping to run a feature on Yelbury fifty years ago. There are plenty of older citizens like yourself with interesting tales to tell. Shall we step along to the Bird in Hand?'

Over the first pint Barnaby skilfully disarmed the old man by asking about his youth, the days spent in the shop when the money travelled from counter to cashier – for a time Donald's mother, her hair in two plaits coiled over her ears – in a wooden drum on an overhead railway. He made notes; the details would be useful if he ever did run such a series, and it would be a pity to let all these old codgers die with their memories unrecorded. He asked questions in such an easy manner that the old man relaxed. He began to chuckle, telling tales of early deliveries in a Ford van which had superseded the horse and cart, of lamps and candles and paraffin, all vital then to their rural customers.

'You must have been sorry not to carry the business on, weren't you?' asked Barnaby.

'Well, I'd been off to the war, of course. That made a difference,' Donald replied. 'And my father had made up his mind.'

'Still, when you had a son of your own you must have regretted it, didn't you?' Barnaby slipped the question in as the second pint went down.

'Not really,' said Donald, on the defensive again.

'What does he do, then?' asked Barnaby innocently. 'Your son?'

Surely he knew Gordon's story? The *Gazette* had reported the trial, but discreetly. Everyone must know what had happened.

'Does he live locally?' Barnaby pursued, still smiling.

'No, he doesn't.' The old man sank his face in his tankard.

'Oh?'

'I haven't heard from him for years,' Donald mumbled.

'Why ever not?' inquired Barnaby guilelessly.

Donald swallowed mightily, then held out his empty tankard.

'Disgraced us, didn't he?' he growled.

Barnaby, who was well known to the landlord, made signs above Donald's bowed head and in no time at all further refreshment arrived at their table.

'What happened?' Barnaby prompted.

Drinking, Donald had forgotten what they were talking about. It was nice having someone to talk to, sitting here by the blazing fire in the snug where he usually drank alone. For once he felt warm and cosseted, and his head swam agreeably, all nasty sensations and thoughts gently blurred.

'Your son,' Barnaby reminded him. 'You said he disgraced you.'

'Went and killed that little girl, didn't he?' Donald said. 'His wife. That dear little Anne. Took her by the neck and throttled her until she was dead. Quite dead. That's what he did.'

The words, coming from this defeated old man now well away with drink, were shocking although their message was not new to Barnaby.

'It was said that she asked for it.' He trawled the remark.

'How? By cowering in a corner, like a puppy that's been kicked? That's all she ever did to provoke him,' said Donald.

'Where's he now, then? Your son? In prison?'

'No. He came out some time back. Wrote to his mother at Christmas, wanting money I daresay. She was always a soft touch about that.' He looked lugubriously into his beer. 'He never held down a job for long before, and I don't suppose things will be different now.'

'Where's he living?'

'I don't know. Never looked at the letter,' said Donald.

Since by this time he wasn't fit to get home on his own, Barnaby sent him there in a taxi. Too bad if Mrs Matthews set about him. Between them, they had raised a son who had killed his wife in a fit of rage and said she had driven him to violence.

Michael West knew that he would find Gordon Matthews eventually, with or without the reporter's help. What then? Would Oliver Randall's natural desire for revenge lead to a further crime? That would do nothing to help the two children. Other families were riven apart by tragedy and somehow the survivors came to terms with what had happened: old aches eased, old griefs became tolerable. He had not been hired to moralize, however; his brief was to trace the man, and if he resigned from the task, someone else would soon take it on.

Perhaps the old man really only wanted to know Matthews's whereabouts, lest he make some claim for his children, though that seemed unlikely. Even in today's climate of doing good to the perpetrators of evil and neglecting the victims, surely no court would grant access to such a man?

Thinking that, Michael was uncertain of the answer.

He prevailed upon a former colleague to run a check on Gordon, and learned that on his release from the open prison where he had served the last part of his sentence, he had disappeared, ignoring plans made for him by the probation officer. He was not on record as owning a car. He might, of course, be using an assumed name in an attempt to start life afresh.

Michael had other work on hand. He got on with that while he allowed Barnaby Duke a few days in which to come up with some news, and he went to see his children.

He drew rather a blank.

Jenny was round at a friend's and Simon was busy making a model aeroplane. He did not want to stop fitting the pieces together, although he was pleased to see his father. Michael stood awkwardly in the living-room of the house where the last four years of the marriage had been spent and on which he was still paying the mortgage, and felt like an intruder. There on the wall were the shelves he had put up to house Lesley's books. After the children had started school she went to adult education classes to study psychology and social sciences, and was now training as a social worker. Though she had been unable to cope with the pressures of life as a policeman's wife, she presumed to advise other people with problems. One of the tutors had moved in with her, a big shaggy man with an untrimmed beard. He came in while Michael made small talk with Lesley and offered him a beer, which Michael declined. It was all very civilized and it depressed Michael utterly; he would have liked to ram his fist into that large, benign face with the rosebud lips lurking amid the whiskers. Didn't they scratch her when the couple kissed?

Perhaps that was part of Roger's fascination for her. Perhaps his hairiness turned her on. He probably had a pelt like a bear. Michael's imagination projected some unpleasing shots into his mind's eye and he switched off quickly, giving Simon a hasty, embarrassed hug and leaving a message for Jenny which she might never receive.

He bought some fish and chips for his supper and was eating them, watching television, when Barnaby telephoned.

7

Carrie bought the microwave oven. When Gordon asked her where she had got the money, she said she had had a bonus at work. When he saw her wearing a new leather coat with a fur collar, she said it had been offered to staff at cut price because of a flaw.

Her day off had become the peak time in her week. First, after a bath when Gordon had gone to work, she had her driving lesson. She was a good pupil and enjoyed progressing sedately through the residential streets of Durford. Soon she was ready to face the challenge of heavy traffic in the town centre and her confidence grew. Three-point turns and reversing into narrow entries had no terrors for her. To vary things, they drove through suburbs of the town including Meddingham. This was where she had done her charity collecting. What a long time ago that seemed! Her trips to London were safer and much more profitable. She was always elated, setting off on the train. At first she booked a room at a cheap hotel where she could take her clients, but after a few weeks she found that, smartly dressed as she was now, she could attract men who could afford to pay her well and for a room. In those early weeks she was always home by half-past seven, and she would tell Gordon she had been to see her mother or Arlene.

If only she could work a longer day! Two extra punters would bump up her earnings very nicely, and it was all free of tax.

She resolved to extend her hours.

She got the idea of telling Gordon that she had begun visiting lonely old people after seeing a story in a newspaper about some woman who had died of hypothermia and had no friends or family or other regular visitors. She'd joined an organisation that helped them, she declared; it ran an evening club they went to, where they got a lovely supper.

Gordon had no reason to doubt her. He was quite taken in, though he did ask why she wore her good coat for her charitable work. She answered that it cheered the old dears up to see someone nicely dressed.

When Gordon lost his job and signed on for unemployment benefit, she kept to her routine, and now her extra income became vital if their account was not to be stripped bare by the mortgage payments.

Gordon told Carrie that he had been made redundant in an office cut-down, and so he had, but he was selected for dismissal because he had never fitted in with the rest of the staff and the policy was last in first out. Added to this, the manager suspected him of not making as many calls in a day as he should. There had been complaints from customers that he was late for appointments and that orders he was supposed to deliver were incomplete. He told Carrie that he had been sacked because the manager was jealous of the way he had increased turnover at the branch and feared to lose his position to Gordon.

Carrie went straight to the point.

'What about the mortgage?'

'What about it?'

'How are we going to pay it?'

'The DHSS will, if we can't,' said Gordon.

Would they? Carrie wasn't so sure.

'You'd better find something else quickly,' she said. 'I'm sure you will,' she added hastily. After all, getting thrown out wasn't very nice, and it didn't seem fair, but then what was?

Now her own life had divided into two definite sections. Every weekday except Wednesday she set off to Brice's in her smart leather coat and spent the day selling fashions to women less pretty than herself, and usually older, who could afford to pay two hundred pounds and more for a suit. Daily, Carrie entered large sums on Visa forms and store accounts. It never occurred to her to wonder whether the buyers could afford the costs they incurred so blithely as she encouraged them when the garments became them.

She never persuaded anyone into making a purchase against their own or her better judgement and she would frankly say if anything seemed to her unflattering to the wearer. This made her a popular assistant. Another of her concerns was to acquire for herself anything that particularly caught her eye, either legitimately or by legerdemain. She stole a blouse, removing its security tag in the cubicle where a customer had been trying it on, and another day she took a black dress with a fly zip all down the front which would be useful for Wednesdays.

Snow fell on Durford several times in the weeks after Christmas, and on a day when the weather was still cold and bleak, with a piercing east wind, Carrie passed her driving test at the first attempt. She was now free of her weekly lesson and could set off for London earlier on Wednesdays. She soon improved her routine.

Carrie would go to one of several hotels where she had developed an understanding with the relevant head porter, and there, among the lunch-time trade at the bar, she found her customers. In this way she could be selective; not for Carrie some sweaty labourer or unwashed drop-out. She preferred the quiet ones who could sometimes, when she felt in the mood, be aroused to heights of passion they had not dreamed of in their dull suburban lives with their house-proud or golf-playing wives. She liked them round the forty-five or over mark; by then they were earning well, and were often quite refined. Carrie would catch the ten o'clock train back to Durford; that was late enough.

Gordon, however, was now often out himself.

When he had found no new job after three weeks, she began to nag at him.

'You could do something temporary,' she said. 'Window cleaning, for instance, or decorating. There's always a demand for work like that and it's cash in the hand – no need for the tax man to know about it.'

But Gordon had had enough of outdoor and manual work at the open prison. He did not care to be exposed to cold winds and rain. He went to a number of interviews but there were always younger applicants with better track records among the candidates, and nothing came his way.

'Well, you could at least do the shopping and cleaning if I'm the breadwinner,' said Carrie.

They began to quarrel, and making up was no longer the delight it had been at first. Carrie, sated by the efforts of her Wednesdays, began to find Gordon's embraces tiresome and her natural healthy response to him diminished. She took to going to bed early, and Gordon went off to one of the pubs within walking distance where he would spend several hours drinking in a corner, rarely talking to anyone. He would get through a whole pack of cigarettes, as well; he'd become a heavy smoker when he was on remand, but he'd never got into drugs, as so many did in prison.

He'd leave the pub at closing time.

It was after one of these sessions that he had the idea of setting up in business on his own.

Carrie approved in principle, but wanted details.

'What as?' she asked. 'You turned down my suggestion about window cleaning and decorating.'

Gordon was vague about where best to apply his talents.

'You need to provide something people want,' said Carrie, who had herself found this extremely profitable. 'A service. Office cleaning, say. Or a shop.'

'I've got no capital,' said Gordon.

Money from the house he'd lived in with Mary had gone towards his legal costs.

'The bank might help, and there's some government scheme, I think,' said Carrie, who had listened patiently while a client droned on about this sort of thing. It was all he'd wanted, that one: just to talk. Poor guy. Married, too. His wife never listened, he'd told Carrie. For a moment, now, the idea of her own fashion boutique rose entrancingly into her mind, to be dismissed at once. Gordon would never play a back-up role in anything like that. Besides, he had proved to be less than reliable as a stayer. It would be foolish to put all their eggs in one basket. She could have her own boutique later, when her Wednesday job began to pall, or she got too old for it, whichever happened first.

'My mother might come up with some money,' Gordon said.

'Your mother! I thought she was dead!' Carrie exclaimed,

astounded. He had led her to believe that he had no one in the world to care for him, now that his wife and children had abandoned him.

'She's not,' he said.

'Why didn't she come to the wedding, then?' Carrie demanded.

'She lives too far away,' said Gordon.

He'd had one or two letters that were unexplained. Carrie had not thought much about them.

'She doesn't know you're married,' Carrie accused. 'Don't deny it. I can tell.' She stood facing him, eyes very bright, cheeks flushed with anger.

'She's very devout. She'd think it a sin,' said Gordon.

His mother never went inside a church, but his grandmother, long dead, had held reactionary views.

'You mean because you've been married before? Come on,' said Carrie. 'That won't do.'

'Some people are like that,' said Gordon. 'So when I go to see her, I can't take you with me.'

'You're ashamed of me!' Carrie understood him now. 'Because I work in a shop and you went to college! That's it, isn't it?' She was shouting in her rage. 'Much good it's done you! I'm the one in work. You go, then! See if I care! I'll have some peace at least, without your filthy cigarettes making the place disgusting.'

Gordon liked to see her in a temper. It put him on edge in a titillating way. But this time she wouldn't let him touch her and stormed off upstairs.

He stayed in the living-room smoking and drinking – he'd brought a bottle of whisky back from the pub – while Carrie went to bed. He heard her crashing round overhead, banging drawers shut and stumping from the bedroom to the bathroom at full volume. Was she packing up and leaving him? The thought that she might do that, that he could find himself alone again, was terrifying. He sat tensely listening until the sounds had ceased.

She'd tried to put him in the wrong, like Anne. It wasn't fair. What had he done to deserve such ill luck? He'd never really had a chance, marrying Anne who wasn't the sort to help a man get on in life, always whining and ailing, and then the kids had come along, and there'd been broken nights and snotty noses. And look at all those things she'd done, like throwing a plate of stew at him and locking him out of the house one night while the children wailed and wailed, all those things that had been described in court and had led counsel to declare that he was a man more sinned against than sinning. She'd broken a picture, too, a view of Grasmere he'd cherished.

The truth was that Gordon had thrown the stew, had shut Anne out of the house and locked the children in their room, and had flung the picture – her property – at her, hitting her on the cheek. But the jury had believed his allegations. There had been no one to come forward and speak the truth for the dead and by this time Gordon had come to believe his own lies.

Nicholas had noticed Carrie on the train. Seconds before it was due to leave the platform, she had got into the coach where he was sitting, looked round breathlessly for a seat, found one and inserted herself neatly into the space available without incommoding the person next to her. Nicholas noticed the glow about her, her flushed cheeks and sparkling eyes, her blonde hair frizzed out in Pre-Raphaelite curls. He noticed her expensive leather coat with the fur collar, and her shapely boots. Other people took heed of her too; it was as though a fresh breeze had entered the stuffy carriage filled with tired travellers. On the journey, people read or dozed; no one talked. Even the blonde girl closed her eyes. She got off when he did, at Durford.

A week later he saw her again. He followed her over the footbridge at Durford, and as he collected his bicycle from the rack she walked off to the bus stop down the road. He had never seen her in the morning, and he had to wait another week before he saw her again.

This time he smiled at her. He'd waited on the platform until nearly the last moment himself before getting into the train. For the first few stops it was fairly full. Nicholas always travelled in the front coach where there was usually some space. Though they were separated by several rows of seats, she smiled back at him, and at Durford he moved along to open the door beside her seat so that they got out together.

'Oh, thanks! They are stiff, aren't they? I'm always afraid of being carried on if I can't open it,' said Carrie, waiting for him on the platform as he stepped out behind her.

They walked together over the footbridge and down the stairs towards the barrier.

'I've got to collect my bike,' said Nicholas, gesturing to the few remaining, each securely padlocked.

'Goodnight, then,' Carrie said, walking on.

He kept her a seat the next week, looking out for her, waving to her as she came along the platform.

'Do you work late on Wednesdays?' he asked her.

'Yes.'

'I have an evening class,' he confided.

'Oh?'

'French,' he said. He'd failed his A level and had decided he must take it again. He'd somehow scraped through his English, just. 'What do you do?' he asked her.

'I'm a temporary relief receptionist,' Carrie told him, inspired. 'At a hotel,' she added. 'I go wherever they're short staffed within the group.' She knew a lot about hotels. 'We do shifts.'

'You must meet some interesting people,' Nicholas supposed.

'Oh, I do.' He could say that again. She chuckled, thinking of the nice plump salesman from Belgium with whom she'd spent some time that afternoon. He'd got a wife and two children in Liège and was devoted to them, but he was lonely in a foreign city and had an hour to occupy between appointments.

'What's your job?' she asked Nicholas.

He worked in the fund-raising department of a charity. If he got his A level, he might go on to some further course, though what he didn't know; he had no very great ambition, but meanwhile he quite enjoyed what he was doing and knew that it was useful. Sending aid to the third world was satisfying in itself.

'Why third, I wonder?' Carrie said. 'Who's first and second?'

'We're first, I suppose, and America. Europe,' he suggested. 'I don't know who comes in the middle.' They laughed together at the puzzle, and when they reached Durford he found the nerve to ask her if she had time to have a drink with him at the Railway Arms.

'Why not?' said Carrie.

In the pub, he took her coat and hung it up. Beneath it, she wore a red fluffy sweater and a narrow black skirt which came to well below her knees. He looked quickly at her left hand, which was ringless. Carrie always removed her wedding ring before her Wednesday work; afraid of losing it if she put it in her purse, she left it at home in a box in the dressing-table drawer.

Over their drinks – she had a spritzer as she had had quite a lot to drink already, and he had half a pint of cider – Nicholas asked about her family, and she truthfully described how her father had left her mother when she was a child and how, years later, her mother had remarried and had another family, with the problems that had meant.

'I expect things are better now that you can help,' he hazarded. One glance at her was enough to show that she was well paid.

He had assumed she still lived with her mother. Carrie let him go on thinking that.

'Yes,' she said, but she'd never thought of giving money to her mother, though she'd taken presents to the children. Her mother would want to know where she'd got it, if she gave her some. Still, she could say Gordon was generous. Perhaps she ought to do it. She regarded Nicholas with some respect and, in her turn, inquired about him.

His parents were in Singapore where his father worked for an American firm. Their family home was let and he was living with his grandmother in Meddingham. His parents had worked abroad a lot on various contracts, each lasting a few years with spells of leave between them, and his grandmother had looked after him during most school holidays; he knew her really better than his parents, Nicholas admitted.

'You went away to school, then?' Carrie asked. She'd had clients who had done the same.

'Yes. It seemed best, with my parents overseas,' said Nicholas. 'They thought it more secure.'

Than what, she wondered; going to different schools in different countries? That could have been exciting.

His grandmother was nearly eighty, he was saying, but extremely fit. She had suggested he should find a place to live in London, but that seemed quite pointless. It would cost a lot and anyway he liked living with her.

'Fares are expensive,' Carrie said.

'Not as expensive as decent accommodation,' he declared. 'Anyway, I'm very comfortable. My grandmother's house is pretty big; much too big for her alone.'

He walked her to the bus stop and waited with her till it came along. From her seat, she could see him mounting his cycle and riding off into the night. He was a funny boy, but nice.

The following Sunday, Carrie went to see her mother and made her accept forty pounds.

'Gordon's doing really well,' she said. 'He gives me plenty for the housekeeping.'

That had never been true. Right from the very beginning they'd had their joint account and now, since he'd been out of work, bills were piling up. Carrie had opened a building society account into which she paid her Wednesday money; otherwise it would simply disappear.

Gordon got work as a barman, but was asked to leave after a week for drinking too much when on duty.

He told Carrie that he'd found the job quite unsuitable.

'I wouldn't stay on if you paid me,' he declared.

'I thought the idea was that the publican did the paying,' Carrie said.

'I'll have no insolence from you,' said Gordon.

'Too grand, are you, to pull pints?' she taunted him.

Gordon tried to strike her then, but, full of drink himself, aimed wildly and she side-stepped.

'Don't you try that, Gordon Matthews,' she hissed at him, and that night she locked him out of the bedroom. He banged on the door for some time, cursing at her, until their neighbour put his head out of the window and yelled at them to cool it, for Pete's sake.

He'd cheated. He'd concealed the fact of his parents' existence.

After her discovery, Carrie's resentment grew. Why should Gordon be ashamed of her? She'd done all right at school; she'd even got O levels, in Art, and Religious Instruction, which was a bit of a laugh but she'd enjoyed those old stories. She hadn't hesitated to take him home to meet her harried mother and well-meaning but somewhat ineffective stepfather who had never treated her badly. Wasn't she good enough to meet the Matthewses? Were they lah-di-dah? Too posh to accept her?

Carrie had learned a great deal in the last few years, and the nature of her part-time work involved being pleasant and friendly. What more did Gordon want? She brooded about it, and was curt to him over the evening meal which they still ate together most nights. He said no more about visiting his mother, and as far as she knew he had not done so by the time he found another job. This one was at a filling station, something he considered very much beneath his dignity. He ran the shop, which sold a variety of motor accessories and refreshments, and supervised the young lad who was on the till.

Carrie hoped that now his temper would improve. She decided to forgive him. Naturally, he'd been worried.

'Let's celebrate,' she said.

Gordon had taken this inappropriate job as a way of staving off confrontation with his mother. He had assured himself that she would help him. She had done it before, and she had visited him in prison once a year on his birthday or the nearest possible date. She'd missed the final year, though, pleading flu at the last minute and had not come down when she had recovered.

If he went to see her, she would cross-examine him about his life, want to know in detail why he had lost his previous job, might disbelieve anything he said. He knew he couldn't stick the filling station for long, but it would tide him over.

He liked the idea of a celebration. He enjoyed being seen with Carrie, who looked good all dressed up with her hair in a golden frizz and her eyes so large and blue. He took her to dinner at the Crown, but having to go there by bus was rather a let-down. He missed his company car.

They took a taxi home, and Gordon said he would buy a car the next day. You were very restricted without some wheels, and he'd need them to get to work.

He bought a third-hand high-mileage Ford Escort on hire purchase, writing a cheque on their joint account for the deposit. It used up most of the balance but Carrie was pleased that they had a car, for she could use it too.

She took it one Sunday to meet Nicholas.

He'd suggested spending a day in the country together the previous Wednesday, when they went from the train to the Railway Arms. He might be able to borrow his grandmother's Metro, he told Carrie.

Why shouldn't she go? Nicholas was a sweet boy, so clean and nice, and so shy. A day in the country would be a real break.

'I can borrow a car from a friend,' she said. 'I'll collect you.' She didn't want him coming to pick her up from home.

'Are you sure?'

'Yes,' declared Carrie. She had provided a lot of the money that had bought the car, so she had every right to use it.

Nicholas gave her his address in Meddingham and they met outside the house at eleven o'clock. Carrie felt rather insecure at the wheel of the unfamiliar car, and she had never driven so far, so she asked Nicholas to take over, which he enjoyed. The car's exhaust was noisy and he told her it needed replacing.

After some discussion they went to a wildlife park and wandered about among large enclosures of grazing animals, some of whom already had young. It reminded Carrie of outings from school when she'd gone to such places. She'd done nothing of the sort since then. The day was clear and cold, the sky a thin blue with shredded clouds scudding above the tracery of trees which, in this late spring, did not yet show any hint of budding foliage.

He'd brought a picnic, which he'd prepared the day before, packing it into his grandmother's picnic basket. Carrie found the hamper with its fitted plates and cutlery a delight. It was chilly sitting out on the grass – he'd even brought a small rug – so they moved into the back of the car, out of the wind. There was cold chicken, rolls, tomatoes, and white wine to drink and a flask of coffee. He'd thought of everything.

'This is the life,' said Carrie.

Nicholas was enchanted by her. Underneath her make-up – he realized that she wore rather a lot of that – she was a nice, natural girl. Today she hadn't done her eyes so much and her nails were pink instead of crimson. Of course she needed more for that hotel in London; it went with the job.

'Gary'd like it here,' she said.

'Who's Gary?'

'My half-brother.'

'Gary and Carrie – that's good,' Nicholas laughed.

'I've got a half-sister, too. Tina's her name,' said Carrie. 'And another half-brother, Jason.' She decided not to introduce her two step-brothers into the conversation.

'We must bring them some time,' said Nicholas, not really meaning it; he didn't want to share Carrie.

She thought him the kindest fellow she'd met in her life, and was ready to bestow on him any favours he might request. She fully expected him to turn into a leafy lane on the way home and park on some grass verge, but he didn't. He filled the car with petrol as they neared Durford and took her to the Crown for a drink and supper in the bar. It was only a few nights since she had been there with Gordon but there was a different barman on duty.

'See you on Wednesday,' said Nicholas as he got out of the car in Elmwood Road and, when Carrie had moved across into the driver's seat, he leaned over and kissed her lightly on the lips.

She moved off very carefully, for she had never driven in the dark before, and she'd naturally had a few drinks.

When she reached home, Carrie found Gordon waiting for her in a fury.

'How dare you take the car?' he fumed. 'And you haven't got a licence.' At first he'd thought that it had been stolen, but a neighbour said he'd seen Carrie setting off in it. The man had looked at Gordon strangely, then had shrugged. Some tiff, no doubt: the bloke looked as if he might have quite a short fuse.

Gordon had gone storming round to Carrie's mother's house to see if she was there, and drawn a blank.

'I'm sorry, Gordon. I don't know where she is.' Carrie's mother was busy in the kitchen, Gary and the other children playing noisily around her. Her husband was painting one of the bedrooms. 'She should have mentioned she was going out,' she added, apologizing for her daughter.

'So where were you?' he demanded now. 'With some man? And what if you'd got stopped by the police? Tell me that?'

'God, you're boring,' Carrie told him. 'Of course I've got a licence, if you'd taken the trouble to show some interest. And I took one of my old ladies to see her son in hospital in Gloucester,' she invented smoothly. 'As I'd have told you if you'd been awake when I left. The car's as much mine as yours.' She flung the keys down on the table. 'The exhaust needs mending,' she said, walking past him, ignoring his uplifted hand. Just let him dare to hit her and see what he'd get in return!

'The insurance,' he said now. 'What about that? It's not insured for you to drive.'

'Then get it seen to,' Carrie said. 'For I intend to use it when I want to. My old dear enjoyed her outing.'

Carrie had refused to go out with Nicholas the following Sunday, saying she must spend the day at home. He fished gently for an invitation, declaring that he would love to meet her small brothers and sister. Carrie, equally gently, refused to be drawn. She planned to spend the day at Arlene's.

'Come to dinner on Saturday, then,' said Nicholas. 'I'd like you to meet my grandmother.'

Why not? Carrie thought dining with an old lady would be pretty dull, but Nicholas was such a pet, she didn't like saying no to him, and she didn't want to stay at home, with Gordon either in a mood, or out somewhere. She accepted.

Gordon's new job meant an earlier start than his former one, and so far he had managed to get up in time, although Carrie had to shout at him after the alarm went. He'd go down and snatch a cup of instant coffee, then, as she heard the car start up, she'd get up and have her bath. She loved that little bathroom and would bath or shower twice a day. Now she and Gordon did not speak. She still produced an evening meal, and on Wednesdays left ready something he could put in the microwave. Most evenings, if he was at home, he sat and watched television, staring at situation comedies and chat shows, chain-smoking. Carrie didn't watch a lot; there was always so much for her to do – the washing, Gordon's shirts to iron and her blouses, her hair to wash and rinse. She went round to Arlene's on Tuesdays, when Tom was at his evening class; he was learning motor maintenance. Carrie thought she might sign on for something to get her out of the house another night. She rather fancied yoga. People said it kept you supple.

She'd noticed that a few of the neighbours in the close were on friendly terms with one another, popping in and out of each other's houses, but most kept themselves to themselves, as she and Gordon did. Carrie wasn't keen on asking people round with Gordon now so moody, but she smiled in friendly fashion at anyone she saw about. At weekends cars were washed and patios tidied; there were no gardens, just a length of concrete slabs extending to the fence at the rear of the row of houses. Beyond that was a footpath leading from the end of the close to the river, an old right of way protected from the planners. Each house had a gate opening on to the path.

On Saturday night, alighting from the bus in Elmwood Road, Carrie suddenly remembered that she was still wearing her wedding ring. She slipped it into the coin section of her purse. At Brice's she enjoyed her married status; it gave her the edge over some of the girls, or so she thought, although things had not worked out as she'd expected.

She couldn't worry about it now. It was time to switch on all her charm for Nicholas's grandmother.

Nicholas opened the door to her. He was excited and on edge, eager for the evening to be a success, bustling about taking her coat and ushering her into the large drawing-room at the back of the house where Mrs Fitzmaurice was waiting. As Carrie expected, she had white hair but also a pair of very shrewd blue eyes. She looked vaguely familiar and with a shock Carrie realised that she might be one of the victims of her charity confidence trick years before. The thought made her want to giggle.

As they shook hands – this clearly expected gesture took Carrie somewhat by surprise – Carrie felt that Nicholas's grandmother could see right through her to her very soul, and her mood switched. She shivered.

'Are you cold, my dear?' Mrs Fitzmaurice was all concern.

'No – no, not at all,' said Carrie, though in fact the house was extremely chilly and she had on only a thin polyester dress with very little underneath, one of the models from her department.

They drank sherry round the gas fire and Carrie cast about for something to say, finally commenting on the water-colour paintings of flowers literally covering the walls. She learned that Mrs Fitzmaurice had painted them. She was a keen botanist who cultivated alpines in her garden and went on annual holidays searching for wild flowers. She was off on such a trip quite soon.

That meant that Nicholas would be alone in the house. Carrie stored away the information, for the problem of how and where they were to get together was exercising her. Odd, really, that she wanted to, but she fancied Nicholas. There was something so fresh and sweet about him.

No, she hadn't been abroad a great deal herself, she replied to Mrs Fitzmaurice's question: just two weeks in Spain three years ago. She'd gone with Arlene who had become enamoured of a waiter but she'd soon got over it and married Tom. Carrie herself had learned a thing or two that summer.

Nicholas and his grandmother talked about France. They seemed to know Britanny well, and they'd visited the Loire and all those châteaux only last September, taking the car. How amazing to go off with your granny, Carrie thought, and as she watched them she was further astonished at the little courtesies they practised. Nicholas deferred to the old lady but he also challenged things she said and didn't hesitate to put his oar in. Carrie supposed that he was sucking up to her because of what he might hope to inherit – the old girl must be loaded, with this big house and all those foreign trips – but they seemed really good together. She began to feel envious and revealed that she had never known her grandparents.

Mrs Fitzmaurice thought this was very sad.

The meal was simple but delicious: spinach soup with cream in it, then chicken in a wine sauce with new potatoes and young carrots. Nicholas had cooked the vegetables, leaving the two women together while he attended to them. Carrie, for a moment at a loss and nervous, called on her professional technique and asked Mrs Fitzmaurice about her forthcoming holiday. While the old lady described her intended Greek cruise with shore excursions to places of historical and botanical interest, Carrie's attention wandered and she felt glad that she'd gone easy with the make-up and had not worn her highest heels; she'd thought the old girl wouldn't approve of anything too modern. What Carrie didn't understand was why she herself had bothered to entertain such considerations, much less bow to them.

There was home-made ice-cream and raspberries from the freezer, then cheese and biscuits, and coffee made in a Cona, something Carrie had never seen before. She felt that she was living in some old film with all the period touches: the old-fashioned radiators and the furniture, so much of it, all antique. You saw such stuff in shops priced very high. It took an awful lot of polishing.

They watched the news on television and after that Mrs Fitzmaurice went tactfully off to bed. Greatly daring, Nicholas then kissed Carrie, coming to sit beside her on the funny old settee with its high sides and back. Instinct told Carrie to take it gently. He'd never, not here, not with the old girl upstairs in bed: not Nicholas.

His grandmother had instructed him to take Carrie home in the car. At all costs, she must hide from him where she really lived. Carrie got him to drop her outside Arlene's house, and when he had driven away – she told him he mustn't wait to see her in – she telephoned for a taxi from the phone box in the road.

She wasn't going to walk to the bus stop at that time of night, not alone. You couldn't be too careful these days and rape was not unknown in Durford.

9

Barnaby Duke decided to give it another try with the old man. He must have some idea where his son was living. A week after their first meeting, he saw Donald Matthews in the hardware shop again, talking to Mrs Francis. In the meantime, Barnaby too had talked to her and had learned that Donald spent a lot of time in there.

'I expect his wife wants him out of the way while she gets on,' Mrs Francis had hazarded. 'It's hard for some when their man retires. They've got used to running their day to suit themselves, you see.'

Now Barnaby picked up a bottle of Dabitoff which he needed, and took it to the till, where Donald was leaning on the counter enjoying the company of Mrs Francis who wore a patient expression.

'Ah, good morning,' said Barnaby brightly. 'Nice weather, isn't it?' There had been overnight frost and now the sun shone in a clear blue sky.

'Not bad, not bad,' said Donald. The young man looked familiar but he couldn't place him.

'I'm going along to the Bird. Care to join me?' asked Barnaby, pocketing his change. He winked at Mrs Francis.

'I don't mind,' said Donald, brightening.

He picked up his basket, which contained two large fillets of plaice, a cabbage and some Steradent, and waddled along beside Barnaby towards the Bird in Hand, a timbered former coaching inn with small leaded windows and a cobbled yard at the rear now used as a car park.

'Heard any more from Gordon?' Barnaby asked, after establishing confidence by way of discussing sport on television. The old man seemed keen on racing and snooker. No doubt watching the small screen helped to kill time.

'Lives in Hampshire, doesn't he?' Barnaby had decided to try bouncing Donald into some sort of recollection.

'Berkshire,' said Donald. 'Durford's in Berkshire.'

He'd seen a letter Hannah had left out for the post. She was probably sending the boy money again.

'Ah, that's a nice county,' said Barnaby, hiding his glee at the success of his tactic. It stood to reason that the old fellow would know something.

Donald suddenly remembered drinking with this young man on another occasion. He'd been interested in the history of the town and they'd had a very nice chat. He prepared to enjoy himself again.

'That's a big house you've got,' said Barnaby, who had been past on a voyage of inspection. 'Keeps your wife busy, I expect, looking after it. Must be a great help you doing the shopping.'

'Hannah doesn't like housework,' said Donald. 'Cooking's different; she's good at that. Mrs Jeffries does the cleaning. Comes Tuesdays. A very reliable woman.'

'Ah.'

It was nice to have someone showing a bit of interest, and the subject had now moved away from the dangerous topic of Gordon. Donald talked freely about Mrs Jeffries and how long she had worked for Hannah, and even told Barnaby where she lived.

'There's no telephone number for him,' Barnaby said when he rang Michael that evening. 'I tried Directory Inquiries.'

'Oh! Too bad,' said Michael. Barnaby was showing a great deal of interest in this project. A suspicion that the reporter might have motives of his own for being so helpful came into his mind. He would be as aware as Michael of the help an electoral roll could be in tracing an individual, though checking the register for every street in a town the size of Durford would take some time.

'I'm pursuing another line,' Barnaby told him. 'I think I'll have the address in a few days. I'll ring you again.'

For his own part, Barnaby was not yet ready to break free and pursue the story he sensed lurked in the wings. First he would need Michael to lead him to the sorrowing grandparents and pathetic, bereaved children. Hunting as a couple was the best way at present, and he could not take the time to go haring off to Berkshire on a whim, whereas Michael could, expenses paid.

Oliver Randall telephoned Michael that same evening. His wife had gone to a parish council meeting as she wanted to hear what was being proposed about an extension to the village graveyard, now almost full. Feelings were running high because nearby land was not available, and future burials might have to be in a neighbouring village where there was the same problem of over-crowding but there was land to spare.

Anne had been cremated. It had seemed the best thing.

The two men met at the café where they had talked before. This time, Michael got there first and was drinking his coffee when the older man came into the small room and pushed his way between the tables. The single waitress came straight up to take his order. He had a presence: Michael noticed that. You'd think he'd been an army officer or something. He'd pass for a trim fifty-one or two, but he must be over sixty. What guts he had to start such a demanding new way of life when most men his age were planning to take things easy.

'What made you pick the grocery business?' he asked as Oliver sat down.

'Had to do something. Needed an occupation that was completely different,' said Oliver. 'We wanted the children to disappear. It was their only chance to get away from the past, and so we had to find a completely new environment. And we wanted to be active, not sitting-in-the-corner grandparents who'd be over-protective and find it hard to make connections with younger age groups. We wanted to stay in touch with life. Of course, my son thought we were mad. He wanted to take the children on, but they'd have been more easily traced there. It only wants some fool newspaper to start the whole business up again.' His coffee arrived and he took a sip. 'Now, you've news for me, you said.' He turned his sharp blue gaze on Michael.

'Yes,' said Michael slowly. 'I think Gordon Matthews is living in Durford but I haven't his exact address yet. I'll have to go down there to find that.'

'How have you got on to this?'

'An agent of mine has spoken to his father.' Michael was not going to reveal that his informant was a journalist. 'He managed to bring the subject up in general conversation. The old man's gone downhill, it seems.'

'Has he?' Oliver showed no concern at hearing this.

'How did you get on with him before all this happened?' Michael asked.

'With Donald Matthews, you mean?' Oliver shrugged. 'We seldom met. You can't be expected to become fast friends with individuals just because your children marry,' he said. 'We weren't acquainted before. Anne met Gordon when they were students.'

'Oh.'

'Well?' Oliver demanded. 'What next?'

'It's up to you,' said Michael. 'I mean, do you want to go on with this?'

'I most certainly do,' said Oliver. 'And please let me have your account to date.'

'I've brought it.' Michael had anticipated this and handed him an envelope. 'He isn't on the telephone,' he added. 'He may have changed his name.'

'Not he. He insisted he'd done nothing to be ashamed of,' Oliver said. 'He blustered at the trial and he'd bluster his way through being recognized. He'd say he'd paid his debt to society – some claptrap of that kind.'

'What will you do when you find him?'

'I'm not sure,' said Oliver. 'For one thing, you've said he's in Durford and that relieves my mind enormously. He won't suddenly turn up in Suffolk looking for the children.'

'You're afraid of that?'

'My wife has nightmares in which he appears demanding them as of right,' said Oliver. 'As if anyone has any rights over another person. Duties, yes; not rights. You married?'

'Not any more,' said Michael.

'Like that, is it? I'm sorry. Any children?'

'Two. A girl and a boy.'

'The same as Anne,' said Oliver. He thought, as so often, that if only his daughter had given up trying to keep her doomed marriage going, she might still be alive.

'Mine are a bit older,' said Michael.

'You don't think you own them, do you?'

'Far from it,' said Michael, and added bitterly, 'I don't see a lot of them. I've only got a one-roomed flat to take them to. My ex-wife has installed her liberal-minded lover in what was my house.'

'Ah,' said Oliver. 'So you feel hatred. As I do.'

Michael stared at him in surprise.

'I don't hate my former wife,' he said. 'I hate what she did.' Hadn't some poet or other said something about hating the offence and loving the offender? That exactly described his predicament. 'You've got more reason to feel hatred than I have,' he went on. 'Your daughter died and she was a lovely person. One of her former neighbours talked to me about her.' He described how he had gone to Gordon Matthews's last known address to begin his search, and what he had been told. Oliver Randall kept his head bowed as he listened. Michael did not mention Barnaby.

'I've got to make Gordon retract his allegations publicly,' said Oliver. 'He's served his sentence. They won't put him back in gaol, more's the pity.'

'How are you going to manage that?' The old boy hadn't thought it out at all; he was merely obsessed with tracking down his quarry because, whilst the man's whereabouts were unknown, he posed a threat. A target in the sights lost some menace.

'I don't know yet. He's a bully. Such people pick on someone weaker than themselves but they crumple if you stand up to them,' said Oliver.

'You mean you'd use violence?'

'I'd go armed,' said Oliver briefly.

What with? He'd probably got a shotgun for potting rabbits, living in the country, Michael thought.

'If you use a weapon on him, the children will be worse off than ever,' he pointed out.

'You mean the police would clobber me? I suppose they would,' said Oliver. He ran his hand through his short white hair and looked suddenly defenceless. 'You're thinking of dropping the case because you're not happy about my motives,' he said.

'If I do, you'll find someone else to take it on,' said Michael.

'That's right, and you're in this now yourself. You've already found proof that what I've said is right – a dreadful thing was done to Anne, not only in killing her but in what was said about her.'

'That's true,' said Michael. 'But even if Matthews had been properly convicted – given life – the chances are he'd have been out on licence after about nine years.'

'Then he'd still be inside now and I wouldn't be worried sick that he'd turn up and upset the children,' Oliver said. 'We'd have another few years' grace at least. And Anne's memory wouldn't be tarnished by vicious lies.'

The vicious lies would still have been used by the defence, whose duty was to do the best they could for their client, not to lay bare the truth.

'It's all right,' Michael said. 'I won't give up if you want me to go on. But I would like your promise not to resort to violence.'

'I can't give you that assurance,' Oliver replied. 'I can't see what lies ahead – what might be forced upon me by the circumstances.' He regarded Michael steadily. 'Take your time,' he said. 'I'll understand if you have more pressing things to deal with – writs to serve – that sort of thing. Are you licensed in any way?' he added.

'No. There's the Association of British Investigators, which you can apply to join,' Michael said. 'I haven't been doing it long enough to be considered.'

'I see.' Oliver sorted out the money to pay for their coffee. 'Don't be ashamed of your own anger,' he advised. 'It may be a deadly sin, but it's natural. Some things are right and some are not, and if your generation doesn't say so, loud and clear, then your children and grandchildren will be the ones to suffer.'

'I suppose you're right,' said Michael.

'You'll see to it, then?'

Michael nodded, not sure if he was agreeing to pursue Gordon Matthews or attempt the moral reformation of the nation.

Hannah Matthews was reading about Princess Maria Volkonsky, who followed her husband, one of the leaders of the 1825 uprising against the Tsarist regime, into exile in Siberia where she raised her children and established a cultured way of life in that unpromising area. In Hannah's view the woman was a romantic idiot to endure such hardship for so foolish a reason; better to have stayed in Moscow with her first child, whom she never saw again because he died during her banishment. Nevertheless, her achievements were remarkable and Hannah admired that.

Rules. People needed rules. She had applied strict ones to her own family but her training had not been enough to keep Gordon from disaster. He needed a strong wife, but he had let that silly little Anne beguile him.

How was he managing now? He wrote that he was sales manager for a large firm and had bought a small house, so he was obviously earning enough to cope with the mortgage. She hoped he employed a cleaning woman for he had never been handy about the place himself, though she had attempted to train him to be more effective than his father. Perhaps he had resumed his studies to occupy his leisure hours; he could better himself with some application. It was unfortunate that he had not acquired any new qualifications while he was in prison.

She had sent him some money to tide him over the first period after his release when things might be difficult. Visiting him had been so dispiriting that she had limited her journeys to one a year. He'd seemed so grey and anonymous there among the other men in their striped shirts and issue trousers. She hadn't been to the open prison; he was near the end by then.

She didn't want to see him now.

She read on about General Leparsky who ruled humanely over the prison fortress in Transbaikalia and later the community at Petrovskt Zavod while her own cleaning woman, Mrs Jeffries, was busy in the kitchen. Chairs were upended on the table; the floor was washed. When the work was done, Mrs Jeffries went along to the study where her employer was reading to collect her pay. Though she had never met Gordon Matthews, she still got a *frisson* from working in this house. There was a thrill in being connected with a sensational crime, however indirectly. Gordon's photograph as a schoolboy stood on the sitting-room mantelpiece. He looked as if butter would not melt, she'd told her husband.

Hannah rose from her chair, stiffly, for arthritis had begun to stiffen her joints, and went to inspect the labours done. Her desk was open, and Mrs Jeffries, following her from the room, glanced at it. Each pigeon-hole held papers; an Intourist brochure was exposed. She was into Russia in a big way, thought Mrs Jeffries, who had studied the titles of the books stacked in piles, some of them paperbacks, some from the library, when she cleaned the room.

Hannah drew her attention to a film of dust on the back ridge of the dresser in the hall, but not harshly. She did not want to lose Mrs Jeffries, who was essential to her own plans for visiting Russia. Someone must keep an eye on Donald, who was incapable of looking after himself. Only a short time ago he had come back from Yelbury disgracefully drunk. He would soon be fit only to live in a home.

A week later, when it was the turn of the study to receive a good turning out, and Hannah was in the kitchen preparing a shepherd's pie, Mrs Jeffries went quickly through the papers in the desk until she found a letter from Gordon, which gave his address in Durford. She memorized it, repeating it again and again in her head until she could find an odd scrap of paper to write it down. Later that day she took her information to Barnaby Duke, who dipped into his savings to pay her the sum he had promised if she were successful.

'When are you going to write the story?' Mrs Jeffries asked him.

'Not yet. Not for some time. There's a great deal to check,' said Barnaby.

'That Anne must have been a dreadful woman,' said Mrs Jeffries. 'Always nagging and wanting money. It's the parents I'm sorry for – all that trouble when he'd been so well brought up. Not that Mrs Matthews is an easy woman herself.'

She pocketed her money, enough to take her and Joe to Malaga for a week. It might be difficult to explain to him how she had come by such a sum, but she would think of something.

10

Michael West's commission from Oliver Randall was to discover the present whereabouts of Gordon Matthews, not to ferret into the past. When he set out to interview Anne's former tutor, his motives were obscure even to himself. This was a trip he could not charge to his client; once again he had allowed himself to become involved with the people he was investigating.

Her father's account of how she had met Gordon had prompted him to ask which university they had attended and a few days after his second meeting with Oliver Randall, Michael was talking to Dr Miriam Fanshawe.

'Frankly, I was horrified,' she told him. 'It was an appalling tragedy and if the evidence given in court wasn't false witness, then I don't know what else to call it. Anne was an excellent pupil – far from brilliant, but conscientious and able, and she had endless patience. I suppose that was what made her stick with the marriage when it was going so badly.'

'You knew that?'

'Oh yes. I went to see her once, not long before her death. I was shocked at the state she was in. In fact, I scarcely recognized her.'

'What sort of state do you mean? Was she hysterical?'

'No.' Dr Fanshawe hesitated, seeking to be totally accurate in her description. 'She was the opposite, I suppose. Extremely subdued, depressed, almost catatonic. I wondered if she might be on tranquillizers. She was still in her twenties, but she could have been almost forty. Her hair was lank and looked dirty. She had rings round her eyes. She was exceedingly thin. The place was clean and neat but very poorly furnished. She'd gone back to work by then – she was the breadwinner, it seemed, though she was too loyal to spell it out like that. She'd got the two children into nursery schools but the little girl was only two years old.' The woman, thickset and fifty-five, her greying hair coiled into an old-fashioned French pleat, took off her glasses and polished them with a tissue taken from her skirt pocket. 'The trial was a travesty,' she continued. 'Maybe Anne did speak out at last, but she could never have been the sort of evil termagant she was made out to be in court. She went back to work not because she was set on her own career, but from sheer necessity. At the trial that vile man made out that he stayed at home to look after the children but the truth was that he couldn't hold down a job. Anne would have returned to work later, when the children were older, no doubt, but not so soon. Frankly, Mr West, I have lost respect for justice. Throw dirt at the victim and get yourself off the hook seems to be the rule, and judges who should know better accept uncorroborated evidence of that kind. Look at what happens in rape cases. Young, innocent girls – and there are still a few of them about – are told they've asked to be raped if they accept a lift home after a party.' She sighed heavily. 'I despair,' she added.

'You said nothing at the time,' Michael mentioned.

'How could I? I didn't know the line the prosecution would take until it was too late. And I didn't know when the trial would be held. If someone had asked me for a statement about Anne, I would gladly have given it. It seems to me that evidence about a victim's character should be mandatory when that is what the case turns on.' She got up and crossed the room to a shelf full of large volumes and extracted one. 'Would you like to see a photograph of Anne? I have some here taken when a group of us went to Belgium.'

'Yes, please,' said Michael, who had seen only grainy newspaper photographs of the dead woman.

Dr Fanshawe turned the pages.

'Do you know Bruges?' she asked. 'Such a lovely city.'

Michael didn't.

'A lot of mosquitoes, though. I remember that Anne got badly bitten and her arm swelled alarmingly. She must have had some sort of allergy.'

She showed Michael several photographs of groups of young women students outside various significant buildings. Anne smiled into the lens.

'She was always a quiet girl. A born victim, I suppose,' the tutor said sadly. 'What's your interest in all this?'

'Like you, I'm concerned about how the law works in such cases,' said Michael. 'Two sets of barristers fight it out in court and attempt to outsmart each other without trying to discover the truth of what really happened. They do things differently in, for instance, France, where they practise the inquisitorial system of crime investigation.'

'You said you were a private detective,' Dr Fanshawe remarked. 'Someone must be retaining you.'

'Yes,' said Michael, and did not enlarge.

'Well, if I can help to set the record straight in any way, I will,' said Dr Fanshawe. 'Anne's children deserve that. How are they? Do you know anything about them?'

'They're well. They're living incognito in another part of the country,' said Michael.

'They weren't at home when it happened. Maybe he'd have done for them, too, if they'd been in the house,' Dr Fanshawe remembered. 'Where were they, do you know?'

'They were at another child's birthday party nearby. According to the evidence, Anne ordered her husband to collect them and when he didn't instantly obey, she attacked him.'

'I wonder what really happened,' said the tutor.

'We'll never know that. Only one person knows the truth and he won't tell. Perhaps he wanted his tea and she hadn't got it ready because she was going to fetch James and Charlotte. Some small thing like that may have been enough to blow the fuse.'

Gordon had left the house afterwards and Anne's body had been discovered only when the parents of the child whose birthday it was had wondered why the two Matthews children had not been collected.

'It's frightening,' said the tutor, who looked as if it would take a great deal to scare her.

'The children have been told their parents were killed in a car accident,' Michael volunteered.

'What, both of them? Both parents, I mean?'

'Yes.'

'Well, I suppose that's good enough, until they get curious. Or until that man seeks them out. I imagine he's still safely in gaol?'

'No. He's been out nearly a year,' said Michael.

'But he was sentenced to seven years, wasn't he?'

'He got remission for good conduct, and the time he spent on remand counted against his sentence,' said Michael. 'And I suspect that those months were the hardest he had to serve. Conditions in Brixton are grim. They're better in the so-called training prisons.' He returned the album. 'Don't get me on to that subject,' he added. 'I could go on for hours about the folly of putting away people who've reneged on fines or stolen a packet of biscuits.'

'And not putting away for long enough people like Gordon Matthews,' said Dr Fanshawe. 'I'm glad to have met you, Mr West.'

After he had gone, she sat for some minutes pondering about her visitor. How odd of him to have embarked on this crusade, for that it was one she had no doubt.

The tutor had given Michael the name and address of a college friend of Anne's and he telephoned her from a payphone.

'Dr Fanshawe thought you might be willing to talk to me,' he said.

'What's it about?'

'Anne Matthews. You knew her as Anne Randall,' he said.

'Oh!' There was surprise and shock in the voice. 'Well, yes, but it can't do her much good now,' said Anne's friend.

She lived in a village some thirty-five miles from the university. Michael wrote down the directions she gave him, and within an hour was ringing the bell at her small stone cottage in a picturesque village beneath the downs. The front door opened straight into the living-room and beyond it Michael could see another room which contained stacked balls of wool and a knitting-machine; he soon learned that Anne's friend designed and made up sweaters which she sold by mail order.

Her eyes filled with tears as she endorsed all that he had already heard about Anne.

'She should never have married him,' she said. 'We all knew it. Some of us tried to tell her but she wouldn't listen. He was a layabout – he didn't stick to any of his courses – changed from one subject to another – physics – sociology – engineering – you name it. I don't know how he got away with it. She thought he'd settle down once he was married – find something which was right for him, as she put it. He used to go on benders even then. It was awful, reading what was said about her in the papers, but by that time it was too late to do anything about it.'

Through her, Michael traced two other friends of Anne's, and their stories were the same. One had visited the couple and had witnessed Gordon breaking a plate because he said it wasn't properly washed; he had thrown the pieces at Anne, who received a cut on her eyelid. She was more upset about the loss of the plate than about her own small wound. The second woman had lent Anne money to pay an outstanding gas bill; the money had been meticulously repaid by weekly postal orders.

'I suspect she did it out of the family allowances,' said the friend. 'I only found out about the bill because I went to see her and she was in tears. Of course I didn't want the money back but she was much too proud to accept it as a gift, and also I was afraid she might not turn to me if it happened again. I was pretty skint, too, of course, but not to the same extent. Gordon was on the dole. He could never hold down any job, or if he seemed to be doing so, he'd get one of these whims to study and sign on for some course or other, which meant buying dozens of books and then giving the whole thing up.' She sighed. 'We actually discussed her leaving him, and she was thinking about it, but it was such a big decision to take and meant admitting she'd failed. She left it too late.'

Michael made careful notes of all these interviews and filed them when he reached home. Then he had to put in an extra effort to chase up some other cases for which he could expect to be paid before continuing his hunt for Gordon.

When Barnaby Duke telephoned with Gordon's address, he felt relief and also a sense of anticlimax. In a way he had wanted to reach the goal on his own.

He told the reporter what he had learned about the dead woman's character.

'It confirms all that her father said,' he declared.

'Interesting, isn't it?' said Barnaby. There was mileage to be got from all this if he could angle it towards the mass market in some manner. Fame beckoned with a seductive finger as he imagined a paperback book with television tie-in and a new career pursuing other cases of a similar nature. Meanwhile, he had to carry on with the *Gazette*, relying on Michael, as the leg-man, to fill in the gaps.

'You'll go to Durford?'

'It depends if the old man wants me to,' said Michael.

But he would go there; he was too curious to stay away, and Barnaby knew it.

When Oliver Randall telephoned a few days later, Michael was spending a rare evening in the flat with his son. Lesley and her partner were at a meeting and Jenny had refused to stay in with her brother as there was a disco she wanted to attend. Michael and Simon were peacefully playing chess when Oliver called.

'I've got the address,' Michael reported. 'Do you want me to go down there and check it out properly?'

'Yes,' said Oliver. 'I want to know what he's doing – if he's got a job – everything you can discover.'

'Very well.'

'I'll ring in about a week,' said Oliver.

'Sorry about that, Simon,' said Michael, returning to the game. It was pleasant, sitting here with the boy; he could pretend for an hour or two that the clock had been put back.

'Was that a customer?'

'Yes. A nice old man.'

'What are you doing for him? Finding a debtor?'

'You could say that,' said Michael. 'Yes.'

He'd managed to conclude the conversation without revealing Gordon Matthews's exact address.

Michael was able to buy a street map of Durford. He traced

Newnham Close and embarked once again on his market-research approach.

Number 9 was a tiny box, one up and one down, amid a row of similar boxes. All the doors were varnished mock oak; window frames were painted white but thereafter individuality was displayed in the matter of net curtains, swathed drapes or venetian blinds.

He walked up to the door of Number 10 and rang the bell, ready this time with inquiries about biscuits.

Anticlimax. No response.

He tried the neighbouring doors with the same result, and at last he called at Number 9 itself, but again there was no answer; the house hid its secrets behind rather surprising muslin frills drawn across the windows. Michael imagined the gas gently pulsing inside, the boiler primed to cut in later on before the occupant's return, the new fitments in the kitchen stacked with pans and utensils for meals, the place poised, a small, convenient nest of cells.

At Number 15 he found someone at home.

'Ah, there you are,' said Mrs Arnold. 'I expected you half an hour ago. Come along in.'

Michael, clipboard under his arm, stepped bewildered but willingly over the threshold.

'What kept you?' went on Mrs Arnold, a plump woman with stiffly set suspiciously dark hair, well made-up, irritated at having had to take time off from her job to await the workman who had said he would call before nine-thirty.

When he had been safely admitted into the house and had penetrated through to the tiny kitchen, Michael enlightened her.

'Who are you expecting?' he asked. 'Because I'm not him.'

'The plumber. There's a leak at the back of the boiler,' she said. 'Well, who are you then?' She spoke crossly.

Michael made his little speech, but abandoned the biscuit script and restored his population theme so that he could refer to the neighbours, and he learned that Mrs Arnold was a divorcée who lived here alone. She worked in an office in Durford.

'You're the only person I've found at home in the whole close,' said Michael. 'I'll have to come back in the evening.'

'Yes. Everyone goes out. I suppose it's an invitation to burglars,' said Mrs Arnold. 'But this is a respectable part of the town.'

'That's no guarantee of immunity. Rather the reverse,' said Michael.

She pouted at him.

'Well, you are a comfort,' she said.

'You've fitted good locks, I see,' he commented.

'I've taken to heart all that on television about keeping the magpies out,' she told him.

A neighbourhood watch scheme, such as operated effectively in parts of Lentwich, would be useless here with the houses empty during the day when most opportunist thefts occurred, Michael reflected.

'No one's on shifts, then?' he asked. 'Or unemployed?'

'Not that I know of,' she replied.

He asked a few more questions of the type that might be expected in a genuine survey, then closed his folder and put away his pen.

'Do you like it here?' he asked her.

'It suits very well,' she said. 'What do you do when your husband takes a fancy to someone younger and as good as throws you out? Makes out he's got no money and can't support you when you know he's pulling plenty, with commission on top?'

'It can't be easy.' Michael was aware that she was reluctant, now, to let him go. He knew what living without a partner was like when you were used to sharing your life, and he had had several skirmishes with other lonely souls, but he had nothing secure to offer another woman. His own livelihood was uncertain and would be hampered by new ties. Casual relationships were not at all satisfying, but for a moment he contemplated trying to warm things a little; he might more easily find out about Gordon Matthews if he made it with this Mrs Arnold, who was attractive enough in a brittle way. She was older than she had seemed at first, and her eyes were sad.

No, he advised himself. Don't get involved like that.

'Are there many single people living in the close?' he asked.

'I don't think so.'

'What about Number 9?'

'There's a couple there, certainly. They may not be married, not that it matters. He's a good bit older than she is. I've seen them at weekends, occasionally. They go out separately a lot. I've noticed that.'

'Oh?' Michael tried to sound as if he could take or leave this news, which explained the unmasculine muslin curtains.

'She's usually on my bus, going to work,' Mrs Arnold informed him. 'We've passed the time of day. She works in one of the shops in town. I don't know which one. She's always very smart.'

'And he's older, you said?'

'Yes. I should think it's a second marriage,' said Mrs Arnold. 'Maybe she took him away from some other woman.' Her tone was bitter.

'Maybe,' said Michael, preparing to go. He mustn't push his luck here and arouse her suspicions by being too inquisitive.

'She might well be two-timing him, in fact,' said Mrs Arnold. 'She's always very late home on a Wednesday. I sing in a choir that night and always go for a drink with some of the crowd afterwards. A friend brings me home and I've seen her walking up from the bus stop. I don't think she goes to work on Wednesdays. She's never on the morning bus then.'

What a lot you could learn by just listening quietly and throwing in the occasional word. Michael bade her farewell and departed, with plenty to think about. It hadn't occurred to him that Gordon Matthews might have remarried or acquired a mistress. There was no point in trailing round the shops in the town looking for her, since he knew nothing at all about her except that she was young and smartly dressed. He whiled away some hours in the museum and visited the cathedral in the old town, away from the brash new shopping centre, then eventually returned to Newnham Close to observe the residents as they returned from work.

He sat in his car in Bridge Street, parked where he could

watch who turned into the close. He saw several people enter on foot, and eventually he drove past the row of houses to the end where the road widened into a turning area. He saw that a footpath ran down behind the boundary fences and wondered where it led. He should have explored it earlier, when there was no one about. There was no need to worry about being recognized; if Mrs Arnold saw him, she would assume he had returned to complete his survey. He got out of the car to carry this out, knocking on all the doors asking minimal questions. Two people refused to reply. He was on the doorstep of Number 3 when a woman walked by, stepped up to the door of number 9, opened it with a key and went in. In the gathering dusk he saw that she was small and moved swiftly; that was all.

Lights went on in the house. Michael allowed her just a few minutes before he rang her bell.

When she opened the door she smiled pleasantly and waited to be told his business. She did not ask him in, but she answered his questions. Michael learned that her name was Carrie Matthews, short for Caroline, and that she and her husband had lived there since their marriage last October. Her husband was out at present and she didn't know what time he'd be back.

Michael wanted to see Gordon Matthews. He waited outside in his car for a long time.

11

From his parking spot at the end of the close, Michael kept
Number 9 under survey. He was used to this sort of vigil; it
figured often enough when he was employed to detect
adultery or to seek evidence of pilfering from construction
sites and industrial premises. Time passed, but Gordon
Matthews did not return. Michael took a stroll up the road
to stretch his legs and had just returned to his car when the
door of Number 9 opened and the young woman emerged.
She walked briskly away into Bridge Street. Well, his
business was not with her.

He waited for another hour, with still no sign of
Matthews. By this time he was feeling hungry, so he drove
back towards the centre of town and stopped at a pub which
advertised bar food. Inside, it was noisy, smoky and warm.
Michael ordered half a pint of mild and steak and chips.
Hanging about achieving nothing was dispiriting, and the
food braced him up. He had had a long day, driving for over
three hours to reach Durford that morning, and it looked
now as if he might have to return to Lentwich without
finding out much more.

He returned to Newnham Close feeling rather sleepy and
saw a beat-up old Ford Escort parked outside Number 9.
Was that Matthews's car? He took down the number. He
could get it checked out the next day. Had the girl returned
too? She had said that she didn't know when her husband
would be home, so they could not have planned to meet in
the town and come back together.

He got out of his car and approached the house. Standing
on the doorstep, Michael could hear the television or radio
on inside. He had to ring twice before the bell was
answered, but eventually the television sound blared more

loudly as an inner door opened. The porch light came on above Michael's head and as the front door was opened, Gordon Matthews stood revealed.

Michael would have found it difficult to recognize him from the photographs taken five years ago which were all he had for identification. The man's hair was grey, almost white, and he had a long, untrimmed moustache.

'Well?' The voice was curt, and Michael caught the whiff of whisky on his breath.

'Excuse me, can you tell me which is Mrs Arnold's house?' Michael asked. Because Carrie Matthews might have returned and would certainly remember his earlier visit, he needed a reason for making a second call at the house.

'I don't know anyone of that name,' said Gordon, and he shut the door firmly in Michael's face.

Well, no one could say that he looked like a murderer, but then, who did? Michael had met several in his police career, and even one who had shot a policeman while trying to escape after a bank robbery had looked quite ordinary without the mask and the balaclava he had worn while committing his offence. Somebody's husband, somebody's son, he remembered: yes, and somebody's killer.

Where had he found this new wife? Was she someone who liked to live dangerously or had he concealed his record from her? Perhaps she believed the version of events given in court and thought herself safe.

Was she?

He drove home through the night feeling oddly deflated. There was no reason to delve further into the matter unless Oliver Randall wanted to know where Matthews was working. He would have to wait for the old man to get in touch with him again. The day had been rather expensive. Michael noted down his costs before going to bed.

He decided to tell Barnaby Duke about Matthews's marriage and rang him the next day. The reporter found the news very interesting and did some quick calculations about the possible profit and loss on the cost of further investigation.

'I'd like you to find out a bit more about her and the set-up in general,' he said. 'I might do a piece on how a wife-killer builds a new life, depending on what you unearth. I can't take the time to go there and ferret about unless there's a story. I can spare a couple of hundred quid. When that's used up, then stop. But see what you can get hold of.'

Michael was very willing to do this. He was curious himself, and ultimately Barnaby Duke might be the means of putting the record straight.

Michael put in some work on other cases and took on two new ones connected with debts. Then he set aside a day to return to Durford. If he made an early start, he could follow Gordon Matthews to work and thus know where to pick him up during the day. He would go on the following Wednesday.

It was a long way. He set his alarm for four o'clock and made good time, reaching the M25 well before the rush of traffic clogged its new lanes. He parked in Bridge Street at half-past seven. Longing for some strong hot coffee, he sat in his car screening his face with a newspaper and watched the residents leaving Newnham Close. They departed in staggered ones and twos. Mrs Arnold went by at eight thirty-five.

Some time later, Michael heard the sound of a car reluctant to start. He wound down his window and listened. Eventually it fired, and the old Ford Escort, which he had confirmed was owned by Gordon Matthews, lurched into Bridge Street and turned right. Michael slipped in behind and followed it past the bus stop towards the main road junction. There was a lot of traffic now, but the yellow Escort was easy to keep in view. It stopped outside a newsagent's where Gordon went in and came out with a paper. Michael, who had pulled into a bus lay-by further along the road, fell in behind again, and finally the car turned into a filling station on the by-pass outside the town. The driver parked at the rear, away from the public concourse, and entered the shop.

There was a queue at the pumps. Michael joined it and while he waited for his turn, peered through his car window into the shop. He could see Gordon Matthews in there, talking to a youth behind the counter. Then he sauntered about among the display shelves before disappearing into some room at the back.

Michael's turn to fill up his car arrived, and when the job was done he went into the shop to pay. A transistor radio tuned to Radio One was playing loudly. The previous customer used his bank card and the transaction took some time; meanwhile, Michael glanced round. He saw that the place sold a fair range of motor accessories, crisps, chocolate, and drinks from a dispenser. After he had paid for his petrol, he fed coins into the machine and received a cardboard cup full of anonymous liquid which was at least hot. He drank it slowly while the rush of business fell away, and saw Gordon Matthews come out of the inner office into the shop. He snapped the radio off and ordered the boy to go into the other room. Now Michael had a chance to study Matthews in the bright light from the fluorescent tubes in the ceiling. He looked a good ten years older than his true age. His hair was shaggy, whereas it had been neatly trimmed at his trial, though then he had worn a small beard as well as a moustache. His manner with his assistant was aggressive, and when the lad returned to the shop he caught Michael's eye and made an obscene gesture before turning his radio on again.

'Thinks he's God, that one,' said the boy.

'Oh?'

'Won't be here long. Says he's only helping out to oblige. He was nearly an hour late this morning and he goes off as soon as the pubs are open. There's supposed to be two blokes here all the time in case we get trouble. Well, I've shopped him to the boss.' He grinned happily. 'They'll send someone round to catch him absent one day. Now he'll be reading the paper and doing the crossword till opening time. And they say young people are irresponsible. What a shower!'

'How long has he been here?' Michael selected two bags of crisps and a Kit-Kat; it might be that sort of day.

'Two weeks. Two weeks too long, if you ask me,' said the boy, and was then obliged to attend to the next customer.

Apart from the filling-station yard, there was nowhere nearby where Michael could park and wait for Gordon

Matthews to leave the shop and head for the pub. He did not want to be conspicuous, so he drove off: in two hours' time he could return and pick up the trail. Meanwhile, he would try to find out more about the unexpected wife. Eating crisps as he drove back towards the town centre, he remembered that Mrs Arnold had said she was never on the same bus on a Wednesday morning and might have that day off.

He drove into Newnham Close and parked at the end in the turning space, as he had done before, where he listened to Radio Two while he waited for some action.

It had begun to rain. What a way for a grown man to spend his time, he thought, and remembered a few of the stake-outs he'd done while he was with the CID. He had thought the work useful at the time. What he was doing now seemed of doubtful merit.

Then his reward came. Carrie came out of the house carrying a big green Marks and Spencer's bag. She put up an umbrella and stepped out smartly. Michael started the car and slid out of the close behind her. She was walking down Bridge Street towards the bus stop, and she had timed her journey well, waiting only a couple of minutes before the bus drew up. He pulled in behind the bus, hoping he would not miss seeing her alight. This sort of surveillance could be difficult; in the police one often had a partner at such a time.

The bus went through the town centre and turned past the new public library. It stopped near the Railway Arms and Michael saw Carrie step down. Cars blew their horns at him as he loitered to see where she went. She turned into the station yard and went into the booking hall.

He made a snap decision to follow her, if he could park the car in time to see which train she caught. This was a far more interesting development than pursuing Gordon, whom he could easily track another day. He drove through a barrier into the station car park and was luckily able to find a small space which would accept his car. The London train was pulling into the platform as he ran panting back to the station buildings. He just had time to buy a ticket and jump aboard. Carrie Matthews might not be going the whole way to London; he would have to stick his head out of the window at every stop to see if she had got off.

This was easy at the first few stations, where no one got into his coach, but at the next there were clusters of passengers wanting to board and he had to remain in his seat. However, looking out as the train moved on, he did not see her moving towards the barrier.

He had some difficulty picking her up at Paddington, for she had exchanged her headscarf for a big black sombrero-style hat, and instead of the carrier she now held a neat zipped bag.

How very curious!

It was easy to lose people in crowds, but he had had plenty of practice at this sort of thing and her hat was distinctive. He followed her into the tube and, standing some distance away on the platform, was able to enter the same coach at the opposite end. He saw how smart she was in her leather coat with the little fur collar. Though most passengers seemed to be sunk in self-absorbed torpor, she attracted a few interested glances.

She must be going to meet a lover! It seemed all too likely, given her appearance, and that of Gordon. Mrs Arnold had wondered if she was two-timing him.

She left the train at Piccadilly Circus and Michael followed her as she emerged from the subway into Regent Street and walked rapidly along various narrow streets, her umbrella up to protect her smart hat from the drizzling rain. She entered a large hotel and disappeared into the ladies' cloakroom.

Michael went into the foyer and bought a paper. The one he had left in his car was the previous day's. Then he went into the bar, which was separated from the main concourse by plate glass. He ordered a beer and took a seat in a corner, hiding behind his copy of the *Independent*.

Carrie came in ten minutes later. She went to the counter and ordered a tomato juice, then perched on a high stool sipping her drink. She did not seem to glance round at all, but there was a mirror set into the back of the bar and he realized later that that was how she had done it. There were a number of men already in the bar, three at a table together and several alone. One of these men got up to join Carrie, and within seconds they had left the bar together.

This was no lover: this was a punter, and Carrie was on the game.

Michael found the discovery extremely amusing and thought that Oliver Randall would enjoy the joke, too. Nemesis had caught up with Gordon this time.

There was nothing to be gained by questioning the barman and making trouble. Michael followed the pair out of the hotel, where they got into a taxi. Luckily for Michael, another one was behind it and he was able to keep up his pursuit. Carrie and her client went to a smaller hotel less than a mile away and by the time Michael had paid off his cab and followed them inside, they had disappeared.

He went to the desk and asked for a spurious Mr Bartholomew, whom he said he was expecting to meet. Was there a message? No.

'I'll wait,' said Michael, and settled down in a comfortable leather chair from which he could observe the revolving doors.

More than an hour later, Carrie emerged from the lift and walked briskly across the hall and into the street. That was a long call, thought Michael cynically. Perhaps they'd had lunch; room service. Hours had passed since he'd eaten those crisps; he could do with a sandwich himself.

Carrie did not return to the first hotel but went on foot to another, not far away. The bar was still open, and Michael saw her put into practice the same routine. This time she left with a spectacled Japanese man and they went straight into the lift, which must mean he was staying here.

Michael had neither the heart nor the stamina to list all her encounters. He went off to have something to eat himself and spent the afternoon in a cinema. Then he caught the train back to Durford where he sat in his car outside the booking hall to watch for her return. From what Mrs Arnold had said, it would be late. No doubt trade got livelier in the evening.

He was almost taken by surprise when she came out of the booking-hall and into the dimly lit station yard soon after half-past ten. She was again carrying her Marks and

Spencer's bag and wore her headscarf, and she was not alone.

Michael watched her and the man she was with, who was wheeling a bicycle, go into the Railway Arms after her companion had padlocked his machine to a lamp-post. They left after half an hour, and the man went with her to the nearby bus stop where he waited and saw her board her bus. Then he mounted his cycle and pedalled off in the other direction.

Michael knew where Carrie lived. He followed the man.

12

Michael saw Nicholas pedal through the gates of his grandmother's house in Elmwood Road and noted the address. Was he one of Carrie's customers?

Michael's years of work on the fringe of crime had innured him to surprise, and this was not his first encounter with the away-day part-time prostitute. A classy-looking girl like Carrie Matthews could set a high price and she clearly had the nerve to ignore the variety of risks she ran, not least being caught out by her husband. Or was this her side of a trade with him, to be set against his past?

Speculating along these lines, with tapes playing when the radio lacked appeal, Michael pushed his car through the night along the M25 and took the Lentwich road.

Even with the windows closed, he liked to imagine that he could smell the sea. He could certainly feel the wind as it struck the side of the car on exposed stretches of road. At last he passed the turning to his own house where Lesley would now be lying tucked up with her lover while Simon and Jenny slept in the rooms that had been theirs through a large part of their childhood. If he'd had a nine to five job, would the marriage have held together? He reflected that the relationship couldn't have been worth a great deal if it could not withstand stress. Lesley had reacted with dismay when finally he left the police; given a chance to support him in a positive manner, she had failed.

Quiet little Anne Randall would not have done that. As the rain began to fall again, sweeping in gusts across the windscreen, Michael wove a little fantasy. He was returning, not to his cheaply furnished shabby flat above the betting shop but to a tiny thatched cottage in one of the inland villages. In a large double bed, almost filling the room, lay a dark-haired woman with big eyes and a wide, sensitive mouth. She was sleeping only lightly because she was subconsciously listening for his car, and when she heard it, she would waken. She wouldn't get up and come down to meet him – well, she might, but he'd rush to reach the bedroom before she got chilled. If she did, he'd soon warm her up. Anne's face, seen only in photographs, floated before his mind's eye.

The car swerved as he almost dozed off. Michael blinked and came back to the facts. He opened the window and let the strong damp night air blow into the car. He was nearly home; a great many accidents occurred when drivers relaxed on familiar ground and he did not want to add to that statistic.

He had plenty to think about before he decided how much to pass on of what he had discovered during the day.

Carrie had had a very successful day and her handbag was stuffed with notes. She would pay most of the money into her building society account. They never seemed to query cash payments. After all, she was only investing her wages.

She and Gordon seldom spoke to each other now. He no longer looked dapper and spruce; his appearance and manner had been what had first attracted her to him, but it was difficult, these days, to see any traces of that early appeal. He went to work in a sweater and jeans and his long moustache now hid his mouth. Some days he didn't bother to shave, much less wash. She could see that he would soon be out of work again, for who would employ someone so obviously casual when there were plenty of better men to choose from?

She still did the washing and ironing, for in a way she felt that his poor appearance reflected on her, but he was so often out in the evening that she had given up any pretext at preparing a conventional meal. If he did come in before she went to bed, she would put something in the microwave for him.

Carrie was aware that if she left him, as she was tempted to do, by simply walking out, she stood to lose the money she had paid towards the mortgage. Her best chance of retaining it was to force him to go, though that could be regarded as a humiliation for her. But if that happened, Nicholas might move in. She played with the idea, not sure if it was a good one. She would have to confess that she had been married, but she could pretend it was all over almost as soon as it had begun, and if she explained that she had not told him about it when they first met because she had not wanted to lose him, he was certain to feel flattered. Nicholas was so easy to understand; he was transparent. Not so long ago she would have laughed at the idea of falling for his style, but it drew her now. You could trust Nicholas.

She had met his grandmother several times. Nicholas had taken her to the house after their now weekly visits to the cinema, before driving her home. She found the rigmarole of returning to Newnham Close from Arlene's house boring, to say the least. Nicholas always watched from the spot at the end of the road where she made him drop her to see her walk up the path. Then she'd have to wait until she saw the lights of his grandmother's car disappear before trekking to the telephone box to call a taxi. He'd commented on the fact that no porch light was ever left on for her, and she'd said the connection was broken, adding that her stepfather hadn't got round to fixing it but summer was coming. It all took ages and she knew Nicholas was hurt because she had not yet taken him to meet her family, but he would have to put up with that. She found keeping the various strands of her life apart exciting.

One Sunday at the end of March she went to lunch at the house in Elmwood Road. Mrs Fitzmaurice was going away in ten days' time, and after lunch, while Nicholas cleared up the rose trimmings from his grandmother's earlier pruning activities, the old lady took out a map and began showing Carrie the route her cruise ship would take. She was embarking from Venice to sail among various Greek islands, with calls at Athens and Haifa, from where passengers would be able to visit Jerusalem and the Lake of Galilee.

'Aren't you afraid you'll get shot or kidnapped?' Carrie asked. 'There's always fighting out there.'

Her geography was a little adrift, Mrs Fitzmaurice

observed, pointing out that on the whole Israel was reasonably stable at present.

'You can run into trouble anywhere, these days,' she said. 'I don't worry about such things at my age, except for possibly giving Nicholas problems to deal with.' She smiled. 'I'm near the end of my journey anyway. At your age life is so sweet that you can't imagine it ending.'

'Well, you're a long time dead, aren't you?' said Carrie. 'It's a pity to go asking for trouble.'

Some would say she did, on Wednesdays, but she'd never yet met a situation she couldn't control.

Mrs Fitzmaurice decided to change the subject.

'I expect you'll see Nicholas while I'm away,' she remarked.

'Oh yes,' said Carrie enthusiastically.

'He's grown very fond of you,' said Mrs Fitzmaurice.

'And I'm fond of him. Of course I am,' declared Carrie staunchly. 'He's the nicest boy I've ever met. He's so kind and thoughtful. Why, he'd give you the shirt off his back if you asked.'

'Yes,' agreed Mrs Fitzmaurice, and added, 'I wouldn't want him to get hurt.'

'Nor me!' Carrie's large blue eyes opened still wider as she spoke.

'I hope you mean what you're saying, my dear,' said the old lady gently. 'If you don't, it would be better to let him go now, before he becomes still more attached to you.'

'But of course I mean it,' Carrie insisted. 'Don't worry!' She smiled at the old lady. 'I'll see he's all right while you're away.'

'I'm sure you will, my dear,' said Mrs Fitzmaurice. She looked steadily at the girl, and Carrie met her gaze without wavering, though she did wonder why she could listen to these admonitions so calmly without wanting to snap that it was none of the old woman's business. I must be getting soft, thought Carrie. If only she could replace Gordon with Nicholas, she might even give up her Wednesdays. Except that the money was nice.

Gordon had come out of prison filled with even more

resentment against the injustice that had dogged his life than before his arrest. It was quite wrong that he should have been convicted of any crime, and it was with the greatest reluctance that he had agreed to plead guilty to manslaughter. His lawyers had insisted that he would receive a far longer sentence if he were to be convicted of murder, and there was no doubt that Anne had died at his hand. However, it had been clearly proved in court that she had driven him to the action that had ended in her death. She had beguiled him into marriage and thus he had been exposed to the stresses which triggered off understandable violence. How could a man of his sensibilities make his way in life when the house was always festooned with damp washing, the children forever snivelling with colds or grizzling, and his wife forever complaining? A man needed positive support, and as women thought themselves the equals of men, they should behave appropriately.

As he brooded about how Anne had expected him to shop and wash up, he forgot that she had returned to teaching and in the last year of their marriage was the sole earner. How could he study to acquire qualifications that would better their lot if he had to waste time on mundane tasks that were her responsibility?

On remand, locked up in a cell with two other men, slopping out, rarely bathing, Gordon had reached a nadir beyond any experience he could have foreseen. When he moved on to his training prison, things were better. He had a cell to himself and had managed to keep out of trouble. He had taken up painting as being a refined sort of activity, but he had no natural talent and his crude, childlike efforts pleased neither him nor the patient tutor who tried to encourage him to persist, so he soon gave up. He had dabbled in several therapeutic schemes that came along but profited from none and he did not get on well with either his fellow prisoners or the staff. He became even more isolated and withdrawn.

Until this happened to him, Gordon had always lived in conditions of comparative physical comfort which he had taken for granted. He had occupied a warm home, with food cooked for him and his washing done. Anne's labours in this direction had compared unfavourably with his mother's, but prison was a reduction to basics. He read a lot, but without any system, lapping up Arthur Hailey and books on war crimes, starting other, more demanding books and abandoning them at the first challenge because his concentration was so poor. He listened to the radio but could not have given an account of a talk or a play he had heard when it was over. Though his crime was serious, his moderate sentence lacked the spurious glamour attached to a lifer. It was only his self-conceit that set him apart from his fellows.

In the final months, when he was at an open prison being prepared for his return to society, he made slight social contact with a few other prisoners. He learned to play bridge and he discussed fraud with a man who had embezzled large sums from the garage where he had worked as sales manager. He had put through bogus paper transactions, allegedly arranging hire-purchase on cars ordered in the names of credit-worthy citizens whose signatures he forged. Gordon was shocked by this dishonesty but at the same time admired the ingenuity that had been behind it, failing to note that the culprit had been speedily caught. If he could do the same sort of thing, acquire a capital sum, he could go abroad to a place in the sun and run a wine bar.

To do this became his ambition. He had spent much time when locked up dreaming of blue seas and warm sands with nothing to do but eat fruit and lie idle. Now, at the filling station, he began reading about how to buy property in Spain or the Canaries and set up in business abroad.

Carrie could be an asset in such an enterprise. Her looks would attract custom, and she could organize the domestic side of things – see to the glasses, clean the place, wait on tables while he presided. She'd like the climate; anyone would.

When his dismissal came, he buoyed himself up by expanding this dream and told his employers that in any case he was planning to go overseas.

'I've given my notice,' he told Carrie. 'I was only doing them a favour, seeing them through in a temporary way.'

It was amazing how he convinced himself that these tailored versions of events were true, thought Carrie, who had heard unlikely accounts of their lives from some of her Wednesday clients and no longer believed him.

Now that he had plenty of leisure, Gordon bought a teach-yourself Spanish course with a book and some tapes to prepare for the rosy future he planned. He could study while Carrie was at work; he might even enrol in a local class. He kept up his new regime for a while, going off to one or another pub before she returned, so that they seldom met.

Carrie was usually home before Gordon, even on Wednesdays; she would be in bed feigning sleep when he came upstairs. He left her alone. Even sex had lost its appeal, now that he had made up for the years spent away from women.

The week after Michael had followed her to London, she came in to find Gordon waiting for her in the living-room, which was full of tobacco smoke. A bottle of whisky, almost empty, stood on the television set, which was showing the late-night film.

'Where've you been?' he snapped at her. 'You're never here when I want you.'

'I've been at my charity job. You know that. I go every week,' Carrie retorted.

'Charity at this hour?' Focusing with some difficulty, Gordon looked at his watch and sneered. 'Fine sort of charity goes on at night.'

'I told you. Believe it or not as you like,' said Carrie and marched upstairs to get ready for bed.

Gordon called after her from the hallway.

'I wanted to tell you about our future,' he said, and his voice took on a plaintive tone as he followed her upstairs.

'What future?' Carrie had entered the bedroom.

'Spain. We're going there,' Gordon told her.

'A holiday?' Carrie's mind tackled the idea, which at first was extremely attractive. She could probably cope with his presence because she would soon make her own circle of friends, but how did he plan to pay for it?

'No. We're going to open a wine bar.' Gordon stood in the

doorway, looking at her as she took off her coat.

'What are we going to use for money?' she asked.

'I'll get some. My mother – I told you.' He moved towards her.

'Get out of my way.' After her Wednesdays, Carrie always liked a good bath, though there had never been a problem about showering after a job since she hit the businessman's trade. Still fully dressed, she pushed past him and went into the bathroom, locking the door and turning the taps on.

Gordon now felt an alcohol-induced lecherousness. She'd be all soft and warm after her bath. It was about time he had a few of his rights. He'd soften her up about Spain with a few smarmy words and she'd be like putty. Then he'd go up to Yelbury and ask his mother for funds.

He started to pull off his clothes, ready for Carrie's return. As he dropped his sweater on the floor he noticed her Marks and Spencer's bag. She usually put everything away before he came upstairs but the routine had been broken tonight when she hurried into the bathroom to dodge him. Gordon lifted it up. Charity work, indeed! She'd been on a spending spree. He looked inside and saw the hat and her large bag, which he took out and opened. Inside were wads of treasury notes, tens and twenties, two fifties, at least three hundred pounds.

What had she been doing? Gambling?

Oddly enough, the true answer never occurred to him.

When she came out of the bathroom he was lying on the bed, still wearing his shirt and trousers, holding the notes.

'Who's a clever girl, then?' he crooned, waving them in front of his face and sniffing at them as if to inhale their bouquet.

'Give me that! That's my money!'

Carrie flew at him, and her speed caught him unprepared. She succeeded in snatching most of the notes from him but he seized her wrist and twisted it savagely, causing her to loosen her grasp on some of them.

Using her as a prop, Gordon levered himself off the bed, but Carrie was screaming at him and tearing at his face with her free hand. Drunk as he was, he was shocked at her language. Such words should not pass the lips of one's wife.

Gordon gave her two swift slaps on the face, and the blows were so hard that she staggered across the room. He came after her, the blood rushing to his head. Something like this had happened before, when he'd taken some money Anne had been saving for Christmas.

But this wasn't Anne. This was Carrie, who could fight back.

She was still yelling as she dodged away from him, but now Gordon had her pinned against the wall by the window and his hands were reaching for her throat while his bulk held her there. Carrie stretched out for anything that could help her, and her hand met a glass bowl that stood on her dressing table. She managed to grab it and raise it, crashing it down on his head. As he reeled back, she kneed him in the groin and he doubled up.

Carrie went on yelling at him as she rescued her money.

'Get out of here,' she cried as he lay on the floor, still writhing. 'Or I'll do that again.'

He went.

13

The idea of a wine bar in Spain wasn't such a bad one.

Carrie thought about it the next day on the bus going to work. Outside, the rain was sleeting down. This was supposed to be spring.

Gordon had spent the night on the settee. The living-room door was closed when Carrie came downstairs and she left the house without seeing him. He'd been really wild. She didn't like to think what might have happened if she hadn't clobbered him with that bowl, which hadn't even broken. She'd won it at a fair some years ago and it was sturdily moulded.

She could divorce him for that sort of behaviour.

It was a consoling reflection, and during her coffee break she consulted another sales assistant who had just gone through a divorce, confiding that she and Gordon had had a fight ending in blows. The other girl told her about divorce based on unreasonable conduct.

'But you'll make it up,' she said.

'I'm not so sure I want to,' Carrie replied.

'Well, you should keep a diary,' advised her colleague. 'Write down every last thing he does that's bad. Does he drink?'

'Yes.'

'That too, then. It all adds up.'

'He's been married before,' said Carrie. 'His wife went off with somebody else.'

'Well, now you know why, don't you?' said her friend.

Carrie had recently begun to feel curious about that unknown woman but there was little time to indulge such thoughts because the present kept her so busy. The store was doing well, with customers buying the new spring fashions to cheer themselves up during the unseasonable late March weather, when there had been freak snow-storms and bitter east winds interspersed with bright blue skies. The house had to be kept clean and polished and she spent time on keeping her own clothes up to the mark, especially what she needed on Wednesdays. And there was Nicholas. He was important.

She didn't even know the other woman's name.

'Where did you get that money?'

Gordon had decided to have it out with Carrie.

'It's club money,' said Carrie. 'Belongs to the old people. They raised it at a sale, and I'm banking it for them. I'm the treasurer,' she added, pleased with her story.

'Where're the books, then?' he asked. 'The accounts.'

'At the centre.'

She had all the answers. He believed her because he thought it was quite impossible for her to be stealing on such a scale from her employers, and he had no reason to doubt her honesty.

But Carrie did not wait for him to continue his interrogation.

'You watch it, Gordon Matthews,' she told him. 'I don't know what your first wife had to put up with, but I can tell you I'm not standing for any rough stuff. I never thought you'd turn out to be useless at holding down a decent job. I was sorry for you because you'd lost your wife and kids, and you came on so respectable. I must have been out of my mind. Look at you now! You're dirty, and you haven't shaved, and your hair needs cutting. Ugh! No one looking at you would give you even half a chance at a job when there's plenty to choose from who're clean and decent.'

Quite suddenly, while she was speaking, Gordon's truculence faded. He had a very bad headache and a sour taste in his mouth, and he longed for someone to swathe him in pity, send him to bed with bread and milk and assure him that everything would be all right in the morning.

'It's not my fault,' he said, laid his head on his hands as he slumped into a chair, and began to weep.

When this happened after rows with Anne, it had always

worked. The silence into which she would retreat after he had berated her, or even struck her, would break and she would forgive him again, although he never apologized. But he never accepted blame, even tacitly; it was always Anne who suggested a fresh start, pleaded with him to overlook her shortcomings, cooked him some special dish.

Now, Gordon expected Carrie to melt, put her arms round him and even lead him up to bed.

But she didn't.

'You make me sick,' she said, and walked out of the room.

She locked the bedroom door again that night.

Nicholas's gentle ways were all the more attractive after Carrie's recent brush with Gordon. She went round to supper with him the day after his grandmother left on her cruise.

'How does the idea of running a wine bar in Spain grab you?' she asked him.

He had cooked *coq au vin* and laid the dining-room table with candles and the best silver. There were spring flowers from the garden in a vase in the centre, tiny daffodils and velvety polyanthus.

'Not a lot. Why?' replied Nicholas.

Carrie had been thinking that it might be more fun with Nicholas than with Gordon.

'Oh – I don't know. Someone I know's thinking of doing it,' she said. 'I wonder what it would cost to start.'

'Goodness knows. You'd have to rent premises, I suppose, and fit it out. You'd need a fair bit of capital,' said Nicholas.

'Like what? Two thousand quid?'

'More than that. You'd need somewhere to live, too.'

'Over the shop,' said Carrie promptly. 'Couldn't you get a loan?'

'Probably.'

'If you don't fancy that, what's your idea of a good life?' Carrie asked him.

'Oh –' he blushed and ran a hand through his hair. 'Getting married and having kids.'

'That's easy enough,' said Carrie. 'Staying married's the problem.'

'Yes, well, it takes two, doesn't it? To make a go of things, I mean,' Nicholas said. 'If both parties mean to make it work, then it will.'

'Maybe.' Carrie shrugged.

'Don't you want to get married, Carrie?' he asked her.

'Most people do in the end, don't they?' she said. 'But it's nice to be independent.'

'I think it must be nice to have someone to come home to who's always pleased to see you,' said Nicholas.

'You've got that. You've got your gran,' said Carrie.

'That's not quite what I mean,' said Nicholas.

She spent the night with him in his room at the end of the corridor, past the bathroom and his grandmother's room, and three other bedrooms which he showed her.

She had lured him upstairs by asking to see the rest of the house, and when at last they reached his room she sat down on the single bed, drew him on to it beside her, and kissed him. After that, Nicholas was lost.

Later, he kept apologizing, but she kissed away his words.

'Why be sorry? It's natural,' she said. He thought he heard her murmur, 'You've a lot to learn,' as he was swept away again.

Nicholas woke at about three o'clock in the morning. He had so often imagined making love to Carrie that at first he thought he had dreamed the events of the night, but as her fine, sweetly smelling hair tickled his face and he felt her small body tucked against him as though designed to fit there, he knew it was real. He held her more tightly and heard her sigh as she snuggled even closer. He was getting cramp in one arm; that must have been what had woken him up. Very gently he moved his position, being careful not to wake her. He lay there fighting the urge to begin all over again, tenderly holding her, and then, without seeming to wake up, she turned towards him and, to his amazement, the miracle was repeated.

No wonder poets raved about this, and half the world seemed to think of little else, thought Nicholas. It was not until morning that he was able to spare a thought for others.

'Won't your mother be worried?' he said then. 'She won't know where you are. Hadn't you better telephone?'

'Oh, that's all right.' Carrie patted his hand as she quickly thought of a way to satisfy his concern. How sweet he was, thinking people bothered about that sort of thing. 'I told her I might stop over with Arlene – that's a friend of mine.'

'Oh.' For some reason this explanation made Nicholas uneasy. 'Well, that's all right, then,' he said.

Later, other worries surfaced, but again she kissed them away and told him she was on the pill. They did not leave the house all day. For Nicholas, whose sexual experience was limited to some inconclusive heavy petting, such rapture was beyond anything he had ever imagined and his instinctive physical response made it easy to suppress any niggling doubts in his mind.

Carrie wanted to spend the next night there, too. It would save her from having to face up to things at home, and anyway he was such a pet that she felt that she loved him a little, whatever that meant; he was certainly different from anyone else she had been to bed with. But Nicholas became suddenly puritan and said it wouldn't do. Besides, they both had to go to work the next day and she needed her own things – a change of clothes and so on.

'What shift are you on tomorrow?' he asked. 'I hope it's a late one.'

'Shift?'

'At the hotel.'

'Oh!' Carrie had forgotten the career outline she had given him. 'Yes – it's an afternoon one,' she said.

'Do you sleep at the hotel when you're on very late?' he asked her. 'You do night shifts, don't you?'

'Yes – oh, yes. Of course,' she assured him, and stretched out a hand to stroke his chest. It was quite hairless. He was worried about her safety, travelling back alone in the dead hours. How touching! 'I don't take any risks,' she said.

She had to give in to his quaint insistence that she went home, and allowed herself to be dropped in Grove Road near Arlene's again.

Later, alone in his hitherto chaste bed which still smelled of Carrie, Nicholas lay regretting his prudence. Still, there would be other nights. His grandmother would be away next weekend, and there was always Wednesday. She might come back with him then. If he could persuade her to do so, he would insist that she telephoned her mother. He lay reliving their hours together and anticipating their next meeting until, with the grey light of dawn, doubts returned. To drive them away, he got up and set about restoring order, changing his sheets and tidying the clutter of dirty plates and cups from the hasty meals they had snatched and eaten in bed. He did not want his grandmother's cleaning lady to suspect what had been going on, and he put on the washing-machine before he left for the station.

'Poor unfortunate girl, I suppose she knew nothing about him,' said Oliver Randall.

Once again, he and Michael were drinking coffee together in the Primrose Café in Rushbridge. Michael had revealed that Gordon was married, and was working in an unsatisfactory way at a filling station.

'They've got a nice little place,' he said. 'A one-bedroomed maisonette. Property's dear down there – it's near the motorway and there's a bit of an industrial boom.'

'What's she like?'

'Small – about five foot two, blonde. Very smart,' said Michael. 'Young. Twenty – twenty-two. Something like that.'

'She's in danger,' said Oliver.

'Not necessarily,' said Michael. 'She belongs to a different generation. She looks well able to take care of herself, whereas I expect Anne was a gentle girl who thought her husband would look after her, at least to some extent.'

'Well, this is an unexpected development, I must say,' said Oliver. 'I hope that girl won't put him up to looking for the children.'

'I shouldn't think she'd want the bother of them,' said Michael. 'Especially if he hasn't told her about his past. He'd have to come clean if he went after them.'

'You're right.' That was a consoling reflection.

'I expect he's told her some fairy tale or other,' said Michael. 'He won't want the truth to come out.'

'What if she discovers it?'

'What indeed, but why should she, unless he somehow blows it?' said Michael.

'I feel she ought to be warned,' said Oliver.

'I don't really think that will help anyone,' Michael said. 'She may be able to manage him.'

'But he's not making out in his job, you said.'

'No.'

'That's typical.'

'I still think Carrie can manage him,' Michael said. 'You won't go down and confront him, will you?'

Oliver frowned.

'I'll have to think about it,' he said.

Michael had to leave it there. He had decided to say nothing about Carrie's extra-marital activities to either Oliver or Barnaby. Such knowledge could be dynamite.

14

'Where have you been?'

Gordon, charged with righteous wrath, turned away from the television when Carrie returned to Newnham Close on Sunday evening. On the living-room floor was a dirty plate off which he had eaten fish fingers and chips. Several beer cans, some of them empty, stood on top of the television set and an empty whisky bottle lay on its side on the floor. A tiny trickle of liquid had escaped from it on to the pale carpet. He had been smoking all evening and the small room was heavy with fumes. Carrie observed him through a grey haze and wrinkled her nose in disgust, walking past him into the kitchen without replying. Things were no better there. A burnt chip pan stood on the drainer and the aura of tobacco was overlaid by the smell of hectic frying.

Gordon plodded heavily after her. He had put on weight and begun to move like a much older man.

'I said, where have you been?' he repeated.

'What's that to you?' Carrie snapped back.

'A man expects to enjoy his wife's company over the weekend,' said Gordon pompously.

'Oh, does he? Well, when did you and I enjoy each other's company at any time, let alone a weekend? Tell me that?' Carrie retorted.

'I demand to know where you were,' said Gordon, and waited to be told she had been at Arlene's, which he knew was untrue as he had telephoned to find out.

Carrie was on the point of saying she had been at the Ritz with her lover, when an instinctive caution stopped her from taunting him. She had learned to gauge the moods of her Wednesday customers and to vary her own response accordingly. Gordon had already exhibited violence towards her, and the best method of self-defence was avoidance of danger.

'Round at my mum's. She hasn't been well,' said Carrie. Her mother, unlike Arlene, was not on the telephone – it had been cut off for non-payment of the account – and he wouldn't have checked on her there, but he might have rung Arlene. There was a box in Bridge Street which they used; Gordon considered installing the telephone a needless expense.

'You should have let me know,' he said.

'I don't see why. You never tell me where you're going when you go off in the evening or don't trouble to come home,' said Carrie. 'For all I know, you're out robbing a bank.' The thought of such a thing made her suddenly laugh; he hadn't the gumption to raid a kid's piggy box.

'What are you laughing at?' Gordon moved towards her, an arm raised.

Carrie had begun to sort out the mess in the sink. He wouldn't do it and tomorrow she'd have no time. If only she were still round at Nicholas's. That was the life. It was a huge, old-fashioned place but you could do a lot with the house, given modern ideas, and it must be worth a bomb. There'd be some future with Nicholas. But she'd tire of him in time; she knew that: the novelty of his innocence would wear off, just as her appreciation of Gordon's maturity had not lasted long.

'You've no right to step out without my permission, even if you are with your mother,' Gordon told her. Anne would never have dared do such a thing.

Holding the frying-pan, Carrie turned to face him.

'Is that so?' she said. 'You think again, Gordon Matthews. I'll do as I like, and you won't stop me. No one would want to spend the weekend with you – just look at you, you're a disgusting, dirty mess. You haven't shaved or even washed for days, and the place is filthy. You might at least wash up.'

'You should have been here to look after me,' Gordon said. 'It's your duty.'

'And what about yours?' Carrie demanded. 'Who's paying the mortgage and buying the food? I don't notice you bringing in any money these days. What about what you get from the DHSS? You've been drinking and smoking that away, haven't you?'

Gordon was standing in the tiny kitchen, swaying slightly, still glaring at her, but the sight of the frying-pan, which she now raised in a threatening manner, warned him off. Anne had never hit back. Carrie had done it once already.

He slouched back to the living-room, banging the door, and Carrie, when she had cleared up the kitchen, went to bed, again locking him out.

Carrie refused to go home with Nicholas after they had travelled back on the train together on Wednesday.

'Do come,' he begged. 'Telephone your mother and say you're with a friend, like before. It'd be true, after all.' White lies were occasionally justified.

'No. I'm sorry, Nicholas. I'm too tired,' said Carrie.

She didn't understand herself why she wouldn't comply. If he'd been a punter and offered enough, she'd have consented. She'd made love with Gordon after several of her London trips and thought nothing of it. But Nicholas was different. He had to be kept separate from that part of her life.

'Well, there's always the weekend,' he said. 'And maybe the rest of our lives.'

There! He'd said it. He looked at her across the table in the Railway Arms where they were having their usual drinks.

'You're much too young to think of settling down, if that's what you mean,' Carrie told him. She patted his hand.

'I'm not all that young. You've never complained about it before,' he said bitterly.

'No, darling, and I'm not complaining now. It's one of the things I love about you,' said Carrie. 'You're so unspoilt.'

These words gave him heart. He'd win her round.

The next two days dragged for Nicholas, who was counting the hours until Saturday. His useful but un-demanding job involved sending out appeals and informa-tion circulars, checking subscriptions, filing, running errands and packing up parcels. The people among whom he worked were mostly amiable unpaid helpers who operated at a moderate pace, though there was one woman with sons his age who was jet-propelled with energy and grew infuriated by the slow tempo of her colleagues. Nicholas was only filling in time with the organization. When his parents came home in the autumn, a discussion about his long-term future would be inevitable. He might have gained his extra A level by then.

If Carrie would only agree to marry him, he would look for a better job now, one with a higher wage. He knew it wasn't the fashion these days to marry; people set up together; but he wanted more than that. He hadn't had a settled home for years, except with his grandmother. Suddenly he wanted to establish one himself and found a family, unusual though this might be, especially at his age. Surely Carrie wouldn't mind being hard-up at first? She'd expect to keep on her own job until they had a baby. This prospect made him blush. Perhaps he could go into the hotel trade, like her; he liked helping people, which it involved. When he'd learned the ropes they could have their own little guest-house in Cornwall.

All this was in his mind on Saturday, and when Carrie at last arrived at a quarter past twelve, Nicholas had been expecting her for over an hour and had been pacing to and fro within earshot of the telephone, afraid she was not coming after all. He had looked for her number but found no one with the name of Foster in Grove Road, where he dropped her. Of course, Carrie's mother had remarried and he didn't know her new husband's name. Still, Carrie could have telephoned him if she'd been delayed. He imagined all sorts of disasters and was edgy with her at first.

'I thought you'd changed your mind about coming,' he said sulkily.

'Silly, as if I would! I've been shopping,' said Carrie blithely, and showed him her laden bag, made of pretty flowered oilcloth. 'Let's go out somewhere for the day,' she went on, delving into it to produce smoked salmon and fresh strawberries. 'We can have these for supper,' she added.

'You'll stay the night?' Nicholas needed reassurance.

'Oh yes. We can have supper in bed,' she said. 'All we need is some champagne.'

'We'll get some,' said Nicholas, happy again.

They set off in his grandmother's car and had lunch at a small hotel in the country. After that he took her to visit a stately home where the season had just begun. It was nice being with him; he always found things to do which were not what she'd have chosen, left to herself, but were not boring at all, and she liked hearing him talk. He'd been to lots of interesting places and knew about painters and how old bits of furniture were, and he didn't just talk about himself, like most fellows did when they weren't trying to get you into bed.

'I like to see these old places,' Carrie discovered. 'I've not been to many. Imagine living like that, with so many rooms!'

Nicholas's social conscience was in an ambivalent state. Such houses were part of the national heritage and it was important that they be preserved; he was quite aware that most of the owners could only afford to maintain them by opening them to the public and devising money-spinning side attractions such as garden centres and craft shops, but the plight of the homeless and of famine victims, and others helped by his charity, made him feel that no one should own so much. He tried to say so.

'Well, you don't do so badly in your gran's house,' Carrie pointed out. 'Two of you in a place big enough for five families. I don't see what's wrong with it. Their fathers and grandfathers made lots of money and earned the right to be lords or whatever. And they gave work to people. Carrying water and things. Not that I'd have liked to be a skivvy.'

She wandered round the mansion eyeing its fittings with a critical eye. The priceless porcelain was too ornate for her, and the curtains were threadbare. Most of the famous paintings that hung on the brocade-covered walls were too dark for her taste.

They went to the souvenir shop where she bought a pot of jam for her mother and a plastic model of the house which she gave to Nicholas, who privately thought it looked cheap and gimmicky. However, he thanked her with ardour. It was odd that she dressed so well but lacked an appreciation of so much else. Of course, he'd had a privileged upbringing; he'd never lived in a very small house like her mother's.

'How's your grandmother?' she asked, on the way back. 'Have you heard from her?'

Nicholas had received a postcard of the Lion's Gate at Mycenae.

'She's having a fine time getting up at six-thirty and spending the day clambering up Greek mountains,' he said. 'All those historic sites were on top of hills, so that the people could watch for attack,' he added helpfully.

'I've never been to Greece,' said Carrie. 'Zeus and all that. He was quite a lad.'

'Well, yes.' This was a new idea to Nicholas. 'He did get about,' he agreed. 'It's quaint, that mythology, but people have always needed gods – something outside themselves to give strength.'

'Like a quick swig of gin,' said Carrie.

He laughed. She was so witty.

After another ecstatic night, he asked her when he could meet her mother and stepfather.

'Oh, I don't want them involved in this,' she said.

'In this? What do you mean?'

'Us. You and me. It's private,' she said.

'Special, you mean?'

'Yes.' She was able to divert him from this unprofitable line of discussion without any difficulty, but he would be certain to bring it up again. Usually girls had trouble getting their fellows to the point of wanting to make things legal; Nicholas was touchingly old-fashioned in this as in so much else.

'Don't you ever have to work at weekends?' he asked her later.

Carrie had an answer.

'No,' she said airily. 'Isn't that lucky? There're two married girls with kids at the place I'm at now. They come on at weekends when their husbands look after the children.'

As long as you uttered it confidently, people accepted

anything you told them, especially if it was what they wanted to hear.

She stayed until ten on Sunday night. They had had a lovely day, getting up late, having a bath together, reading the papers and concocting some sort of a meal before making love again.

'Till Wednesday,' he said, as he stopped at the usual place on the corner of Grove Road. He had hoped she would forget her shopping bag, which was in the back of the car, and then he could hurry after her with it. It would give him a chance to meet her mother, unless she had already gone to bed. But she didn't forget.

Instead of going straight home, he drove round the bend out of sight, locked the car and walked back towards Grove Road again, intent, like many a lover, on gazing up at her window.

Ahead was a telephone box, and someone was in it.

Not wanting to be seen hovering about like Romeo, Nicholas retreated into the shadows on the opposite side of the road where there was a gap between two blocks of houses. Whoever was in the telephone box stayed there until a taxi approached, coming from the direction where Nicholas had left his grandmother's car. It pulled up by the box from which, to his astonishment, he saw Carrie emerge. She got into the cab and it drove on down the road.

He came out of his hiding-place and stood staring after its departing tail-light. Where could she be going at this hour? There hadn't been time for her to go into the house at all. He drove home in a confused state of mind and spent most of the night thrashing about sleeplessly, wondering what she could be doing. At five o'clock he abandoned the quest for repose, put his sheets in the washing-machine and cleaned up all traces of the weekend's activities.

His grandmother would be back on Friday. He'd said this to Carrie, who had told him that she could always creep out quietly, if she came round and stayed until after Mrs Fitzmaurice had gone to bed.

'The house is huge. She'd never know,' said Carrie.

Nicholas was shocked.

'We couldn't,' he said. 'Not with her here.'

This was only what Carrie had expected, but she thought it would add spice to their intrigue.

'Well, never mind. We'll think of something,' she had said, and kissed his nose.

On Wednesday, he took the car to the station. Why hadn't he thought of this last week? Carrie could escape her bus trip once, at least, if he took her home. But to his dismay, she wouldn't agree. She accepted a drink at the Railway Arms but that was all.

Thwarted, he followed her bus, soon catching up with it once he had left the station yard. There was no other bus in sight at that point and he kept well back, not wanting her to see him, and not really knowing why he was doing this. He was not very familiar with the bus routes across town and he expected this one to go past the hospital and the fire station, which was the way to Grove Road. To his surprise it turned into the old town by the cathedral and went along Bridge Street, through a residential area that had been developed in recent years. When his grandparents had first come to Meddingham this had been open countryside but now there were rows and rows of new houses of varying kinds and sizes radiating back to form whole colonies.

Each time the bus stopped, Nicholas stopped too, waiting at the kerb some distance behind it and peering ahead to see if Carrie alighted. He annoyed some of the other drivers and horns were blown at him more than once, but at this time of night the traffic was not heavy. Luckily there were no police cars about. He almost missed the moment when at last Carrie did leave the bus. What if she came towards him and saw him spying on her? That was what she would think he was doing and she would be right. He ducked down, ready to hide. She might not remember the number of the car.

However, she continued in the same direction as the bus for three hundred yards or so, and then turned into a side road. Nicholas parked under a tree and, in darkness lit only by the widely spaced streetlamps, followed her along a short street of very small, new terraced houses, each separated from the pavement by about a metre of front area roped off with a chain linked on foot-high posts. As in Grove Road, there were no garages and cars were strung along the kerbside.

Carrie stepped up to a front door two-thirds of the way from the end of the line and opened it without any delay; she'd had her key ready.

There were lights on downstairs in the house. Nicholas approached and stood outside. He could hear the television, turned on loud. He saw a light go on upstairs and shrank back against the wall of the next house as a figure – Carrie's – quickly drew thin curtains over the gathered muslin already across the window. Nicholas hurried on to the end of the row and turned to his left past the last house where a footpath ran behind the houses.

Nicholas walked along the path in the dark. He counted the black shapes of the houses lying close to the fence. She had entered the ninth house. He located it and looked up at the single lighted window at the rear, a frosted one, the bathroom.

She wasn't alone. Someone was in the house watching television. Who could she be visiting now? Was this where she had come in the taxi on Sunday? Why? It was not easy to think of an innocent reason for visiting anyone so late at night. If one did exist, why had she not told him where she was going? Why had she not asked him to take her there last Sunday?

He could think of no answer.

15

Mrs Fitzmaurice arrived home on Friday after spending the night at a hotel near Gatwick as her plane from Dubrovnik, where the cruise ended, flew in too late to let her travel home.

She had met stimulating companions and found many pleasing varieties of plants on her cruise, and had enjoyed speaking the small amount of Greek she had managed to learn during the years she had spent travelling to the Eastern Mediterranean. Now, after an interval, she was refreshed and could look more objectively at her own life and that of her grandson.

She had no other grandchildren, and he had occupied a large part of her thoughts and affections since he had been a very small boy. Sometimes, especially in the very early years, he had accompanied his parents during their tours abroad, but at eight he went to boarding-school and thereafter flew out to join them at most twice a year. The Easter holidays were always spent with his grandmother, who at other times dispatched him to wherever his parents were working, and met him on his return. Her house was his home and he lived comfortably. Until he met Carrie, he seemed to spend very little time with other young people, and Mrs Fitzmaurice thought this was a pity. He lacked the aggression that had ensured his father a successful career. He must extend himself after his exam in the summer. If he meant to take up some further training by going to a polytechnic or other college, he should soon apply. It was not always kind to take too much care of a young person but she loved his company and would miss him desperately if he moved out.

Her husband had managed a furniture factory which he had inherited from his father, and they had come to

Meddingham with their first child, Nicholas's father. A second son, who had died as a baby, had been born in the house where she still lived. Meddingham had been a village then; now it was a suburb of Durford. The factory had been taken over during the fifties; so Nicholas's father had trained as an engineer and followed a different path to commercial success.

If Nicholas were to move, she would have no good excuse for remaining in such a large house alone. She could sell it and hand over some of the proceeds to either her son or even to Nicholas. What would he do with it, if she were to take such an action?

Buy a house and marry that girl, most likely, she decided, thus tying himself down far too early. A young man should be free to roam the world. She knew the boy's parents were disappointed that he had not done better at school and showed no special aptitude in any direction, but he had gentle qualities which might be lost if he were to compete in the real rat-race.

It was that girl who made her uneasy. Carrie seemed very pleasant, was polite, had good manners and was very pretty, but Mrs Fitzmaurice, who over the years had learned to trust her own instinctive reactions, felt that her grandson might seriously burn his fingers at that particular fire. Still, he could profit from the experience. Mrs Fitzmaurice had a very good idea of what might be going on while her back was turned and as long as he was careful about the consequences, she thought no harm could result.

She had bought him a Greek shirt, and two tapes of bouzouki music which they listened to together that evening while they caught up with each other's news. All had been well at the house; he had kept the garden under control and the cleaning lady had turned out various rooms and washed curtains and covers.

'And what about Carrie? Have you seen much of her?' asked Mrs Fitzmaurice at last.

'Oh yes,' said Nicholas, turning away so that his grandmother should not see the colour which flooded his face. He told her about their weekend's visit to the stately home.

'Would you like to invite her to lunch on Sunday?'

'Oh – thank you, but we thought we might go off somewhere for the day,' said Nicholas. 'If you don't mind,' he added.

'Not at all, dear, but in that case I think I'll go over to visit Marjorie as I haven't seen her for some time. So I'll need the car.' Marjorie was a friend of Mrs Fitzmaurice's who lived in a comfortable flat in Oxford with a warden to whom one could turn if in trouble, and there was a communal dining-room. In Mrs Fitzmaurice's opinion, the warden merely replaced the former dependable hall-porter and janitor system which still prevailed in rare areas. Mrs Fitzmaurice herself treasured her own independence and dreaded the day when increasing frailty might force her into such an establishment. Though still very active, she had neither the wish nor the energy to cultivate new acquaintances. It took years to build up a friendship; if untended, it could wither away, and surviving links were precious. Old age was a lonely time but the mere fact of sharing it did not mean one had tastes in common. One of the merits of her recent cruise was that it brought together people with similar interests, but there had been so many elderly widows among the passengers that she had felt quite depressed as she watched the newer ones timidly circling about with their grey heads, and often grey faces until the sea air took effect. Many had walking sticks, and moved stiffly.

She was tired. The schedule was exhausting if you went on all the shore excursions, sometimes two or three in a day with early starts each morning, but now she would soon catch up on her arrears of sleep. It was good to be home, and it was good to see Nicholas.

If she went out for the day on Sunday, he could bring that girl back to the house. She would make quite clear to him how long she would be out.

Because she explained her plans so precisely, exactly what Mrs Fitzmaurice foresaw took place. Nicholas had taken Carrie out on Saturday night; they went to the cinema and then to a Chinese restaurant for dinner. He dropped her in Grove Road again and drove straight home, not waiting to see if she caught another taxi, and because she had agreed to spend Sunday with him, sheer physical anticipation enabled him to put her deception out of his mind.

When his grandmother returned from Oxford they were both in the drawing-room listening to Greek music and looking at the newspapers. Nicholas's well-brushed hair, still slightly damp from his recent shower, and his spruce appearance – he was wearing a different shirt from the one he had on that morning – confirmed Mrs Fitzmaurice's diagnosis of the situation. Nowadays it was called having a relationship, she reflected. Were couples never friends as well? She could not feel that Carrie would remain interested in Nicholas for long. She was probably only two or three years older than he was, but she was much too experienced and worldly not to wish to move on to someone who could offer her more. The girl sat in a large armchair looking neat and demure and asked about Mrs Fitzmaurice's trip, wanting to see the postcards she had collected from each port of call and the sketches she had made. All this took some time, and afterwards they had supper in the kitchen, soup and bread and cheese. Then Mrs Fitzmaurice went up to bed, telling Nicholas to take Carrie home in the car.

This time, after dropping her in Grove Road again, Nicholas drove straight to Bridge Street and parked near the river. He blundered along the dimly lit path on the bank until he came to the junction with the footpath which ran behind Newnham Close, hurried along it to the end where it joined the turning bay and was in time to see Carrie walk jauntily down the road and enter Number 9, as she had done before.

So it wasn't a one-off thing. There had been no sudden emergency calling her to this address. She lived here.

And why hadn't the taxi – for she must have taken one again – brought her right to the door?

Nicholas did not sleep that night, and the next morning he telephoned the office from a call-box to say that he was unwell and would not be coming in. He had left the house at his usual time as he did not want his grandmother to realize that he was breaking his usual routine.

He cycled into Durford, through the centre of town and across to Grove Road, the route along which he had driven Carrie so many times when he thought he was taking her home. This morning he parked his bike by the kerb and walked up the path to the front door of the house outside which he had so often dropped her. Musical chimes sounded when he pressed the bell.

The door was opened by a plump young woman with untidy dark curls, big brown eyes, rosy cheeks, and a small child tucked under one arm.

Carrie's sister? But they were all small, the step-brothers and sister she had mentioned.

'Yes?' Arlene beamed at him. He was probably selling insurance or something.

'Is Carrie in?' he asked.

'Carrie?'

'Carrie Foster.'

'Goodness, you are out of date,' said Arlene. 'You can't have seen her for ages. She's married now – her name's Matthews.'

'Married?' Nicholas felt the blood surge into his head at the same instant as a cold sickness entered his stomach.

'Yes. Last October, it was. She still lives in Durford, but right across town. Are you a friend of hers? Well, you must be, to ask for her.' Arlene didn't remember him, but then Carrie had had so many boyfriends over the years, none of them lasting long.

'Yes. I – er – I was nearby and thought I'd look her up,' said Nicholas. He made an effort. 'Can you give me her address?' He may as well have it confirmed.

'Yes. It's in Newnham Close – Number nine. That's off Bridge Street. It's a new development. She's got a lovely little place. And she's working at Brice's now.'

'Brice's?'

'Yes. In the fashion department. She left Marks a bit ago.'

'I thought she worked in a hotel.' Nicholas gasped the words.

'Whatever gave you that idea? She's never done that.' Arlene found the idea entertaining. 'If I see her, who shall I say was asking?' she added.

'Don't worry. I've got the day off work and I'll catch her at Brice's.' Nicholas managed to speak in a level tone.

He pedalled away.

Nicholas was well acquainted with Brice's. As a small boy he had been equipped there with trousers and pullovers. He had graduated through Teen Togs to the menswear section and still occasionally shopped there.

There were some women's fashions arranged on racks on the ground floor, among jewellery and cosmetics, cheap bright lines to appeal to young office and shop workers hurrying in during their lunch hour. He peered around for Carrie but could not see her. There seemed to be no assistants about except for one at a till, with a queue forming in front of her counter. He took the escalator to the first floor and skulked among the raincoats, trying to locate her. He didn't want her to see him. And he didn't really want to see her, because he didn't want what her friend had told him to be true.

But it was.

He moved cautiously forward between racks of garments and saw her fair froth of hair as she tidied a rail of separates. Nicholas ducked behind the nearest display and looked past it to observe her. He saw a customer approach her and ask her something. Carrie smiled at the woman and led her to another rail.

He supposed she was nice to everyone, and that included telling them what they wanted to hear. She knew he wouldn't have liked learning that she was married, so she didn't tell him, not even when he more or less proposed.

But he loved her, and he thought she loved him. She'd said she did, more than once.

He spent the afternoon in the safe darkness of the cinema, among a scattering of senior citizens, and watched *Crocodile Dundee* without taking in any part of the action.

Perhaps Carrie and her husband didn't get on and they had parted. But there had been someone in the house watching television, and that girl would have known if they'd split up. Any theory that Carrie might have left the television and the lights on to scare away burglars wasn't convincing. When the film ended, Nicholas pedalled sadly away through the town. She'd be going home before long. It was still daylight; the days were lengthening and the clocks would be going on soon.

He decided to go and see her.

Nicholas turned down Bridge Street and when he came to the river, he pushed his bike along the embankment path and turned up the footpath behind the houses that formed Newnham Close. He left his machine at the end of the road, not bothering to fasten the padlock. Then he waited until she came into sight.

She was wearing her leather coat with the fur collar and carrying the bag in which she had brought the smoked salmon and strawberries on Saturday, only two days ago. Nicholas moved forward as she was inserting her key in the lock and arrived on the step as she turned to close the front door behind her.

'Hullo, Carrie,' he said, and put his foot through the gap to prevent her from shutting the door.

'Oh!' Carrie's eyes widened in shock as she saw him. 'Oh, Nicholas!'

'Yes, it is "Oh, Nicholas" isn't it?' he said. 'You don't live in Grove Road at all, do you? You live here.'

'I can explain,' said Carrie.

'Can you?' he asked. 'That'll take quite a bit of doing.'

Carrie glanced up and down the street. There was no knowing when Gordon would be home. He'd been sitting in front of the television full of drink and snoring when she returned the previous night, and she'd managed to get to the bedroom without him waking. She hadn't seen him this morning.

'You'd better come in,' she told Nicholas, and stood back to let him enter.

The hall was so tiny that there was only just room for the two of them. Nicholas noticed the smell of stale cigarette smoke as he waited while Carrie put down her bag and took off her coat, which she hung over the banisters. She opened a door on the left of the hall and went into the living-room. Nicholas followed. The place was frowsty with smoke. There were blankets heaped on the sofa, and a grubby pillow lay on the floor.

'Phew,' said Carrie, waving her hand in front of her face. 'Gordon's a chain smoker,' she added. 'He's been sleeping down here for a while.'

That was some small comfort to Nicholas.

'Why didn't you tell me you were married?' he said. 'Oh, Carrie!'

'I thought you wouldn't want to be friends if I did,' she said. 'You're such a prim one, Nicky.' She had started to call him Nicky in bed. She laughed at him, the little tender mocking laugh which always made him want to kiss her. He wanted to now.

'You said you worked in a hotel and you don't. You work in Brice's,' he accused.

'I see you've been spying on me,' said Carrie.

He couldn't deny it.

'I went to the house in Grove Road,' he said. 'I saw your friend.'

'Well, I do work in a hotel on Wednesdays,' Carrie said. 'Gordon's out of work and I go to make extra money.'

'You said you did shift work as a receptionist and that married women with children took over at the weekends,' he reminded her.

'I had to tell you something,' said Carrie. 'You were so sweet and I liked you. It was fun meeting you on the train every week. I knew if I told you the truth it would be the end.'

'What is the truth?' Nicholas demanded. The smoke was tickling his throat and he coughed.

Should she maintain that she was a receptionist? Insist that part of her story was true? He would probably believe her. She looked at him and saw an outraged boy, hair on end, eyes large in a white face. His charm for her evaporated as she recognized that he had already begun to bore her. His hitherto appealing sweetness had suddenly become juvenile stupidity.

'You really want to know?' she asked.

'Yes.'

'Well, I'll tell you. I'm on the game. Know what that means? I go up to London every Wednesday and I meet rich businessmen and they pay me to go to bed with them. There! That's the truth!' She looked at him defiantly, her small body rigid.

'No. No, that isn't true!' he exclaimed. 'You're saying that to shock me, so that I'll go away and stop being a nuisance.' Nicholas's voice rose shrilly.

'It is true,' Carrie declared. 'They pay me at least fifty pounds a time.'

'No!' Nicholas took her by the shoulders and shook her. 'No, Carrie, you're lying!' he cried and began to shake her. 'Say it's not true,' he urged. 'Oh, Carrie!'

How light she was in his grasp, and how often he had held her soft little body, but so had others, dozens of them, and for money! The enormity of what she had told him overwhelmed him as he went on shaking her. She tried to move his hands and he closed them round her throat, still shaking her and moaning her name.

Carrie had felt no fear of her gentle Nicholas and was quite unprepared for his sudden savagery. As she tried to writhe away from him, choking, her head pounding, he tightened his grip until she suddenly slumped and went limp, her arms falling to her sides and her head dropping back.

Nicholas did not immediately understand that she had lost consciousness but he moved his hands to her shoulders to support her weight. Then he shook her again, this time to rouse her.

'Carrie, I'm sorry. I didn't mean to hurt you! Oh, Carrie, wake up!' he besought her now, and tried patting her cheek, but she did not stir. Half-sobbing, he dragged her across to the sofa and laid her down, putting the pillow beneath her head. Her face was a strange purplish red. She'd soon come round. He knelt beside her and picked up her hand, but when he let go her arm dropped back like a dead thing.

That was what she was: a dead thing.

Tears poured down Nicholas's cheeks as he stood looking at her. How could she die so easily? What should he do now? Call an ambulance? But it was too late. He listened for her heart-beat and heard none.

Slowly he sat back on his heels and looked round the small

room with the empty beer tins on the floor and a soiled plate with a dirty knife and fork askew. What a mess! How squalid and awful!

Bile rose in his throat. He rushed from the room and out of the house, banging the front door behind him. For a moment he stood outside inhaling great gulps of fresh air.

Then the instinct for self-preservation took over. He ran back to where he had left his cycle, jumped on to it and pedalled off down the footpath, the way he had come, nearly knocking over two schoolgirls on their way to the library and disobeying their parents' instructions to keep to the road.

Further on, he stopped and vomited into the grass on the river bank. The girls saw him and thought he was drunk.

It was a little while before he felt able to mount his bike and ride off.

16

Nicholas pedalled away through the streets where Durford's rush hour was now at its peak. As he swerved among the traffic, he almost wished some passing car would knock him down and obliterate the last hour. But in spite of hooting horns and flashing headlights, he survived.

He went to a public lavatory where he washed as thoroughly as he could. After rinsing his mouth out, he felt less physically soiled but his soul, he was sure, would be tarnished for ever by what he saw as Carrie's betrayal.

He would never see her again, never kiss those soft lips nor hold that small warm body close. She was gone for ever, but then she had never really existed, not as he'd thought her to be. How she must have been secretly laughing at him during all those moments that had been so precious to him.

He rode slowly back towards Meddingham, for there was nowhere else to go, but he must time his return to fit in with his usual train because his grandmother supposed him to be in London as usual.

Hatred and revulsion carried him through that first evening as he began to recover from the immediate shock of what had happened. He had not meant to hurt her, much less kill her; it had been a total accident. Perhaps she had had a heart attack, brought on because he had frightened her by being so rough and shaking her like that. He'd felt so angry! She'd been taunting him, or so it had seemed, by showing him how easily he had been deceived. What a fool she must have thought him! It was all like some terrible dream but one from which he was not going to wake.

There were bits of the past that he didn't want to forget: those hours spent together, their shared delight when her pleasure had been as great as his, or so she had said. But perhaps those were all lies! How could he believe anything good about her now, when she had proved herself so false? She was a whore! And married, too! What about her husband? Did he know how her Wednesdays were spent? Perhaps he was her pimp and they counted her takings together. After today's revelations, anything seemed possible.

How long would it be before her husband came home and found her? He would phone the police, and Nicholas's fingerprints would be all over the room. He felt cold at the thought, until he remembered that nobody knew about him in relation to her. He had met that girl this morning, the one in Grove Road, her friend, but he hadn't told her his name. Those two schoolgirls on the path might have noticed him, but he didn't live in the area so they would have no idea who he was. He had never been in any trouble with the police, so there would be no record of his fingerprints for comparison. Nicholas's knowledge of how the police traced suspects was gleaned mainly from television; his grandmother liked a good thriller.

He went home at last, tired out, and told his grandmother it had been a hard day at the office.

He ate very little supper, and, excusing himself, went straight off to bed.

'I hope you're not sickening for something, Nicholas,' his grandmother said as, white-faced, he left the room.

Gordon had been to the Job Centre, where there was no vacant post that attracted him, and had then gone to the library to look at advertisements in the papers, but his mind was still on Spain. Once he'd mastered the language, he would be able to dispense philosophy as well as *sangria*. In the warm sunlight he would get the chance to express himself fully at last; he might start writing poetry, for example.

Because smoking was not permitted in the library, he had gone out to a café where he had drunk several cups of coffee and smoked seven cigarettes in a row. This, he realized, was the place where he had met Carrie on the day he had bought his new suit.

Those first weeks with Carrie had been good. After years inside perhaps almost any woman would have had the same effect, but she had been pretty and affectionate, even enthusiastic, unlike Anne who had very soon begun to shrink away from him, cold, frigid thing that she was. After James was born he had felt no particular desire for her, but she was his wife and intimacy between them was his right. Besides, it was physically good for one's health.

With Carrie, it had been very different.

He stayed in the café until it closed, reading a book he had purloined from the library, wrapping it in his raincoat when no one was looking. It was a historical novel about the Incas and well written enough to absorb him, though he didn't approve of fiction. He had also taken a Spanish language primer to supplement what he had at home already. He should really have been a don, of course; safe in a university, doing research, he would have led a dignified academic life and been a respected scholar by this time if he had only been directed aright in his youth. He had received bad advice at every crossroads but there was still hope for the future, if he could get away.

From the café, Gordon went to a nearby pub. He could not get through the day now without alcohol. It had long been his crutch. He had missed it in gaol but at the open prison he had been able to get it again. Downing his beer – he had no money left for spirits – he resolved to assert himself when he reached home. There would be no more nights on the sofa. A man had his rights.

He parked the car outside the house and levered himself out of it on to the pavement. There were no lights on in the house, but Gordon did not take that in as he pealed the bell for Carrie to admit him. No one came to the door, and at last, cursing, he fumbled for his key and let himself in, calling her name.

It echoed back from the empty house.

Then he saw her coat, draped across the banisters at the foot of the stairs. Carrie always went straight upstairs and hung it up. She took good care of her clothes.

'Carrie?' he called again.

No reply.

Gordon went into the living-room and turned on the light but he did not glance at the sofa, whose back was towards the door. The room seemed just as he had left it that morning. He went upstairs to the bedroom. It was empty, the duvet neatly in place, frilled pillows undisturbed.

He would be here in the bed, waiting, when she returned from wherever she had gone.

In the bathroom he urinated extravagantly, sighing with pleased relief, and then, suddenly hungry, went down to the kitchen to look for something to eat. The breakfast things stood where they had been left that morning, Carrie's neatly stacked on the drainer, his own on the worktop – sliced bread in its packet, a mug, marmalade and butter, the jar of instant coffee with the lid off, a half-empty milk bottle, just as they were when he went out of the house that morning. She hadn't even cleared up, the slut! He'd soon show her where her duty lay. He buttered two slices of bread, spread them with marmalade and made a sandwich which oozed at the sides.

Biting into it, Gordon went into the living-room and turned on the television for the late film or whatever else might be on offer at this hour. He backed towards the sofa without looking at it, lowering himself on to it with the familiarity of long practice.

His buttocks sank down on something – some obstruction which was firm and yet soft. Odd! Gordon raised himself awkwardly and felt beneath him. His hand encountered fabric and thin flesh over a bone. As he rose fully to his feet and turned to look round, his half-eaten sandwich dropped from his hand and a high scream escaped him, bitten back as soon as uttered.

She lay there, livid-faced, her eyes slightly protruding and staring straight at him. Gordon stuffed his fist into his mouth to stop himself screaming again. Then he rushed to the window to draw the curtains before anyone passing by could look in.

She was dead. There was no question about that.

She was lying with her head on the pillow, as if she had been resting. Her skirt was drawn down over her legs and she wore her fashion boots. One hand hung towards the floor, her bracelet drooping from her wrist. Gingerly, Gordon touched her arm and met resistance. Her body was cold, and rigor was already setting in.

Then he saw the marks on her throat.

No!

This was like some ghastly repeat! Similar marks had shown up on Anne's throat, and her face, too, had been suffused, purplish. Gordon peered at Carrie's eyes and saw tiny red flecks in the whites.

Someone must have broken into the house and strangled her. Yet there were no signs of forced entry. The place was a mess, but not the sort of mess made by an intruder. Had some mad rapist followed her home and forced his way in? Yes, that was it. That must be what had happened.

But her legs were neatly together, her clothes not in any way dishevelled.

Gordon had met rapists in prison. Though communicating little himself, he had heard cruder men talking. He knew that Carrie had not been raped, though she might have made willing love with someone she had let into the house.

But she would never have allowed anyone in with the place in this state. She was no great cook, but she kept the house clean. She'd have tidied up if someone had called.

The police. He must ring the police.

Gordon went into the kitchen and sluiced his face with cold water. Then he walked out of the house, closing the door, and hurried up the road to the telephone box. He had lifted the receiver ready to dial 999 when he realized that the police would think he had killed her. Gordon remembered how he had wept after Anne's body was found, then the police grilling him without considering his natural grief. He had admitted his responsibility fairly quickly while insisting that it had been an accident.

They would never believe that he had not strangled Carrie, even though it was the truth, not when they checked his record. Tough CID men would keep him up all night putting words in his mouth, trying to break him, and however much he stuck to his story they'd look for evidence to convict him. They would soon find something to connect him with what had happened, planting it if there were no other way. He would never be able to prove his innocence. Even if people swore he had been in the pub and the café and the library, the police would insist that he could have come home and killed her. They would bend anything to fit their case.

He would be sent to prison again.

Gordon walked slowly back to the house. He stood looking down at Carrie until her dead gaze unnerved him and he covered her with the blanket under which he had slept for so many nights. Then he shut her into the room, leaving the light on because it seemed wrong to let her lie in the dark, and went into the kitchen to think. He made some strong black coffee to help clear his head for he needed his wits.

At last he evolved a plan.

To take her out of the house by the front door was too risky, in case a neighbour came home late or looked out of a window, so he would have to use the gate at the rear which led to the footpath. All the bathroom windows were frosted with fixed glass except in the fanlights, so no one caught short in the night would be able to see what he was doing.

He found a roll of big black refuse bags in a drawer. Carrie often had more rubbish to dispose of than would fit in the weekly bag left by the council. He bundled her into two of them, putting one over her head and the other over her feet, tying them round her body where they met in the middle. Her shoulders and upper body were already beginning to stiffen, but not her legs. Then he wrapped her in the blanket and lashed that around her, using two of his own ties because he could find no more string.

It was a clear, cold night, and dry. Gordon heaved Carrie over his shoulder. Though small, she was now a dead weight and he was surprised at how heavy she was. The rear gate squeaked slightly when he opened it. Unless it was the day the garbage collectors called, it was always kept bolted and never used. Gordon carted her along to the end of the path where he dumped her while he collected the car. Her head hit the pavement with a hard, dull thump. Then he drove the car up past the row of houses to where he had left her and, with the engine still running and exhaust fumes fanning out into the chill air, loaded her into the boot.

He drove rather noisily out of the close.

All it wanted now was for some nosy copper with nothing better to do than harass the motorist to trail him and breathalyse him.

But in that respect Gordon was spared. No one did.

17

Hannah Matthews had been reading about the siege of Leningrad which lasted for nine hundred days during the Second World War, and the horrors endured by the starving population as their city was bombarded and its buildings devastated. A million and a half people perished, and yet there was no surrender. It was all very well to remember the Battle of Britain and the Blitz: the two could not be compared, she decided, and wondered if her countrymen would have endured similar experiences so long. In those days, it had to be remembered, moral decadence had not set in the way that it flourished now, and an island nation girt about by the sea had a natural protection.

Soon she would set foot in the mighty streets laid out by Peter the Great, would see for herself the vast country where unemployment did not exist and where materialism was not a religion, as it had become in the west. She had made a journey into Yelbury, something she rarely did, to obtain visa photographs, and her travel documents were due from the agent any day now. She looked at the wall, where a chart of the Cyrillic alphabet was suspended. She was finding it difficult to master: all those curiously varied sibilants signified by ornate characters were not easy to remember. Each day she studied them and repeated them aloud. She was engaged in this task when the doorbell rang.

Donald had gone out shopping, and it was not Mrs Jeffries' day, so she would have to answer it herself.

A man stood on the step, an ashen, puffy-faced, elderly-looking man in a crumpled suit. His grey hair needed cutting, and he wore a long, drooping moustache. It was some seconds before she identified her son, who was equally astonished by the change in her appearance since she had last visited him in prison. Hannah, who had never taken much exercise, now weighed over thirteen stone. She had grown her hair and wore it in a bun, *babushka* style, and she had on a navy crimplene dress with a matching jacket. Her painted brows were too fierce crescents above her button eyes.

'Well, Gordon,' she said. 'And what has prompted you to visit me now?' For of course he had not come to see his father.

Gordon had been working on his self-image as he drove towards Yelbury. He had put on his grey suit and had shaved carefully, even trimming the ends of his moustache which he had been allowing to cover ever-increasing areas of his face. He had sucked peppermints to mask the smell of the drink he had consumed on the way. His mother would be delighted to see him, he told himself firmly as he followed the A34 road north. She had always understood that his marriage to Anne had been an appalling mistake. Disguising from himself the fact that now, in a new crisis, he had come running for reassurance, he strove to believe that she would find funds to enable him to get out of the country. He wouldn't feel safe until he had managed that. He intended to say that Carrie had left him, if anyone asked where she was, as, one day, her mother or Arlene was certain to do.

He had rung Brice's and explained that Carrie was ill and wouldn't be in for a week or so. It was a pity that he didn't know the address of the charity she worked for on Wednesdays. Someone there might get nosy. There was the money, though, that Carrie had been handling. If she was the treasurer, there might be inquiries about that. He would simply say that he knew nothing about it. She'd gone off, he would add, perhaps with some man, and he didn't know where she was. He'd be pitied, then.

'Well, come along in.' His mother opened the door wider. 'I needn't ask how you are,' she continued. 'I can see that you've let yourself go.'

Deflated already, Gordon followed her into the house, transformed back in those seconds into the schoolboy in trouble for poor work, a failed exam, torn trousers.

'Things have been difficult,' he said, and took out his pack of cigarettes.

'Put those away,' said Hannah. 'They ruin your health and they make your clothes smell extremely unsavoury.' She sniffed. He had brought his ashtray aroma into the house with him. 'Ugh,' she added, and went on, 'You're out of work.'

'Yes. It's not easy when you've got a record. People pick on you.' Gordon hurried to defend himself.

'You had a good position, you said, with those office suppliers. Why did you leave?'

'The manager took a dislike to me. He was jealous – afraid I might get his job.'

Hannah had heard this sort of tale before. She ignored it as he followed her into the study. In spite of his self-absorption, Gordon noticed the piles of books heaped on the desk and a table, and the Russian alphabet adorning a wall.

'I see you're learning Russian.' He tried to smile, but his moustache concealed the movement of his lips. 'I'm learning Spanish,' he told her, and waited to hear her commendation.

'Why Spanish?' she asked curtly.

'I want to open a wine bar in Spain,' he said.

'A wine bar?' From the tone of her response, he might as well have said a brothel.

'Yes.' His voice wavered. 'One could do very well in a tourist resort, or an area where there are time-share villas. I need to make a fresh start, you see.'

'And you want me to provide the money, I suppose?'

'Just to start me off. I'd repay you,' he replied.

'Hm. What about your house? Can't you sell that?'

'There'll be nothing left after I've paid off the mortgage,' he answered. 'It's a ninety per cent one.'

'That leaves ten per cent,' she told him. 'Use that. I can't help you any more. Not again. You must cut your coat according to your cloth, Gordon.'

She gave him lunch – stew, which, judging by its texture, was being reheated for the fourth or fifth time. She had cooked well when he was living at home but it was obvious that recently standards here had declined, and the notion of moving back temporarily which Gordon had been nurturing became an unlikely solution to his immediate problems. There was even the possibility that his mother might refuse to take him in, if he were to ask her. Such an idea terrified him; if that happened, his last prop would have been knocked away.

'How's Father?' he asked.

'Drinking himself silly,' she said. 'He goes off shopping and spends his time in the Bird in Hand. He'll have to go into a home if this goes on.'

She spoke so coldly. Gordon shuddered. How ruthless she was, like all women. He left without seeing Donald.

Hannah gave him fifty pounds to tide him over, and on the way home he stocked up with alcohol, buying whisky as well as beer. He'd always preferred spirits. Then he returned to the house. There were things that had to be done and he could postpone them no longer.

First, he cleaned up. He knew that he would be removing any traces that might have been left by Carrie's killer, but that was irrelevant now because her body would never be found. It went against the grain to be sweeping and dusting so vigorously. He sprayed on Pledge and polished it off every exposed surface, put his empties and stub ends into a refuse bag, even opened the windows to let out the stale smoke. Then he went upstairs and packed a suitcase with Carrie's washing things, her make-up, a skimpy nightie – she wore those little shorties – and some other clothes. What a lot she had! There were slinky dresses with scooped-out necklines which he had never seen her wearing, several pairs of shoes with very high heels, and three spectacular hats. His own garments took up very little space beside this array.

If she'd gone for good – left him for a lover – she would take all her clothes. In a frenzy of decision, he piled everything that was hers and which wouldn't fit into the case into refuse bags and carriers. There was an Oxfam shop in Durford. Gordon drove there and left all the packages outside it. It was three o'clock in the morning.

When he came home, he found her leather coat still draped over the banisters. With its fur collar, it might be valuable. He would sell it.

He felt better after obliterating every trace of her. Now anyone could call and it could easily be proved that she had gone for good. Gordon would look noble and sad as he revealed her betrayal. He poured himself a tumbler of whisky and as he did so the question of how Carrie had managed to buy so many clothes rose in his mind. He knew she got a discount at Brice's but even so, her wardrobe seemed excessive. It was a little while before he remembered her handbag. He had put it and her printed PVC shopping bag into a kitchen cupboard while he cleaned up. He took them out now, and tipped the contents of her handbag on to the worktop.

There was a purse, her keys, make-up. And there was a building society deposit book. He looked inside it, and when he saw the sum entered to her credit, he could not take it in. Since just after Christmas, she had paid in weekly amounts, often two hundred pounds, sometimes more, and this was not her salary. That went straight into their joint account at the bank to meet all the bills.

Where had she got all this money?

Gordon swallowed more whisky as he wondered about it. Then he had a more positive thought.

How could he withdraw it?

18

Nicholas listened to the late news on the local radio on Monday night but there was no report about Carrie's death, nor was there the next morning. He set off for work as usual and was in his office in London by the time Gordon was motoring up to Yelbury.

There was no mention of a murder in Durford in the *Daily Mirror*, which he bought with his usual *Guardian* to read on the train. Perhaps the police hadn't told the press about it, though usually they seemed to learn about such things straightaway.

Somehow he got through the day, making mistakes on the new computer which was the pride of the place and having to sort out the resultant confusion before serious harm was done to the system. One of the women in the office commented on his pallor, and teased him, but kindly.

'Quarrelled with her, Nicholas, have you?' she quipped.

'With who?' Nicholas's face flamed.

'Whom. Your girl friend. You've been going steady for quite a while now, haven't you?' There had been all the signs: absent-mindedness, moods of elation.

'I don't know what you're talking about.' Nicholas bent his head over his work.

'Sorry, I'm sure,' said his colleague, affronted, and later mentioned to one of the others that young Nick had got it badly over some girl and things seemed to have gone wrong.

Wednesday was worse, because that night Carrie would not be on the train. Nicholas thought of abandoning his French class and going straight home, but he must stick to his routine. The fact that people at work had noticed that he was disturbed was worry enough. He avoided the usual coach at the front of the train, however. He could not expose himself to the curious scrutiny other regular travellers might bend upon him if he was there alone. He quite expected a police car to be parked outside his grandmother's house when he reached it, but there was nothing out of the ordinary to be seen.

Carrie's husband must have come home and found her. She'd said they didn't get on, and that he had been sleeping downstairs, which was obvious from the condition of that squalid, grubby room. Perhaps he had discovered what she was doing and had left her? In which case her dead body still lay on that small sofa.

When there was no news by the weekend, he decided that must be what had happened. How long would she lie there before anyone came to the house?

He felt an urge to go back, to ring the bell, find out for certain, and resisted it successfully throughout Saturday, when he worked hard in his grandmother's garden. Mrs Fitzmaurice had deduced, from his haggard appearance and the fact that her name was not mentioned, that the affair with Carrie was over, but the sudden break must have been the girl's doing; otherwise Nicholas would show less distress. It was a pity that he was the rejected and not the rejector; his broken heart would take all the longer to mend and at the moment he probably didn't believe that he would ever get over it. He might well never forget Carrie entirely as she was his first real romance. Mrs Fitzmaurice decided to adopt a tactful silence on the subject, since his pride as well as his emotions had taken a battering.

On Sunday, when she came downstairs, there was a note to say he had gone off on his bike and would be out all day. It was unlike him to give so little warning if he was going to miss a meal. Mrs Fitzmaurice sighed; poor boy, but he would recover in time and be all the better for such an experience. She hoped the next girl would be rather different. As she had bought a small shoulder of lamb for them both, she rang up Marjorie and invited her to come over and share it. The weather was fine so the drive would be pleasant, and Marjorie accepted.

Nicholas pedalled to Bridge Street through the slack

Sunday morning traffic. He was too early to meet the regular attenders at the cathedral, or the devout Baptists who parked their cars bumper to bumper outside the chapel, but he saw a few faithful souls on their way to Mass at the Roman Catholic church.

Newnham Close was quiet. Nicholas cycled down its short length. It seemed as if everyone was still asleep in the row of small houses, for all the curtains were drawn.

They were drawn at Number 9.

Nicholas remembered entering the house with Carrie. It wasn't dark yet and she had not pulled the curtains.

She'd recovered.

That must be what had happened. She wasn't dead after all. She had only fainted, and after a while had come round, and decided not to tell the police that he had attacked her. A warm rush of love filled him again until he remembered how she had lied to him; he realized that if she put the police on to him, their affair would be discovered and her husband would learn about it.

If she'd gone to London on Wednesday, she must have come back on a different train.

Nicholas pushed his bike along the path behind the close and joined the track by the river, then turned away from Bridge Street and pedalled along its bumpy surface until he met the next bridge, where he rejoined the road and cycled out of town into the country. After a few miles he branched into a minor road and went on until he came to a village. Because she was not dead after all, at last he felt hungry and stopped at a pub for some food. Then he wandered round the nearby churchyard looking at tombstones, finally sitting inside the church for a time giving thanks for his own deliverance. Well, he had been punished for his black act. However badly she'd treated him, there was no need for violence; he could have just said, in a dignified way, that they'd come to the end, and left.

He rode back along Newnham Close after dark and saw lights on in most of the windows, including Number 9.

She was in there. If he were to ring the bell, she would come to the door, just the same as ever except, perhaps, for a fading bruise on her neck. Maybe she'd made things up with her husband. That would be for the best, really.

He convinced himself that this was the truth and pedalled back to Meddingham in a mood of precarious calm.

Inside the house, Gordon was practising Carrie's signature. He had traced it from her driving licence, which was in her handbag. How sly she had been, learning to drive and not mentioning it to him. Much good it had done her. He was far better off without her; in fact her unknown assailant had done him a very good turn.

Gordon had collected a sheaf of withdrawal forms from the building society and had filled one out for almost the whole amount, over two thousand pounds. He thought this might look less suspicious than emptying it completely. He had the cheque made out to Carrie. He could pay it into their joint account at the bank, then draw it out again a day or two later, in cash. It would take him to Spain.

Gordon was enjoying the peace of the house. He found it quite simple, without Carrie there, to be reasonably neat. After all, he had kept his prison cell clean. You had to see to such things if there was no woman about. He still smoked as much as before, but from time to time he emptied the saucers he used as ashtrays, and he washed up after his meals. Now he had reason to appreciate the microwave cooker; the food packets all bore instructions for use. What a mistake he had made in getting involved with Carrie. It was understandable after his celibate time in prison, but he needn't have married her. He conveniently forgot the contribution she made to the mortgage.

He would find a new job and establish a respectable routine while he made plans to leave the country. His passport had expired while he was in gaol. The wisest thing might be to get a temporary one; he must find out how to do so.

After he had made out the application form for the money and posted it in the nearest letter box, Gordon settled down with some beer and put on his Spanish lesson tape. He opened the textbook at the relevant page and settled down to his studies.

*

A few days later Arlene took Jackie into town to buy him some sandals. Having found a suitable pair which she hoped would last through the summer, she decided to call in at Brice's to see Carrie. If it was near her lunch break, perhaps they could all eat together in the Happy Snack Bar on the top floor of the store.

Carrie was not to be seen in her department, and when Arlene asked another assistant where she was, she learned that she had been away ill since last week, when she had come in only on Monday.

'What's wrong?' asked Arlene.

'Can't say,' said the assistant.

She might be pregnant and suffering from morning sickness, thought Arlene. Carrie had never had more than a minor cold in all the time she had known her, whereas Arlene was prone to earache and sinus problems.

'I'll go and see her at home,' said Arlene.

What a nuisance it was that Carrie and Gordon were not on the telephone. As she couldn't go round there that day, Arlene bought a get-well card and sent it to Carrie.

It arrived by the same post as the cheque from the building society.

Gordon found the two envelopes when he came home from his new job as a warehouseman on a small industrial estate near the filling station at which he had spent two ineffectual weeks. His references were inadequate but the personnel manager, who was also the invoice clerk, held enlightened views and prided himself on his sound judgement. When Gordon, taking a gamble, confessed that he had been inside for a very short time for drunken driving but that he was now on the wagon, he decided to give him a chance.

Full of good resolutions, Gordon had now completed three days' work.

He mustn't destroy her mail. If she had really gone off somewhere, the natural thing would be to keep any letters until she either returned or supplied a forwarding address. He could tell this was some sort of card and it had a local postmark. It wasn't her birthday. It might be from someone at work.

He propped it up on a shelf in the living-room and opened the building society letter. The cheque was there, safely enclosed with the book.

He paid it into the joint account the following day, during his lunch hour. It would take a few days to be cleared. Then he went into a travel agency and inquired about flights to Spain. With Carrie's money and what he would get from the sale of the house, he could easily start a whole new existence – write poetry, paint. You could live cheaply in Spain.

He wouldn't get mixed up with a woman again.

Arlene telephoned Brice's on Saturday morning to find out if Carrie was back at work, and learned that she had not been seen at all, nor had there been a further message.

'I'll have to go round, Tom,' she told her husband. 'If she's been away that long she must be quite bad, and I don't trust Gordon to see that she goes to the doctor.' Neither she nor Tom had taken to Gordon, which was a pity because it meant they didn't meet in the way that they kept in touch with other couples. Arlene had always enjoyed Carrie's company and had envied her spunk; she was game for anything legal – and maybe not so legal, too. Arlene had suspected that one or two things had happened in the past about which Carrie had been less than frank.

'We'll pop round in the car,' said Tom.

Accordingly, that afternoon, they drew up outside Number 9 and rang the bell.

Gordon was watching the racing on television. He had been out that morning to buy some supplies – more frozen meals and beer, and some bread – and he'd taken Carrie's coat to a shop called Second Choices which dealt in second-hand clothes. The woman had admired it but said it must be cleaned before she could put it on sale. She thought it would fetch about twenty pounds, out of which she must take her commission, but as summer was coming it might not go for a while.

Gordon said he would return it when it had been cleaned. He put it on the back seat of the car and drove home.

'How's Carrie?' Arlene asked when he opened the door.

'Oh – well –' Gordon was very surprised to see her and he floundered about trying to say the right thing. Then he took a grip on himself. 'You'd better come in,' he said.

Gordon led the way into the living-room. He turned the sound down on the television as Arlene glanced round. Her gaze fell on the envelope, in her own writing, propped up on the shelf.

'She's not had my card!' she exclaimed.

'No.' Now came the test. Gordon swallowed. 'She's gone, Arlene. She's left me. Packed everything and gone.'

'But Brice's said she was ill!'

'I know. I told them that. I had to say something. I thought she'd be back,' he said.

'Didn't she say where she was going? Is she at her mum's?'

'I don't know,' answered Gordon.

'Do you mean to say you haven't been round to ask?' Arlene cried. 'Why, surely her mum knows where she is!'

Gordon had made a mistake there. He should have gone round to that messy, crowded house and made anxious noises.

'There didn't seem much point,' he said, and added, 'She's taken all her things.'

'Don't you want her back?' Arlene was staring at him in disgust. Carrie had done the right thing, even if she'd gone about it the wrong way; there was no life for her with this man. 'You'd quarrelled, I suppose,' she said.

'Not really. I'd left my job and she didn't understand why. It was quite unsuitable for me,' said Gordon. 'I've got another one now.'

'Didn't she leave a note?'

'No. That was what was so hurtful,' said Gordon. 'I've been very worried.'

'Oh yes? That's why you haven't been round to her mother's?'

'I think there might be someone else involved,' said Gordon delicately.

'Someone else? You mean another man? Was she seeing someone?'

'I don't know.'

'Well, was she out late sometimes?' His woodenness was exasperating.

'Oh, she was often late. She was seeing you on Sundays and her mother on Saturdays, and there was that old lady she visited on Wednesdays after work,' Gordon said.

'What old lady?' Arlene kept to herself the fact that she hadn't seen Carrie on a Sunday for some time.

'She said she was helping a charity that worked with old people,' said Gordon. He decided not to mention the large sums of money Carrie handled on its behalf, and in that instant realized that this was the money she had paid into the building society. She'd stolen their funds!

Arlene was sure that Carrie had not worked for any charity. She had obviously told Gordon that lie to conceal what she was really up to on Wednesdays and now she had made a run for it with her lover. Good luck to her, then, thought Arlene. But she'd been gone so long without a word. Surely she would have let her mother know where she was?

Still worried, Arlene left the house.

Tom and Jackie had been walking up and down the road while she was talking to Gordon. They got into the car, strapping Jackie in his child seat in the rear.

'She's gone off with someone,' Arlene said. 'Cut and run. Can't say I blame her. Gordon's turned into such a shower. Knowing Carrie, she's probably found some rich guy who's taken her off to Cannes or somewhere. She always lands on her feet. I expect her mum knows where she is.'

'Let's go and see, shall we?' said Tom.

'All right. Good idea,' said Arlene.

'Packed her things, has she?' Tom asked casually.

'So he said.'

'She didn't take that leather coat of hers. The one you fancied, with the fur collar. It's on the back seat of Gordon's car.'

Arlene stared at him as he started up the engine.

'No!'

'Yes.'

'If she'd only taken her summer clothes –' Arlene began. 'But he said she'd taken everything.'

'Let's get round to her mother's right away,' said Tom.

19

They found Carrie's mother busy icing a birthday cake for Gary, who was eight. It was shaped like a racing car, iced in red and yellow, and had a small figure sitting in the driver's seat, an effort of love and artifice. Her husband had taken the children to the cinema as the birthday treat and the cake was to be consumed when they returned.

'Arlene! How lovely to see you!' Carrie's mother was tired and harassed, and could have done without this interruption, but she smiled at her daughter's friend. 'Do you mind if I go on with this? It's got to be ready in an hour or so.'

'You carry on,' said Arlene. 'I'll watch.'

They had followed her through the untidy little house into the kitchen at the back. There were bits of Lego and small model cars on the floor, and a cat streaked past them as they crowded through the door. Jackie was offered some fruit juice with a flexible straw to drink through. Carrie's mother gave him some trimmings from the cake.

'If you'd put the kettle on, Arlene, we could all have a cup of tea,' said Carrie's mother. She stuck some chocolate peppermint creams in position as wheels. 'Have you seen Carrie lately?' she asked.

'No,' said Arlene. 'Have you?'

'I haven't, and she hasn't sent Gary a card. When you rang the bell, I thought it was her with his present, seeing it's Saturday. She never forgets. Of course, last year she wasn't married, but still, you'd think she'd remember.'

'I'm sure she hasn't forgotten,' said Arlene. She glanced at Tom. 'She hasn't been at work for a bit. They said she was ill, so we called at the house.'

'Yes?' Something in Arlene's tone warned Carrie's

mother that she was going to hear worrying news. 'She's not in trouble, is she?'

'What sort of trouble were you thinking of?' Tom asked carefully.

'Well –' Carrie's mother turned to the sink with her equipment. As she ran water into a bowl, she said, 'She can be a bit silly sometimes.' She was thinking of Carrie's expensive clothes and the presents of money she had recently received from her daughter, but she could not bring herself to voice aloud her dread that Carrie might not be entirely honest with other people's cash and possessions.

'Gordon says she's left him,' Arlene told her.

'What!'

'He says she went on Monday. He came home that evening to find her gone and all her clothes. The lot.'

'She's found someone else,' said Carrie's mother instantly. That would account for everything: the clothes, the presents. She'd never believed in Gordon's generosity. 'Some rich fellow,' she expanded.

'But don't you think she'd have let us know? You, anyway,' said Arlene. 'She didn't even leave Gordon a note.'

It took Carrie's mother a little while to understand what they were trying to say, but when they explained about the coat, and she remembered Carrie's failure to send her little brother a birthday card, she turned ashen and sat down abruptly.

'I think we ought to tell the police,' said Tom. 'If she's all right – and she probably is – they'll soon find her.'

Arlene had made the tea. She poured it out and made Carrie's mother drink hers.

'Don't worry,' she advised. 'Carrie's pretty good at taking care of herself.'

'But what shall I do? There's Gary's tea –' Carrie's mother glanced round distractedly. 'I can't ring up. The phone's been cut off,' she told them.

'You see to Gary and the others. We'll pop round to the police,' said Tom. 'You can't do anything about finding her. We don't know where to start, but they will.'

'Tom's right,' said Arlene.

'Got a snap of her?' Tom asked. 'They may want that.'

That evening, after the police had checked the hospitals, a uniformed officer called at Newnham Close.

Gordon had been dozing by the television set. It was pleasant at home now he had the place to himself with the whole bed to stretch out in at night, and no frilly bits of clothing draped about the place. He might go down to the pub later, but again he might not; he could drink more cheaply here, and now had no need to escape.

He cursed under his breath when he saw the police constable. He knew whom he had to thank for this: that nosy Arlene and her sanctimonious husband, prying into other people's business. Without their curiosity weeks, or even months could have passed before anyone wondered seriously about Carrie's whereabouts.

The officer formally told Gordon that there had been a report about his wife and that he had come to ask where she was.

'I don't know,' said Gordon. 'She's left me and she didn't leave an address. One of her friends was round here today, wanting to see her, and I told her. She took everything with her,' he added. 'All her clothes.'

'Except her coat. She left that in your car, didn't she?' said the constable. 'In the Ford Escort parked outside.' He had checked the car's ownership on the computer and had seen the coat for himself before ringing Gordon's bell.

Gordon fumed inwardly, then came up with an excuse.

'It was at the cleaners,' he said. 'I collected it this morning.'

'I see, sir,' said the constable. 'Which cleaners was that?'

'I don't remember,' snapped Gordon.

'Come now, Mr Matthews. If you collected it this morning, you can't have forgotten already,' said the constable.

'That place in the High Street, then,' said Gordon. It was the only cleaners he knew of in Durford.

'I see. Well, you'll let us know if you hear from your wife?' said the officer.

'Certainly. I'm anxious to know that she's safe,' said Gordon.

'Have you reason to think she might not be?' asked the constable smoothly.

'No, of course not. But it's natural to worry when

someone goes off without even leaving a note,' said Gordon.

'You didn't get in touch with her mother?'

'I didn't want to upset her,' Gordon answered. 'I thought Carrie would soon be in touch.'

PC Kent wrote a full report.

'I didn't like that bloke, the husband,' he told the sergeant. 'And fancy making out that he couldn't remember which cleaners it was. A coat like that must have cost a bob or two to be cleaned.'

'No harm in popping down to Sketchley's and asking about it,' said the sergeant.

The cleaners had closed for the weekend but on Monday morning when it reopened, PC Kent was waiting outside.

At first the police did not take Carrie's disappearance very seriously. A wife who packs all her clothes and leaves her husband commits no offence. A woman who ignores her small half-brother's birthday is probably only forgetful. A sick shop assistant who fails to notify her employer about her condition after the first call is negligent: no more.

But Carrie wasn't ill, although Brice's had been told that she was. Arlene had given the police this information and after PC Kent's fruitless visit to the cleaners, he went to the department store where he learned that the original message had been given by telephone not by Carrie herself, but by a man.

If the caller was the rich boy friend in whom Carrie's mother was staunchly trying to believe, why had there been no further communication?

If such a man existed, it was possible that the pair were living it up abroad and that Carrie would send a postcard to her mother, or that they would eventually return. It was always difficult to be certain that a missing person had genuinely vanished; people went away on whims and came back just as suddenly. Time often provided a straightforward explanation.

All the cleaners in Durford were checked but none had any record of processing a leather coat belonging to a customer named Matthews. Indeed, no leather coat with a fur collar had passed through their hands for quite some time.

PC Kent decided to run a check on Gordon Matthews, and when the results came up things began to look ominous.

Inspector Benton remembered the case.

'He was lucky not to go down for murder,' he recalled. The case had not been in their area, but reports of the trial had made headline news in the tabloids, and no one seriously thought that even the worst virago deserved strangulation. The Detective Chief Superintendent in command of the Durford area ordered a full-scale search for Carrie and two officers were dispatched to Newnham Close to take possession of the coat.

It had disappeared.

Gordon declared that it had been stolen from his car, together with some language tapes and a pair of shoes, but the police found his explanation far from satisfactory and he was taken to Durford Central police station for questioning. Meanwhile, the police searched the house thoroughly for Carrie.

There was no trace of her.

As a result of these developments, door-to-door inquiries were begun in the area around Newnham Close and Carrie's description was circulated to police forces throughout the country. Staff at Brice's were interviewed. No one knew of any romance Carrie might be having on the side. She had been quite popular in the store, where she was cheerful and efficient, but she had seen none of her colleagues outside working hours. Bus drivers and conductors were questioned, and Carrie's photograph was recognized by several who worked on the route which daily took her from Bridge Street into town and back. She travelled regularly on the last bus from the station on Wednesdays, and she had made her normal morning and evening journeys on the Monday when she had last been at Brice's.

Local television put out a report on the news programme.

'Fears are growing for the safety of Mrs Caroline Matthews who has not been heard of for going on two weeks,' a young reporter intoned into the camera, and gave details. Carrie's photograph – not a very good one – was flashed on to the screen and it appeared the next day in a number of newspapers. An appeal was made for her to come forward if she was safe, and failing that for anyone who had seen her after six o'clock on the relevant Monday to let the police know.

Gordon could not be held for more than three days without being charged, and, without a body or some better evidence, the police had no firm case against him. He told himself that he had only to keep his head. She wouldn't be found. There had been murder charges brought without a body, and convictions, too, in the past, but Gordon had not murdered Carrie and in the end he would be safe. It was easier to stand up to cross-examination now because the interrogating officer had to note down every exchange under the new PACE act.

After his three days' absence, he went back to work and explained that there had been a serious misunderstanding; his wife had left him and couldn't be traced, although he was sure she was with some man. Her family had stirred things up with the police and because he had a record for a trivial offence, they had subjected him to an investigation, alleging that he had harmed her.

This was the truth.

'What have you done with the body?' they had asked him again and again, and 'Strangled her, didn't you, like the other one? Anne, her name was, wasn't it? What about this one? Another nag, was she? Don't you ever learn?'

He'd painted Carrie's character in glowing terms. She was a lovely little housekeeper, he had said, and pretty and charming – yes, and sexy, too, he'd agreed, when taunted, for Anne's frigidity had been one of his complaints that other time.

'Who would want to hurt a girl like Carrie?' Gordon had exclaimed in the interview room, forgetting how he had attacked her.

'Every man's dream, was she? You were luckier second time round, eh?' asked Detective Sergeant Shaw.

'Indeed I was,' sighed Gordon.

Though he held out, he knew they wouldn't let up. They would have him in again and again, worrying on about it until at last they were forced to give up – as in the end they must.

What about the real murderer? How would he be feeling, knowing that an innocent man was suspected of his crime? One thing was certain: he was a very fortunate man.

At work, Gordon adopted an appropriately tragic demeanour, and the personnel officer, who had no reason to doubt his story, was sympathetic.

'She'll turn up,' he consoled Gordon. 'When she sees all the fuss in the papers, she'll come forward. Didn't think. That's what it was.'

'She was a lot younger than me,' Gordon admitted. 'She may have got bored with me, and I had been unemployed for a while. She didn't like that. What woman would? Couldn't have her little treats.' He sighed. 'My first wife left me,' he confided.

The personnel manager was shocked at the treatment Gordon had received from the police. It was too bad.

Gordon remained calm when police frogmen began looking for Carrie in the river. He knew they would not find her there.

'Why would she take all her clothes if she was going to drown herself?' he asked a constable at the scene. A small crowd had gathered to watch what was going on, though they were not allowed near the bank. Gordon stood on the fringe of the group, registering grief, and was photographed there by the press.

He had drawn all the cash out of the joint account that morning. He would be leaving the country soon.

That night the personnel manager, remembering his conversation with Gordon, realized that he had referred to his wife in the past sense. The knowledge made him uneasy.

When Nicholas saw a blown-up, grainy photograph of Carrie staring at him from the tabloid press under the headline HAVE YOU SEEN THIS WOMAN? his precarious calm was shattered. At first he did not recognize her; it was only when he looked for a second time at the paper that he realized it was Carrie with her hair cropped short, a year or two younger. In a daze, he bought the *Daily Bulletin* and read the text. Caroline Matthews: that was her name, not Foster, as she had told him. She was twenty years old, and her husband, Gordon, a warehouseman, was thirty-nine.

A reporter had been to Brice's, where the missing woman had been employed, and talked to Carrie's workmates, one of whom knew where Carrie's mother lived. He followed the trail.

A MOTHER'S AGONY was splashed across a centre page and below it was printed CARRIE COME BACK. There was a picture of Carrie's mother and the three other children, two boys and a girl. Well, that part of Carrie's tale, at least, had been true. All her clothes had vanished, the paper disclosed, and it was thought she might have gone off with some man, but in that case why hadn't she remembered her little brother's birthday, which she had never forgotten before?

It didn't make sense.

As it was Wednesday, Nicholas stayed up in London for his class. He must not do anything out of the ordinary. Not now, not when someone might remember seeing them together and tell the police. Once again, he travelled back at the rear of the train.

His grandmother was still up when he reached home, which was unusual when he was late like this. She heard his key in the latch and came to meet him, her face grave.

'Nicholas, dear, come in a moment before you go up to bed,' she said. 'I have something to tell you.'

Nicholas knew what it was. What if she wanted him to come forward and tell the police he had known Carrie? Hardly able to breathe, he followed her into the drawing-room, where daffodils from the garden stood in a bowl on the round table by the window.

'It's about Carrie, isn't it?' he asked. A sudden pain in his chest was so severe that he thought he was going to choke. Perhaps the police had found out about him and had been to the house already.

'You know, then? It was on the late local news,' said Mrs Fitzmaurice.

'I only know what I've read in the paper,' said Nicholas. 'I saw it at the station. There was a photograph, not very like her.' His voice trailed away.

'I'm so sorry, Nicholas, dear,' said Mrs Fitzmaurice. 'You didn't know she was married, did you? You said her name was Caroline Foster. But I'm sure it's the same girl. There was a wedding photograph on television.'

There was no point in remarking that she had always had her doubts about Carrie. Mrs Fitzmaurice took a positive line.

'I expect she'll turn up, safe and sound,' she assured him. 'She deceived you about her husband, and she deceived him with you. There may well have been someone else.'

There were countless others: her clients.

'It's possible, I suppose,' Nicholas allowed.

'You'd quarrelled, hadn't you? Was that the reason? Because of some other man?'

In a way, it was.

'Yes,' said Nicholas. 'I thought she wasn't being quite straight with me,' he managed to say.

'Her poor mother. They showed her on television. She pleaded with Carrie to get in touch if she's safe. So thoughtless to go off without leaving any sort of message.'

'Yes.'

'When did you last see her?'

He had worked out what to say about that, in case the police challenged him.

'On Sunday night,' he said. 'I took her home.' He swallowed. 'She told me a lie about that. I always dropped her in Grove Road. She said she lived there with her mother. But that's not where her mother lives, or where she – Carrie – was living with – with her husband, according to the paper. She wasn't on the train last Wednesday.'

'There's no need for you to get in touch with the police about her,' his grandmother said. 'The time they are interested in is after that Monday – over two weeks ago now.'

On the news she had heard that a man was being questioned. Perhaps things would soon be straightened out.

The two schoolgirls whom Nicholas had nearly knocked

over as he fled along the path behind Newnham Close on the evening of Carrie's death, and who had seen him later vomiting into the grass, had wondered about him as soon as they heard the news of the missing woman. He might know something about her disappearance.

'She lived along there,' one told the other, and they goggled at Number 9 from the road.

'She hasn't been seen since that evening,' said the older of the girls.

'But he wasn't carrying a body.'

'Of course not. He was riding a bike. He may have stolen a car and gone back later to take it away. Or perhaps he dug a hole and buried it in the garden.'

'Those houses haven't got gardens,' said the younger girl. 'Only back yards.'

They had discussed it for several days, and at last they decided to tell the police because the man's conduct was, to them, bizarre, and they had not seen him in the neighbourhood before.

A constable noted their words and took down a description of both Nicholas and his bicycle. He made sure the girls themselves had not been the target of insulting or threatening behaviour from the man, and said he had probably been drinking and that was why he had been sick.

'That's what we thought, but it was only about a quarter past six in the evening,' said one girl.

'That's late for some folk, where drinks are concerned,' said the constable, but because the girls were so sure of the date and the time, he took careful note of what they had told him.

20

Michael West, on his way to meet a solicitor in Lentwich about delivering a writ, stopped to buy his copy of the *Independent*. Ranged beside it were the tabloids bearing Carrie's photograph, and he glanced at them. He did not recognize her straightaway, but her name, printed below, jumped out at him. He seized a bundle of papers, paid for them, and went back to his car to read them. The hairs on the back of his neck seemed to prickle as he took in what had happened, and the only thing that surprised him was that the press had not got on to the story of Gordon's first marriage and Anne's death. They would, and very quickly: some copper would tip them off if they didn't drop on it themselves.

This time, the routine supposition that until it was proved otherwise, the spouse was the likely killer would be justified if Carrie Matthews was dead.

As soon as his discussion with the solicitor was over, Michael telephoned the *Yelbury Gazette* and asked for Barnaby Duke.

'He's not in the office,' a girl's voice said. 'He's gone rushing off on some big story. Said he might not be back for a day or two. Can I help? I'm covering for him,' the girl, a new recruit, added importantly.

Michael did not need to be told where Barnaby had gone.

If Oliver Randall hadn't seen the news, he must be warned. Barnaby in pursuit of a scoop would be ruthless and as he knew where Michael lived there was the risk that he might pick up the trail leading to Anne's children.

Oliver was slicing bacon when Michael came into the shop. He had driven fast, ignoring the pale green of the budding trees and the fresh glint in the hedges which ordinarily he would have enjoyed. He found the shop, in the main street of Little Foxton. It occupied the ground floor of a long, low stone and timbered house with a thatched roof. Michael parked the car outside and went into the rather dark small store with its closely packed display of produce. A small woman with straight grey hair cut in a fringe was ringing up a long list of purchases on the till. Three customers were roving round selecting goods from the shelves, and Michael, noticing a stack of wire baskets by the door, saw that the place was semi self-service. He picked up a basket and put bread and biscuits in it, with a jar of instant coffee and some Flora. Then he approached Oliver, whose bushy white eyebrows had shot up when he recognized him.

'Seen the news?' Michael asked, having requested a quarter of streaky bacon.

'What news?'

'Can't tell you here,' Michael murmured.

'I can find you a box or two, certainly,' Oliver said in a normal voice. 'I've got some at the back. Would you like to come and see for yourself? Packing's such a bother, isn't it?'

The old boy was certainly inventive. He went on talking about the problems of moving house as Michael followed him through the back of the shop to a rear lobby used as a store.

Michael had one of the newspapers, folded up small, tucked under his arm. He gave it to Oliver, who made no sound as he ran his eye quickly over the full story and then read it through more carefully.

'He's done it again,' he said. 'Just as I feared.'

'She could have gone off with someone else,' said Michael, who thought it highly likely. He considered telling Oliver about Carrie's spare time activities and decided against it for the moment. 'If so, she'll turn up soon, but it won't be long before the media gets hold of Matthew's past history.'

'Can they print it?'

'Oh yes, if he hasn't been charged with another offence. It's not libel – it happened. But if he has killed her, and he's charged, they'll have to sit on it until after the trial.' He paused, then added, 'The man who helped me trace Gordon

Matthews is a reporter on the *Yelbury Gazette*. He's left his desk to chase off on some story and I'm sure he's gone to Durford. He knows about Anne, though – the truth, I mean. I've told him.'

Michael knew that nothing would stop the newspapers from dropping hints or tracing the children, and printing poignant photographs under cryptic headlines about doomed orphans who had lost their mother and now might lose their father too, if they chose to do so.

'We can't run away again,' said Oliver. 'If they find us, we'll have to ride it out. We'll have to tell the children the truth and hope they're old enough now to handle it.'

Both men were silent, imagining the possible taunts the children might receive at school, their shame and humiliation.

'Kids are extremely resilient,' Michael offered. 'Mine seem to have survived their mother and me splitting up. Of course, that's happening to kids all the time these days. Murder's something else.'

'It's probably been harder on you than them,' said Oliver surprisingly. 'You and their mother will both be busy trying to make up for it all. You're the one who's come off worst, aren't you?'

'You could say that.' Astute old man! 'I don't know if there's any way I can help,' he went on. 'But I'll do what I can – as a friend, I mean. I don't want paying. I'm involved in this now and I'm responsible for alerting Barnaby Duke. I'll do my best to muzzle him, at least as far as you and the children are concerned.'

'Thank you. That's good of you,' said Oliver. 'I'll have to tell my wife about all this,' he added. 'I'll leave it till tonight.'

Michael nodded.

'I quite expected you'd already have heard,' he said.

'We don't read the paper till the evening. Even then, sometimes we don't bother. I hope the story isn't in the *Times*.'

'Why the *Times* specifically?'

'That's what my son reads. Anne's brother.'

'He might think it was a different Gordon Matthews,' Michael said. 'Lightning not striking in the same place twice, and all that.'

'It can,' said Oliver.

'I know.'

'Carrie may have already reappeared,' said Michael.

'That's not going to stop somebody resurrecting the old story,' Oliver declared. He straightened his back. 'Perhaps it won't be such a bad thing after all, now that we've had a chance to put ourselves together again. There'll be a chance for someone to tell the truth about Anne, speak up for her. Those friends of hers you've seen. They might come forward now and help to put the record straight.'

He made it sound quite simple. Michael wondered how such witnesses could be provided with a platform. Would Barnaby be able to do it?

Several other people saw Carrie's photograph and thought her very like someone they had seen, but the hair was different. Among them were the staff and customers of the Railway Arms, and people who had seen her on the train. None had seen her after the relevant Monday; there was no need to get involved.

Hannah Matthews saw the newspaper headlines at Heathrow, where she was waiting to catch her flight to Moscow for the start of her Russian holiday.

Sitting in the departure lounge, she read about the disappearance of her son's wife – the wife of whose existence she had not known.

Hannah had filled in the complex questionnaire as required from those travelling to the USSR. She had declared upon it what money and valuables she was taking into the country, aware that failure to do this with accuracy might mean the loss of even a wedding ring when it was time to return. On her sturdy knees she held her large handbag which contained her travel documents, cash, washing kit and her Russian phrase book, and with nothing to do but wait for the flight to be called, her attention was caught by the headlines in the paper the person sitting next to her was reading. She noticed the name Matthews, her own, in the small print below a picture of a young woman. It was a common enough name; Hannah felt only mild curiosity until her neighbour turned to a centre page where the details were set out, and she read the words 'Gordon Matthews, 39, a warehouseman.' Her son Gordon was not a warehouseman; he was an unemployed representative. Even so, she had better know what this was about. Hannah lumbered to her feet and plodded across to the newsstand to buy a paper. Slowly, she perused every word of the report, and had just finished when her flight came up on the indicator.

Hannah laid down the paper and set off on the long march to the allotted departure gate. Gordon's sudden visit was now explained; he was seeking her help for something quite other than his wine bar idea but he had not been able to confess his true predicament.

This time, he would have to manage alone. She was not going to abandon her long-standing plans because he had got himself into new difficulties.

She put him and his muddled, ineffectual father out of her mind and settled down to enjoy her first taste of Russia as the Aeroflot plane taxied down the runway and finally bore her aloft.

Barnaby had taken a camera to Durford. He snapped the house in Newnham Close and rang neighbouring bells to ask about Carrie but, on a working weekday, he found no one at home. He photographed Carrie's mother's house, though not the woman herself since she was now refusing to come to the door and had kept the children back from school because they might be badgered by either the press or their fellows.

He snapped the exterior of Brice's and went in to talk to Carrie's colleagues, noting down their shock. Then he rang a news desk in London and made a deal, exploding the truth about Gordon, beating by a whisker a tip-off from a policeman working on the case. After that he returned to Yelbury, planning to write a feature that would be unique in the history of the *Gazette*. First, though, he went round to the Matthews's house, determined to get Hannah to talk. He would frighten her by threats of what the press might make up if they did not receive some nuggets of fact on which to base their pieces. He would telephone through a 'human' story to London.

A light was on in a downstairs room. Barnaby rang the bell several times before he heard shuffling steps, the chain was pulled back and the door was opened. Donald Matthews, in a shabby grey cardigan with dried food spills smeared on its front and baggy, sagging tweed trousers, stood blinking at him.

He let Barnaby in and explained that Hannah had gone to Russia.

'Been planning it for ages. Went this morning,' he said. 'Tee hee – it lets me off the lead till she comes back, doesn't it?' he cackled. 'I can tell you I'm already enjoying myself.'

It seemed a pity to spoil his delight, but Barnaby did not relent.

'You've obviously not heard the news about Gordon,' he said, and proceeded to reveal what had happened.

'Didn't know he'd got married again,' said Donald in an uninterested voice. 'Boy always was stupid. He should have been properly punished the first time and then this wouldn't have happened. It was murder then and it's murder now, you can be sure.' He looked slyly at Barnaby. 'I don't think he was my son at all,' he remarked.

21

The following morning all the tabloid papers carried a photograph of Gordon Matthews as he had appeared at the time of his arrest for killing Anne. A full account of the case, varying only in degree of sensational presentation, revealed his past to the nation, and even the more serious papers included the news. A posse of reporters waited outside the house in Newnham Close when he left for work. He almost retreated, but the thought of being hemmed in all day, unable to escape, was more daunting than pushing through them. Once at the warehouse, there would be some protection.

However, the personnel manager was no longer so kindly disposed. He taxed Gordon with lying about the nature of his conviction.

'You wouldn't have given me the job if I'd told you I'd gone down for manslaughter,' said Gordon.

'I might have done. You'd paid your debt to society,' said the man sententiously.

'I haven't killed Carrie,' Gordon said sulkily. 'She's gone off with somebody else. You'll see.'

The man decided not to send him home at present. Matthews's homicidal tendencies seemed only geared towards wives, so no one at the warehouse would be in any danger from him. Even so, he was treated warily, although he was on his own for most of the time, in his part of the store.

'I'm not a leper, you know,' Gordon told him. 'It could happen to you, if your wife drove you round the bend, like Anne did. Nag, nag, nag, as soon as I came home, and she was a shocking housewife. Drank, too.' He had repeated this so often that he had forgotten the truth, which was that Anne rarely touched even a glass of wine.

'Your wife drank?' counsel had asked, and when reproved by the judge for putting a leading question, had phrased it, 'Did your wife enjoy an occasional drink?'

Gordon had replied with fervour.

'She drank. She liked her port.'

Anne consumed perhaps three glasses of port every year, when her father gave them a bottle at Christmas. But the damage was done. The jury concluded that she was a near alcoholic.

'I never meant to hurt her,' he'd added, looking as abject as when caught out by his mother in some misdemeanour. 'I'd just had enough and lost my temper.'

No one had asked him if he had ever struck Anne before the fatal occasion.

During a lull at work, when he was able to get to the telephone and use it unobserved, Gordon telephoned a solicitor, one whose name he found in the yellow pages, to ask if the press could be stopped from running that old story. He was told that as he had not been charged with any new offence, there was no contempt. The matter of Anne's death and the trial was recorded fact. Only if fresh charges were brought would the press have to be silent. The solicitor professed himself willing to act for Gordon and suggested applying for legal aid.

Someone out there in the world was walking about laughing today because he could see that Gordon was in line to carry the can for his crime. Gordon fumed at the thought.

But she wouldn't be found and they wouldn't charge him without a body.

Mrs Fitzmaurice read the *Daily Telegraph*'s concise account of Gordon Matthews's conviction for causing the death of his first wife with horrified incredulity. After bracing herself with an extra cup of very strong coffee, she set off to the newsagents to pick up a paper with a fuller account of the fate of Carrie's predecessor. The business concerned her grandson: if Gordon Matthews had found out about the romance, he could have been provoked into killing her, always assuming she was dead. It seemed all too possible that he had repeated his earlier crime and invented the tale that she had gone off with another man. She certainly hadn't gone off with Nicholas.

When he arrived home that evening, she made him sit down to discuss the matter calmly, for of course he would have seen the papers, too.

'It's tragic,' she said. 'That unfortunate girl! We must hope the police clear things up quickly. They don't seem to have charged the husband yet. I suppose that's because they haven't found her.'

'She may not be dead,' said Nicholas in a faint voice.

'In that case, she'll come forward,' said his grandmother.

But now Nicholas understood what had happened after he left Carrie on that fatal Monday evening. The husband had come home and found her, and to avoid suspicion falling on him had got rid of the body. It might all blow over if she was never discovered. His own safety depended on the actions of an unknown man who was a convicted killer, though as unintentional a one as Nicholas. What a curious bond!

'I can hardly believe it's happened,' he said, truthfully.

He must continue to act normally. That would be easier if he could only get some sleep, but ever since the event he had spent his nights tossing and turning, wakeful, or plagued by horrific dreams.

His grandmother, imagining him to be consumed with grief, decided not to put into his mind the possibility that he might be involved in any investigation into Carrie's disappearance. If Gordon Matthews knew about him, he would soon tell the police. She realized that reports of the release of a man who had been helping the police with their inquiries implied that this was the husband. Perhaps he had known nothing about Nicholas.

She clung to this hope as she tried to console her grandson, telling him that although he might think at the moment that he would never get over what had happened, in time he would recover.

She was so innocent, Nicholas sadly reflected. What would she think if she knew the dreadful truth?

Arlene heard the news from a neighbour who had met

Carrie and who came round to show her the *Sun*. Tom had already left for work, and Arlene immediately bundled Jack into the pushchair and set off to see Carrie's mother, who was almost hysterical.

'I never liked him,' she wept. Now she had lost all hope of seeing Carrie alive. Arlene was soon sobbing, too, as they compared their reactions to Gordon and found incidents to tell one another which confirmed their misgivings about him.

'But they said his first wife was a slut and a drunkard,' Arlene pointed out. 'That he was a decent man who was pushed beyond all endurance. Carrie wasn't like that. She couldn't have provoked him.'

'They may have been two of a kind, him and his first wife,' said Carrie's mother. 'He certainly liked his drink. Maybe he got away with it in court, being painted whiter than white because she was worse.'

'I wonder if she really was,' said Arlene slowly. 'You can't believe all you read in the papers, and you know what can happen in rape cases. They make out the girl was asking for it because she was a bit silly, accepting a lift or something like that.'

'That's true. Oh, Arlene, she wasn't a wicked girl.' Carrie's mother blew her nose. 'If – if she is dead, and he's killed her, we mustn't let them turn it round like that in court and blacken her name.'

'You're right,' said Arlene. 'We must stop them from doing that.'

Barnaby Duke extracted a great deal of information from Gordon's father. Tales of his son's youth emerged, his quarrels at school, his few successes and his constant changes of direction as he chased a degree in vain. Then came his disinclination to hold down any job for long, and his lack of friends. He had never had any other girl friend but Anne and Donald had already spoken well of her. He did so again.

'She was much too good for him,' he said. 'I expect he punished her for that.'

Barnaby had warned Donald that the London papers

would soon be after him, perhaps offering large sums of money for exclusive rights to his story, something Barnaby could not do. But he meant to get in first, for it wouldn't be long before Gordon was charged, with or without a body, and then the whole story would be under wraps. Not much about the past would come out at the preliminary hearing and the main trial would not be held for months, even a year or more.

He rang the *Daily Bulletin* with whom he had already made a deal and gave them his story about Gordon Matthews's background, taking care to avoid libel and omitting Donald Matthews's theory that Gordon was the result of an extra-marital liaison on Hannah's part. The old man had not produced any likely candidates for the role of her partner. There would be time to pursue the theory later.

Barnaby was preparing an instant book. If Gordon was not convicted it would be short and would merely prove how his first wife's name had been blackened during the court proceedings. Perhaps he would cite other similar cases. But if Gordon were sentenced for a second time, he would cover that trial and he would make not only his journalistic reputation but also a lot of money. He would tell Michael West his plans for he would need the detective's help in tracing and interviewing Anne's friends.

And he must look for an interested publisher before anyone else had the same idea.

After days of drenching rain the weather had at last improved and there was warmth in the May sun. Two women out walking their dogs in woodland twelve miles from Durford found Carrie's body. The animals, running on ahead through the beech trees and snuffling about among last autumn's fallen leaves and the superimposed, more recent deposits, caught the whiff of something unusual. The golden Labrador dug busily in absorbed silence; the Jack Russell yapped excitedly, paws frantically burrowing alongside. Usually both dogs were reasonably obedient to their owners' commands, but this time they were deaf to all whistles and calls.

Irate, the two women, both widows, one of an insurance

consultant, the other of an admiral, approached their recalcitrant pets to haul them off whatever attraction they had discovered.

But they had already exposed it. Gordon, ill-equipped for his undertaking since he owned no spade, had delved into the loose earth near a clump of brambles using the wheelbrace from his car to get some depth, and had scooped out the soil with his own hands. The result was only a shallow grave.

Carrie's skeleton fingers, some flesh still adhering to the bones, poked through the dead, sodden leaves and thin covering of earth which the dogs had disturbed. The insurance expert's widow looked away quickly, her hand to her mouth; there were maggots and flies. The admiral's widow was made of sterner suff. Setting her lips, she succeeded in hauling her Labrador away from his prize, and the Jack Russell was then soon secured.

'It could be that missing woman,' the admiral's widow said. 'One of us had better stay here while the other notifies the police.'

'Do you mind if I'm the one to go?' asked her friend, who was trying hard not to retch. 'You're wonderful, Angela,' she added, and meant it.

'Not at all. It's a matter of genes,' said Angela. 'You go, Pam. My dog's bigger, too, in case some ne'er-do-well comes by.' She smiled grimly. 'If you've got some sweets in the car, better have one, my dear,' she advised. 'Good for shock.'

Feeling craven and swallowing hard, Pam hurried away, towing her small dog who was most reluctant to leave this intriguing scene. The admiral's widow paced up and down a short distance away from the body. She knew you must not disturb the area lest you destroy vital clues, but time and the weather, not to mention the dogs, must have done a good deal of damage. Round her, the woodland rustled with sounds of wild life: a jay screeched and smaller birds twittered; a pheasant croaked in the distance. Moles and weasels burrowed beneath the ground.

The two women often walked this way. Once, they had felt threatened when a group of youths on motorbikes hared past them down one of the rides. The bikers had shouted at them and yelled mocking remarks, some obscene, but had ridden on, more intent on pitting their skills against the terrain than intimidating the two elderly women, who had been lucky that day; the youths' mood could easily have swung in another direction and walkers were very vulnerable. It was dreadful to think that surroundings of such beauty held menace, but then forests and woodland had always been linked with horror in legend: one had only to think of Little Red Riding Hood, and of Hansel and Gretel.

Angela walked to and fro, talking softly to her dog who was whining and tugging at his lead, anxious to investigate further. It seemed an age before Pam returned with a very young policeman who was the nearest mobile patrolling officer and had been sent to meet her at the callbox from which she had dialled 999. Reinforcements were following, he said, and after gingerly glancing at the dead, extended hand, took over guarding the body. The two women went back to the road where his white patrol car was now parked beside their vehicles.

More cars soon arrived, and a thickset man in plain clothes who said he was Detective Inspector Benton came to speak to the women. They explained what had happened, and he took their names and addresses. It was decided that they should both go to Pam's house, which was the nearer, where an officer would be sent to take their statements.

'You must have had a shock,' said Benton.

'Yes, well.' The admiral's widow had been a Wren serving in Malta during the war. She had seen worse. Young men (the inspector was certainly forty years old and would have been flattered to know that this was how she regarded him) and young women, too, forgot that one had not always been old, grey-haired and a grandmother. Still, he was right, it had been a shock.

'Is it that missing woman?' she asked.

'We won't be able to tell for a while,' said the inspector. 'It'll be in our minds, of course. The doctor will have to decide.' Visual identification was no longer possible.

'It's a very small hand,' said Angela.

'Yes,' said Benton. 'Ah, here he is,' he added as an old blue

Honda drew up. 'Funny thing, in a case like this he has to certify that the corpse is just that – dead – even though putrefaction has set in – even if the head is detached from the body.' He laughed, mirthlessly, and then, noting Pam's shudder, commented, 'Strange job, ours. It may be some vagrant. Excuse me,' and he went to greet the doctor.

The two women drove in convoy to Pam's house, a modern one in an exclusive group of five built in the centre of an expanded village four miles from the woods. Angela lived in the other direction and the two had originally met playing golf, which they had both now given up. Their friendship, however, survived, and they met regularly, each needing companionship more than either cared to admit.

A woman police officer arrived while they were drinking strong coffee in Pam's expensively fitted kitchen. After taking their statements, which were quite short, she warned them to be ready for the press. Their names would not be divulged by the police but it was amazing how journalists discovered these things and if the body turned out to be that of Caroline Matthews, the media would be down in droves.

'How soon will you know if it's her?'

'Quite quickly, I expect,' said the girl. 'It depends a bit on how long she's been there.' She did not want to go into details about animals devouring the remains and rendering the face unrecognizable even if it had not decomposed to any great extent. 'There are always the teeth,' she added. 'And the clothing. Rings. That sort of thing.' She told them to telephone if they were unbearably hounded; the police would attempt to stop any harassment of such a kind, and when she left they began to discuss avoiding the immediate fuss by going away to spend a few days in some comfortable country hotel where dogs were made welcome.

Gordon had given up going to work just before the personnel manager decided to end his employment. Each day he had more trouble passing the phalanx of reporters and photographers outside the house.

He made a final foray to buy stores, food and drink and enough cigarettes to last for some time, until things blew over. He'd got enough money now to get out of the country. He'd be all right then, living somewhere in the sun.

But at dawn on the morning after Carrie's body was found, the police came to arrest him.

22

Since Carrie's disappearance, Oliver and Mary Randall had taken to turning on the early morning radio news while they drank their tea. Until then, they had preferred to lie comfortably among the pillows enjoying a chance to talk quietly before the demands of the day began.

Today, they learned that Carrie's body had been found.

'Poor girl,' said Mary. She had accepted Oliver's explanation about tracking down Gordon with calm understanding. One day the children would have to discover the truth and now it might be necessary to protect them from ruthless media sleuths determined to lay bare the past.

'This will give us a few more years' grace,' said Oliver. 'When they lock Gordon up again, I mean. James and Charlotte will be grown up the next time he comes out.'

'They'll sentence him properly this time,' said Mary. 'Even the most out of touch judge will know what he's done.'

They speculated on the likely reactions of their son, the children's uncle, to the news. Luckily he and his wife were now on holiday in Cyprus and unless they read the English papers would not hear about it until they returned. Oliver and Mary were still deciding how to deal with the next anxious days when the telephone rang. They had a bedside extension; Oliver wanted to be able to summon help if anyone broke into the shop below.

The caller was Michael West.

'You've heard about the girl?' he asked. 'She's been found.'

'Yes,' said Oliver.

'I've got some more news for you,' said Michael. 'There's a

piece about Anne in the *Daily Bulletin* – that reporter from the *Yelbury Gazette*'s done it. He got it in just in time. They're certain to pick up Matthews and charge him. I'll come round with a copy of the paper when the children have gone to school.'

Oliver could not wait until then. He went straight along to the newsagents two hundred yards down the road and bought the *Bulletin* plus several other papers, all of which merely reported that a body had been found in beechwoods in the Chilterns and surmised that it might be that of the missing woman. They had gone to press before the victim's identity had been confirmed.

Barnaby's piece in the *Bulletin* was brief. It contained textual imperfections due to hasty composition, telephone transmission and arbitrary editing, but described how the legal system had permitted allegations that Anne Matthews was a bad-tempered, dictatorial and drunken woman to be accepted in court upon the sole testimony of her killer and revealed that there were other witnesses willing to testify that the truth was otherwise.

When Michael arrived at the shop just before nine, he found the elderly Randalls wearing restrained, if anxious smiles.

'Matthews has been arrested,' he told them. 'I've heard it from a contact in Durford. The press won't be able to refer to the previous case now until after his trial, if he is charged. It might preclude a fair hearing. That's the law. But afterwards – wow!' He grinned at them, looking carefree himself for the first time since Oliver had known him.

'I hope they get him for murder this time,' said Mary.

Michael knew that if Carrie's lifestyle was revealed, Gordon Matthews might plead manslaughter again due to provocation, and this time there might be sound grounds for such a plea, but whether it would be accepted a second time was another matter. Was there any chance that the police might not discover the truth about her activities?

'I'm going down to Durford,' he said. 'I want to find out what sort of case they've got lined up. Matthews may crack. If they keep on at him they may break him down into confessing, but of course he could recant by the time the case comes up. Anyway, Anne's name will be cleared now.'

'But at what a price!' said Oliver. 'That poor girl.' If he'd intervened, taken the law into his own hands, she would still be alive. But had he really ever intended so drastic a vengeance? He'd never know, now.

Michael wondered what the old man was thinking. He was glad he had not told Oliver about Carrie's moon-lighting. It was possible that Matthews knew nothing about it and that he had caught her out over the young man she had been with in the Railway Arms.

'You're a father,' Oliver said. 'What would you do about the children? Would you put their headmaster in the picture?'

'I think I'd hang on for a bit,' Michael answered. 'You may have to, later on. I think they're safe from the media for the moment.'

'I wonder if they're old enough to understand why we kept the truth from them?' said Oliver.

'They trust you, I'm sure. Perhaps they're young enough not to question that trust,' Michael said.

By means of the electoral roll, Michael had discovered that Helen Jane Fitzmaurice and Nicholas Bruce Fitzmaurice lived at the house in Elmwood Road to which he had followed the young man he had seen with Carrie.

At seven-thirty that evening, Michael rang the doorbell. The young man, presumably the son of the house, should be home from work by then.

Michael had made himself up a small identity card with a photograph and typed details which gave his address. He kept it in a plastic case and used it to establish his credentials, though it was in fact utterly valueless. If and when he became a member of the Association of British Investigators, he would possess their official card, an authentic record; meanwhile, bluff usually carried him through and it did when Mrs Fitzmaurice opened the door to him. He waved it under her nose, and used his most policemanly manner to inform her that he was inquiring into the death of Caroline Matthews, whom he had reason to believe was a friend of Nicholas Fitzmaurice.

Mrs Fitzmaurice never challenged his identity. All along she had feared that Nicholas would be drawn into the investigation. Plenty of people must have seen the two together.

'A tragic business,' she said. 'Poor girl. Nicholas is upstairs. I'll fetch him. I'm his grandmother, but I expect you already know that.'

She showed Michael into a room that had been her husband's study and now was seldom used, and went to tell Nicholas that he was wanted.

Two minutes later a pale, dark young man entered the room. Michael had only glimpsed him before, in the dark, and scarcely recognized him because he looked so ill.

'I know nothing about it,' he said at once, saving Michael from having to introduce himself in some way.

'But you did know Caroline Matthews?'

'Oh yes. I didn't know she was married, though. She told me her name was Foster. That was her maiden name, as I've learned now from the newspapers,' said Nicholas.

'I see. How did you come to meet her?'

'On the train. We travelled regularly back from London on the same one on Wednesday nights after my evening class and her – er – some work she did in London,' said Nicholas.

'Did you know what that was?'

'She told me she was a hotel receptionist,' Nicholas said.

'Did she?'

Nicholas pressed his lips together. He must not tell this policeman that he had discovered Carrie had lied.

'How can I help your inquiry? You've arrested her husband, I believe,' he said. His voice sounded very calm.

'Do you think her husband found out that she had been meeting you and killed her in a fit of jealousy?' Michael asked.

Nicholas looked startled. If Gordon had discovered what had been going on and told the police, they might think along those lines.

'I hadn't thought of that,' he truthfully replied. 'He must have found out or you wouldn't be here.' How else could the police have traced him?

'She had another side to her life, didn't she, apart from working at Brice's? And she wasn't really a hotel receptionist, was she?' Michael said.

'I don't know what you mean,' said Nicholas. 'I only know that was what she told me. What other side was there?'

Unless he had been one of her London clients, the boy might really not know. Michael changed tack.

'When Matthews was arrested after his first wife died, he confessed to manslaughter,' he said. 'The plea was accepted because the defence successfully vilified the victim's character. Have you read the piece in today's *Bulletin*?'

Nicholas had. He was reading everything about poor Carrie, putting newspapers in his briefcase with his French texts on which, since Carrie's death, he had been unable to concentrate. Upstairs in his room a drawer was filling with cuttings.

'He got away with it that time. He may try it again,' said Michael.

Nicholas was staring at him in some bewilderment. None of this seemed to be the sort of line the police would pursue. The man had not asked him when he had last seen Carrie or if they had quarrelled.

'What did you say your name was?' he asked faintly.

Michael told him.

'I'm a private investigator,' he said. 'Your grandmother assumed I was from the police, as I must admit I hoped she would initially. I was hired by his first wife's family to find out where Matthews was living after his release. They don't want him bursting into their lives again. There are two children to think of, both quite young.'

Nicholas's heart began to thump harder as waves of relief surged through him.

'Well, he won't, now, will he?' he managed to say.

'I hope not.' Michael paused. 'The police may not inquire too closely into how Carrie spent her spare time,' he said. 'They know about her job at Brice's, of course. They've probably got no cause to look further as there's sure to be plenty of evidence to convict. It's likely to be a straight up and down case against Matthews, but the defence is another thing. If Matthews knew anything that could be used to discredit Carrie, they'd make the most of it.'

'What could he know?' Nicholas said steadily. And what could this man know, either? He'd been hired to investigate the husband, not Carrie. He wouldn't have discovered what she did in London. 'I don't see how he could have found out about me. Carrie –' He swallowed, mentioning her name. 'Carrie made sure that he didn't. We did meet sometimes, apart from Wednesdays. I never took her back to her own house – always to another address where she told me she lived,' he said. 'A friend's place.'

'I see. Well, you're not going to tell them about that, are you, unless they come asking?' said Michael. 'Matthews is a cowardly bully. He didn't need a reason to kill her. She may have simply annoyed him and he lashed out.'

But he hadn't. Not this time. Only Nicholas knew the truth.

'That's possible, I suppose,' he allowed.

'Well, let's hope no one else thinks of mentioning it,' said Michael. 'Did her mother know about you, or that friend?'

'I don't think so,' said Nicholas. 'We went out together on a few weekends, but mostly we met here. My grandmother's been away,' he explained. 'I'd only known Carrie a few weeks.' He thought of telling the detective that their affair had ended, then decided against it. The safest course was to say as little as possible.

'I very much doubt if the police will cast their net widely this time,' said Michael. 'They're not obliged to discover the whole truth behind a killing, as they would try to in France, for instance. They might try, there, to establish a *crime passionel* if they knew about you.'

'Oh.' Nicholas had no interest in the niceties of criminal law. 'Well, I don't intend to advertise anything I know about Carrie which they could use to get him off. It's not much, after all. Just that she didn't tell me she was married and you imply she wasn't working in a hotel in London.'

'I didn't say that.' Michael picked him up. 'I just asked you if she was really a receptionist. I don't see why she shouldn't have had some sort of part-time job, do you?'

'Not really.' Nicholas must keep quiet about not knowing that Carrie had worked at Brice's. How complicated avoiding the truth could become.

'I'm glad to have seen you,' said Michael. 'Here's my card,' he added, taking one out of his wallet. 'Just in case you want to get hold of me.'

Only after Michael had gone did Nicholas wonder how the detective had found out that he knew Carrie.

23

Nicholas's load of guilt felt lighter after Michael's visit and he even managed to sleep for several hours that night. Gordon Matthews was not a blameless man being made into a scapegoat; moreover he deserved further punishment for what he had done to his first wife. And he, Nicholas, had meant Carrie no lasting harm.

The next morning Gordon Matthews was taken before the magistrates and charged with the murder of Carrie. There were shots on the local television news of his arrival at court with a blanket thrown over his head, to the accompaniment of catcalls and jeers from the crowd of spectators always present on such occasions, kin of the knitting crones beside Madame Guillotine. He pleaded not guilty and was remanded in custody.

In time, Gordon might have killed Carrie, like his first wife, Nicholas reflected. In their last conversation she had said that she was going to leave him and if she had done that, she would have escaped with her life. But had she meant what she said? She'd proved herself to be a liar.

Well, let Matthews try to talk his way out of this one, as he'd done before. It was not worth wasting sympathy on someone so thoroughly evil.

While Nicholas braced himself with such rallying thoughts, the painstaking police investigation was proceeding in its routine way as evidence was collected against the accused man. A number of facts supported the case. Carrie's body had been transported in the boot of Matthews's car. Because of the covering polythene bags, her clothing had left no contact traces but there was a wisp of the polythene itself where a bag had snagged on the catch. Of course no one could prove it was from the same bag, only that it was of n identical variety. One of the ties Gordon Matthews had used to lash round her had come from Austin Reed's and in fact Carrie had given it to Gordon. The other had come from Marks and Spencer's. They were being examined to see if traces from Matthews could be found in the fabric; there might be a thread from a sweater or shirt he had worn. Such scientific testing took time.

There was no blood. Death was due to strangulation; that was established on several counts and, as in the case of Anne Matthews, the hyoid bone in the neck had been fractured. There was also a depressed fracture of the skull but that had occurred after death. Due to tears in her polythene shroud and the shallow depth of her grave, Carrie's body had attracted predatory animals and it had been impossible for the pathologist to discover evidence or otherwise of recent sexual intercourse, but she was not pregnant.

Even before the body was found, while the police were searching for Carrie, they had found evidence that her marriage with Gordon was stormy. The pair had been known to quarrel. One neighbour declared that there had been a row when Carrie took the car without her husband's permission. The couple in Number 8 had heard yelling and thumps late at night and had seen Gordon Matthews flounce out of the house after this noisy disturbance. A colleague of Carrie's from Brice's declared that she was contemplating a divorce, complaining of Gordon Matthews's drinking and generally inconsiderate behaviour. Just after Carrie's disappearance, the neighbours on both sides had heard him plying the vacuum cleaner and running quantities of water as if he were giving the place a good clean. Carrie's leather coat with the fur collar had turned up in a skip on a building site in the town. Some rubbish had been pulled on top of it, but a workman had seen the fur collar poking out. He had taken it home to his wife who had been delighted with this unexpected present and she took it to be cleaned. The cleaners had remembered earlier inquiries about just such a coat and had informed the police, who had taken it away for testing. A hair matching Carrie's had been found clinging to the inside of the collar, and it was being checked for other traces.

The most damning evidence of all against Gordon was the building society cheque. Police searching the house after Gordon's arrest had found Carrie's book in a drawer showing the withdrawal dated two days after she was last seen alive. The request had come by post and the clerk had routinely checked the signature against the original held in the files before passing it. Further inspection confirmed that it had been forged. Then the bank, always so reluctant to yield information, conceded that Gordon had paid a large sum into the joint account and had later withdrawn it in cash. Gordon would not disclose what he had done with the money, but detectives sent to the house for a renewed examination found it hidden under the carpet in the living-room, beneath the small settee.

Evidence was piling up against Gordon Matthews but no one was going to say, this time, that the wife had got what she deserved.

In Moscow, Hannah Matthews had been to the ballet and also the circus. She had travelled alone on the Metro, map in hand, descending on very long steeply pitched escalators to platforms resembling cathedrals in their splendour. She had visited GUM and seen there the shortage of consumer goods, but man did not live by bread alone. The great roof of the building, a triumph in glass, amazed her. She paced round Red Square, marvelling at its size and at the magnificence of the gold cupolas and minarets behind the high walls of the Kremlin.

She travelled to Leningrad by train, passing through seemingly endless forests of silver birches. In Peter the Great's city she went to St Isaac's Cathedral and to the palaces devastated in the Great Patriotic War and now perfectly restored. Felt overshoes fixed to her feet, she shuffled around in awe.

In spite of her hours of study, she could understand very few words of the language. She tried to speak to the maid in the hotel and the waiters in the dining-room. The maid wandered around in knee socks wielding a shaggy mop as she transferred dust from one part of Hannah's room to another and showed no interest in Hannah's careful remarks about the beautiful city. It never occurred to Hannah that she was deaf. The waiters, with large numbers of tables to tend, were simply concerned with avoiding complaints from visitors who seemed to expect their meals to arrive with unnatural speed. She ate caviar spread on hard-boiled eggs, and consumed delicious bortsch, and she enjoyed the black bread and the blinis. The meat, swimming in greasy gravy, was another thing altogether and she left it untouched.

If you cooked it more carefully, it would be tastier. She looked about and saw plenty of food for sale, though there were often queues.

All the time she kept her son Gordon out of her thoughts, and while he was being arrested for murder for the second time in his life, she was at Petrodvorets admiring the fountains.

On the last morning, as she packed her suitcase, it all came back. She was returning to another catastrophe, one she had no power to amend, and, this time, not even the wish. And there was no longer any goal ahead: for years she had focused on her desire to visit the Soviet Union and now it had been accomplished.

Why go back at all? Why not stay here? Work was guaranteed for all: she had seen ancient *babushkas* minding the treasures in galleries and palaces; she could do that. She could continue to study the language and there were plenty of English-speaking people to talk to among tourist guides and assistants in the hard-currency shops. She might even earn her living by giving lessons.

There was no time to make a plan, to seek out the appropriate official or report to some specific bureau. Hannah went down to the reception desk and, in English, told the startled clerk that she admired Russia and had no wish to return to the decadent West. Then she sat down on a leather-covered settee to await developments.

She would not budge when the harassed courier responsible for shepherding her group to the airport came to look for her, and the bus left without her, but almost immediately two men appeared who bundled her out to a car. They were very polite and Hannah thought that they were taking her to a government department where her action would be applauded and she would be processed for admittance to the Soviet Union. Surely they would be pleased to secure a defector, even one who was only an elderly civilian?

She was hurried into a large building and taken to a small windowless room where she was given a cup of coffee. It contained a powerful sedative, and when the drug had taken effect she was buttoned into her serviceable raincoat and driven to the airport, where she was put in a wheelchair and pushed out to the London plane, clearing customs without formality and delaying take-off by only a few minutes. Her guards watched with relief while this problem departed to be dealt with in her native land.

Hannah slept throughout the flight and at Heathrow she was taken from the plane on a stretcher, put in an ambulance with a policewoman as escort, and driven to hospital where she remained under further sedation. When she woke and found herself in a high hospital bed with curtains drawn round her, she thought she was still in Russia. Her confused remarks led to the administration of further sedating drugs.

The newspapers loved it. An enterprising member of the group with whom she had travelled rang one of them to report that a member of their group had wished to remain in Russia but had been summarily sent home. When her identity was disclosed, all was explained. Hannah knew what her son had done and was so anxious to avoid the consequences that she was even prepared to remain in Russia.

A reporter interviewed the informant and learned that while in the Soviet Union Hannah had behaved oddly; she was unsociable and went off on her own a great deal. She was able to read the alphabet and could speak a few words of the language. His paper, foiled by the *Bulletin*'s early capture of Donald Matthews's story, decided to make sure of Hannah. She had clearly had some sort of breakdown and could not yet be allowed home. In order to protect her from other media visitors and preserve their prize, they had her transferred to a private hospital deep in the country but not too far from London, and arranged to pay her expenses. The Foreign Office learned this with relief.

Someone went to tell Donald what had happened and get his response.

'I'm the *Bulletin*'s property,' he said cheerfully. Barnaby had already made sure of his exclusive story for the paper. Much relieved at the postponement of Hannah's return, Donald added, 'You'll have to ask them what I think about this,' and he went off into town to give Mrs Francis the astonishing news.

Mrs Fitzmaurice had expected Nicholas to pass on the gist of his interview with the man whom she had assumed was a plain-clothes detective. When he did not, she took comfort from the fact that he seemed brighter and for a few days ate a reasonable meal in the evening. However, soon he relapsed again and his pallor returned. She broached the subject herself.

'Do the police need you as a witness in any way?' she asked him at breakfast on the Sunday after the preliminary hearing when Gordon Matthews was remanded in custody.

'What? Oh!' Nicholas had been chasing muesli in a sea of milk round his plate, like a four year old. 'No. No – they haven't said so,' he answered, and then, understanding what had prompted her question, added, 'That wasn't a policeman the other day.'

'Wasn't a policeman? Who was he, then?' his grand-mother demanded.

'Some sort of private eye,' said Nicholas. Making an effort, he added, 'He'd been asking about – er – that man – on behalf of his first wife's family.'

'Oh!' Mrs Fitzmaurice took in this news. 'How did he get on to you, then?'

Nicholas had wondered a good deal about that.

'I've no idea,' he said. 'He must have seen us together, I suppose.'

'I do hope you won't be involved,' said Mrs Fitzmaurice.

'Why should I be? I had nothing to do with it. Her husband was obviously vicious,' snapped Nicholas.

Mrs Fitzmaurice was startled at hearing him speak in such an untypically harsh, almost rude way, but he must be beset by conflicting and very distressing emotions.

'You're right, of course,' she said. 'But he'll be properly punished this time. It seems as if he got off too lightly before.'

'Are you for hanging, then?' Nicholas asked. He wanted to know the answer, and anxiety made him speak truculently.

'No. Mistakes have been made and there can be no amends after something so final as death,' said Mrs Fitzmaurice. 'But I'm in favour of very severe punishment appropriate to the crime. Aren't you?'

'Yes, of course I am,' said Nicholas.

'This is dreadful for you, Nicholas,' she said gently. Poor boy: amorous skirmishes were normal, but this was beyond imagining. 'It's the first time anyone you've been fond of has died, isn't it?'

'Except Grandfather, yes,' said Nicholas.

'Well, he was old. Poor Carrie has been cut down by violence and in her beautiful youth. That's very difficult to accept.'

'Oh, don't be nice to me, Grandmother,' Nicholas burst out desperately. 'I just can't stand it,' and he leaped to his feet and rushed from the room.

His grandmother sat there, stunned. He was never rude or abrupt, and she had always felt they were on some shared intuitive wavelength, but this time she had failed to receive the proper signal. When she had recovered from her first shock and the pain caused more by his mannner than by his words, she began listening to the inner voice which was telling her that Nicholas knew more than he was admitting about what had led to Carrie's death. Perhaps she had ended their relationship because she feared her husband's jealousy, and Nicholas now felt residual guilt as well as grief.

Very severe punishment appropriate to the crime: those were his grandmother's words and they echoed in Nicholas's head.

His was the crime, and he was going to escape retribution.

How had it happened? Again and again Nicholas relived that final meeting with Carrie, her surprise, her blunt words, then her horrified eyes seeming to grow slowly even larger as he strangled her to death.

For that was what he had done, and in seconds. He had had no idea that life could be snuffed out so easily and fast. If she had not been married to a man convicted of another killing, the police might by now have tracked him down. Or would they? One of the reports about the case had said that domestic murder was almost always between spouses. Perhaps any husband would have been similarly charged. It just showed you could not trust in the process of the law.

His work was deteriorating. Daily he made small errors, and at length the office manager spoke to him about it, suggesting that perhaps he had outgrown the scope of what was a strictly routine job.

'Are you dismissing me?' Nicholas asked. He spoke curtly, surprising the manager who had often found him almost too deferential.

'Of course not, Nicholas,' said the manager. 'We have enjoyed having you working here among us, but we knew you wouldn't be with us for ever. Perhaps the time has come for you to move on.'

'Very well,' said Nicholas. 'I'll go.'

And he must leave Meddingham, too. He could not face his grandmother's wise, troubled gaze; if he remained in her house he might end by telling her the whole story.

He agreed a date for leaving and in that instant said goodbye to his French A level. If he were to sit the exam, he would fail. Instead, he must look for a job with a future.

It was one of the women in the office who suggested the hotel business, which she had heard lacked promising recruits because young people were reluctant to adopt serving roles. Nicholas had no such attitude and his good manner and appearance would be assets in that career.

He applied to a large group and was soon accepted as a potential management trainee. The job included accommodation so that problem was also solved.

Mrs Fitzmaurice was, to some extent, relieved by this

development. Nicholas had made a positive decision and that must mean he was beginning to recover from the depression into which he had sunk after Carrie's death. Even so, there was still a blankness in his expression which alarmed her; it was as if some part of him had died with the girl. Of course, it had: his heart had broken and he was too young to know that though it might remain for ever scarred, it would heal.

She hid her sorrow at the prospect of losing him.

'I'll often come and see you,' he assured her.

He probably would, at first.

She wrote circumspectly to his parents who were certain to deplore this change of direction. His probationary period would be over by the time they returned.

One day, just before he was due to move out and start his new job, Nicholas walked into Durford Central police station and asked to speak to a senior officer.

He was dressed in a clean pullover and jeans. He wore no earring; he had shaved and spoke with a classless accent. The desk sergeant was joking when he said, 'Come to give yourself up, have you?'

'Yes,' said Nicholas.

'Well, what have you done, then?' asked the sergeant. Nicked a bar of chocolate from a supermarket, probably.

'I killed Carrie Matthews,' said Nicholas steadily.

The sergeant rolled his eyes up to heaven. The lad was probably one of those mental patients sent out of institutions to cope alone and longing to get back. They'd had several other confessions, too; it was amazing how nutters with some in-built self-destruct syndrome appeared at such times. To humour him, the sergeant noted down his name and his address in Meddingham, and sent him on his way.

'But I did do it,' Nicholas insisted. 'I strangled her and left her dead on the sofa. All her husband did was move the body.'

'Kind of him, wasn't it?' observed the sergeant. 'I wonder why he went to such pains to oblige you? Now, run along, lad. I'm too busy to waste my time with such nonsense.'

Well, I tried, Nicholas told himself as he walked away. He

had left his bicycle at his grandmother's house, sure that he would be locked up at once. He could do no more.

He began his training at a hotel near Heathrow, starting work in a dulled, unemotional state as if he were some sort of automaton. His first duties were to help the hall porter and he spent his time fetching and carting luggage about, running errands and answering guests' inquiries. He was physically tired by the end of the day and slept heavily for a couple of hours when he went to bed. Then he would start awake, roused by the dreams which before this had been spasmodic but now came nightly. Sometimes he would see Carrie in a weird green garment looking like the drowned Ophelia and calling his name, while her eyes started out of her skull. Sometimes he saw a man in grey whom he knew to be Gordon mounting a scaffold. But that wouldn't happen, he told himself as he sat up in bed, gasping with panic. Even if Gordon Matthews were to be sentenced to life imprisonment, he would go to gaol just for a few years, and after all, he'd been there before; he would know the ropes.

And he, Nicholas Fitzmaurice, would escape punishment.

One evening he went to a local Catholic church. Though brought up in the Church of England, Nicholas knew that Catholics went into wooden sentry-boxes where a priest was concealed behind a grille and could not observe the penitent's face. You said, 'Bless me father, for I have sinned,' and related your list of offences. Then you were absolved, forgiven, unburdened of guilt.

There was a smell of incense in the church. Along the walls lurid paintings representing the stations of the Cross created an impression of doom. Clusters of candles burned here and there. A huge plaster image of Christ on the Cross with blood pouring horribly from the spear wound in his side over his otherwise spotless loincloth was attached to the wall in the chancel. A small queue of penitent sinners waited in various pews.

Nicholas sat behind them while three supplicants were processed, the third taking over twenty minutes. Then, unable to endure the threatening atmosphere and his own mounting tension, he fled, unshriven.

24

He could not bear this load of guilt for the rest of his life.

Nicholas struggled through the days, managing his work reasonably well because most of it required little mental application, but he would be walking along a corridor with a guest's luggage when suddenly Carrie's features would seem to appear before him, her eyes full of reproach. He was not good at joining in the free and easy friendliness among the staff. Some of the girls, who thought him very good-looking in a sad, Jeremy Irons sort of way, decided he must be in the midst of an unhappy love affair; they were not so far out.

He went to visit his grandmother and managed to talk with enthusiasm about his work; two waiters had suddenly left and he had been sent to help in the restaurant which had added variety to his duties. He had met some interesting guests and had already discovered what a big operation was involved to keep a place of such size with a quick turnover of visitors smoothly in operation.

He remembered how he had thought of running a hotel with Carrie, and shivered at the irony of fate. His grandmother, who was shocked by his gaunt appearance, felt a chill of apprehension. His ghosts were not laid.

'When do you think the trial will be?' he asked her, when she had just commented on his remarks about the dietary foibles of some of the guests.

His question was quite inconsequential. He was still obsessed by that girl and her death. Perhaps when the man had been sentenced and sent off to some secure prison, he would be able to put it behind him.

'I don't know,' she said. 'I suppose the lawyers have to get all the details together. It might take some time.'

'The police haven't been to see me,' he said. 'They haven't asked for me here, have they?'

'No. Why should they?' she asked. 'If they were going to talk to you, they would have done it by now.'

But I killed Carrie, he screamed in his head, and I've tried to confess but no one would listen.

After a night in his own bed, the scene of his precious moments with Carrie, Nicholas returned to London. He was not on duty until the evening so he decided to walk to Piccadilly Circus. He took a roundabout route which led him through various residential streets, and he noticed the prostitutes only because they were so blatant, most of them very young girls in short skirts and shoes with very high heels. There were one or two older women, so raddled-looking that he could scarcely believe they ever found clients.

'Hullo, darling. Want a good time?' one woman called out to him quite loudly as he walked past on the other side of the road staring at them in fascination. Such women were outside his experience, although at the hotel he was aware of some dubious pairs who entered together and sometimes did not stay long. Was this how Carrie had found her customers? She was much prettier and smarter than any of these women. As he walked on, hurrying to escape from the importunate girl, a car pulled up at the kerb and one of the girls hopped in and was driven away.

Then he had the idea. He drew a resolute breath, turned back and approached one of the older women who told him in a bored voice that they could go to a place round the corner.

'Cost you twenty quid,' she said.

'Right.'

A pulse throbbed in his head as they walked together to a shabby hotel in the next street. Had he got twenty pounds on him? Just about, he thought, but if his plan worked he need not pay her at all. She was expendable, surely, this drab, weary woman tittuping along beside him on stilt heels beneath skinny bowed legs. Wouldn't he be doing her a favour by putting her out of it all? Then he'd be arrested and that would be that: no need for further concealment. His grandmother would be upset, naturally, but it couldn't be helped.

How was he to do it? Go the whole way and then strangle her in post-coital exhaustion?

The woman did not collect any key but led the way straight upstairs. He wondered dully how many other clients had been there with her already that afternoon. As he followed her, he saw that she wore nothing under her brief jersey skirt. Now he understood a remark she had made when quoting her price, about standing up.

The woman pulled a key from her bag and opened a door. The room within was tawdry and far from clean, and the bed was dishevelled.

'Go and wash,' she ordered, pointing to a basin in the corner.

Nicholas found himself gagging. He drew out all the money he had on him, flung it down, and ran.

But although this effort had proved unsuccessful, Nicholas did not give up the plan. It needed more thought, that was all. He must take a weapon – a knife. That would show his intent, when he was charged. He would pick a woman who looked really bad – either old or ill, or both, one who perhaps was diseased and might pass on infection, so that attacking her could harm no one else and might benefit some. The important part was to do it. He could have knifed that first woman as they went up the stairs. He needn't look at her face, see her eyes, and he needn't kill her; all that was necessary was a wound serious enough to get him gaoled. A mere scratch would do. Whilst ostensibly serving his sentence for this, he would really be doing penance for Carrie.

He thought of little else until he had another stretch of off-duty time long enough to let him go into central London.

He got out of the tube train at Piccadilly Circus and walked about until he found a shop selling knives. He chose one with a long, strong blade, paid in cash and put the receipt in his pocket. Then he asked the assistant the best way to King's Cross and made her tell him twice over so that she would be certain to remember him later. After that he walked north to the area which even he knew was a hunting ground for prostitutes.

Any woman who looked remotely young was out. Nicholas eyed the older ones who stood about in groups of twos and threes, smoking and talking. Eventually he selected a blowsy one who looked about fifty. She was fat, with a big stomach like someone pregnant, and thick bare legs knotted with varicose veins. Her bleached hair hung in straggles to her shoulders, and she wore a skirt that had once been white and a yellow and white striped sweat shirt over enormous breasts.

How could such women ever find men who wanted to sleep with them? Perhaps they were very cheap, catering for the unemployed and the rough trade.

He was just about to speak to her when he realized that she was, after all, not fat but what he had thought at first, in an advanced state of pregnancy, and a good deal less than fifty.

It took him an hour and two cups of black coffee before he found the nerve to try again.

This time he got as far as the hotel once more – a different one, but resembling the other. He pulled out his knife as he walked up the stairs behind the thin woman with ginger hair whom he had selected for sacrifice.

But he couldn't do it. His hand refused to move towards her. He could not, in cold blood, stab that defenceless creature who had done nothing to hurt him; he could not even deliver a surface wound to her calf or buttock, one she would scarcely feel and from which she would soon recover.

He turned and ran. She had taken his money before entering the hotel, so he lost that too.

Carrie Matthews was discussed from time to time in the Railway Arms, where she had been recognized from photographs in the newspapers. A selection had now appeared, culled from family albums.

'Haven't seen that young fellow in here lately,' said a regular. 'The one she was always with on a Wednesday.'

'I daresay he was the cause of the husband doing her in,' said another.

'Very likely,' the barman agreed.

The matter was referred to again now and then, and one evening when an off-duty policeman who lived locally was in the bar, he was asked about it.

'Who was her boy friend?' someone wanted to know.

'Whose boy friend?'

'That Carrie whatever-her-name-was. The one who was strangled by her husband who'd already murdered his first wife,' said the man. 'They were in here every Wednesday night for several weeks. Very affectionate, they were.'

'What was he like?' the policeman asked idly. He was not concerned with the case, and it hardly mattered now that the perpetrator had been charged.

His informants described Nicholas accurately, and one of them knew that he bicycled away in the opposite direction after seeing Carrie on to the bus. Someone else knew that he travelled to London each day.

The officer, who was conscientious, reported the conversation when he was next on duty, and it was referred to the team handling the murder inquiry, who decided that the young man should be traced. Since he travelled regularly by train he probably had a season ticket and could soon be identified by station staff.

None of this percolated to the desk sergeant at Durford Central who had heard and ignored Nicholas's confession, but the ticket collector confirmed that the pair had regularly travelled back together on the ten o'clock train, and the booking clerk was able to provide the young man's name and address.

An officer went to Meddingham to interview Nicholas. This time Mrs Fitzmaurice checked his warrant card thoroughly before letting him into the house.

'My grandson is living in London now,' she said. 'He has a new job. Perhaps I can help you.'

'We believe he was acquainted with Caroline Matthews, of whose death you may have heard,' said the officer.

'Yes, indeed. Most distressing,' said Mrs Fitzmaurice. 'Nicholas knew her slightly.' She tried to conceal her dismay that the connection had been discovered.

The police already knew that the two did not make the outward journey to London together.

'Do you know why she went to London each week?' asked the officer.

Hadn't Nicholas said she worked in a hotel? But she had been an assistant at Brice's. This must have been another of the girl's deceptions, perhaps said to impress him.

'I've no idea,' she said. 'It was none of my business. My grandson hadn't seen her for some days before she disappeared,' she added.

'I see,' said the officer. He asked for Nicholas's address in London, and Mrs Fitzmaurice was obliged to supply it.

'He comes down to see me from time to time,' she said. 'If you still want to see him after what I've been able to tell you, perhaps he could call in next time he's down, unless it's urgent? Which it can hardly be now, with the poor girl dead.'

'That would do very nicely,' said the officer. 'It may not be necessary at all.'

The officer made his report and as routine it went into the file. He had no knowledge of the large sums which Carrie had paid into her building society account so regularly every Thursday. Meanwhile, however, Detective Inspector Benton, who did, thought that Carrie might have been killed for her money. The police had decided to find out how she obtained such large, regular sums.

The idea of approaching Michael West came to Nicholas in the night, when he woke drenched with sweat from more terrible dreams.

If he made a clean breast of the whole business, perhaps the private detective would take him seriously and persuade the police to listen to him.

Most people would think he was foolish. Why not let Gordon Matthews take the blame? He was an evil man who should never have married Carrie, and he should still be inside serving a proper sentence for what he had done to his first wife, if Michael West were to be believed. But it was guilt that had driven Macbeth to ruin, Nicholas remembered, having studied the play for O level, and it was doing the same to him. 'Macbeth does murder sleep,' wasn't that how it went? It seemed to Nicholas now that he would willingly surrender the rest of his life for a night of uninterrupted, dreamless oblivion. Even the prospect of avoiding disgrace to his parents and grandmother could not compensate for his present distress. His grandmother might, just possibly, understand.

He telephoned Michael several times but always got the answering machine. How could he leave a message on that? At the third attempt he managed to give his name.

25

Hannah looked in bewilderment round the room. It was small and high-ceilinged and had a big window with thin beige curtains patterned in tiny splodges set in one wall. She had no memory of her trip here by ambulance from the first hospital, and thought that this was the same high bed in which she had first woken, as she dimly remembered, after her defection. Everything must have been too much for her and made her ill, for there was no doubt that this was a hospital bed and she certainly felt extremely odd.

On one side of the bed there was a locker with a tray bearing a jug of water, some of which had been poured into a glass containing a flexible straw. On the other there was a hinged table which, if she extended her arm, she could draw closer until it was across her body. There was a box of tissues on it, a magazine and a television remote-control switch. What a luxurious place! She hadn't known the Soviets went in for this sort of thing, but of course the important people would want the best and they were giving it to her. How very gratifying!

The events of the last days were hazy. She could remember the two men driving her off in the car. They had taken her to some official building and given her coffee; after that she had only a hazy recollection of being wheeled somewhere on a trolley; of a nurse holding a cup to her lips; the sharp stab of a hypodermic in her arm.

She picked up the magazine. It was a recent copy of *Harper's*. She was surprised to find this sort of publication from a capitalist country available in Leningrad but there again, perhaps such luxuries were permitted for the privileged, though this was not one that appealed in the least to her.

They might bring her the *New Statesman* if she asked. There was a bellpush pinned to the sheet. She pressed it, and while she waited for someone to come, she wondered if any of the nurses spoke English.

A disembodied voice spoke from somewhere in the wall above her head.

'Yes?' it inquired.

'Oh – please, if it's not too much trouble, could I have something to read?' she asked. What was the Russian for please? She remembered it and uttered it proudly. '*Pazhalsta*,' she added.

'I'll see what I can do,' said the heavenly voice in a strong Scots accent.

While she waited, Hannah tested her limbs to see if any were out of action. All seemed to be working: toes flexed and knees bent, though stiffly; her legs felt heavy. Nothing hurt but she was still drowsy. Why had she bothered to ask for something to read? She was too sleepy to attempt anything so positive.

Now she could see that there was a television set fixed to a bracket on the wall opposite her bed. She was about to test the remote-control switch when the door opened and a small red-haired nurse came in carrying a pile of magazines and two books.

'There we are. Feeling better, are we?' she asked, beaming at Hannah. 'Ready for some tea and toast?'

Now that girl mentioned it, Hannah did feel hungry. It must be some time since her last meal. She had eaten blinis and black bread for breakfast, with fragrant rather smoky tea.

'That would be nice. Thank you,' said Hannah graciously, and added, 'What excellent English you speak.'

The girl looked surprised, then laughed.

'Och aye – well, I've been staying here a wee while now,' she said.

'Ah!' Hannah understood. Another defector. She nodded wisely.

'I'll bring you a tray shortly,' said the nurse. 'Do you want to go to the bathroom while I'm here? It's just there, you know,' and she indicated a door in the wall beyond Hannah's bed.

'I think I can manage,' said Hannah.

'I'd better help you till you're a wee bit stronger,' said the girl. 'We don't want any tumbles, do we?'

Hannah submitted. The girl helped her into some slippers – her own, and the nightgown she was wearing was hers, too; they must have managed to intercept her luggage. Walking into the bathroom, she found that she was glad to have the nurse's support; her legs were distinctly wobbly. However, she made the girl leave the room while she attended to intimate matters. She felt rather tired after this little expedition and forgot about the television, dropping off for a snooze when tucked back into bed.

The nurse returned with a tray of tea – cup and saucer, teapot and everything daintily arranged, and two digestive biscuits on a plate. She had left *Woman and Home, The Field, Country Life* and *Punch* for Hannah's delectation. The books were Mills and Boon novels. Orders had been given to keep all newspapers from Hannah in case there was any word in them about either herself or her son. She had been prescribed further drugs and she did not, after all, turn on the television that day.

Mrs Francis felt sorry for Donald Matthews. Poor old man, with his son arrested for what seemed like a repeat of his earlier crime and with Hannah acting up like this, wanting to stay in Russia: he had a lot to bear. He was baffled by his wife's conduct, and privately regretted that she had been unsuccessful, but there seemed no imminent prospect of her returning home. He had been told that she still needed medical care and was content to let matters ride. He had not been to see her in the private hospital although the *Bulletin* had suggested he should go. He certainly had no wish to make the journey nor even to see her ever again.

'I never raised my hand to her in all these years, though many's the time I was tempted,' he told Mrs Francis as he leaned against a rack of saucepans in the shop.

Mrs Francis was shocked.

'I should hope not, indeed,' she said sternly.

'Gordon shouldn't have done it,' said Donald. 'It's easy enough to get a divorce these days. I expect this new wife was another pretty little thing who wouldn't say boo to a goose. I never met her, you know. He didn't tell his mother or me he'd married again.'

'Dear me,' said Mrs Francis and turned away to deal with a customer. She could not help feeling a morbid interest in what was happening to the unfortunate family, although she was ashamed of this vulgar reaction. But everyone liked reading about murder as long as whoever did it got suitably punished.

Donald told her that a newspaper was paying for Hannah's treatment and would ghost her story when she was able to tell it.

'And Barnaby Duke is going to write a book after the trial and he's promised me a cut. It'll be a best seller.' He beamed, anticipating wealth. 'The *Bulletin* will probably serialize it, I shouldn't wonder.'

Mrs Francis deplored his attitude, but then the son had brought nothing but trouble upon his parents. Why shouldn't poor old Donald cash in?

'What will you do with the money?' she asked, for he was already quite comfortably off, though he looked so shabby.

'Go to Australia,' he said. 'Finish my days down under. Monica's there, you know. My daughter. She's married to a property developer and lives in a smart part of Sydney. I could have a nice little flat not too far from her with a view over the harbour so that I could watch the ships coming and going. It must be a great place to live.'

'What a good idea,' said Mrs Francis.

'I've written to her about it,' said Donald. 'Of course, Hannah doesn't know, and I shan't tell her till it's all settled.' He tapped the side of his nose. 'Mum's the word.'

Mrs Francis hoped the old fellow would last long enough to achieve this ambition.

A doctor had been to visit Hannah. He spoke excellent English and wore a very well-tailored suit with hand-stitched lapels. He took her pulse, nodded, then murmured to the staff nurse who was with him. He told Hannah to get as much rest as possible – superfluous advice since she was seldom awake – nodded wisely and departed, telling the patient she was coming along well.

Hannah had not seen him again, and the red-haired nurse had not reappeared after the first day, but everyone who came into her room spoke fluent English. It puzzled her. Could they all have sought sanctuary in Russia like herself?

In wakeful moments she glanced at a magazine, and at last she summoned the energy to turn on the television. She was in time for the Six O'Clock News on the BBC. There was the familiar figure of Sue Lawley with her catalogue of mainly woeful events to relate. There had been bloodshed in the Middle East, political mud-throwing, scandal in the city, and a missing child remained unfound.

Hannah slowly took in that she had been rejected by Russia. When her supper tray arrived, she asked the overalled helper who brought it where she was, and was told that this was the Bellevue Private Clinic in Sussex.

Hannah ate her supper, but she did not swallow the sleeping pill that came later with a cup of warm milk, holding it in her mouth until the nurse had gone and then spitting it out. She was so full of accumulated sedatives that she drowsed off again, but she woke at two in the morning, still confused and with shreds of dream images in her mind. There were memories of buildings and traffic, of being carried somewhere, and of newspapermen.

There had been newspapermen when Gordon did that terrible thing to Anne. And now he had done it again to another young woman. It had been in the paper when she left for Moscow and the Russians must have found out about it, considered the connection unacceptable and sent her home. Such a shock would have certainly made her ill, and it seemed she had lost her memory since several days were quite unaccounted for. She lay against her pillows thinking about Gordon. Was anyone seeing that he received advice? This second wife, about whom he had kept so quiet, had probably been just as trying as Anne: people never learned from their mistakes and he would have picked another weak, malleable girl. He must plead provocation again.

Having decided this, she fell asleep and when she next woke her head was clearer than it had been since she left Leningrad. Sue Lawley had given the date; she had been in the clinic for nearly a week and it was time to get out.

Her clothes were neatly laid in a drawer. It took Hannah some time to dress, for she was still weak and her movements lacked co-ordination, but eventually she was ready. She put on the flat-heeled shoes and the raincoat in which she had walked about Russia. Then, for the first time since her arrival at the Bellevue, she looked out of the window and saw that her room was on the ground floor.

It would be better to leave that way than try to find the main entrance. She had not been into the passage at all and she might meet a nurse who would challenge her right to discharge herself.

She pulled the one chair in her room to the window and climbed stiffly on to its seat, reaching up to unlatch the clasp. The window slid open without any noise, leaving a gap at the bottom. It was not easy for Hannah, getting on for seventy years of age, stout and arthritic, to climb over the sill and descend to the flowerbed beneath the window, but somehow she managed to heave her cumbersome body across, scraping one leg as she did so, and lower herself to the ground.

Unseen by anyone in the building, she wandered away across a vast lawn in search of the road.

Michael West heard with surprise the recorded male voice announce that it was Nicholas Fitzmaurice speaking. It said no more.

Why had he called?

Had the police discovered his connection with Carrie? The boy had not left his telephone number. Michael dialled directory inquiries to obtain it and rang Mrs Fitzmaurice, who told him that Nicholas was no longer living in Meddingham.

'Why do you want to speak to him?' she asked warily.

'He left a message on my answering machine,' said Michael. 'But he didn't say he'd moved.'

'Oh.' During the pause that followed, Michael could almost hear Mrs Fitzmaurice's thought processes operating as she pondered the wisdom of making her grandson's new whereabouts known to this possibly dubious inquirer. In the end she decided to do so and explained that it was difficult to get him on the telephone.

Michael made a note of the details.

'He'll ring me again if he really wants to get hold of me,' he said, and with that they concluded their conversation.

He had plenty of work to do, some of it routine, some rather more interesting. Cases like that of Gordon Matthews were, perhaps fortunately, rare. He was writing a report on a bankruptcy case to background music from the radio when he heard a news item.

A woman's body found earlier that day in a river in Sussex had been identified as that of Hannah Matthews, aged sixty-nine, the mother of Gordon Matthews, presently on remand on a charge of murder. Mrs Matthews had disappeared from a clinic where she had been receiving treatment for a nervous disorder.

Michael immediately telephoned Barnaby Duke and learned that the reporter had already gone dashing down to Sussex pursuing the story.

'She'd gone potty, poor old thing,' said the girl who answered the phone. 'They think it may be suicide. Shocking, isn't it?' She sounded exhilarated rather than dismayed.

Michael asked her to let Barnaby know he had called.

A police officer had been sent to the hotel to interview Nicholas. He had made it quite clear to the anxious manager that his promising if over-quiet recruit was in no trouble; the visit was merely in order to clear up some matters relating to somebody else, now dead.

The manager hoped sincerely that this was true. It would be regrettable, to say the least, if Nicholas turned out to be mixed up with thieves or drug pushers. He put a small room at the policeman's disposal and sent for Nicholas.

In order to keep the files straight and the record up to date, officers preparing the case against Gordon Matthews had decided that as a connection between Carrie and Nicholas Fitzmaurice had been discovered, it must be explored.

Detective Sergeant Price first asked Nicholas if he had

known Caroline Matthews.

'Yes,' agreed Nicholas.

'You travelled regularly together on the ten o'clock train from London on Wednesday nights?'

'Yes,' said Nicholas. 'I'd been to my evening class.'

'What had she been doing?'

'She told me she worked in a hotel,' said Nicholas.

'But she worked in a store in Durford.'

'I know that now. I didn't then,' said Nicholas.

'She was regularly paying large sums into a building society account,' said Price. 'Every Thursday. Two or three hundred pounds each week. Did you know that?'

'No, I didn't,' said Nicholas, truthfully.

'Was she on the game?' said the officer.

Nicholas stared calmly at him. Carrie's reputation was at stake.

'Of course not,' he said. 'What a scandalous suggestion.'

She had died, and her squalid secret had died with her. He wanted to protect the false, idealized image that he had cherished, and that wish guided him as he denied having a sexual affair with her himself when Price asked him.

'We were just friends,' he said. 'I was fond of her, but she was married, you see.' It was easy to bend the truth to give a false slant on events.

Detective Sergeant Price left at last, and as he drove back to Durford decided to suggest asking the Met to make some inquiries around the London hotels. Someone might recognize the dead woman's photograph. But his superiors might not think it worth while spending valuable police time following this line when they had got their villain safely locked up awaiting conviction.

Barnaby telephoned Michael that evening.

He had got most of the story from one of the nurses at the Bellevue. The old woman had been very muddled mentally, and it was hardly suprising that she had felt unable to bear the idea of her son's second trial. The staff were afraid that heads would roll over the fact that she had been able to escape unobserved, but then she was not being kept in a cell. The woman was only old and ill. During the night she had climbed out of her bedroom window and wandered across the grounds to the boundary fence, which she had crossed. As soon as she was missed, a search party had set out to look for her: they had seen her footprints in the flowerbed under her window and headed at once in the right direction. She was found lying face downwards in reeds at the edge of a river which ran through a field beyond the grounds of the clinic. She may have had a heart attack; the post mortem would reveal if that had killed her or if she had drowned. It was feared that the inquest might attract adverse criticism of the clinic's supervisory arrangements.

'It'll make a good story,' said Barnaby cheerfully. 'I'll be at the inquest, and the funeral too. I wonder if they'll let the son go to that.'

Would they? Probably, if he so wished.

The tabloid press posed the same question the following day, when Hannah's fate made almost as dramatic a story as the arrest of her son had done earlier.

Nicholas could not have missed learning about it, passing the newsstand in the hotel lobby as he did several times an hour.

He had missed the previous report of Hannah's unusual return from Russia; now he read with astonishment about her death. It was difficult to accept the notion that Gordon Matthews had parents. Fresh interest in Carrie's murder was aroused by this incident and when the point was raised in the newspaper as to whether her killer would be allowed to go to his mother's funeral, some of the hotel staff said that if he were refused permission, it would be an offence against human rights.

A few days later the *Bulletin* and other papers reported that the inquest had been opened and adjourned after evidence of identification had been given. Nicholas telephoned the *Bulletin* to ask about the funeral. He thought it might not take place for ages, but soon learned that permission for burial had been given. He said he was a friend of Carrie Matthews but would not give his name. The *Bulletin* gave him full information about the funeral arrangements, for the paper had made them on behalf of their property, Donald Matthews, and they hoped for a good attendance.

Donald Matthews had not intended to go to his wife's funeral. Hannah had died in Sussex; let her obsequies be concluded there. He thought it amazing that any paper considered her story worth paying for in such terms as treatment at a private clinic. When he was told that she had died, he felt only relief; now he could sell the house and take the proceeds to Sydney when Monica had made the arrangements. He wrote to her accordingly and agreed to the *Bulletin*'s plan, made to cut the ground from under their rivals' feet, for the funeral to be held in Yelbury at the parish church where Gordon had sung as a choirboy. How could he object, when they would see to everything and meet all expenses?

'They've thought of everything, even to ordering a wreath,' he told Mrs Francis, inspecting a plastic water-filter jug. They were all the rage now, but it would be wasteful for him to get one when he would soon be leaving the country. 'I doubt if she did it on purpose. I expect she was trying to find her way home.' He had refused to go to the inquest, despite the *Bulletin*'s attempts to persuade him to attend in a hired car which they would provide.

'It's all very sad,' said Mrs Francis in a tone of reproof. Donald's attitude, and his cheerful face, were not seemly at such a time. He had even spruced up his appearance and bought a new raincoat.

'They asked about hymns but I said leave all that to the vicar,' said Donald.

'I'm surprised she's not being cremated,' said Mrs Francis, who preferred this method of tidying up remains.

'She never fancied it. I remembered that,' said Donald, who had been reminded of it in a letter from Gordon in prison. He seemed upset by his mother's death which was surprising, really, thought his father, as he hadn't been home since he came out of prison the first time. Donald had never learned about Gordon's brief visit after Carrie's death.

'It will be a good thing when it's all over,' said Mrs Francis.

'I hope you've got a respectable black tie.'

Barnaby told Michael West that Gordon Matthews would be going to his mother's funeral. The *Bulletin* had suggested to the accused man's solicitor that his client should press for permission. As he had not yet been tried and was unlikely to show violence to anyone except a wife, there could be no grounds for opposing such a request.

Michael decided to be present, too.

It was a wet day, and drab raincoats predominated over black among the mourners who shook out their umbrellas and left them in the porch while they went into the fourteenth-century church for the service. A number of curious citizens who had not known Hannah but were loth to miss such an unusual occasion swelled the congregation which would otherwise have been sparse. Journalists and photographers clustered by the gate to watch the arrivals and take pictures of the coffin. The widower, with a new black tie and wearing his old dark suit beneath the new raincoat, looked trim and tidy. Barnaby, who had suggested a haircut, escorted Donald to the front pew and sat beside him. The vicar kept the service as short as he could decently contrive. He was appalled at the notoriety of the affair, and was finding it difficult to maintain an attitude of Christian charity. When he had called upon Donald to offer condolences, he had found the bereaved man rather the worse for drink and very cheerful. No member of the Matthews family had attended church during the vicar's incumbency; today he offered no eulogy but read Corinthians I, chapter 13, a safe choice when in doubt, in a sombre tone. He tried not to look at the flabby-faced, grey-haired man standing between two stocky police officers in plain clothes. Were they handcuffed to one another? The vicar did not want to know. There were other problem members of his flock, but none had killed two wives. Provocation was no excuse; a soft answer turned away wrath.

He led the way out of the church for the interment, the undertaker's men lifting the coffin from the bier and shouldering it with some difficulty as they stepped through the falling rain across the rough ground towards the raw grave by the wall at the northern end of the cemetery. Donald followed, looking solemn, then came Gordon, with his escort.

Nicholas had been sitting at the back of the church. He had seen Gordon enter and take the front pew across the aisle from an old man who was probably his father. He had listened to the familiar words about charity, and his hand, in his raincoat pocket, had grasped the knife he had bought when he thought he would be able to wound a prostitute.

Now he knew why he had come to the service. Here was a man whom no one would miss and whose death would secure for ever the safety of two innocent children. If Gordon Matthews were to die today there need be no trial, no defence in court, no public exposure of Carrie's secrets. Even her hoard of money might go to the children, unless Gordon Matthews had already spent it. And at last he would receive his own appropriate punishment, although no one would know the full extent of his crime. He would plead guilty to murdering Gordon Matthews and he would go to prison. Somehow he would endure the time there and use it to good purpose. You could study, he knew. One day, when at last he was released, he would be able to sleep without bad dreams.

He waited until the final words of the committal were spoken and there was a moment of quiet. No one saw him take the knife from his pocket and flick it open. It was easy in the respectful hush, with the rain pattering down on bent heads and open umbrellas, to move up behind his target. The two officers were as surprised as the victim when, as it seemed without cause, their charge suddenly sagged between them, uttering a low gurgling moan which at first they took for an expression of grief. Nicholas, aiming wherever he could, had struck just beneath the shoulder and, entirely by chance, the slim blade had penetrated Gordon's heart.

Stunned witnesses saw the young man who had inflicted the fatal injury stand swaying slightly, smiling, as he watched the prisoner take two stumbling steps between his guards and then collapse.

Michael had not noticed Nicholas until he moved up

behind the group at the side of the grave. As small agitated cries broke out among the spectators – for of all the mourners perhaps Gordon himself was truly the only one – he came up to Nicholas and led him aside, back to the church to wait for the arrest that would be almost instantaneous.

'I did it, you know,' said Nicholas. 'Killed Carrie, I mean.' In his briefly elated state he stared at the detective. 'No one must ever find out what she really did in London. You know, don't you?'

Michael nodded, in that moment seeing it all.

'You won't tell?'

'No,' said Michael. 'I won't.'

'And don't tell my grandmother. Let her just think I was mad with rage.'

'Well, you were, weren't you?' said Michael slowly. 'You'll be all right now.'